WANDERING STARS

STARS

THE BEST OF THE ZODIAC SERIES

THE ZODIAC SERIES

The Zodiac Series is a collection of twelve speculative fiction anthologies, each focusing on one of the Zodiac signs. The anthologies feature short stories and poems inspired by each sign, and retellings of the various myths behind those signs.

\#

Capricorn Aquarius Pisces

Aries Taurus Gemini

Cancer Leo Virgo

Libra Scorpio Sagittarius

\#

The Zodiac Series has been produced by Australian Speculative Fiction, and each anthology contains a diverse selection of tales by talented writers from Australia and New Zealand.

First published by Deadset Press in 2022.

Isbn: 978-0-6450228-6-5

Cover design Copyright © Austin P. Sheehan.

Edited by Austin P. Sheehan

ACKNOWLEDGEMENT OF COUNTRY

In the spirit of reconciliation, Deadset Press acknowledges the Traditional Custodians of country throughout Australia and their connections to land, sea and community. We pay our respect to their Elders past and present and extend that respect to all Aboriginal and Torres Strait Islander peoples today.

ACKNOWLEDGEMENTS

Wandering Stars is the culmination of The Zodiac Series, a collection of twelve anthologies each focusing on the one Zodiac sign, with a total of 178 stories in all.

We must acknowledge those who made this all possible. There were many editors who helped fine tune each story in each anthology, including Helena McAuley, Nikky Lee, Leanbh Pearson, Mikhaeyla Kopievsky, Neen Cohen, Matthew P. Copping, Alanah Andrews and Jocelyn Spark. Without the writers, though, there would be nothing to edit. So we must acknowledge all writers who contributed those 178 stories, with a special mention to Nikky Lee, Helena McAuley, Sasha Hanton and Zoey Xolton who featured in every single anthology.

Most importantly, we acknowledge and thank the readers who picked up these collections. Those who are curious, brave or foolish enough to try a Zodiac-themed collection of fantasy, sci-fi and horror stories are the people we publish our books for!

- *Austin P. Sheehan, on behalf of Deadset Press.*

CONTENTS

CAPRICORN
DECEMBER 21 - JANUARY 20

LORD OF THE DEEP

Marcus Turner

The deep trembles. So it begins anew, rippling the still waters of both thought and space with its idiot mewling—a newborn screaming its way into existence.

Endless hunger, the bawling darkness that precedes all things.

Chaos born yet again.

The deep trembles, and the hoary eyes crack open, crusty with the sleep of ages. Hunger, and hate, growl awake. Entwined lovers shiver in trepidation and lunatic lust; infants start screaming—nameless terror vexing soul and sinew. Fathers grind their teeth in unplaceable rage and despair, calamity shivering in their bones. Mothers hold their bellies, a graveyard rotting foreshadowed in their wombs.

The waters ripple, quivering like stricken flesh. A new age, a break in the eternal conflict, is imminent. Such darkness—something has shifted.

So it begins anew . . . to end at long last.

The creature was back, watching him as he slept for the fourth night in a row.

It looked like a man at first, ripped out of time. A thick, plaited black beard, dark kohl-rimmed eyes. Bare-chested and bronzed, he stood wearing only a long, rough-spun skirt, and a horned helmet shaped like a sharply ridged turtle shell. Its presence in the shadowy corner pricked Magnus awake through the blanket of sleep. The stranger stood smiling, lips pallid and bloodless in the small spot of moonlight illuminating its face, making silvery flares of his eyes.

What made Magnus' blood freeze wasn't the uncanny fact of a strange voyeur invading the privacy of sleep, but the instinctive awareness that it wasn't a man at all. It was a rind, a skin to be peeled back from some rotting fruit.

At last, the entity didn't seem to care any longer to pretend. The giveaway was the horns. Gone were the horns and helmet of previous nights; tonight, *real* horns emerged from the figure's forehead, thick and long, curving back like a ram's. And then there was the auburn-coloured fur sprouting from what had previously been smooth skin—threading through pores before Magnus' eyes, like watching a time-lapse video, until eventually no skin could be seen at all.

The face was changing, too. The nose and mouth were drawing closer together while the face elongated. The eyes changed from brown to a harrowing ice-blue, while the pupils contorted into horizontal slits. The creature's lips turned black, became leathery and animalistic—but that leering smile did not change.

It lapped up his fear like milk, and it was *thirsty*.

The devil, he thought. *I'm being haunted by the devil.*

2

The skirt became leather; the bones beneath fused together, a grotesque syndactylous digit, before the flesh took on an oily shimmer. Scales—a thick tail tapering into a broad fan of pearlescent black fins.

He had seen photos of the Horned Goat, Baphomet, Satan . . . but this wasn't any of those beasts. This was the Goat of Waters, the Living Capricorn. Lord of the Deep.

How the hell did I know that?

A shiver prickled Magnus' arms. "Who are you?" Magnus demanded.

The creature's smile split open, but instead of worn, square goat's teeth, its mouth was filled with daggers. It flensed the air with them, stretching and testing its jaws, before it finally rasped a single guttural word:

"Apsuuuu."

"What?" Magnus cried, revolted by the horrible voice.

"Apsu." The Goat of Waters lifted its clawed arms to the ceiling. A rush of waters—a sloshing of waves breaking against walls and bed-posts.

Black water disgorged from the carpet, flooding the room at alarming speed. Water seeped through the mattress, spilling over its edges. Magnus cried out, but the moment the water touched him, his body refused to obey his screaming mind. He was anchored to the bed by some invisible force while the water engulfed him, pouring down his throat. It rose past the window, obscuring the moonlight. The inky form of the Lord of the Deep continued to watch Magnus as he drowned.

The Apsu, *the Apsu . . .*

Magnus woke like a man rising from the bottom of a lake, coughing and spluttering. The sun coming in through his window couldn't cut through the chill permeating his skin. But it had been no dream—he knew that as well as he knew the lines on his hand, the moles on his face and neck. He could still feel the icy water pouring down his throat, the sodden sponges of his lungs . . . He'd drowned. He'd *died.* And yet here he was.

How strange that a dead man could feel so fresh and energised, so *alive*; born anew from the baptismal waters of terror and pandemonium.

Magnus got out of bed and headed to the bathroom, wondering why his relatively dry sheets were at such odds with his memory. *The room flooded. I drowned. It wasn't a fucking dream.*

I'm not crazy.

The person looking back at him in the mirror looked surprisingly fresh for a man drowned by a murderous, evil presence. But then dreaming of drowning probably hurt a lot worse than *actual* drowning, because the brief terror overloaded the senses, made what was merely common and pedestrian somehow special, meaningful. But there was nothing special or exceptional about death, the brief, clawing struggle.

But you know it wasn't a dream. Something happened. Something has changed. You know it, don't you?

And then, the burning question: *What is the Apsu?*

The Apsu. The mere thought of the word covered his skin with gooseflesh, and a formless dread twisted in slimy coils in his guts. It had awoken. It was hungry—and he was the prey. The Goat of Waters smiled again in his memory, flashing its rows of long, needle-like teeth. *Why me?*

Surely a god did not register a man, the slimy afterbirth of the universe's womb. *Unless you're not a man. Not anymore.*

Magnus backed away from his reflection. *Maybe you are losing your marbles, son.*

He went downstairs into the kitchen. His sister Leila was already at the table, scrolling through her phone as she nursed a cup of coffee in her free hand. Magnus went to the cupboard, took out a bowl and joined her at the table, reaching for the box of Corn Flakes.

"You're up late," Leila said, without looking up.

Magnus stood back up and went to get the milk and a spoon, then returned to the table without replying.

"You missed the bus, *and* the train. You're going to be late for work. Again. It's—"

"Nine thirty-seven a.m. I know." He glanced at his naked wrist. He'd left both his smart-watch and his phone upstairs, but somehow, *he knew.* He knew the exact second of where they stood in time.

Leila looked at him with a lopsided frown. "Yeeeah. Anyway, you're late. You're probably gonna get fired. This is, what, the sixth or seventh time in a month?"

"I'm not going in today," Magnus answered through a mouthful of milk and half-chewed cereal.

Leila threw up her hands in exasperation. "Even better."

Magnus continued shovelling food into his mouth without rebuttal. Leila stood up—she was already dressed for work in her black pencil skirt and collared shirt. The diamond pendant on her white-gold necklace gleamed in the morning light. "Anyway, some of us have to get to work."

Magnus grunted. It was his go-to communication with his sister—he knew she hated it, though he never intended to bait her. But the shark was ever circling, and as always, she lunged.

"Do you even care?" Leila blurted.

"About what?"

"About *anything?* Fucking hell, you live your life in a daze. Zero consideration for the impact your actions have on anyone else." She wrung her hair in her hands. "I'm not your mum, Magnus."

"I know that," he replied peevishly.

"Well, when are you going to start acting like you realise that? I'm not her replacement and I don't fucking want to be. We're supposed to be in this together, helping each other get by until we're in a position to go our separate ways. But you act as if it's an option. It's not."

"What do you want me to say?" *That I don't care, because as of 2:44pm today, both our worlds are about to change.*

Whoa, where did that come from?

"That you'll call work, *apologise profusely* for being late yet *again*, and beg them not to fire your ass—if not for your own sake, then your sister's," said Leila.

It won't matter. I won't need food or shelter after today. Neither will you, because you'll be dead.

"Are you going to say anything at all?" she demanded.

"Like what?"

"'Sorry' might be a good start."

Magnus turned his head and rolled his eyes, so she wouldn't see; but she probably knew anyway. If she hadn't sensed his absolute indifference at this twilight hour of her life, she never would. "Well, sorry, then."

Leila scoffed, unimpressed. "It's only our lives, for God's sake."

At 2:44pm, it'll only be my life. And in the blink of an eye, the future unspooled before his eyes, a ribbon ripped by tragedy. *An accident. A car is going to crash through the window of Michael Hill's. It's not a hit-and-run robbery as the media will speculate, just a stupid accident. The tank is going to catch on fire. That whole corner of the Westfield is going to burn. The driver, and all the Michael Hill employees are going to die, including Leila.*

Leila screwed up her face. "You're being even weirder than usual."

"Don't go to work today," Magnus said.

"What? Why?"

"Just a . . . bad feeling, that's all."

Leila grinned, hand on her hip. "Right. So I'm supposed to risk losing my job for your *feeling?*"

Magnus shrugged and turned back to his cereal.

"No, really. What's going on?" she asked.

You won't listen. You never do, and you look for any excuse to get away from me, because secretly I've always made you uncomfortable. You asked Mum about it once, and she said you were being silly, that I cared and felt things, I just didn't show it. You weren't convinced—still aren't. Magnus' mind overflowed with secret knowledge, past and future gleanings. *I could tell you, but you won't believe me, and you'll go to work to die anyway.*

My God, what is going on with me? Where is all this shit coming from?

"Nothing. Sorry," Magnus said. "Have a nice day at work."

It was hard to feel guilty, no matter how hard he tried to force the feeling, to forcibly will it to galvanise him into action before it was too late. But it was no use, he realised as he stared at the blank TV: you couldn't change what was already future-past.

God damn it, where was all this *coming from?*

He lit up his phone screen and checked the time: 1:32pm. He set an alarm and put the phone back down on the armrest.

2:44 came and went. Magnus didn't turn the TV on straight away, knowing it wouldn't make the news for a little while yet.

At 2:55pm he turned on the TV.

"Breaking news now from Westfield Airport West in Melbourne's north-west," the blonde anchor-woman said, staring solemnly down the camera, "a car has reportedly crashed through the wall of the shopping centre and ploughed into the Michael Hill Jewellers, before exploding moments later. Witnesses allege the car lost control and veered off the road. It does not appear at this time to have been a deliberate 'ram-raid'. We have no further information on casualties right now, stay tuned for more as this story develops."

The Goat of Waters watched from beside the entertainment unit, smiling.

"You motherfucker," Magnus growled, though he knew the Goat had nothing to do with it—blaming the creature simply made him feel better. He'd tried to convince himself of his own guilt, too, but he didn't believe that either, even if others might see fit to blame him. But they didn't see what he saw. They didn't *know*.

He knew this because knowledge was the gift of his awakening. The workings of the universe's machinery, the weave and weft of fate, the mysteries of creation—secret and forbidden things he had no earthly way of knowing. It was through this he understood that

9

fate was as solid as stone—it could be broken, worn down with enough time and energy expended, but it would always reform; fate, once written, would come about, one way or the other. Understanding bloomed like a kaleidoscopic rainbow bursting outwards at light speed, fractals exploding upon fractals with every heartbeat—yet understanding did not make the truth any less galling.

He was becoming a *god.*

How is that even possible? Not because the idea was impossible—many had come before him—but at the same time, there were no gods . . . None *living,* anyway. None but the Apsu, the Primordial Remnant, the Goat of Waters, Lord of the Deep. *Until now.*

Magnus' mind recoiled, warring against the forces of creation and destruction oscillating in his fevered mind like converging galaxies, a cosmic collision of his humanity and nascent godhood—and a few lingering splinters of confusion and self-doubt for good measure—vomiting out of his egg-shell skull.

He sat and mourned his sister in the only way his soul permitted: a complex equation not fully grasped.

Magnus sat on his bed, his hands circling around an orb of light like a miniature sun. Slowly, he flattened his palms and spread his hands apart, stretching the light along with it. This was the stuff of creation: the mesh beneath physicality; the invisible force binding all matter made incandescent and malleable like molten iron.

His phone screen lit up and vibrated for the twentieth time. He did not answer—the call would contain nothing meaningful to him.

His right hand glided along the bottom edge of the bar of light, began to hone it into a sword's edge with his fingertips—a smith playing in the forge of the gods.

Why was this happening—to *him*? How was it even possible? Although knowledge continued to explode within him, each detonation igniting the next, like an AI hurtling towards singularity, the answers to those questions still eluded him. It was as if some *other*, some power beyond reckoning, deliberately obfuscated him, a bulging black abscess in his mind. Something didn't want him to know. But still, *why?* Why him? He was not special.

Maybe your mind is perfectly suited for what's happening to you. Wisdom and perception unmarred by sentimentality.

The Goat of Waters came and went, flickering in and out of reality to watch him. *An avatar, not the real beast.* Magnus ignored it as best he could, though he felt ill at ease practising his new powers with it watching. It was sizing him up. But Magnus was feeling less disturbed by its presence as he grew more confident in his experimentations. Could its increasing presence, its boldness, be nothing more than posturing? A mask for its fear?

No, he decided, as he met the Goat's gaze, evaluating its smirk. *Not fear—excitement. It calls to me. It wants me to come.*

Apsu, Apsu, the Goat hissed in confirmation as the twilight

11

filled his bedroom with ominous shadows.

The Apsu—the one thing he needed to know, to understand; yet it was the one thing hidden from his newborn eyes. *A blockage.*

Magnus went to his desk, sat down and opened his laptop. He typed *Apsu* into the search bar and scanned the results page. An acronym for some type of business—nothing useful there. Above the search bar, Google asked, *Did you mean "abzu"?* Magnus clicked the link. *Abzu* and *Apsu*—used interchangeably in Sumerian, Akkadian, Babylonian mythology: the primeval sea in the bowels of the world, the void space between the earth and the underworld.

Magnus frowned. Aquifers? Underground seas between the earth and underworld? It still didn't explain why the Goat kept haunting him, nor the monumental powers transforming him.

Wait . . . What if the Apsu is the place where it lives, the primeval sea? Is it trying to make me go there, to meet it face to face?

A scan through Wikipedia and then a website on Mesopotamian mythology brought more information: the Apsu wasn't just a place, but an entity existing within it—a primordial chaos god. Several references caught his eye: *Apsu,* the Begetter. The Dreamer.

The Devourer.

My father. The thought screamed through his limbs, searing nerves like arcing electricity.

It didn't make sense. If the Apsu—the Goat—was the Begetter, the Father, then . . . where were all the other gods?

The names are not mutually exclusive, but parts of a process: there are no gods because the Apsu births them and then devours them. It devours its children because it is afraid of them.

Magnus turned his head. The Goat of Waters loomed again beside his bed, smiling. He ignored it and continued reading.

The Apsu feared its children, feared their rising power, and so it devoured them, to maintain its dominion. And yet in its slumber it continued to spawn new gods beyond its control, born from its dreams and nightmares. It woke only when its newborn progeny let out their birthing wail . . . to murder them, to *eat . . .*

An icy knife cut all the way down along his spine. So even gods could know fear.

Magnus rose and approached the Goat, mere inches away from its undulating fangs. The creature's smile yawned wider. Only a projection, an extension of the real demon, but it could speak . . . and it could listen.

"Tell me where to go," he demanded, jaw clenching. "Tell me how to find the Apsu."

The Living Capricorn reached up with a clawed finger and pushed it through Magnus' brow as if skin and bone were soft butter. Magnus cried out softly in alarm, before the finger anchored itself in his cortex.

To pursue the Apsu is to march willingly to the grave, the Goat whispered—a complexity and humanness of thought that its crude

13

mouth could never have imitated. *So many have come before you—Enki, Zeus, Horus, Loki, Quetzalcoatl, even the Judeo-Christian upstart—all have fallen to the Apsu. So is its decree—all gods must die. None are suffered to live but the Apsu; none escape the Devourer's gaze. And yet you would offer yourself up, a babe begging the slaughterer's knife?*

You are but a squalling newborn. What power do you have to battle the Apsu? What inkling *have you of the madness?*

Magnus could not find words to answer. A litany of the dead, the names of extinguished gods from every human pantheon—even names of gods in a thousand alien tongues from places beyond the visible stars—babbled through his mind like a river of ghosts. And the implications! A godless world, a godless *universe,* except for the Apsu: a predatory, megalomaniac force of chaos and darkness. *A prophecy.*

A prophecy he unwittingly accelerated with idiotic bravery.

"Tell me," Magnus insisted against the creeping despair frosting his insides. "Tell me where to find the Apsu. Where to find *you.*"

The Goat flashed its unholy rings of teeth—whether in delight or mockery, Magnus couldn't tell; perhaps they were one and the same. Images flooded through the Goat's invading finger into Magnus' mind: a peninsula; a massive freshwater lake. A place he recognised from family holidays with Leila and his mother.

River grass waving gently in the murky depths.

He knew where he had to go, what he had to do.

Magnus didn't call work or stay to organise his sister's funeral. Such things seemed irrelevant, so small, in the light of what lay ahead. For all the immense power that coursed through his limbs, all the preternatural intelligence now setting his every neuron aglow, nothing could alleviate the sense of doom crushing down on him like the full weight of the ocean.

Human concerns simply *did not matter.*

After a three-and-a-half-hour road-trip out of Melbourne, the massive body of water, and the knobby finger of land extending across it, soared into view: Lake Eildon.

Magnus turned off the highway away from Eildon and continued down towards Jerusalem Creek. He parked the car inside the holiday park and strolled through to the lake's edge. The park was only half-full, being outside the holiday season—mostly caravaners stopping over for the night, and a few permanent residents. Except for a lone fishing boat far out beyond Gerraty Bay, the lake was lonely and still; ominous, as if all souls sensed the cataclysmic echo of what was to come, and though unable to explain their misgivings, stayed away.

He made sure no-one was out walking by the lake before stepping into the water, not bothering to take off his clothes or shoes. He waded out past the shallows, then broke into a freestyle swim towards the deeper, darker cobalt waters. The water soon swelled as a monstrous black mouth beneath him—he'd come far enough.

Magnus stretched out on his back, floating for a moment before bowing his torso and allowing himself to sink. The Goat of Waters slipped into view from the darkness below, swam over and placed a hairy claw on his chest, pressing him down. A moment passed between them, a kind of candour: whatever happened today would change the world forever.

His lungs suddenly cramped. Magnus forced more air from his lungs, but his body refused the dreadful demand heaped upon it. *Relent,* he whispered . . . But the crazed animal inside him struggled, frothing in desperate fury.

Magnus sank faster. The Lord of the Deep smiled. The shell yielded at last, expelling the last motes of air inside its lungs. A second baptism before a passage opened into unfathomable darkness. Into death.

Magnus thrust himself upwards, exploding across the surface of the subterranean lake like a great white shark, thrashing with alarm. Another death, another baptismal drowning—and yet he could breathe. No coughing, no water flooding his lungs. Strange.

It was so dark that it was impossible to tell where the water ended and the cavern began. It took several moments for Magnus' eyes to adjust, to separate the water and the void to discern his surroundings. Thin grey stalactites dangled above like wheeling chandeliers of knives. The cave walls curved round and extended into the distance like the gullet of a monstrous serpent. A little further into the cavern, an even darker shadow rose up out of the lapping waters—some kind of edifice. Trudging closer, through the waist-deep water, squinting against the gloom, he saw it was a squat stone temple, encrusted with calcium and other mineral growths. No braziers glowed inside its gates; no hymns resonated from its hidden cloisters. A forgotten, forsaken place.

What men would have—*could* have—built a temple in such a place?

Unless the builders were not men at all?

Magnus knew the answer as soon as the thought crossed his mind. *The first gods. They built this.*

But if they honoured the Apsu . . . why did it destroy them? Why does it continue to murder us?

Something rose from the shallows he'd just departed—something far too big to be concealed even in such depths. A famished rumbling; the saurian crackle of a disused throat; a hot, rank exhalation like wind through a bushfire.

Suddenly the braziers along the temple's staircase erupted to life: it was not fire, but living *water* that took the shape of flames, flickering, scintillating with bioluminescent light. It did not glow as brightly as flame and threw the temple and the nearby rock formations into greater relief—and everything else into greater shadow.

Slowly, Magnus turned. A barely perceptible form slithered

and shifted its massive bulk in the darkness; a miasma of death and rotting, eons-old god-flesh wafting on its breath.

The Apsu.

Its ancient and reptilian voice ground like tectonic plates inside Magnus' skull. *Newborn. What do you call yourself?*

"Magnus."

A deep, rumbling growl. *Not your before-name.*

"This is my only one." All the power inside him became like water, threatening to flow down his legs. Whatever strength he had, here in this demon's presence, it counted for nothing.

What were gods compared to *this?*

It matters not. Curious as this one may be, it will not change the cycle: you will die, as all gods must. I will eat, and then sleep peacefully for millennia to come. It is the natural order.

"I didn't want to be a god. I *don't.*"

Desire is irrelevant. You are a god. That is all that matters.

"Why must the gods die?"

Another disdainful growl. *Why do you ask such questions? Knowing is your Aspect: this I know as well as you.*

"I can't see everything."

You lie.

"You fear competition."

The Apsu's six black eyes, like teardrops of polished obsidian, bolted open. Magnus sensed a sneer on its scaly lips.

You scratch at the surface of things possessing depths you cannot fathom. I am older than time, boy: I have watched, for endless ages, the turmoil the gods would wreak upon the universe; seen the greed and lust girding their loins to rape the world and its people.

This one made a choice: to deliver the cosmos, they must be empty. The evil children must die.

"Is it not the role of fathers to guide their sons and daughters, to discipline and tutor them? Don't children emulate the natures of their parents?"

The Apsu hissed in disgust. *You know nothing, infant. The first children proved only the error of such notions as control. They could not be contained. Tiamat and I, our union—one of love—it created monsters! It begat fickle, wicked creatures that would bring order only to serve their own ends, to enslave softer, more gullible beings. At first they honoured us, but it was a deception: the children declared war against us, led by Enki. Enki killed Tiamat, cut her body into a hundred pieces and mortally wounded this one with his blasphemous weapons.*

I brought a thousand hells' worth of wrath crashing down upon them. Death, and oblivion.

How I mourned! Tiamat, ripped to pieces by the fruit of her own womb! In despair, I consumed her pieces, so that my consort might live on forever inside my belly, be one with me always. That was my mistake: the children should have ended with Tiamat's avenging. Instead the mother's fertility took root in this one's slumbering mind—the Apsu bore more children, more wicked gods to plague the cosmos, through its dreams.

So began this one's purpose: a bulwark to guard against the savage gods; the preservation of a peaceful, unsullied universe.

"But the world *isn't* peaceful, Apsu. Humans kill each other, wage war, steal, rape. Their cruelty knows no bounds. What does your murder achieve, then?"

The universe does not need gods to magnify what mortals do perfectly well on their own. Your argument yet justifies my end.

"Gods might instruct them—lead them away from their darkness, if given the chance—"

Enough! I weary of this prattle.

"So that's it?" Magnus snarled, shaking his head. "I'm sentenced to die because I was selected by the universe's cosmic lottery? It's not fair."

I must prevent the pestilence, as only I can. I am the Primordial Vestige—the last remnant of Chaos. The only one strong enough to end the madness . . .

"The Goat of Waters, The Living Capricorn, Lord of the Deep—all your stupid names. I don't care what you are. *You* are the evil one. *You* are the monster."

The hidden serpentine head turned on its side; the black eyes, glossier than the surrounding darkness, narrowed to suspicious slits, scrutinising him for a long time.

Then, the voice, limned with something unfamiliar: doubt. *You don't know who you are, do you?*

"What?"

The Goat stood watching him from the Apsu's left flank. The bearded man with the four-tiered crown—its earlier manifestation—stood on the Apsu's right, holding a spear. Both beamed tight-lipped, sinister smiles—as if privy to some terrible secret.

I am not the Goat of Waters. That was Enki's first form. It is **you**, *newborn. Enki, my first spawn, reborn.*

"What?" Magnus' eyes widened. How had his *gift* not made any of this known?

The Apsu shifted closer. The first clear impression of a horned black-scaled dragon head twisting lifted from the shadows like crags rising from the primordial soup. Innumerable fangs glistened in the soft bioluminescence cast by the temple's braziers. The Apsu's growl sounded almost like a long, throaty cackle.

I shall enjoy devouring you once more, my murderous son. Eating you a thousand times over is not enough to avenge all you have done . . .

The Apsu charged forward, open maw dripping. The cavern shook; stalactites broke from the ceiling and sent geysers exploding from the waters. The stench of dead gods flooded the cave.

Magnus smiled.

A spark of light as the Apsu loomed over him—a radiant bar that vanished impossibly fast but for a tiny remaining splinter in the burgeoning black.

The Apsu let out a cavern-shaking roar. Oily black blood boiled from its mouth into the water.

The abscess, the black fruit of ignorance, was suddenly gone.

The Apsu wailed and stamped its feet but could not move. The haft of the spear of light jutted from its back, pinning it to the floor. Magnus grinned. It had suspected—now it *knew*.

If only it hadn't been blindsided by that flicker of doubt.

"You should have swallowed me when you had the chance."

Deceiver! the Apsu screeched in outrage. *How? How!*

"Knowledge is my Aspect, Father. It helps me see a great deal—perhaps too much. You would never have believed my ignorance . . . unless I really *was* ignorant. You have lived too long to be fooled so easily. But if I could fool even myself, then I could fool *you*." His smile broadened in triumph.

"From the moment I drew breath, before you'd even rubbed the grit of sleep from your eyes, I placed a block in the shell's mind, so it could not know who and what I was, or what you were. Only impressions could be permitted. A gambit—so much depending on but a moment of apprehension, a sliver of weakness . . ."

You truly are Enki, little deceiver.

"No," Magnus replied, the mirth sliding from his face like melted wax. "Enki is dead. But all newborns are echoes of those that have come before. Sekhmet, Ares, Huītzilōpōchtli, Týr—all shades of the only true-born god of war, Irra. Thoth, Apollo, Odin, Fukurokuju—spectres of Enki! Ghosts of the past born into reality by your frightful dreams.

"But this time, you had a particularly bad dream. In it you saw

22

Enki and Irra—relived your wife's murder at Enki's hand all over again; witnessed once more the devastation Irra wreaked upon ancient Babylon—and then you imagined something *inconceivable*:

"What if Enki and Irra were *one*?"

The Apsu roared, spraying black spittle. It squirmed upon the impaling spear, thrusting up on its thick legs, trying to unpin itself. With a sliding of the hands and a simple thought, another incandescent spear appeared in Magnus' hands and he drove it through the Apsu's flank, piercing all the way through its ribcage. The monster screamed and dropped to the floor, shivering. *No . . .*

"I have no name, Father—but I will give myself one fit to honour the delirious horror of your nightmares." His voice boomed: *"I am Enkirra—Scourge of Chaos, Avenger of the Gods; the All-Knowing, All-Seeing Avatar of War and Plagues, The Goat of Waters, The Living Capricorn . . ."*

Magnus was gone. Enkirra swelled within its host shell, luminous like a thousand suns. He smiled, and his shell's mouth bristled with rings of the Goat's needle fangs. "The *new* Lord of the Deep."

The Apsu struggled but the fight was draining from it, oily ichor pouring from its wounds. The obsidian eyes were losing their sheen. Enkirra conjured a third spear and calmly approached the Apsu.

23

The world deserves better than you, the Apsu groaned. *You will bring nothing but destruction and despair!*

"No. They will fight each other to win my favour, but in their worship, their savage devotion, there will be unity. Through love and fear I will bind a hundred warring nations, a thousand errant faiths. I will be the only god: the god of everything.

"And *you,* Apsu, will be nothing but a brief memory. A forgotten myth on a dusty, broken tablet."

Enkirra spread his hands slowly, conjuring a broad pane of light, and with a single practiced curve of the flat of his hand, he honed it to a sword's edge. Incandescent blade in hand, he approached the monster and laid an almost tender hand upon its head, stroking one of its yellowed horns.

So it ends at last, the Apsu whispered.

Enkirra nodded, almost with deference. "You were a worthy foe."

The sword of light flashed up—a hot knife through scaled and ridged butter. The Apsu's eyes bolted open, then its head and long neck separated and splashed into the waters.

"Now the Deep, and everything on either side of it, belongs to me."

A collective tremor passed through every cluster of humanity, in every corner and cranny of the earth. Intensified in the manic lust of rutting bodies, woken in their beds from the fever-dreams of some imagined doom, or an involuntary shiver dismissed as some vague, foolish dread, all sensed something had changed—

some fundamental fact. A whirlwind on the horizon, an eclipsing of their collective suns.

Oh, what a glorious age it would be.

About the Author:

By day, manager of a well-known bookstore chain in Melbourne, Australia, ghoulish horror author by night.

Whether it's in carefully selected books someone else has written or the delectable thrills delivered from his own, Marcus lives to bring words to people: words and stories bring us together; they are the nexus between past, present and future and the symmetry and asymmetry of human thought and experience, cataloguing our greatest triumphs, our hopes, hubris and failings.

Marcus is an avid gamer, metal-head, reader and horror film aficionado who may be a little too obsessed with Cthulhu, the apocalyptic hubris of mankind and the inevitable heat death of the universe.

Marcus lives on Wurundjeri Willum land and acknowledges the resilience and dignity of its traditional custodians and pays respect to its elders past, present and future.

You can follow him on Twitter: @MarcusTurnerAu and Facebook: https://facebook.com/MarcusTurnerWriter/.

THE PACT

Dee Cheers

"That's an interesting image." I pointed to the painting over the fireplace. "I don't think I've ever seen anything like it." The artist had depicted a mythical beast—part goat, part fish—set against an estuarine landscape of mudflats and wheeling sea birds. The overwrought baroque frame, all gilded cherubs and acorns, seemed at odds with the overt menace of the subject.

Iain laughed, handing me a glass of wine. I tried swirling it as I'd seen on the vid, nearly slopping it over my new dress.

"Yes, there's a funny story about that." His wine moved in glorious eddies of red and purple, without any conscious effort on his part. I could study etiquette for months and never achieve the careless perfection Iain and his family displayed. I took a large gulp, hoping that sufficient alcohol might compensate for no class and little money.

"So, tell me? I like a good story."

Iain cradled his glass and stared up at the painted beast. The fire crackled and spat, illuminating the planes of his face, accentuating sharp cheekbones and designer stubble.

"My ancestor, the first Lord Ambrose, had it painted." He raised the glass to his lips. I watched, spellbound, as he swallowed.

"The legend is . . ." He paused, with a half chuckle. "The legend is that he gained these estates—and all his wealth—by making a pact with a sea monster."

"A sea monster." I moved closer to the fire, the heat warming my flesh. "I read that he gave King Louis the design for a new weapon. Demanded these lands as the price."

"Well, of course, that's the official story." He finished the last of his wine. "Our family is hardly going to tell everyone their ancestor made a deal with a monster to gain political advantage."

"And what did the monster get in return?" I turned, basking in the warmth of the fire. The mudflats are always so cold. Above me, the vaulted ceiling and painted frescos of the Great Hall soared above me.

"There, see, that's the funny bit. The legend is that the monster asked that in two thousand years, it could have one thing standing in the great hall."

"That's a bit obscure. That could mean anything." I really liked Iain. Unlike the rest of the family, he never intentionally made me feel less than them, just because I was poor and lived in a tiny village at the mouth of the river.

"I don't think my ancestor thought that far ahead. I mean, two thousand years. Anything could happen by then. It's far too long for anyone to worry about."

"I don't know." I put the glass back on the table. The crawling, shivering of the change raced under my skin. "It didn't seem that long to me."

About the Author:

Dee Cheers has been reading, watching and writing science fiction since childhood. Currently writing her first full-length novel, she describes writing as the most frustratingly rewarding thing she has ever done.

In real life, her work takes her to some of the most remote areas of Australia. Dee lives in Brisbane, with a dog and two cats.

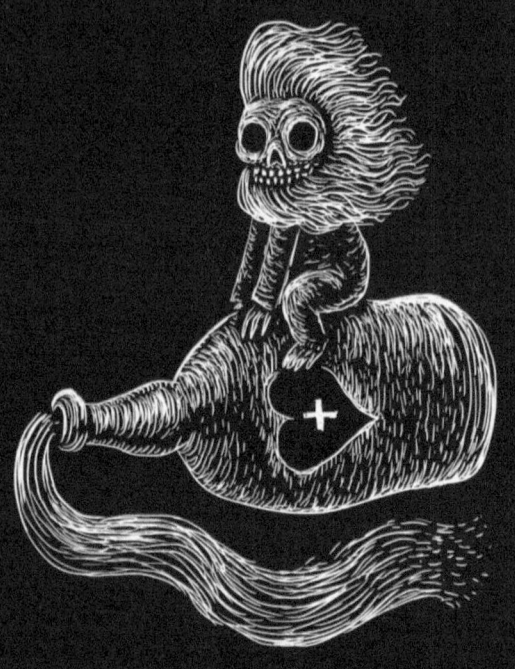

AQUARIUS
JANUARY 21 - FEBRUARY 18

She Walks on Frosted Fields

Aiki Flinthart

Her bare feet leave no prints in the snow. Her pale body casts no bruised shadow on the field of broken diamonds. She smiles back at me, with teeth white and sharp, and eyes of green ice and darkness. The weak sun turns her white hair into a crown of glittering glass knives.

I must be delirious. There's no other explanation. Altitude sickness. Dehydration.

"You're not real," I mutter, holding on to sanity. "I'm Andrea Chen I live in Sydney. I just have to get off this glacier. Tell people that Michael's dead . . ." I grit my teeth against the lump in my throat. Tears will only steam up my goggles. Guilt is pointless. The best I can do is get to town and find people to retrieve his body.

She gestures with a slender hand and drifts across the glacier like a snowflake. Wafting downhill. Towards the valley, maybe? I've been on the ice so long I can't be sure which way leads to safety. The clouds have turned me in circles. Now they've parted maybe I can find my way out.

She waves again. Urging me on. Such a beautiful figment.

I follow, compelled. She's the first . . . person? . . . I've seen in two days. Light glints off snow. Blue-shadowed, fae light; dimmed by my goggles to bearable levels. Clouds close overhead and dull the anaemic sun.

My chest aches and I press a hand to my side as I hurry to catch up. I shouldn't have come hiking with fractured ribs. But I'd spent months planning this trip. The injury had only made me more determined. I'd missed too much of life, already. No more. I touch my belly. Is the flutter there just my imagination?

My breath mists the air, obscuring the figure gliding away. Panic swells in me. "Wait!" I call. My voice is lost in the vast, broken whiteness; captured and returned distorted by the stony arms imprisoning the glacier.

But she pauses. Gestures. Her long grey skirt sparkles and floats about her ankles like snow. How can she possibly be warm enough? Even in the sun it's barely above freezing.

I squint at the sky and check my watch. Maybe an hour until sundown. The sun abandons the world for longer each night. And half the day it cowers, like a frightened child, behind the black stone ridges that slice the sky on three sides.

I need to pitch my tent soon and get some rest. Eat the last of my rations. I've miscalculated. Michael carried more of the food. His pack is at the bottom of a crevasse.

Clouds thicken and tumble lower in the valley; a tide, surging over the foot of the glacier, swelling up toward me, drowning the world. They smother me and she's gone. I yell a hoarse cooo-eee. Roiling clouds suck the sound from my lips. I'm alone again.

I shove the goggles onto my forehead. Bitter cold stings my eyeballs and tears form. I rub them away and hiss as my clumsy, gloved fingers press against the bruise on my left eye. The week-old cut on my cheek is closed, at least. No stitches needed this time.

I stumble onward, peering at treacherous ground obscured by shifting mists. Ice crunches underfoot with the unsteady rhythm of my steps. In a cocoon of swirling grey, that's the only sound: crunch, crunch, crunch. Steps eating distance, carrying me closer to . . . to where?

I don't know which way to safety. Is there such a thing, anywhere? At any moment I could misstep and plummet to my death. Then the glacier would have two more victims. Three, instead of one. Guilt and despair close my throat and curl around a knot in my stomach.

My thighs burn. My lungs ache in the thin air. My icebound heart drags at heavy feet and a boot catches in a crevasse. I stumble, collapsing into the snows. The backpack lurches forward, pressing my face into the ground. The weight pins me in place. I fist handfuls of snow and crush it into hard lumps. The snow stifles my scream. Cold soaks through my pants, through my jacket, eating into bone and flesh hardened by guilt and grief.

I shatter again. I cannot go on. But I must.

A thousand regrets pin me to the ice. Things I should have said to him. Things I should have done for him. To him. But he's gone.

The glacier speaks in deep groans and creaks. It sang to Michael. He swore he heard voices in the clouds; followed them. Fell. I couldn't stop him. Didn't.

I don't care anymore. The glacier can take me if it wants. Suck me into one of its thousand, groaning mouths—as it did Michael. Chew me up, swallow me into its dark bowels—as it did Michael.

The ice growls at me, echoing my despair, my hope. The fluttering sickness, low in my body, pushes me to rise; to carry on; to start a life after Michael. I roll stiffly and scramble to my knees. Half-healed ribs grind painfully together.

The pale woman . . . creature re-emerges from the swirling cloud, her head cocked to one side, white brows raised. A faint, uncertain smile curls the corners of her pale mouth. She waves me on, urgent, frowning now.

"Who are you?" I call.

She drifts away. I stagger after her. Is this wise? Should I find somewhere sheltered to pitch the tent? But another endless, solitary night huddled around the tiny burner, listening for Michael's voice in the creaking ice holds no appeal. My rations are almost gone. My butane tank almost empty. Without food, I can maybe last another couple of days. Without water, less. My mouth is parched. Surrounded by endless frozen water. Unable to drink. The irony doesn't escape me but I fail to appreciate it.

On I trudge, tripping over shattered ice, following a broken dream and a fantasy. Is that the faintest sound of laughter? Or true delirium setting in? She glides ahead of me, one with the mist; her outline a blur of wet grey paint on a white canvas.

I follow the snow-sprite. What other choice is there? This is insanity, but so is the entire trip. The madness of the desperate. The desperation of the fearful. The fear of the wounded.

At this point, I have little to lose by following a delusion. But if she saves me, will I be truly saved? Guilt gnaws at my stomach, eating me from the inside out. I miss him. Not what I expected when I started planning this journey three months before. Anticipation, excitement, relief—yes. Not pain and guilt.

The light fades. I stumble on. The air is slightly warmer now. Thicker. With a faint tang of salt. Or that could be my imagination.

Decisions are too hard. They involve thinking, which triggers memories. Walking is easier. No thought required. The adrenalin has long since worn off. The nausea in my stomach after Michael fell is a dull, distant uneasiness. Bearable if I ignore it.

A chasm looms at my feet and I gasp, teetering on the edge, flailing at air not thick enough to grab. Her white head appears from within the gaping crevasse. She points to my right. In the last glimmer of daylight, I make out what seems to be a rough set of stairs, carved in ice. She smiles and nods.

I fumble in my pack and pull out a torch. The stairs are little more than tumbled blocks of ice, arranged and chipped into risers. The brilliant white of my torch illuminates blue walls, smooth and carved into gleaming sculptural curves. The crevasse descends into the body of the glacier. When I look up, the sky is indistinguishable from ice and I'm entombed.

Snowflakes drift down and wind wails an eerie chorus across the opening high above. Too late to go back up. I can't set up the tent in a blizzard. I continue down. The ground levels out and I stamp my crampons so I don't slip on the smooth floor. Chipping away at blue diamond-hardness with teeth of steel.

The walls widen and curve into a hall that appears almost man-made in its perfection. Ice underfoot gives way to grey, tumbled rocks. I unclip the crampons and stuff them into my pack, then tug off my ski-mask. The flutter of a pale skirt ahead draws me on.

A rushing sound overwhelms the glacier's groans and crackles. The roar grows louder. I emerge through an arch, into an enormous cavern of ice. The torchlight plays across a cathedral ceiling carved of glistening concave gouges. Water drips occasionally, but it's lost in the gurgling wash of water tumbling over the stones at my feet. A river, deep under the glacier. Milky blue-green; the colour of blindness.

I fill my water bottle, keeping my gloves out of the icy chill. The water makes my teeth ache, but I gulp it down anyway. And shiver as it hits my stomach.

The tunnel extends beyond my torchlight in both directions. Downriver should lead me out, into the valley and the little town at the foot of the glacier. To questions about Michael's death.

I hesitate and flash the light upstream again. She flinches, raising a hand to shield her eyes from the glare. She seems more substantial down here. Her skin gleaming with moisture. Her dress heavy with damp.

"Sorry," I say, but the word is lost in the waterfall of noise.

She dances lightly from rock to rock, heading upstream. I follow.

Another graceful arch leads to a smaller tunnel that twists into the glacier's belly and emerges into a new cavern. The river is now a muted rumble in the background. The blood of the glacier pumping through its artery. Around me, the ice-bones creak and crackle, complaining of age and unwelcome warmth.

The floor of the cavern is level and reasonably smooth. Warmer and less terrifying than the blizzard raging above. She nods and smiles as I pitch my tent and unroll my sleeping bag. My legs give out and I sit on a rock, head hanging. The relief of being off the glacier after three days sets my body trembling. I hold back a sob with my gloved hand.

I'm dimly aware that I need to eat to help stave off hypothermia. Rummaging in my pack results in two muesli bars and a silverfoil pack of food. I tear open a bar and movement catches my eye. She's still here. Standing just outside the beam of my torch, watching me. I offer her the muesli bar.

She creeps closer and sniffs it. A small nibble and she screws up her nose. Up close her skin is a bluish hue and she has four slits in the skin under her jaw, low behind her ears on each side.

"What's your name?" I ask. I point to myself. "I'm Andrea." I can't believe I'm having a conversation with my hallucination.

Her mouth opens and closes. Squeaks emerge. I shake my head.

"I can't understand." I wave a hand at her, and myself, and at the cavern. "Thank you for this, though. For saving me."

She smiles gently. I hope she understood, but I doubt it. She touches the cut on my cheek. Her fingers are cold and webbed up to the second knuckle. Her green eyes widen. A milky lens, the same colour as the river, sweeps briefly across them. She touches the bruising again. Harder. I pull away with an indrawn hiss.

She cocks her head, frowning.

"Yes," I say wryly, pointing to my yellowing black eye. "Let's just say you have the right idea—living down here alone." I press at my ribs, testing them. The pain isn't any worse than ten days ago when it happened. I'll survive. I lay a hand on my belly and smile for the first time in months.

I open my pack and pull out a small cooking pot. She watches in apparent fascination, following my every movement. I set up the butane stove and empty my last packet of dehydrated unlabelled something into the pot. Stir water in. She screws up her nose again. I sniff the pot. Curry. Again. But I haven't eaten all day and I'll need strength to make it out of here in the morning.

I light the stove. The flame hisses blue-yellow in the arctic darkness. She squeals. So high-pitched it drives through my skull like a hot wire. She vanishes down the hall. I wait but she doesn't come back.

Left alone in the splintering darkness, I eat and try not to think about him. Every time I do, guilt twists at my stomach and I want to beg for his return. But I can't. He's gone. I ache for his guidance. Why wasn't I better? Was it my fault? Did I do the right thing?

I methodically pack away my cooking gear and curl up in my sleeping bag. There, nestled in the womb of the old woman glacier, I rest well. Fear, my bedfellow for over twelve months, has fallen from me.

When I wake my watch says it's six am. Down here the darkness is absolute. I flick the torch on and strike camp. I eat my last muesli bar and drink again. I need to pee but I don't want to pollute her home. I'll hold it until I reach the river.

I want to say goodbye but she's nowhere to be seen. Not surprising, given she was all in my head. Michael would have known that. He would have set me straight.

I stand at the exit from my shelter and stare into a future with no Michael. A future full of interrogation and tears and endless guilt . . . and hope. A future that cannot be avoided. I need closure and the world will need answers. Demand answers.

Answers to the wrong questions. Questions asked of the wrong person.

Lifting my chin, I shoulder my pack and follow the tunnel back to the river. But I choose the wrong path and step into another chamber. A thin fall of sunlit water cascades through a hole in the ceiling. Diamond drops of light coruscate and dance through the air. A fragile squeal echoes over the noise of water. I swing the torch around and the light bends into a deep, clear pool beneath the waterfall.

Five of my hallucinations float in the water, their white hair swaying like seaweed. They climb from the pool and gather around me. I swallow and hold still as they touch my clothes, my face, my hair. They are smaller than the one who led me to safety. Children of varying heights. Female. Unclothed. All with the same green eyes and webbed fingers.

They don't seem to mean me harm but I back out the door, my heart racing. Not hallucinations. Real. These are real beings. But how?

I can't deal with this. My mind is too full of Michael. He would know what to do. He would tell me what to think about this. I run back down the tunnel. And take another wrong turn. Overhead a narrow crevasse lets watery blue light fall into the tunnel. A huge boulder blocks my path. I swear and turn around.

She's standing silently behind me. I squeak and she flinches, eyes wide.

"Sorry," I say. "I have to go. Can you show me the river?"

She smiles and touches my face, gently. I recoil. I can't help it. She steps past me and leans her shoulder against the stone. Why? It's too big to move. The rock grinds against the granite underfoot. I edge backward, gaping. The boulder rolls aside, revealing a dark opening. She waves me in.

Hesitant, I flash the torch. Dark piles of what looks like fur lie mounded against the walls. The scent of animal and death wafts out. I'm reluctant to go any further. But she's in there, waving me on. I step in, half-expecting the door to rumble closed. It stays open.

I pan the torch around. The light wavers in my hand. Curled against a rock, a man lifts his head and blinks. Hopeful fear lights his face and he holds up a hand, squinting.

"Who's there?" His voice is thin and quavery, made old-mannish in his fear. His blond hair lank and oily. Blue eyes shadowed with sleeplessness and pain.

She urges me in. I resist, trembling. The torch falls from my hand, tumbling and dancing over the rocky floor. It's unbreakable, unlike me. It comes to rest with the light shining in my face.

"Andrea! Thank God! Get me out of here." Michael's voice takes on the command tones I'm used to and my feet move of their own accord. Two steps towards him.

I stop, torn. Ripped asunder. I want him. But he's gone. I was almost used to the idea.

"Andrea." He sounds confident. Certain of me.

I collect the torch and shine it on him again. She stands before him, one hand pressed against his chest. She's looking at me. There's an unmistakable question in those green eyes.

"Andy? C'mon, sweetheart." That wheedling tone gets under my defences. "You have no idea how glad I am to see you! I told you this trip was a bad idea. Dunno why you were so dead set on it. But I came, right? Now let's go home. I promise I won't be mad at you."

He loves me. I know he does. I take another step towards him. He nods, eager.

"When I fell into that crevasse, I thought this . . . this . . ."

"Woman," I say.

"Whatever." He dismisses her with a flick of a hand. "I thought it was rescuing me. But it dragged me down here. I thought I was a goner."

She cocks her head and utters a sharp, lilting creel. She's still looking at me, still pinning Michael to the wall. Michael shoves at the arm holding him in place.

She doesn't move. Isn't affected. He's taller and broader in the shoulder but she holds him like he's half her size. His brow clouds and I cringe back.

"Let me go, you bitch!" He swings at her, fist balled, aiming for the cheek.

She blocks his arm with casual ease. Slaps him so hard his knees sag and he half-slips down the boulder face. His eyes roll back and he groans. She straightens and dusts her hands.

Looking in my direction, she points at Michael. Then at herself. Her hands outline a lump over her belly. Then she mimes rocking a baby in her arms and smiles, crooning.

Michael groans. His hands flex and curl into fists again.

"Andy." My name emerges thick from his bloodied mouth. He scowls. "Don't piss me off. No more games. Just call it off and get me out of here."

My ribs twinge. The cut under my eye throbs. I stay where I am.

He regains some of his power and straightens. Wiping at his mouth, he sees the blood and grimaces. "See what it did to me?" He touches a fingertip to the cut on his cheek again, anger gathering in his eyes. And just a hint of fear.

I shiver. I recognise that look.

Her lips draw back in a knowing smile and she leans closer to him. Michael recoils. She casts a knowing, glittering grin over her shoulder at me. She touches the cut on his face, then the same spot on her own cheek, leaving a dab of scarlet on her pale skin. Then she points at me, and at the door.

"Andrea!" Disbelief tinges his cry.

I hesitate. All the early days of our time together flood into me, filling me with the memory of warmth and laughter. Then the torchlight catches the crimson spot on her face, and on his. My fractured cheekbone aches. The child in me is a little storm; a sickness in my stomach at the promise in Michael's eyes.

I swing the torch around the chamber. Michael's not the only inhabitant; just the only living one. The piles of fur are eight mummified bodies. They lie against the walls, curled into foetal positions. I light up Michael again. His eyes are wide, stark.

"Michael," I say, rolling his name on my tongue, tasting it again. "Did you know that eight men have gone missing on this glacier in the last twenty years?"

"What the hell are you talking about? Get her off me, damn you." He shoves at her arm again.

I back away. The chamber opening is right behind me. The river's breeze tosses hair into my eyes. Cool, fresh, clean. Water rushing towards the ocean.

"Do you know what the locals call this glacier, Michael?" I ask.

"What the hell? Stop blathering. Get back here! Andy!"

I'm outside the chamber, standing free of darkness, bathed in light.

"The Widowmaker," I say. "They call this glacier the Widowmaker."

About the Author:

Aiki Flinthart was both a writer and editor from Queensland, (Turrbal/Jagera Country) with 13 published novels, two non-fiction books and numerous short stories published in various anthologies and e-magazines.

Her work as an editor received recognition in the 2021 Australian Aurealis Awards, seeing her win the award for Best Anthology with her book 'Relics, Wrecks and Ruins'. Her own stories have been shortlisted for multiple Aurealis and Ditmar Awards and she was twice a top-8 finalist in the USA Writers of the Future competition.

When not writing, Aiki liked to practice fantasy-approved hobbies such as martial arts, archery, knife-throwing, lute-playing, and belly-dancing. More information about her can be found at www.aikiflinthart.com, or on Facebook, Twitter, and Instagram—she's the only Aiki Flinthart.

A Pitcher of Water at the End of Days

Pamela Jeffs

"Aquarius?"

The name my mother gave me in the hope that I would adopt the traits of the sun sign concludes too much. I am no airy-minded dreamer. I am a space explorer. And one focused on fighting to survive.

"Aquarius?" My husband, Aeon, calls out again. His voice cracks, throat thick with the red dust that gathers in the air. I glance up from the blanket panels I am joining and out the shuttle's port window. My fingers still work the metal needles as I watch the blood-dark dust storm crouching on the horizon.

"In the control room," I reply.

Aeon's boots thud up the metal ladder. Muscled and barrel-chested, he squeezes into the cockpit. He is too large for the small space and his body knows it. I can tell in the way he holds his shoulders hunched forward.

He looks weary, only half the man he was when he flew us out from Space Dock 10. His cheeks are heavy with lines and his bright blue eyes are dulled to grey. Even his uniform looks tired, holes and oil stains marring the knees. "You got that blanket ready?"

I knot the last thread and snip it with the pliers from the console. "Yeah. Ready."

"Good." He dips his head to look out the window and rubs his dusty knuckles under his nose. I notice blood on his wrist, the place where perhaps a wrench tore a hole as he fixed the sub-thrusters. Watching the approaching dust storm, he nods. "It'll be here soon. Better go cover the condensers."

I lay my weaving needles aside and fold the blanket into quarters. "On it," I say.

The air outside smells like petroleum, bitter and burning on the back of my tongue. I swallow, trying to remove the taste but it sticks there. I clutch the blanket to my chest as I head along the side of the craft. Its giant silver hull towers over me like a metal cliff. Scrapes mar the bright steel, scars earned in our forced landing three days ago. Most of the damage is to the rear of the ship. As I approach it, I see Aeon has been busy. The sub-thruster plates are back in place, meaning the focusing crystal cradles have already been re-aligned.

I move past the plates and on to the condensers. Work is ongoing here. The medium sized units, with their shallow funnels and wide turbines, are exposed from behind broken hatches. Usually used to convert ice molecules from interstellar dust into fuel, the components now collect and process water from sand particles. Both units are covered in a thick layer of dust. Too much dust. Not ideal for the working mechanisms and as our only source of water, all the more reason to get them covered before the storm hits.

The breeze kicks up as I approach the units. The storm moves closer. Shards of lightning skitter and circle the dense mass of dark air hanging low in the distance. I turn my face away from the stinging grains of sand carried on the wind. Grit crunches between my teeth. There is a bad feeling to this storm. Uneasy, I unfold the ion blanket I pieced together from four separate sheets. The interwoven metal links clink as I tuck the edges into place around the condensers. I reach into my vest and grab my pocket welder. A green light flicks on when I activate it. The glowing tip makes short work of fusing the blanket to the hull.

I look up and notice the quality of the light has changed. The bright daylight from the planet's three suns has dimmed to dark orange. With the suns obscured behind the approaching dust cloud, the landscape is suddenly far more ominous.

Aeon waits at the gangplank. His broad hand reaches down for me. The wind grows wilder, snapping at my hair. "Hurry up!" he says, "We need to secure the hatch."

I start to run.

I almost reach his hand.

But the dust beats me.

With a sudden drop in atmospheric pressure, the storm is on us. I am flung from the gangway and tossed against the ship's landing strut. Pain lances along my ribcage but soon fades. I look for Aeon. He is still on the gangplank. In shock, I watch him turn and stumble back into the cargo bay. The shuttle door grinds shut. *Is he leaving me out here to die?* All I can do is clutch at my anchor.

I never thought Aeon to be a coward.

My thoughts circle. Perhaps he only left Earth for the glory, to find evidence of alien species to further his own career. Maybe it was never about us taming the universe together. Maybe I was just a contingency plan— something to sacrifice if it was needed.

My anger sits like a rock in my belly.

And the wind is just as angry. It roars around me, twisting and turning like the currents of Earth's far oceans. Waves of sand buffet against me. I squeeze my eyes shut against the stinging onslaught, but the backs of my hands, cheeks and neck suffer the brunt of its vicious touch.

I sob.

Damn Aeon. Damn him to hell. I'm going to die out here.

I force my eyes open to a blurred view of lightning lashing against the dark sky. It is almost beautiful, the way the edges of the electricity skitter and are shattered by the errant winds. Squinting, I look to the ship. Panels are peeling off the hull like scales torn from a fish. I watch them twist up into the sky, before they are thrown away like ruined toys.

A shriek of metal. I glance back at the gangway. The door to the ship opens and Aeon, dressed in his space suit, emerges. My heart leaps. He hasn't abandoned me.

His steps are laboured as his huge bulk presses against the force of the storm. I sob again, guilty for doubting him. He is carrying something. Metal winks in his gloved hand. Another ion blanket.

My desperation turns to hope. If he can get the blanket to me, I can make it to the ship. I close my eyes, huddle my chin to my chest and with hair whipping around my head like serpents, I wait for Aeon.

His hand is like a vice on my shoulder. I look up and see myself reflected in the mirrored surface of his helmet's visor. The blanket falls over my shoulders and head and the stinging of the sand fades. Aeon pulls me to my feet and leads me toward the gangway. The wind pounds our backs, pushing us up toward the open door. I reach out and grasp the pillar. I turn to Aeon. But as I do, he slips. I can't see his face, but I sense his desperation in the way he grips at my arm. But his gloves give him little purchase. His fingers slip, his boots scrape on the gangway and then he is torn away for me.

I watch in horror as he is pulled upward into the sky. Gusts of wind, spinning like a tornado, fling him against the back of the storm like a broken doll.

Then he is gone.

I make it back into the ship. I press the button and the door closes. The forces of nature fade to a distant sound rattling against the hull. I sit with my back against the door and cry.

The ship will never fly again, but the condensers survived the storm. Heart-sore and weary, I pull away the blankets that held the units safe. Aeon's laser cutter, pilfered from his toolbox, fires up at a touch of the button. He always looked after what belonged to him. Guilt washes over me again at the thought.

The cutter sears the condensers free from their cradles. They thump to the ground, moisture leaking out from their collection canisters. I sit the unit up and trickle a handful of sand into the funnel. The turbines grind as they spin, but still water begins to form on the blades. I breathe a sigh of relief. They still work.

I get to my feet and lift the unit to my shoulder. It's heavy, but its value on a world like this is priceless. I look up into the now clear sky. The three suns blaze down on my forehead. I close my eyes then open them again. Time to go. I step away from the ship and head toward the distant horizon. If I am lucky, I will find the aliens we came looking for. Perhaps they might find my gift of water a fair trade for my life. Or perhaps this may be the End of Days for me.

As I walk, heading for the far horizon, I am struck by the irony that on this desert planet, I have become what my mother named me for. A woman holding a pitcher of water on her shoulder. I have become Aquarius, the Water Bearer.

About the Author:

Pamela Jeffs is a speculative fiction author from Brisbane, Queensland (Turrbal/Jagera Country) with a love for writing short fiction. She has published five short story collections and has 80+ short stories featured in various national and international magazines and anthologies.

She has been shortlisted for multiple awards throughout her career including numerous Aurealis and Ditmar Awards and has also been twice noted in the Writers of the Future Competition. For more information, visit her at www.pamelajeffs.com.

PISCES
FEBRUARY 19 - MARCH 20

SCALES AND SAND
AND SORROW

Rebecca Dale

He was right about me. That's what hurt the most.

Here I was, a hair's chasm away from the most clichéd suicide in the world and all I could think was that he'd been right about everything.

I laughed and looked over the city as the sun set. New York was the place where dreams came to die, and maybe if I ended here, I was some semblance of a dream too. The kind of dream you forget, perhaps. Running in the forest. Drowning. A blurred smile. Something tired and well worn. That was alright.

At the top of the Empire State is an ocean. Horns and engines and the shifting of concrete come together. The sounds of New York coalesce and cadence into waves. It is unspeakably peaceful.

I crammed myself between warm bodies, strung together by errant scarves and coat tails. Couples brought their heads together to talk in whispers. My breaths shallowed. I stood still with my head bowed and waited.

And then the throng parted, pulled by the gravitation of the earth and my own fate. I stepped into it, letting the New York summer leave its bitter taste on the back of my tongue. I slipped beside a set of coin-operated binoculars. There was bile in my throat as I steadied my foot against the stone and wrapped my fingers around the metal lattice.

Nobody noticed. Or maybe they didn't care. Isn't it strange how much Americans talk to each other in elevators but not in crowds? The grate hurt my hands. Obviously it was designed to prevent someone like me doing something very stupid.

I'm not stupid, I'd said once, and without a pause he'd turned his head, big blue eyes burning into mine, the question coming out of him slow and quiet.

Aren't you?

I shook my head because that was over now. Fear knotted up my stomach and I swallowed it down as I climbed. The hands, at least, were strong. They knew cold tiles and the precise texture of blood and how to get back up again and how to pull, pull, pull.

But my limbs paused at the precipice. The ocean sound crashed over me and the lights of the city glimmered like glowing microbes. My knees and thighs spasmed from the awkwardness of the climb. Almost over the edge and down, down, down and I didn't dare to look. It was okay. It was okay. I looked to the sky instead.

And I saw something wrong, cut from the other cloth of the universe.

There are ancient responses to such sightings. Not flight, not fight, but freeze. The brain knows, at the back where the medulla sits, when it beholds something that is not meant to be seen. A primordial freezing took hold of me. I was the ancient rabbit caught in the headlights.

Eyes and fins and scales and starlight. It loomed over me, monstrous and beautiful. A first I thought it was a blimp burning to the ground. But the movement was too wrong and too elegant.

It drifted in front of me, its eyes glistening, pushing forward. As it draws near my hand, clutching the top of the rail recoils backwards. But it persists until my open hand is full. The gentlest nudge, cold and slick and wet, urges me backwards.

And as I fall, there is release. The endless chanting in my head—*stupid, stupid, meaningless, worthless, stupid*—softens and quietens.

Strong hands catch me and turn me on the floor. An attendant dressed in a crisp scarlet uniform and a bell-boy cap shakes my shoulders. His eyes are frantic and wide as leans over me.

"What are you doing?" he screams, "are you stupid? *Are you?*"

Maybe I am. And maybe I'm also crazy, exactly like he said, because when I close my eyes the dreams are the same as always, except the blood is water, and the whisk of a gold fin fans the rivulets away from me.

The phone rang. I put it down on the pillow and stared at the screen until my eyes hurt.

Children thumped down the hall beyond the hotel room door. I wanted to go out there, with the veins in my temple building, and demand their silence. But I hadn't left this bed in three days. I hate hotel rooms, but I can't go back to that apartment on Statton Island, where the heat slides over my skin and leaves residue.

My head pounded as the air conditioning unit near the window blasted icy air into the room. I reach for it again but fall quiveringly short. All the strength I have left is preserved in my fingers, resevoired into simple acts; plugging in the phone when the battery gives out, pulling it back to my chest, tapping at the screen until it pressing the ringer button.

How many times had I pressed it, only for the call to ring out? I've lost count.

That thought filled my chest with tightness and frayed nerve endings. My heart *literally* hurts. I imagine him looking at my name as his phone rings, as he swipes the call away. And at least he thinks of me. If nothing else. He will not speak to me. But this ritual is better than nothingness.

A click.

"I'm recording this conversation," he says.

My haze of nightmares and firm pillows dissolves. His voice is quiet and firm. My fingers fumble and the phone drops to the floor. When I pick it up, a shattered screen scatters the display, breaks up his name into ancient symbols.

I couldn't remember what I was saying. The words left my lips and were gone forever, even though their internal workings were the same. They were words of begging, and weeping, and confusion. Pleas given at a disinterested temple.

But every word of his singes the delicate skin of my eardrums and is intoned there forever.

It's not my fault, he said. You've changed, he said. You used to be a free spirit.

But then you wanted me to be somebody I'm not. You wanted every part of my life to belong to you.

You made every little thing an explosion.

Like the goldfish. It was just a mistake. I forgot. People make mistakes. But you cried and you cried. Do you know how ugly you are when you cry? You were ridiculous. Sometimes things are broken. It's not anybody's fault.

You just wouldn't stop talking. You were always talking. But none of the words were important.

Like now.

You blame me, but it was your choice to come here. It was your choice to be with me, no matter what. I'm not your knight. And you cried about everything. It was impossible.

You're gaslighting me, do you know that? You keep telling me my actions hurt you. But did they really? Aren't you responsible for your own emotions?

If you had only just left me alone. If only you'd gone away when I told you.

Then this would never have happened to you.

Then those little goldfish would be alive.

In a slow place, I saw it for a second time. There were voices there, distant and fleeting, asking me to stop. There were hands, reaching. They receded away with the tide. It was hard to blink, as if my eyelids were glue. I groaned and tasted the salt spray on the back of my tongue. At first, each step I took was a laboured thing. There was sand beneath my feet, sinking down around my toes.

Reality rushed back over me. Sight and sound pounded at my temples and I wanted to go back there, where it was soft and quiet. Rocks and ocean tempted me, with only the boardwalk of Coney Island behind me, glittering and blaring and all too much. I bolted to the water. Shivers took over me. I gusted along with the wind until the waves closed in.

Further and further I pummelled myself into the foam. My hands clenched and grasped and gripped for a handle on the waves. Salt water burned my lungs and my throat closed itself off against the rising tide. Only my constant coughing ensured that I was still pulling breath. But I wanted it that way. This was good. I swallowed down the acid rising in my stomach. I expected the beach to be dirtier, poisoned like the Hudson. But there was none of the havoc of New York City here. Just the rolling clouds above me ghosting over the setting sun, splaying shades of rose quartz and blue tourmaline. There was peace and stillness and the kindest kind of momentum. I spiralled in. It was okay. It was okay. It was okay.

No-one tells you about the warmth. How it feels when you finally let yourself think about letting go. I closed my eyes and thought about a little golden bed of light where you put your head down and just stop. I don't know when I started thinking about that place. I don't know when I started looking for it. But the water was warm, gliding over my skin. It pulled me in and pushed the world further away. I was wrong to search upwards. This was it, this was so much closer than that night at the Empire State.

Soon I was weightless, both floating and sinking. The cold fell away. Goodbye, goodbye. It didn't hurt and it hurt a lot. My lungs screamed. The back of my head tilted backwards and backwards, as if it was trying to adhere itself to the backs of my shoulders. My eyes forgot how to close. Darkness and stillness surrounded and the endless pinprick of stars. Stars above and below. This was sanctuary. This was a place to rest.

And yet there was movement.

Do you remember when you were a child, and stepping into the ocean, when it happened? Maybe it wasn't your first time. Maybe you'd been in water time after time after time. But then you looked down, and the water was dark and you couldn't quite see, and in the depths there was something. *Something.* Inexplicable. All the calm in you shrivelled away when you realised how wrong you had been, to trust that water. Something reached for you, and even though it only touched your skin for the briefest moment, you recoiled and ran and screamed and never quite trusted again?

That moment is yours and mine and belongs to more, a common thread between us.

And there I spun that thread out again, and pulled surrender and slumber back into myself as I realised the darkness was wrong. Something had slipped past me and knocked me off my axis, leaving me tumbling and reeling into starlight.

My arms thrashed of their own accord as *it* approached for the second time, curving around me in a wide arc. Lights danced across its body, its giant tail as thin as a piece of paper, voluminous and liquid and soft. Fins in equal measure billowed out from its body. This was not the sort of being that hurried, its scales and delicate appendages each built from dreams. Each part of it glittered and melded and made one final rupture through the water with its tail. Darkness rushed to fill its wake and pulled me alongside, barrelling me forward until I faced its magnanimous eyes.

I opened my mouth (to scream?) but there was no air left. Instead only the memory of air, tiny bubbles like pearls, spiralling out and leaving my body in all directions.

The eyes are gold, not the silver of whatever faced me in the sky.

And they both won't let me die. They want me to go home.

It drifted over me until its belly was close enough to brush the tip of my upturned nose. Thunder clapped, a dull, horrendous sound that sliced across my skin and it descended. I was smothered in its fins, inhaling scales, its massive body dragging me endlessly down. Or is it up? I don't know anymore.

Nobody likes having two sisters. It leaves you outnumbered.

Why did you stay in the first place? asks the first. It is not a question. Her voice is anger and tightness and trembling sadness.

I love him, I answer. Because even now it is still true.

Get on a place, she says. Just get on a plane. Forget him.

It's not just his fault, I explain. I did things.

None of that matters, says the second. She is stillness. She is the silver moon hovering over the ocean. She is my home town on a Friday night, when the sun has set and the beaches are empty. I can taste the sea spray. It seems like a memory borrowed from somebody else.

Come home, she says, we will take care of you.

But that's worse. Once they set their laser gazes on my ruined body, that's all I'll ever be. I will be a hushed conversation hidden between hands. This worldwide ditch between me and my beautiful sisters will widen to a chasm, their sighs of horror echoing out across the valleys of what's left of me.

They are right. It's incredibly stupid to stay here. This isn't my city. Even the light is wrong. I need the Australian sun. I need to lie down in it and sleep.

But I put down the phone and walk away every time, until my beautiful sisters sob and hang up. Or the phone runs out of power. Whichever is first.

This is not fair on them. Everything that I am. I should go home and face them. They deserve that. When I think that, I realise whatever is holding me is not enough.

But the moment passes, and I linger on.

I don't want to open my eyes. I've adjusted to the void and leaving it behind burns. But soon enough there is sun and wind and water gliding over my body and pushing darkness away. Gravity cannot be denied, it is the only goddess that insists.

There are hands too, pulling me up from the sand. When I swallow I taste salt and stars. But the aftertaste is different somehow: crisper, brighter?

Homelier.

So are the voices that clamour around me. I don't understand how it's possible, how I could have gotten here so quickly. But their faces can't be denied. I find my feet, stand up, teetering precariously as I reach for them. I breath in my sister's hair and smell the geraniums in her garden. Behind me, a second pair of hands laces its fingers with mine, clutching me the same way that they used to, when we were all small, full of giggles, tucked away in a blanket big enough for three little ones.

How can you be here? asks the first. You're in New York. You cannot be here. This is bloody Fairy Meadow.

The only answers I have are laced across my wrists. Red curves littered on top of one another, pressed hard into my skin and leaving eternal impressions. I cannot tell if I cut these myself, in slips of northern darkness, or if they're as fresh as they look. Perhaps it's some kind of reminder.

I don't understand, says the second. But let's get you home. Her eyes are glimmering and gold.

We're all together now, says the first. It'll be okay now. Even if it hurts. We'll be okay.

She's right. I smile and that hurts too.

About the Author:

Rebecca Dale is a speculative fiction writer living on Dharug Country. Visit rebeccadale.com.au for more information.

THE BETRAYAL OF IKHTHUS

Austin P. Sheehan

We were defeated. I knew it in my bones. Looking back, our
mission had been doomed from the start. When our fleet left the
bay of Timos, we had been beset by ill omens; portents of failure,
portents of doom. Not that there were ever shortages of those in
times of war.

The war between Thalassia and the treacherous Valakians
had gone on for years, and the once fertile stretch of land that
joined our two kingdoms was knee-deep with the dead. But
during the dark and bitter winter, the Valakians had invaded the
neutral island kingdom of Orten, attempting to intimidate them
into an alliance. Royal messengers arrived—disguised as
merchants—who called upon our leaders for aid. They outlined a
clever strategy: thirty Thalassian ships and three of our precious
magi—Wind, War and Sea—in a mission to free their kingdom,
win their alliance, and thus tip the balance of war in our favour.

As winter loosened its hold upon the earth, our thirty ships
had left the Thalassian bay on a mission to turn the tide of war
against the Valakians. Three brave leaders lead our forces, each
with ten ships of fighting men and a magi. Tesserarius Encanno's
magi was the Servant of Tyndaridae, third of the ancients, ruler

of the wind. Tessararius Homata was appointed the Servant of Toxotes, the ninth ancient, the God of war. Tessararius Nahuma was appointed the Servant of the twelfth ancient, Ikhthus, whose domain was the sea.

Before we had lost sight of our homeland, the fleet encountered ill omens, which foretold betrayal, fire, and an angry, bloodthirsty sea. Thinking to outwit the gods, the Tessararia Encanno, Homata and Nahuma decided to split the fleet for a three-pronged attack. Only the mages—elderly, wizened and bitter—urged caution, warning that the gods do not like to be tricked.

Two days after the fleets separated, the southerly skies turned dark and we were assailed by heavy gusts of wind. Trierarchus Massai, who had traversed these seas before, gave the order to furl the sails, hold our course and row. Strong winds were not uncommon at the end of winter, so Tesserarius Nahuma heeded his advice.

Huddled belowdecks, there was little for us soldiers to do but play dice or watch the rough sea and grey sky from the ship's sidescuttles, which let light and fresh sea air into the cramped quarters. Before long, soldiers—on the lookout for land, fish or sea siren—saw fog approaching, surrounding us. *Another ill sign.*

"These winds, the rough seas, and now fog." The deep voice of Kova, our keenly-forged Decanus, rumbled behind me. "I do not hold with this talk of omens, but how can we be certain of our bearings?" His query echoed my own, though I was in no position to voice it.

We were near the stairs the deck and were fortunate to hear Tesserarius Nahuma ask the same question.

"Trierarchus, what is this fog? How has it not been blown away by the mighty wind?"

"That's the Notia Omichlia, the fog of the southern ocean." Massai's voice was full of confidence. "These seas are full of mystery, Tesserarius Nahuma. But have no fear, we have not been blown off course."

"Thank the ancients, thanks to Tyndaridae," said Nahuma.

As Decanus Kova reassured the soldiers with Massai's words, mutterings of thanks to the ancient ruler of the winds echoed amongst the soldiers, and our concern eased.

For the next hour, despite the ship rolling against rough seas, we relaxed. We were confident in Massai's words, assured of the protection of the gods.

With a bone-jarring crunch, the ship jerked to the side, throwing us against the wall. Salt water sprayed through the sidescuttles, covering us all without regard to rank or honour.

"The fog has concealed a violent tempest!" Treirarchus Massai's shouted from above. "To the deck, soldiers!" roared the Decanus. "Perhaps our strength can assist in this battle against the sea!"

I fought down the fear in my stomach and followed Decanus Kova. As we reached the open sky, the heavens opened up and rain sheeted down on us. Howling winds tore at our sails and ferocious waves burst through the fog, towering over our ships.

"Decanus, go rouse Magi Algerbon," Tessarius Nahuma yelled. "Have him call upon Ihkthus to soothe the treacherous sea!"

As Kova returned below decks, we were hit by another wave. The force jerked soldiers off their feet and into the dark, churning depths. I slipped, crashing to the deck, the weight of my armour dragging me towards the edge. Tessarius Nahuma's hand reached for mine as I slid past, destined to the depths. I caught his hand, righted myself and grabbed the mast, shaking with fear.

"Grab ahold of something or go downstairs!" the Trierarchus shouted as we were hit by yet another wave. "My crew and I will try to turn us against the waves and the wind, but only experienced seafarers should hazard our aid."

"I will stay and help," Nahuma declared.

"Very well, but I suggest the rest of your soldiers go and pray with the Servant of Ikhthus!"

From belowdecks came the murmured incantation of Magi Algerbon. As the ship pitched and tilted, I did not loosen my grip on the mast. Below me, the voices of the soldiers repeated the chants of the mage, amplifying his pleas to the ancients to calm the seas. With my knuckles white against the mast, I did the same.

After several harrowing hours the tempest died away and the seas calmed. Our fleet had been reduced to six ships: two had snapped their masts when the powerful gusts had caught their poorly furled sails. Two more were lost to the waves. But we took solace; we had faced the worst of it and the other two fleets would have been unscathed by the storm that caused us such harm. We had no way of knowing how wrong we were.

The next day we sighted the coast of Orten; mountainous and rugged, green and full of life. A bay surrounded by dense trees and steep hills was where the Royal Messenger suggested a fleet land. It felt as if the gods had smiled upon us again. Tessarius Nahuma sent a scouting party into the mountains. As we awaited their return we unloaded our supplies.

It was the glow of fire in the hills above that was the first sign we had yet again been deceived, been betrayed.

The familiar shriek of a Valakian war trumpet split the silence of the secluded bay. In an instant, the sky was full of flaming arrows. Thin trails of smoke described their passage as they passed overhead and down towards the ships.

Tessarius Nahuma jumped into action, shouting orders above the chaos. "Soldiers, defensive positions! Archers, draw."

We rushed into our defensive formation, four ranks of one hundred soldiers, bristling with sword and spear, two rows of a hundred archers behind us.

There was no movement in the hills, just another volley of arrows.

Nahuma glanced at the ranks of soldiers, then up at the hills surrounding us. "Decanus Kova, take your soldiers into the mountains and engage those archers."

I swallowed, and following Kova's lead, rushed for the cover of the trees. We saw even less under the thick branches, which had kept their leaves despite the recent winter. The dense foliage muted the sounds of our comrades, all we could hear were our own footsteps, our own panicked breaths.

"What are the Valakians doing here?" I asked in a whisper.

"What happened to the arrangement the Ortens made?" Sophanus asked.

"Shh," Kova hissed. "The only way to find out is to get through this." He signalled for us to press on.

The hill was steep, and we had to sheath our weapons and use the trunks and branches of trees to pull us up. Every sense I had told me something was wrong. The Valakians should not have been there, should not have been ready for us.

A low rumble shook the ground, accompanied by the sound of tree trunks splitting. *Oh no.*

"What's that?" Sophanus asked as our eyes scanned the mountains above for the source of the noise.

"There!" A sphere of light—a ball of fire—was hurtling towards us. It crashed into trees, threw them out of its way.

"Return to the boats!" Decanus Kova yelled, recognising the threat.

72

We turned and ran down the mountain, straight into a row of advancing swords and shields.

"Tessarius, we must return to the boats!" Kova urged, panic rising in his voice.

"I say when we retreat!" Nahuma said, his voice firm.

"We have no—" Screams from the soldiers drowned out Decaus Kova's voice as three fireballs burst through the trees, cutting through rows of warriors, and continued on towards the ships.

"Soldiers of Thalassa, return to the boats!" Nahuma cried, too late.

Our ranks broke just in time to see a ship explode in flames. Treirarchus Massai and his men pushed a ship out of the way of the second fireball, and the third narrowly missed another ship.

"'Ware the archers!" roared the Decanus and Tessarius, to no avail. In a panic, we waded into the sea, so preoccupied with returning to the ships that many forgot to defend themselves from the arrows falling from the sky.

By the time another of our ships had been destroyed and the last of the men had boarded the remaining four ships, the beach was covered with corpses, the sea red with blood.

Tessarius Nahuma, Magi Algerbon, and the Trierarchi of the surviving ships debated long about the disaster that had befallen us, about we should do. Either the King of Orten had allied with the Valakians and had betrayed us, or the Valakians had overrun Orten during the winter, either learning of our arrangement or chancing upon us. They made the decision to travel north, find where Tesserarius Encanno had landed, and join our forces. Together we would get our revenge on the Valakian horde.

That night, those of us who could sleep dreamt either of bloody revenge, or of the ancients turning upon us and leading us to our ruin. No matter what our dreams, we woke to the sound of wood splintering, of our ships shuddering. My heart sank. We had run aground. The angry seas were not done with us yet. Only one of the ships had avoided the submerged reef, and it was not big enough to carry the surviving soldiers. Nahuma ordered the soldiers to shore, and many voices asked if we had angered the ancients, whether the Servant of Ikhthus had done enough to ask for the sea God's blessing.

Magi Algerbon's response was curt. "The Gods' plans can be hard to fathom. And Ikhthus, the ancient in all his power, does not control the shape of the land. Hidden reefs do not answer to him."

Nahuma urged haste. He had no doubt that the Valakian army was watching our fleet and would soon be on our heels. We began our trek through the low hills of Orten towards the city of Akagine, where we hoped to find sign of Encanno's army.

For over a week we pushed north. The Valakian horde pursued us, and we had to fight just to survive, barely escaping the clutches of the enemy time and time again, and we had still seen no trace of Tesserarius Encanno's army. Our mighty force, once numbering one thousand, had been reduced to just eighty, and none of us were without our scars.

As the sun set, casting an unearthly orange-red glow, hundreds of Valakian soldiers appeared from the low hills to the south. The silver of rectangular shields, the tips of countless spears and curved blades reflected the sickening orange glow. From the north came the sounds of hundreds of marching feet. Another army. My heart rose, surely this must be Encanno's force. But no, I looked north to see the pennons and bandums attached to their spears were the grey and blue of Orten.

As the two armies linked up and surrounded us, I knew it was over. We were defeated. We had been betrayed from the start. My tired, aching muscles wanted to give up, to lay down in the sand like so many of my comrades. Like them, I wanted to be carried by the ancient ones to the eternal battle grounds, to feast with the worthy. My time had not yet come, but it was close, so close.

The enemy soldiers shuffled aside and a wheeled platform was pushed forward. On the platform were three iron cages, two occupied by the emaciated figures of the Magi who had travelled with Tessarius Encanno and with Tessarius Homata; the Servant of Tyndaridae and the Servant of Toxotes. Their hands were bound, their mouths gagged.

"Soldiers of Thalassa, Defensive formation!" Tesserarius Nahuma shouted. We formed two lines of thirty in front of our archers. Behind them stood Magi Algerbon, the proud and defiant Servant of Ikhthus, the twelfth of the ancients, the ruler of the sea.

"Your other armies have been beaten." A rough voice boomed from the Orten line. "You cannot hold any hope of victory!"

"Tesserarius Nahuma, you are surrounded. Surrender your magic-maker, your evil one, and we will show you mercy." The strong voice of the Valakian cornicern echoed above the crashing of the waves. "You have been betrayed. Your gods are dead."

Nahuma ignored the taunts from the enemy commander's herald, as he had before every battle. My eyes met his; haggard, grey and defiant. A hint of a smile on his dry, cracked lips. I prayed he would live to ignore the cornicern yet again.

"Magi Algerbon, our need is mighty. You must try again to call upon the ancient Ikhthus for aid!"

"I will do what I can, Tesserarius," the mage replied, his voice fraying against the wind. "But the lives and wishes of men matter little to the gods."

"Perhaps, yet they matter a lot to me. You must do this."

Algerbon—weak of flesh but unyielding in faith—began his murmuring of an invocation, filling the air with his potent chants, making my hairs stand on end. From the ranks of enemy soldiers came the slow rhythmic banging of war drums, trying to drown out his voice. He would not be cowed and his fraying voice rose, chanting in rhythm with the drums, accenting and strengthening his invocation.

A shrill trumpet blast filled the air. The Valakian forces pressed forward. Step by step they marched down to the beach, the sunset reflecting off their armour, and the leather-bound ranks of the Orten soldiers followed suit.

Snakes of fear burst to life in my stomach, constant companions over the last weeks of endless conflict. I clutched my shield, already dented and scarred from countless blows, and prayed to the ancients that it would protect me again.

Nahuma stepped forward, commanding our attention. He spat towards the line of overwhelming enemy soldiers. "We'll not be defeated by these bastards."

His calm defiance soothed the snakes in my stomach. He was not afraid. Perhaps there was still a way out of this. Perhaps he had faith that the ancient Ikhthus would sense our need, would respond. And if not, we would die as heroes and join the eternal feast.

"Archers ready!" Nahuma's voice was cold and firm. There was no one who could hear it and not obey.

My heart beat faster as the soldiers approached and I tightened my grip on the handle of my sword.

"Archers, release!" A volley of arrows shot overhead. As they hit their mark and enemy soldiers fell, inspired by Magi Algerbon's frantic chanting, the eager fire of battle coursed through my veins. I was ready to defend the Tesserarius, my comrades, and the Magi of Ikhthus to the death.

Before the archers launched another volley, the approaching soldiers faltered, a peal of thunder sounding over the ocean.

A silver flash split the dark sky, heavy clouds full of rain, full of anger. The Valakian war drums were silenced, the only sound over the waves crashing was the Magi's fierce cry, "It is done!"

His words filled me with a dreadful, dark hope. As I turned to look, my heart sank. A mountain of water sped towards us.

"Soldiers of Thalassa, servants of the ancient twelve, pray to Ikhthus and you shall be spared!"

I bowed by head, welcoming death. Welcoming the arrival of the ancient and powerful Ikhthus.

My heart beat once, twice, and the wave was upon us, rushing through us with a bone crushing force, as if all the anger of the sea had been united into one unstoppable wall of death. I heard nothing but an ear-splitting roar and screams of terror.

The smell of the sea was stronger than I expected in the afterlife. I knelt on the damp ground in prayer, in gratitude. It was finally over. Familiar cries of pain and fear broke through the thunder. I opened my eyes, ready for a glimpse of the eternal battlegrounds.

My heart lurched. I was back on the endless Orten beach, the sea lapping at my wrists. Before me, Magi Algerbon knelt in the water, arms raised to the heavens. Surrounding us were countless enemy bodies, their faces contorted in expressions of terror.

Something dark stirred in the ocean's depths, and the familiar snakes of fear returned. The water parted and a grotesque, gigantic figure burst from the waves, towering over us. I wanted to turn, to run, but I was like a stone, unable to look away from the creature's massive head with a wicked elongated face and black eyes.

Icicles of fear raced down my back as the creature's body emerged from the depths. Muscular arms, as wide as the trunks of the oldest trees, ended in massive serrated crab claws. *What was this monstrosity?* Its body was at least twenty spans across, covered with hair like seaweed, thick and black.

"Sons and daughters of Thalassia," intoned Magi Algerbon, his deep voice breaking through my fear. "Behold Ancient Ikhthus, Ruler of the Deep, Twelfth God of the Eternal Twelve." *No!* The monster was a mockery of the icons of the benevolent sea-centaur. This thing was grotesque and radiated a sick malice. It just couldn't be.

The creature's eyes bored into me. Its laugh, like the crashing of the waves, echoed through my soul.

"Ikhthus the Ancient, the Victorious, the Ruler of the Deep," my voice intoned, in chorus with the other surviving Thalassian soldiers. I tried to close my mouth, to stop the words that had come, unbidden, from my lips.

"We look upon you and know salvation." *No!* "We will follow you to the darkest core of creation. Until our last breath, we will be bound to you." *NO!*

The ancient God turned, its long finned tail flicking out behind. Cascading laughter echoed through my skull as it sunk back into the dark, angry sea.

As the night chased the last of the sun's rays from the sky, waves crashed against the empty beach. All remnant of friend and foe had been claimed, and any trace of the betrayal of Ikhthus had been washed away.

About the Author:

Austin P. Sheehan is a writer of speculative fiction and lives just north of Melbourne on Wurundjeri Woi Wurrung country with his wife and their greyhounds.

Austin's debut novella 'Submerged City' *was published by Deadset Press in 2019. His work is also featured in* 'From The Waste Land' *by PS Publishing which celebrates the centenary of T S Eliot's poem, and Planet Scumm and Etherea magazines, as well as anthologies by Black Hare Press, Deadset Press, ScoutMedia, Fantasia Divinity, and Blood Song Books.*

Find him on twitter @AustinPSheehan, or go to www.austinpsheehan.com.

ARIES
MARCH 21 - APRIL 19

WITCHFINDER'S LOVER

Stephen Herczeg

"Good evening Miss Audrey," said William as he helped the young woman into the front seat of the small horse-drawn wagon. His bright blue eyes shone with an inner glow even in the dim afternoon light.

"Thank you, William. Damnable horrible night for it." Audrey looked up at the darkening sky and threatening clouds building on the horizon.

William sat down beside her and took up the reins. "That it is Miss Audrey. That it is. We should make good time. If it holds out, we'll be in Ipswich before midnight. If not, then there are a couple of inns along the way. Small towns but nice enough. Mr Hopkins has told me to look after you as if you were me own daughter, so nary a hair on your head will be mussed if I can helps it."

Audrey glanced around the wagon. The tiny market town of Lavenham wasn't much to look at and she was quite glad to leave. The townsfolk weren't happy when they arrived and were even angrier now, they were going.

Granted, Matthew had executed justice on the town and found five of their women guilty of various acts of witchcraft.

Audrey Mayfair was proud of her role as chief investigator for Matthew Hopkins, the Witchfinder General. Her job was to unearth the rumours, gossip and scuttlebutt in the towns they visited and locate the practitioners of witchcraft and devil worship.

It mostly involved finding those who had been wronged in their dealings with the miscreants. Her methods ranged from bribery to seeding doubt in the minds of the townsfolk. When small minds were reminded of the commitment to their Lord, they were quick to denounce criminals in their midst.

Upon Audrey's recommendation, Matthew brought the accused to trial. The defendant was offered a choice. Confess and burn at the stake or be dunked in a lake. If the waters rejected them, they would be hanged, if not they were deemed innocent and given a proper Christian burial.

After many successes over the last few years, Audrey had come to Matthew's attention and been elevated in his ranks. Eventually, she had been raised in his affections as well, spending the last year as Matthew's lover. Even though, Matthew operated above the church and was immune to much of their prescribed doctrine. Their life together enjoyed all the characteristics of a married couple, except in the eyes of the Lord.

"Hold on Miss and we'll be away."

William's voice shook Audrey from her reveries.

She held onto the side rail as the horse kicked and the carriage jolted forward. Soon they were away from Lavenham and trotting along through open countryside.

William raised his voice over the horse's clopping, "so, you'll be joining Mr Hopkins up in Norwich?"

"Yes. We are expecting to unearth a lot of witches and Mr Hopkins wants me to bring Shelley and Caroline."

"You'll be using the closed carriage, with young Rodgers driving it, then," he said as he looked over his shoulder at the darkening sky. "Least it will keep you out of this sort of weather." He lashed the reins to spur the horse on. "Come on Nobby, you dozy mule, get a wiggle on. There's a tankard of ale waiting for me, I can feel it in me bones."

The wagon rocked and jumped over the uneven and rutted road. Audrey and William held on for dear life, crashing into each other numerous times to avoid being thrown from the seat.

A drop of rain landed on Audrey's neck and she peered over her shoulder. A dark thunderhead rolled across the fields, chasing them with outstretched arms of black cloud. The wind picked up and made desperate grabs at her hat and coat. The rain started in earnest and soon they were both drenched to the skin.

Nobby galloped on through the torrent, his steady feet finding footholds on the muddy track where none appeared to be.

Until it happened.

A bright bolt of lightning blasted down and smashed into a gigantic oak tree on the apex of a tight corner. The trunk ignited into the shape of a flaming ram's skull, with curling horns on either side, and glowing ovine eyes that stared straight into Audrey's own."

Nobby skidded away from the spectre, galloping off the road and into an adjacent gulley.

The wagon twisted sideways, launching both Audrey and William into the air. As she flew, time slowed, extending her moment of terror. The wagon crashed and the terrified horse screamed in pain at the bottom of the hollow. William landed with a bone crunching thud, and Audrey upon meeting the sodden earth, heard her leg crack as it struck a protruding rock. Her mind exploded with fire and pain as her head hit the ground.

It was extinguished as the darkness consumed her.

Audrey's eyes flickered open. A pale blur hovered nearby framed against a dark background. She blinked several times to clear the crust from her eyes. "William?" she said.

The pale figure shook its head and spoke. "No, no. I'm Maggie."

Audrey lifted a hand that felt like a dead weight and rubbed at her eyes. She blinked and peered at the figure.

"M-M-Maggie?" Audrey asked, her throat raw. "Where is William? He was driving. I saw him fly. Where am I? Is Matthew here?" The figure came into focus, and Audrey saw she was a beautiful young woman.

"You are in our house. A little way from where your carriage crashed. I don't know who Matthew is, perhaps you can tell me about him when you're a little better. As to your driver, William is it? We will talk later. You are still weak. Rest a while and I'll bring food to help build your strength up."

Audrey slumped back into the bed. She closed her eyes to seek more sleep. Voices drifted into the room.

"Well?" said a deeper, older voice.

"She has awakened but is still exhausted. She asked about William. That would be the driver I'd say. I've told her to go back to sleep. I'll take her some food in a while."

"It's a waste of our food," said a gruff voice.

"Esme, what a horrible thing to say. We have more use for that young lass than we do for the food. She will be important in the coming days," said the older voice.

Audrey's mind trailed off as sleep claimed her once more.

She awoke with a start and looked around the dark room. Her head still throbbed, and she found a huge egg-shaped lump on her forehead that was tender to touch. She winced and cried out in pain.

A noise grabbed her attention.

Moonlight filtered through the gaps in the window shutters and cast bright lines across the sheer curtain and onto the floor.

A shadow fell across the window. Audrey gasped, as she watched it sway from side to side before moving away. A crunch of gravel and a scraping noise followed its withdrawal.

Audrey sat still, her eyes fixed on the window as the crunching footsteps receded. For what seemed like an eternity, she held her breath, alert for any sign of return.

Finally, she let her breath out. She thought about looking outside but fear got the better of her. She lay down and pulled the bed covers over her head.

Bright light exploded across Audrey's closed eyelids. She turned her face away from the sunlight that streamed into the room, opened her eyes, blinked several times to adjust her focus and peered back.

Maggie stood in the middle of the open window, her arms stretched up to the ceiling welcoming the bright daylight onto her face and the green dress she wore. "Ah, nothing better than a beautiful sun-filled day," she said over her shoulder.

Audrey peered past her and spied the rolling fields stretching out toward the distant hills. Seas of long grasses and crops swayed in the light breeze and dazzled in the sunlight. "It's beautiful," she said.

Maggie turned and smiled. "It is," she said. "Today we'll get you up and about, so you can enjoy it and take your fill of the mother's gifts."

"The mother?"

"Yes, Mother Nature, silly."

Audrey mouthed a silent, "Oh" as Maggie moved across to the bed. She pulled back the covers and Audrey saw that she was now dressed in an unfamiliar plain spun smock that reached to just above her knees, and that a bandage had been wrapped around her right calf. She winced as the memory of pain spiked in her brain.

Maggie undid the binding around Audrey's leg and drew the bandage away. Audrey reeled back at the foul odour and closed her eyes to protect herself from what was sure to be a hideous sight. The young woman removed the dressing from Audrey's leg revealing long ropes of thick yellow fluid which smelt revolting. Audrey reeled back at the smell and let out a disgusted cry.

Maggie chuckled and said, "Oh, it's not as bad as all that. Esme's poultices are always a little smelly, but they do the job. See for yourself."

Audrey opened her eyes to see the thick fluid on her leg as Maggie dropped the dressing into a bucket by the bed. As Maggie gently washed away the remains of the foul-smelling poultice with a wet rag, Audrey winced, expecting more pain, but there was very little. Once clean, the devastation she expected on her leg was nothing more than a mass of dark but fading bruises.

Audrey stared in surprise. "But I heard it snap. And the pain. I was sure it was broken. How?" she stammered.

Again, Maggie chuckled. "Oh, no. It wasn't broken, just a fair bit of bruising and some small cuts. We cleaned you up, put the poultice on and bandaged it. You slept for the most part, but that looks like it's healing very nicely," she said.

Audrey was dumbstruck. "How long have I been here?"

"Just two nights. You're young. Strong. You heal quickly. Esme's poultice worked a treat as well."

Audrey was about to ask more, but Maggie reached out for her arms.

"Let's see how it holds up to some walking." She slipped Audrey forward until her feet touched the floor.

"I don't know. I don't think I should just yet."

"Nonsense, just put some weight on it and see how it goes."

Audrey placed her feet flat on the floor, leaned forward and tentatively stood up. She expected searing pain to lance up her leg, but there was none.

Maggie led Audrey with no problems. She smiled. Audrey smiled.

"Excellent, let's go out and see the others," Maggie said.

The pair stepped through into a room devoid of humans. Maggie frowned. "I thought they were here. I wanted them to finally meet you face to face," Maggie said as she moved across to another doorway and looked through.

Audrey followed Maggie into the plain but functional room. Its simplicity was in stark contrast the large ram's head carved above the door. The detail was striking, with eyes that seemed to fix on her own gaze.

Maggie suddenly pulled back from the doorway, as two men burst through carrying a third. They lifted the man and dumped him onto the table. He cried out in pain.

His lower leg was a mess of blood and torn tissue, a jagged piece of white bone stuck out of the wound. Audrey turned away with an audible gasp, but the disturbing sight dragged her attention back.

Maggie moved across to the table and patted the man's forehead, cooing to him to allay his pain. "It will be alright Sam. Gertha and Esme will be here soon. You will be fine in no time."

The man's only response was to cry out again. As he began squirming in pain, Maggie looked up at the two men. "David, Michael, hold him still. Otherwise, he'll hurt himself further."

They nodded and took Sam by the shoulders and thighs to stifle his movement.

Just then two more women entered the room, a matronly woman in her late forties and a withered old crone that must have been well past eighty. The matron held a basket of herbs and mushrooms. She went to the kitchen cupboard and placed it down.

The old crone turned to Maggie, "Maggie. Hot water and some clean cloth." She craned her ancient neck to the matronly woman. "Gertha, prepare a porter's poultice."

"Already on it, Esme." The matron pulled down a mortar and pestle and several jars of herbs and grains.

Audrey watched her as she ground and stirred up the mixture.

The crone moved across to the cupboard and pulled out a pottery jar. She extracted a couple of dried leaves and moved back to Sam. She grabbed his mouth and popped the leaves inside. "Chew on this for a bit," she said.

Sam obliged. The action of chewing tore his attention away from the pain. As he chewed, Sam's eyes rolled back as if drawn into a dream-like state. A powerful stench of strange herbs filled the room. Esme placed a small cylinder of leather into the injured man's mouth.

Esme looked at Michael. "Make sure he bites down on this while I fix his leg, he's gonna need to," she said. The man nodded and managed to hold Sam down with one hand and the leather block with the other.

Maggie arrived with the hot water and cloths. Esme dunked a cloth into the water, wrung it out and slopped it onto the leg. Sam cried out in pain, his teeth clamping down hard on the leather.

"Good boy," said Esme. "But we've only started."

"Should we get a Doctor?" Audrey asked, grabbing Maggie by the arm.

The young girl shrugged her off, a hint of smile on her face. "No Doctor can do what Esme can."

Horrified, but fascinated, Audrey watched as Esme went to work. She quickly cleaned the area around the wound, revealing the extent of the injury, then dropped the blood-soaked cloth into the bucket and prepared herself for the next stage.

"Hold him down boys. Tight," Esme said, pressing her fingers against the protruding bone and pushed it back into the wound.

Audrey gasped and clutched her hands to her face. They slipped away and folded together as she let out a silent prayer for the poor man.

Sam screamed out, the leather bite-block exploded from his mouth and landed on the floor. He struggled against Michael's hands for a moment then flopped back unconscious.

"Well that makes things easier," said Esme. She quickly pushed the two pieces of leg bone together, using her palm to finish the job. The bones ground together horribly as they slipped back in place. Bile rose in Audrey's stomach.

"Needle and yarn."

Maggie pulled out a long needle with the yarn already threaded from a nearby sewing basket. Esme pinched the skin together, grabbed the needle and sewed the wound shut. When finished, she gave the bloody needle back to Maggie.

"Gertha, poultice."

Gertha brought the mortar over and placed it on the table. Esme slopped the thick mixture across the entire area while Gertha placed wet strips of cloth across the wound, then tied them up with dry strips.

The whole process lasted less than five minutes. When finished, Esme stepped back, washed her hands in the bucket and wiped them down her apron.

She turned to the men and said, "Right, take him home. Bedrest for a couple of days. I'll see him tomorrow to check on the wound. Tell Mabel I'll expect a healthy spring lamb come April."

Michael nodded his head and said, "Thank you, Granny. Will do." The two men bowed, carefully picked up Sam and headed for the door.

Audrey stood in the shadows near the wall, a dumbstruck look on her face.

The crone turned towards her. "You'd be Audrey then," she said.

Audrey lay back on the bed and digested the events of the day. Her head swam.

How did I end up here? I should be in Ipswich, ready to join Matthew in Norwich.

Her thoughts turned to Matthew.

Would he miss her yet? Would he be worried? No, too early. He'd be preparing to seek out the coven of witches.

The crone had introduced herself as Esmerelda. Granny to many, Esme to some. Esme and Gertha said they had lived on the farm for decades, Maggie only joining them the previous

94

year. She had run away from her own parents and found solitude
and safety with the two older women.

They talked for ages with Audrey, about her background, her
childhood, her time with Matthew, the witch trials and various
other small topics. But the three women didn't talk much about
themselves. Audrey knew almost as much now as she had this
morning.

When Audrey raised the subject of William, her driver, the
older pair made excuses and left. Her heart sank when Maggie
said they had found poor William at the scene. He had broken
his neck and was beyond even Granny's healing skills. They'd
buried him near the road and placed a small cross as a marker.

Audrey cried, for William, for Maureen his widow, and with
the realisation that it could have so easily been her. William was
a friend of Matthew's, but only a colleague to her. It was those
piercing blue eyes that would remain in her mind as a reminder
of him, but his face would fade with time.

Finally, Maggie led Audrey outside into the light of the day.

The farm was small. The women raised some pigs and sheep
and tended a small vegetable and herb garden. They were women
of limited wants and means, and the farm satisfied most of them.

During the day, a constant dribble of visitors from nearby
farms and villages came to the farm. Maggie said most came
because of health problems. The three women studied the
healing arts and were happy to offer their services to folk. They

asked for no money, but any donations of food or other items were always welcome.

All the visitors followed the path from the north, as the southern end of the farm was bordered by a deep, thick forest that stretched off into the distance. Audrey peered towards it.

Maggie noticed and said, "The wood is ancient. Filled with the power of nature. There we seek the special herbs and mushrooms for our poultices and medicines."

Audrey concentrated harder, but her eyes failed to penetrate the darkness of the trees.

"The folk around here fear the wood. Which suits us as they leave it well alone."

Audrey eyes opened wide as she caught sight of a tall, gnarled figure standing near the edge of the trees. She blinked several times, but by the time she looked back, it was gone.

I must have imagined it.

Audrey snapped awake. The last vestiges of a scraping noise died away in her subconscious. A loud clap of thunder erased any further memories.

She sat bolt upright and listened to the sounds of the night. Rain sheeted against the thatched roof of the cottage. A stiff wind blew the curtains away from the window opening. Lightning lit up the gaps in the shutters.

Audrey rose and stepped across to the window. She pushed on the shutters, but they were locked on the outside.

Strange. Why lock it from outside? It's as if to keep someone in.

She peered through the largest gap. The night was pitch black, everything outside was obscured by the driving rain, only the lightning providing brief illumination.

A sudden clap of thunder shook her to her marrow. Lightning lit up the barren hill to the north-east of the farm.

A figure, slim and small, stood naked on the summit.

She stared at the hill, waiting for another flash of lightning. It came. She saw a woman. Young, slim, lithe but muscular. Her long tresses stuck to her naked back.

Maggie?

Another flash revealed a second figure. A huge, hulking form that towered over the smaller. Its humongous claws outstretched towards the woman, ready to strike.

Audrey screamed, "Maggie, watch out!"

Another crash of thunder and the lightning showed the slim figure alone again. The woman—Maggie?—turned towards Audrey. In an instant, Audrey saw her mistake.

The figure was ancient. Its skin wrinkled and sagging. Its breasts flopped like bags of soggy meat. The thin, grey hair hung in lank clods across the scalp and shoulders.

It wasn't Maggie but Esme. Eighty-year-old Esme. Standing naked in the rain.

Her bedroom door flew open. Maggie charged in carrying a candle, her face tired but frightened by Audrey's screams. "Audrey? What's wrong? Are you alright? Is your head paining you?"

The candle threw strange shadows across the room and made the young woman look ancient.

Audrey turned and pointed at the window. "I saw Esme. In the rain. Naked. There was a beast. I was afraid for her."

Maggie peered through a gap in the shutters. Her calm façade dropped for a moment. "There's nothing there. Why would Esme be out in this foul weather? See for yourself," she said, a touch of anger in her voice.

"But I'm sure I saw someone out there. I thought it was you, but then it looked more like Esme." Audrey peered out again. The storm raged on, but there was nothing there. She turned back to Maggie, a sheepish look on her face. "I'm sorry. I must have dreamt it all."

Maggie nodded, a smile returning to her face. "That must be it. Sleep again. We can go look outside tomorrow if that would comfort you."

Audrey nodded as she climbed back into bed. She laid back and closed her eyes. As soon as Maggie stepped out of the room, she sat up and stared at the window.

The storm raged on. Lightning lit up the night. Audrey began to tire, and her lids grew heavy. She failed to notice the shadow thrown across the window by one massive sheet of lightning.

By the next flash it was gone.

Audrey shuffled into the empty living area. The sun shone bright and high in the sky outside. She spied the hill off in the distance and her mind filled with images of a naked Esme and the towering hulk lit by the storm.

Maggie's voice broke her reverie. "You're up then, sleepy head?"

Audrey turned to see the young woman enter with a basketful of fresh vegetables. She moved to the cupboard and put the basket down.

"How is your head this morning?"

After the excitement of the thunderstorm and Audrey's visions of a naked woman, she hadn't even remembered about lump on her head and the headache it had caused. The pain had reduced, but a fog remained. "It's better. I just feel a little groggy," she replied.

Maggie gathered some items and set the table with a loaf of bread, a pot of marmalade and cutlery and crockery. She placed a jug of water and cup beside them. "Here, have some breakfast. It will settle your stomach and help your head." Maggie looked around, then sat and cut herself a slice of bread and piled on some marmalade. She sat back and took a bite, her eyes closed in bliss as she ate and moaned with pleasure. "Mrs Johnstone from two farms over makes this marmalade. It is wonderful," she said pushing the pot and bread towards Audrey. A cheeky grin came to Maggie's face. "Esme and Gertha are visiting a new mother at a nearby farm, so have some before they return. It's Esme's favourite. She's very protective of it."

Audrey smiled despite herself and prepared a slice of marmalade bread. She realised how hungry she was and wolfed down the first slice in no time. Once she was halfway through a second, she began to feel much better. She looked down at the simple homespun smock Maggie had loaned her. "Do you think we could find my carriage and bring back some of my things? I'm very thankful, but don't want to impose too much," she said.

Maggie's face changed from offended to a broad smile. "Certainly," she said. "We can visit that little hillock where you thought you saw Esme as well. It's on the way."

The small hill was nothing out of the ordinary. It was more the location that made it stand out. The immediate area surrounding it was flat and low, providing Audrey with a wonderful view across the farm to the deep dark wood. Audrey shielded her eyes and peered in the opposite direction. She noticed a narrow dirt track winding off into the distance.

Maggie's voice snapped her attention. "That's where your carriage left the road, where we found you and your poor driver." Maggie pointed towards a small copse of trees with her right hand while fingering the odd amulet she wore around her neck.

It was a small stone carved into a curved three-pronged triskele. In the middle was a carving in the same style of ram's head as that above the kitchen door. Audrey thought it a pretty but queer looking object.

After a short trudge across the muddy field they came upon the overturned carriage and the remains of the horse. Audrey cast an eye over the corpse of poor Nobby. The local foxes had found him and had their way. Flesh gave way to bone and sinew across the length of the animal. She turned away in revulsion and breathed deeply to maintain her composure and keep her breakfast intact.

"Poor animal," said Maggie. "It doesn't look like it suffered, and it has provided others with food, so all is not lost."

Audrey shot her a withering glance.

Maggie shrugged. "It is the way of the Mother. Of nature. Eventually we all become food for the worms." She pointed at an overturned trunk nestled against a tree. "Is that yours?"

Audrey looked over and nodded. They both made their way to the trunk. Audrey kept her back to the decimated body of the horse and swatted at several flies as they sought out fresher meat.

Maggie turned the heavy trunk over, showing a surprising amount of strength. "It doesn't look damaged."

Audrey hunkered down and unlatched it. Her clothes and possessions were all still in place, if a little mussed up from their journey down the hill. She peered back up the slope and sighed. "How will we get this up to the road? And how will we get it back to the farm?"

"Together," said Maggie, grabbing a handle with one hand and hefting her half of the trunk up with ease.

Audrey stared in disbelief for a moment then grabbed her side with both hands and managed to repeat Maggie's feat.

By the time they reached the roadside, Audrey was bathed in sweat, her smock sticking to her in several unwanted places. Maggie showed no sign of fatigue.

"How are you not sweating?" Audrey asked, but was cut off by a shout from behind. A wagon approached, driven by Sam.

The same Sam who had been lying on a table, his leg a mess of rent flesh and splintered bones, not more than a day before. He smiled, waved and shouted, "Hello there, Miss Maggie. What are you doing down here?"

Maggie waved back. "Well met, Sam. We came to collect some of Audrey's belongings from the wagon down the bank."

"Aye, nasty that was. I feel for the poor driver," he said looking across the road to a small pile of dirt marked with two sticks tied into a simple cross. It was nestled back from the road in a small clearing bordered on three sides by short flowering shrubs.

Audrey followed his gaze and saw the grave. Shock blossomed on her face. "William?" she gasped and made her way to the graveside. She knelt and the tears flowed. "Oh, William. I'm so sorry."

Maggie stepped up next to her and stood quietly to give Audrey a moment of grief. "When we found him, he was already gone, much like the horse. We thought this was the best for him," she said looking around at the beautiful surroundings.

Audrey looked up at Maggie then around the area. She slowly stood, dropped her head and said, "Thank you. I think he would have liked this place."

A torrent of tears spilled forth again. Maggie placed an arm around Audrey and brought her face to her shoulder. Sam stepped up next to the pair, removed his hat and dropped his head slightly in deference to the dead man.

After a while, Audrey's tears subsided, and she pulled away. She took one last look at the grave and moved towards the wagon.

"I've loaded the trunk and can take the two of you home, if you'd like," Sam told Maggie.

Audrey climbed up into the wagon, her heart heavy with sorrow for poor William. She looked back towards the grave and vowed to come back and pay her respects once more before leaving the farm.

Audrey watched, astounded, as Sam carried her heavy trunk in from the wagon. He strode past the table where, only the day before, he'd writhed in agony as Granny Esme pushed the exposed pieces of his leg bone back together and bound his gaping wound. There was no limp. No wobble in his stride. Just a confident man full of health.

Maggie stopped him and told him to sit up on the table. He duly complied and stretched his leg out for her.

She unbound the bandages and Audrey expected to see a bleeding, weeping wound with puckered skin, but was astonished to see that the leg was healed. The flaps of skin sealed back together with a slight ridge where they joined.

Maggie smiled. "That's healed nicely."

"You can thank Granny for that. A miracle worker if you ask me," said Sam.

Audrey remained silent. Her eyes wide in shock.

Was this magic? Real magic?

Maggie cleansed the remains of the poultice away from the Sam's wound and went to fetch some instruments to remove the stitches.

Audrey took her chance. "Has this happened before?" she asked Sam.

He smiled. "Oh, yar, Granny Esme and Mother Gertha have been helping us folk for years. They never ask for much but when we is sick or injured, they do what they do and pretty soon we're right as rain again."

"Is it magic?"

Sam looked a little puzzled by the question, then brightened. "I don't think so. They always use ointments and such like. They don't do no spells or naught. So, I wouldn't call it magic. They are magical I suppose, but t'ain't magic."

As Maggie returned, Audrey stepped away and fell silent.

"I heard voices, what were you two talking about?"

"Nothing much Miss, just a bit of this an' that."

Maggie eyed him for a moment then set about removing the stitches. Sam winced a couple of times but remained silent.

When finished, Maggie stood up, gathered the discarded bandages and stitching and took them away.

Audrey spoke quietly to Sam, "The ladies have been wonderful in helping me recover, but I feel I've encroached on their kindness quite enough. Would you be so kind as to take me into the nearest sizeable town? From there I should be able to find someone to take me to Ipswich. I really must be getting back."

"Oh, aye, that should be fine. I can probably take you now, if you'd like. Or in the morning if you want to be having your goodbyes," he said.

Audrey was about to speak when Maggie returned. She stared at Sam and raised an eyebrow.

Sam's demeanor changed completely. "I . . . I just realised I won't be able to take you for a while. I'll be out for the next few days. I've got to go north and help out at my brother's farm." He replaced his hat, shifted towards the door and bid Maggie goodbye. "Thanking you again, Miss Maggie. You, Granny and Mother Gertha. Thank you again. We've started fattening up one of the lambs ready to bring across to you in a month or so." Sam almost collided with the door frame in his hurry to exit.

Audrey watched him go then turned back to Maggie, a look of severe disappointment on her face. "How?" she said.

"How what?" Maggie answered.

Audrey studied her for a moment before replying. "How did his leg heal so quickly? There's no way on God's Earth it could have healed by itself in such a short time."

"It may be that the problem lies is in your choice of God."

"What do you mean? There's only one God"

"Some think that, but we do not follow the teachings of the carpenter's son. Our Gods were here long before him and will be here long after he has faded from the memories of man."

Audrey's eyes opened with her mind. "Witches," she said. "You are witches."

Maggie grimaced at the name. "That is a name ascribed to us in Christ's book. A foul name but not of our choosing. We know no name. We are just as we are." She pointed towards the carving above the doorway. "Our Gods are old. They draw their power from the Earth. We seek that power from Lord Atho, the old god of the forests. We are his children. We harness the power of Atho and of Hecate, the mother, to heal the sick and lame. Much like the stories of the Carpenter, but his power was attributed to a higher being. Truth be told he was more like us than not."

Audrey was affronted by the accusation. "Blasphemy. You're saying Jesus was a witch," she spat.

106

"That or a fraud. Perhaps his lover, the Magdalene, was one of my sisters and performed the miracles in his stead. Stranger things have happened through the ages."

"Enough!" shouted Audrey. "I'm leaving. This is insane. I will bring Matthew Hopkins the Witchfinder General to this place, to rain his judgement down on you all." She strode to the door of her bedroom. A final rebuff came to her mind and she stopped to address Maggie once more.

As Audrey turned, she was shocked to find the witch standing close behind. She opened her mouth to speak but Maggie raised a hand and blew yellow powder into her face.

Audrey was in darkness when she awoke. Moonlight filtered through the shuttered window. She sat upright; the fog of her dreams still bound her mind in a cloud of murkiness.

Was it all a dream? Am I still in Lavenham? Am I in Ipswich?

The murmur of the three women's voices filtered through from next door. Flickering candlelight seeped into the room from the base of the door. "It must be tonight. The moon is high. The night is still," said Esme.

"I'm so sorry. I lost my temper. She won't come willingly now like we planned," said Maggie's softer voice.

"Foolish child. It doesn't matter. Once Hecate possesses her, it won't matter how upset she is," said Gertha.

What do they mean 'once Hecate possesses her'?

Audrey backed away from the door and stared at it in shock. A chill ran up her spine. The three women had healed her only for their own means. Hecate. Maggie had mentioned Hecate. She'd also heard it called out by many of Matthew's accused. That was their god or their demon.

They mean me harm. They want to sacrifice me to this Hecate. I must get away. I must find Matthew.

She spied her trunk and pushed it against the door to stop it from opening. The scraping noise was a deadly cacophony in the quiet room.

"What was that?" Gertha shouted.

"She's awake," cried Esme.

Audrey spun for the window and pushed at the shutters. Behind her, there was a thump at the door. The shutters were locked tight. A crack of light appeared as the door was inched open.

"No," she cried and pushed again. The shutters bulged outwards but held fast. She kicked them. Only pain greeted her.

Another thump echoed through the room. The crack was wider as the heavy trunk was forced back.

Audrey spied a thin rod of metal in the gap between the shutters.

The bolt outside has been thrown.

She pushed her fingers into the gap and tried to move the rod. It jiggled in its holder.

Another thump. Maggie's face appeared at the crack.

"Audrey. Stop. It's not what you think. We mean you no harm. We only want you to help us."

Audrey concentrated on the bolt. She jammed her hand though the shutter and wrapped a finger around it. Finally, it slid out from the bracket. She flung the shutters open. A cry behind her and Maggie squeezed into the room followed by Gertha. Audrey sensed freedom and turned back to the window.

Standing before her was a demon from Hell. The hulking form she'd spied on the hill. A giant covered in a coat of coarse dark wool. It's long, pointed face stared down at her with two great ram's horns curled on either side of its head.

Audrey backed away at the sight. A scream caught in her throat. As she turned away, her gaze were drawn to the creature's eyes. Sparkling through the gloom like diamonds made flesh were the palest blue eyes she had ever seen. Eyes so alien in this beast's head, nestled under the thick brow within a cowl of dark wool.

Her terror faded as realisation dawned in her mind. Those eyes. She had seen those eyes so many times but in another's face.

William?

"Oh, William? What have they done you?" she said.

Suddenly, William's monstrous face disappeared as a thick sack was thrust over her head. Stars exploded across her mind as pain erupted in the side of her head. As the darkness closed in, she heard the women argue.

"You didn't have to hit her," said Maggie.

"Much easier to handle this way," said Gertha.

"That was foolish, I just hope you haven't damaged her. Hecate won't be pleased," said Esme.

"You can always fix her up afterwards," said Gertha.

"True that," answered Esme.

The flickering flames of an oil burner atop an iron tripod cast dancing shadows and light upon the thick canopy of branches and leaves above. The sweet smell of the oil pervaded the underlying odour of rotting leaves and mulch. Audrey found herself in a clearing surrounded by a thick, dark border of trees. She realised she was inside the forest near the witches' farmhouse.

"She awakes." Esme's gravel voice echoed across the area.

Maggie, naked except for her triskele amulet and a daisy chain in her hair, stepped into Audrey's view. She smiled a placating smile. "Welcome back Audrey. It is time for you to join us."

"No," Audrey said weakly. She tried to raise her hands. They were bound as were her legs. She, too, was naked and lying on a rough and cold stone slab. A ram's skull stared back at her from the end of the altar.

Esme and Gertha stood naked to one side. On the other side, partially hidden in the trees, was the hulking form that had caused Audrey to faint.

Esme turned and motioned to it. "Lord Atho. Come forth. Your bride awaits."

The beast stepped into the light and stood to its full height. Audrey gasped. William's bright blue eyes peered out from each side of the long ovine face. Two large curled horns grew on each side of his head, their tips ending in sharp points jutting forward of his brow.

The creature stood seven feet tall with a light covering of dirty brown wool. To Audrey, it looked like an overstuffed sack, as if the beast beneath was too large for its own skin. The beast walked forward with an awkward gait. The body fighting against the actions of the mind.

Oh, William, thought Audrey as she stared at the possessed and corrupted body of her once proud friend.

Lightning split the sky. Thunder cracked through the silence. The Horned God stood and reached towards the sky beyond. Power leapt up from the ground and into his form. The muscles in his arms and legs rippled and grew, straining further against the tautness of his skin. His barrel chest expanded and filled his lungs to feed the fire within. He bellowed, either in pain or triumph.

Atho stepped next to Audrey. She gasped and tried to pull away from him, turning her head aside.

Esme appeared on that side of the altar. Her sagging skin and breasts providing only a slightly more palatable view. The old woman held a short bone-handled knife and a carved stone triskele similar to Maggie's, complete with a ram's head at its centre. She placed the triskele on Audrey's chest and before Audrey could reel back, touched it with the tip of the knife.

Sparks flew through Audrey's body and she could only move her head to one side. There, she spied Atho's bright blue sparkling eyes.

Esme raised her face skywards. "Hecate. We have prepared a vessel for your entry into this world."

Thunder cracked outside the forest and lightning shone through the gaps in the canopy.

"Hecate. Your King awaits. This vessel is ripe for your taking. Come now and claim her for your own. Then cleanse this world of those that would destroy your servants."

Audrey cried out, "William. William, I know you're still in there. I can't save you, but you can still save me. It's what Matthew would want. It's what he asked you to do."

The great horned beast drew back from the altar. Its clawed hands grasped at its head and an anguished cry left its lips and filled the clearing.

Esme turned towards the beast. "Atho, my Lord, ignore this petulant child. Your Queen will arrive soon. You will be together again in flesh."

The beast tore its hands away for a moment and looked at Esme then Audrey. Its eyes sparkled brightly in the firelight.

"Fight it William. Fight it."

The Horned God howled and grasped at its head.

Gertha stepped up to the altar. "Be quiet child. Your friend is no match for the Horned God. He who walked this world when man still swung from the trees."

"Fight it William. You are winning. Fight!" Audrey cried.

Gertha slapped her across the face. Audrey yelped; a spray of blood splattered the altar.

The great beast stopped and turned towards Audrey's cry. The eyes sparkled electric blue. It let out a terrible roar and stepped forward, swiping Gertha out of the way and sending her flying across the clearing. She slammed into a tree with a resounding crack, slid to the base, and lay still.

"No," shouted Maggie. She ran towards the horned God and beat her tiny fists against its back. "You killed Gertha. Why?"

The beast rounded on her, one thrashing arm sent Maggie's thin frame sailing over the altar and toppling into the oil burner. The oil sprayed Maggie and the surrounding grass. Flames engulfed the young girl, setting her hair ablaze and spreading across her skin. She scrambled to her feet and ran from the clearing, a bright trail of flame in her wake. The grass caught alight and fire ignited across the clearing.

The thunder and lightning raged above the forest adding a strobe effect to the bright yellow of the inferno within.

"No, you've broken the spell," Esme screamed. She stared at the hulking beast for a moment before raising her knife. "Hecate will not come if you cannot fight the man inside you. Atho you must have control."

The great beast bellowed in rage, grasping at his head as the two halves of his nature fought against each other.

Esme looked at the broken body of Gertha, at the fire encroaching on the entire clearing and back at her knife. She peered up at the beast's back and nodded to herself. "There is nothing left but to start again." She stabbed the knife deep into his back.

The beast howled in pain.

"William, no!" shouted Audrey.

The beast turned. Tried to reach for the knife, but the blade stuck deep, just out of reach. Blood poured down its back. It roared its anguish.

William grabbed the frail figure of Esme in one gigantic paw and squeezed. The old witch cried in pain. Her eyeballs bulged with the pressure.

"No, great God Atho, no. I am your servant. Fight the puny human within, or Hecate cannot return," she pleaded.

The beast reached up with his other hand, grabbed Esme around the chest and pulled. The ancient witch tore in half, spraying the burning grass with her life blood.

The thunder reached a crescendo and went silent. The night beyond the forest turned dark. The magic was gone.

The Horned God turned and stepped towards Audrey. He stumbled and dropped to one knee. He reached back and tried to grasp the knife to no avail. Behind him the flames started to take hold of the trees surrounding the clearing.

"William. The fire. We must get out of here," Audrey cried.

William regained his feet and staggered towards Audrey. He managed to slide a long vicious claw under one of the bindings. It gave way with the slightest tug; within seconds she was free.

The beast held out his hands to Audrey. All around the clearing, the fire raged as it took hold of the grass and raced up the trees. The leafy canopy was alive with fire.

Audrey climbed into the beast's hands and he turned towards the nearest gap. The fire bit into his feet and soon his lower body was bathed in flame. He howled but trudged forward holding his prize before him.

As they reached the edge of the flaming clearing, William tripped and fell. Audrey was thrown from his hands. She landed on a dry patch of dirt and rolled into the darkness, then staggered to her feet.

William, her friend, in that horribly distorted body was ablaze, his hands held out before him in a last heroic gesture. Her hero. Her protector. His duty fulfilled.

A tear sprouted from her eye and slid down her cheek.

She turned away and made for the starlight filtering through the edge of the forest. Once clear, she dropped to her knees, bowed her head and cried tears of relief and pain.

A sudden noise grabbed her attention. A dark figure moved against the bright orange background of the burning forest.

Audrey stood and stepped backwards. "William?"

The figure moved slowly forward. Audrey stared closer and it came into focus. "Maggie?"

The flaming oil had destroyed the girl. Her hair was gone. Her face a melted miasma of liquefied skin and flesh. She stopped a few paces from Audrey. Her mouth moved but failed to make any noise.

Audrey leaned closer.

"We meant no harm," Maggie whispered. "We are only here to heal. To help. Never to destroy. We only sought protection from those who would destroy us." She sucked in a lungful of air, the breath rattling in her fire-ravaged throat. "This was wrong. Esme was wrong to do this."

She brought her hand up and opened it. The melted skin split and bled with the effort. The triskele amulet sat in the middle of her black and cracked palm. The eyes of the ram, holding whatever moonlight it could capture, shone brightly against the gloom.

"Take this. It will protect and hide you from our enemies. Matthew Hopkins is wrong. He kills innocent old ladies. He cannot see the true servants of Lord Atho and Lady Hecate. He cannot see the true meaning of magic. He cannot see the truth."

Audrey picked the amulet out of Maggie's palm and stared into her eyes.

"Spread the word. Spread the truth. We only seek to help. We do not deserve to die," she whispered, then fell forward with a sickening thud.

Audrey tried to turn her over, but Maggie's skin sloughed off in her hands. She reared away in disgust. There was no helping the young woman now.

The amulet felt heavy in her hand. She opened her fingers and saw sparks flash across the surface and into her hand. There was power in it. The power of nature. The power of truth.

Audrey looked out of the carriage window as the dirty, poverty-stricken streets of Ipswich passed by. A light rain washed the worst of the stench away. Urchins played in the mud and effluent coursing its way down the ruts of the roadway. Their mothers watched from the nearby doorways; most held another babe in arms.

These are the people most in need of help. Not persecution for seeking aid from so-called witches. These are the people Maggie, Esme and Gertha would have gone out of their way to help. To nurture. To protect.

She gazed over at Matthew beside her, staring at his profile. Handsome. Confident. Committed to his cause. To seek out those he believed to be witches. To break their spirits and bodies until they confessed to their accused crimes.

"You've achieved so much. Do you still need to pursue more?" she asked.

A flash of anger ran across his face before it resumed its impassive expression. They'd held this conversation many times since Audrey's return. It was only because they headed to another mass-trial that she brought it up again. "Witchcraft is blasphemy in the eyes of the Lord. It is my God given duty to root it out and bring the accused to justice. We have talked about this enough. You have your own duties to God in this. Do you wish to cast aside all the gravitas that your responsibilities bring you?" He smiled, a lascivious smile. A smile that once caused Audrey to tingle in certain places and yearn for his touch. Now that smile only brought a feeling of disgust. A feeling she hid behind fake smiles and pleasant expressions.

"I think you are wrong," she said. "Those you accuse are simple old widows and spinsters. There is nothing blasphemous about them. They merely help the poor unfortunates with the troubles of their simple lives."

"You accuse me of false justice?"

"Rather, misplaced justice."

His eyes drilled into her the same way he had faced down tough old ladies and driven them into snivelling messes.

Audrey held firm. She knew the reality. She knew the truth. A simple look would not bow her will or resolve.

"I think you had better watch your tongue. You speak like many of the accused before they are brought to justice. One day it may be you who stands before me. Have you thought about that?"

Audrey sat straight up. The time had come. "Yes. Yes, I have." She thumped on the roof of the carriage and shouted above the din of the horses, "Rodgers, please stop the carriage."

They slowed down. Matthew's expression grew puzzled. "What are you doing?"

The carriage drew to a stop. Audrey opened the door.

Before she could leave, Matthew grasped her arm. "Where are you going?"

"If you will not be swayed, then it is time I left. My future lies not with you. I will not be a part of this charade anymore." She tugged her arm from his grasp and hopped down from the carriage.

Matthew poked his head through the window. "You will regret this, Audrey. If you help the blasphemers, I will find you. I will bring you to justice."

Audrey smiled and watched the carriage disappear around the next corner. She drew the triskele amulet out of her small purse and gently placed it around her neck. "I doubt it," she said. Bright blue sparks ran down the ram's horns along the three spiral arms and across her chest. She shivered with the feeling. "Now to find others and spread the truth," she said.

About the Author:

Stephen Herczeg is an IT Geek, writer, actor, filmmaker and Taekwondo Black Belt from Canberra, Australia on Ngunnawal land, who has been writing for well over twenty years, with sixteen completed feature length screenplays, and numerous short and micro-fiction stories. Stephen's scripts, TITAN, Dark are the Woods, Control and Death Spores have found success in international screenwriting competitions with a win, two runner-ups and two top-ten finishes.

He has had over a hundred short stories and micro-fiction drabbles published through Hunter Anthologies; Things In the Well; Blood Song Books; Dragon Soul Press; Oscillate Wildly Press; Black Hare Press; Monnath Books; Battle Goddess Productions; Fantasia Divinity; The Great Void Books; DeadSet Press; Eerie River Press; Belanger Books and MX Publishing.

In 2021, his collection of stories – The Curious Cases of Sherlock Holmes was published through MX Publishing, plus his novellas, After the Fall Part 1 and 2 were published by Black Hare Press.

He lives by the creed Just Finish It, and his Mum is his biggest fan.

MADE

Zena Shapter

Niam

Around the fire, in the night, with drums beating, I sit on my throne of wood and bone and grip its smooth armrests, pushing my heels into soil as warm as wounds. Orange flames whip at the black night, glowing over my tribe as they leap and twist, banging their bare blood-stained shoulders to the rhythm . . . *my* rhythm. Not so long ago, I was the uneasy one in the corner, wary of my king. Now they all cower from me—even the warriors—and when I command them to dance, they dance. Their chants fill the air while feet stamp dirt, sending billows of dust into crackling fire until the air smells of burnt earth, and I am left amazed at why they don't challenge me. I am merely a man, same as them. I am their king, but only just. I am strong, though weakened in this moment, more than they must realise. So I take up my chalice and sip at the honey wine we seized today from our enemies, and relish both its sweet taste and my victory . . . while it lasts.

Beyond the blaze of the celebration sits a yellow grass plain. No one can see it in the dark, but it is there and, as of today, it is mine. Beyond that plain there is a stream, and beyond that a mountain. After today, those are mine too. Behind this village is a forest and a path that leads down to the sea. In every direction, as far as my eye can see, I am king now—a king taking a deep breath, easing back into his throne, and wondering what comes next. What lays beyond my sight, beyond the mountain and the seas . . . the stars beyond Serein even? I have often wondered what awaits out there, what tomorrow will bring me.

Tomorrow I shall of course demand my tribe haul the salvages we seized from our enemies and take it to the place the gods call their landing pad. When they descend from the sky in their silver beast, they will see how grateful I am for today's victory, for the wrath they gave me to make it so, and they will stare into the eyes of my tribe and entrance them all to follow me for another moon. The gift of mesmerism is the price they pay for whatever 'old tech' we kings can salvage from across our lands.

What comes after that though, given I have so much more wrath to share? Today was only the start . . .

"Niam," my brother whispers, easing close. He hasn't yet washed, so the smell of battle sweat and blood is thick and sticky on him.

I wait, then nod to indicate he may continue speaking.

"Ule has done as you wished." Bowing, he holds out the dagger of my vanquished enemy, covered in the blood that proves my son has done as I commanded.

I take the dagger and admire its balance. Its weight is perfect. I wish I could see the body myself, witness the proof that my boy is now a man, but I cannot move. Victorious as I am, under my clothes my body shakes. No matter how fierce the fire crackles and burns, I feel cold. If I were to stand now, I might collapse. The legs that served me well today on the battlefield now ache like an old man's, and in places, throb as if the flesh has been sliced down to the bone.

In places, it probably has.

So for now I don't stand. I concentrate on breathing, slowly until my shaking stops; I breathe in my reign . . . slowly so it lasts. I replaced our last king a mere moon ago, when he showed weakness. He had been king himself only a year. My reign will last longer and be more glorious. It will because it must. I have more battles to fight, more darkness to alight.

Indeed, it matters not that dancing warriors glare at me now, as they move with apparent abandon to drumbeats. They may search for weakness, as I once did, they will not find it easily. In an hour my legs will be strong again, and tomorrow, after my tribute to the gods, my power will be greater. I am not afraid of these men. I am the leader they need, a monster, a killer—just let them try.

Across the fire, in the night, I search instead for my son, Ule.

Flying embers dance across black air and lead me to his face, a man's face, aglow in the flames, watching his king. His chin low, one hand on each knee, he looks like he wants to kill me himself. Over time I will teach him how to channel that rage, as I have taught myself. There has always been this war; there will always be a war. A death on our side begets a death on theirs, and so it goes on. Ule will soon learn that what happened to his sister wasn't my fault; that what I did to him was for his own good. One day, his mother will understand too. I did it for them.

Across the fire, in the night, I see my wife dangle an arm around Ule's shoulder. When his focus does not shift, she whispers in his ear. Turning, he smiles at her and, as their eyes meet, they laugh. I can hear their laughter in my memory, though have not heard it in my ears for a long time.

It's amazing how long it has been.

Too long?

How different our lives have would been if I'd listened to her when she tried to warn me, before what happened with Lana . . . I would have more than wrath and regret for company. We would still be a family.

A family. Could that be what comes next? If only that were possible. War is one thing, but the way my son used to laugh is another.

I blink, long and with purpose, remembering.

The air fuzzes.

The very next second I am living a different life, another chance, dancing around the fire myself, in the night, with drums beating, this time alongside my boy, who is not yet a man. I may not be a king, but to Ule I am a god—at least that's how he looks at me

with his eyes shining, face smiling, and his laughter, gentle yet
playful like the rippling of a stream.

Beside us, my wife and daughter dance, drinking the honey
wine our current king seized today from our enemies. Our
cousin lost his life in battle, though I try not to think about that.
The deaths are getting closer. I want to push it all away. Yet what
can one man do? Our king has his reasons for battling on, for
refusing any peace or truce. Moons ago, he lost loved-ones to the
fighting. I can only imagine what that did to him. Just watching
the danger creeping ever closer makes me fume. This is my
family. I must protect them.

I lead my wife away from the fire so we can sit and watch our
children dance, breathing in their laughter like air, feeling lucky
to hear it. Tomorrow we must scavenge for more of what the
gods call salvage, technology from the time before memory,
scattered across our lands. The more salvage we gift to them
when they descend in their silver beast, the more powerful our
king will be and the further we can push death from our village.
At least for this night our children are both safe and happy. It is a
time for celebration, so celebrate we do.

Until Ule spins around so fast he falls into us, knocking wine
from my wife's hand.

He laughs at his own foolishness.

"Why do you laugh at this?" I ask, standing. Does he not realise
the danger around him?

"It's okay, Niam," my wife whispers, tugging my arm.

But I can't have our son being so careless. Carelessness like that could get him killed—on the battlefield, or here. What if he'd fallen into our king? "Do you think *this* funny?"

Ule straightens and stops smiling, sensing I'm serious.

Though already a woman, my daughter Lana doesn't realise. "Yes!" she laughs, bumping into me and spilling my wine too.

"Niam . . ." my wife says, staring at my clenched fist.

I try to control myself but it's hard. Why can't my children see how dangerous the village is becoming? If they don't learn respect, our king will want to teach them and he won't be as merciful as me.

I shake wine from my hand and think how best to explain. But when I hear my son and daughter sniggering, all thoughts abandon me. There is only wrath.

"This is not funny!" I yell, gripping Lana's arms and shaking her. I turn to grab Ule too, but he pushes me first.

"Get away from her!" he yells, standing in front of his sister.

It gives me the excuse I need and I drag him away. "Then you will take the lesson for both of you."

Lana cries, yelling after me—something about my being a monster, about wanting to leave the village forever.

My wife catches up to me, grabs my arm and wrenches Ule free of my grasp. "You're just like him," she hisses, gesturing at our king. "Go back to the celebration, Ule. In the morning, your father will apologise. Keep going the way you are," she warns me, "and you'll lose everything you hold dear."

She doesn't understand—I'm trying to teach our children how to survive.

The next morning though, around a weak fire, my heart beating, I search for Lana. She is not in her bed, my wife cannot find her, neither can I.

I am too harsh on my children. I love them so much. I will never again touch either of them. It was a mistake. I will control the darkness in me, my outbursts, my temper.

We race around the village, the beach, the yellow grass plains . . . Lana is nowhere. She's run away.

"This is all your fault!" my wife screams, tears streaming down her face. "She's as brash as her father!"

I say nothing, knowing she's right. Born under the same moon, it's in our nature.

By the stream, near the battlefield where our enemies were retrieving their dead last night, we find a torn corner of fabric. It resembles Lana's clothing and is covered in blood.

"No!" my wife sobs, sinking to her knees.

Our enemies have taken an opportunity and brought death closer.

And so it will go on . . . If only I hadn't lost my temper.

I blink, long and with purpose, full of regret.

The air fuzzes.

The very next second I am living a different life, another chance—it is night again, and I am standing around the village fire while drums beat and my wife warns me of my future. Ule has just bumped into her and I'm still trying to control myself, fists clenched. Do they think this funny?

"Sit back down, Niam," she mutters, "or you will become just like him." She gestures at our king. "Is that what you want?" And she tells me how monsters are made, that they fail to control their nature. They act before they think, then have only regret and wrath as company.

As I listen, I see imaginings from a future I do not want and feel the rage ease. I don't want to hurt, or lose, my children. I want my wife to always whisper in my ear and make me laugh. So I let her pull me back down beside her, unclench my fists, and together we watch our children dance. Wine spills, but not their blood. They are safe and happy.

Still, I cannot live like this anymore, this village is baiting my fury.

So I take a deep breath, and decide. Gods or no gods, tomorrow we pack.

Leaving is what one man can do.

Lana

I wait until my mother and father think I'm dancing once more, until my brother Ule is surrounded by others, then I leave. It's only a matter of time before my father loses control and I will not wait for when he does. I saw him tonight, fists clenched, boiling on the brink. He burns hot, hunting for a way to unleash his rage. He's a monster waiting to be made. He thinks we should all fear our king, yet he is the one I fear. So I run across the yellow grass plains, away from everything I know, and sprint until I reach the stream.

There I slow, though only to hitch my skirt and focus my footing. Stars beaming brilliant above light my wade across the water. Currents cool my careful feet, hot from running, dirty with soil and grass. On the opposite bank, I go to run again, but a warm breeze brings the beating of drums. I turn to see the distant glow of our village fire, its smoke scented with burnt earth. My father knows how dangerous the village is becoming yet will never leave – my mother says it's because he can't. The gods have looked into his eyes, deep into the eyes of our whole tribe, and entranced them all to follow our king to the death. She and I are the only ones impervious to their stares.

"This is the only way I'll ever be safe," I mutter, looking skywards to gain direction.

"Safe from what?"

I jump at the voice, spin around to search for a source. Stars shine enough to light blades of grass on the riverbank, boulders upstream, and outlines of mountain peaks in the night beyond. Yet there is no one, no animal even, nearby. Did I hear a voice at all?

Water babbles softly.

Wind plays with my hair before passing.

I recognise a nearby ridge. I'm further west than I thought. Today's battle was fought near here, which means our enemies could still be close. I edge back towards the water. I should have been more careful. I've been too brash. My mother says I often act before I think, just like him. She says it's in our nature, born as we are under the same moon.

"Are you lost?" the voice comes again.

This time I turn to see a man standing on a boulder beside the stream. His beard covers as much of his face as his yellow war paint, the colour of our enemies. Metal glints at his belt.

I stumble backwards. My foot twists on uneven ground and I fall onto the bank. When I go to stand, my ankle gives way.

"Stop," the man says, jumping off the boulder.

The sound of him striding closer makes me scramble into a crawl.

"Stop!" He catches my skirt underfoot to anchor me still. "Who are you?" He leans to peer at my face. "One of them?" He gestures at the distant fire.

I breathe steadily to stay calm, nod, then think better of it. "But no more," I add.

"What do you mean, *no more*?"

"I ran away."

He straightens up and reaches for his dagger. "That is not possible. The gods assured me it wasn't." He glances behind him, listening to the night.

I say nothing; keep still. Only kings can speak with the gods, when they descend in their fearsome machines to look into the eyes of our tribes. If this warrior has spoken to the gods, he must be Eirlu, king of our enemies, ruler of a tribe entranced to be as angry as ours.

I should have said I was lost.

"I—"

"Shh!" he snaps, looking over his other shoulder, his dagger ready. "Are you alone? Don't lie! Who's with you?"

"No one!"

"Then what are you doing here?"

"I told you, I'm lost."

"No, that's not what you said before." He grabs my arm. Half lifting, half dragging, he hauls me to a boulder. He searches around, then leans close. "How did you leave them?"

My breath catches. What does he want to hear? "I, I waited until no one was looking and then . . ."

"No, I mean how *could* you."

I shake my head, confused. "My mother wanted me to be safe. In the village, there is only anger. All the deaths . . . I thought it safer out here."

"So you just . . . left? You didn't feel any need to stay." He rubs his chin, "to follow your king?"

I shake my head.

"No, no, this isn't right," he mutters. "This isn't right. You are to follow your king to the death, as my tribe is to follow me, and the other tribes are to follow their kings. The gods told me you cannot simply leave." His grip on my arm tightens. "I should kill you now."

"No, please! I'll look into their eyes again! I made a mistake, I'll make it right."

"No. *They* will." Finding his solution, he falls to my feet and rips my skirt, using his dagger to cut off a corner. Then he slices the shin of my leg.

I scream.

He clamps my mouth with a hand that tastes of dirt and death. Air invades my wound, stinging and throbbing. I reach to grip at the gash, but he pushes my hands away and holds the ripped corner of fabric to my blood until it's soaked. Then, while I rock myself in pain, he pierces the bloody cloth onto the branch of a nearby bush.

"You never ran away," Eirlu says, grabbing my arm again. "I *took* you, understand? To incite your tribe to fight. Say you understand, or I will kill you myself tonight."

"I understand."

"Good. Now come, for we have gods to meet. They *will* grant me greater power for this contravention," he mutters, dragging me into the night.

Niam

Around the fire, in the night, with drums beating, I paint my face red. Long have I waited to unleash the darkness within; now tonight there is nothing more my wife can say. She may predict her futures again and again, and I may have my many imaginings, rethink my actions, try to change; but it is no use, for I am who I am. Last night I controlled my temper with Ule. I let the rage ease and sat back down.

This morning Lana was missing anyway, a bloody scrap of her dress found by the stream.

There is no future now worse than this. So tomorrow I will scavenge lives, not salvages.

Spear in hand, I set off towards where the gods land in their silver beast. There I will pray for my fury tomorrow to be great.

Stars beaming brilliant above light my wade across the water. The gods' landing pad sits in open land between our village and that of our enemy. Lana probably came this way last night to pray at the pad herself. I think about the hand that caused her blood to spill and grip my spear tighter. At the pad, I approach the silver altar where tiny specks glow blue and green. Kneeling, I present my offering, a metal board the colour of grass, dotted with tiny silver squares, black lines between them. It is my apology for doubting the gods' righteousness, for even considering leaving the village. I should never have provoked their anger. Lana's demise is my punishment. My retribution will be in their glory.

"Hear me, oh gods," I say, "grant me the anger to seek my vengeance, cloud my vision with wrath."

Gods speak only to kings; but I do not need them to answer me, merely to hear. I tell them of my love for Lana and the reckoning I now deserve. As I pray, I cannot know if they listen, yet feel as if they do. There is a tightening inside me, a tension in my muscles that wasn't there before, a focus in my mind. I visualise faces I do not know and swinging fists into them. Each whack frees more fury. As my knuckles collide with imagined skin, I feel myself float, slipping into a trance, and in that intoxication I sense the gods telling me something.

When I hear footsteps, and voices with the accent of my enemies, I realise what meaning the gods speak . . . My king is weak, for it was under his rule that Lana was taken. I have come here to pray for justice, yet the gods are giving me more. Our village needs a stronger leader, bold and determined, outspoken and brash. The men now approaching are a gift—a sign of what the gods want me to do. My rage will not have to wait until morning. Tomorrow is already here.

So I hide behind the altar, balancing the weight of my spear in one hand while in the other I clench my dagger. I focus my fury. My vengeance will not stop at these few, it will weed out the weakness that brought it into being. After I am done here I will seek out our king and teach him what his weakness has meant for me.

Finally the voices are so close I can make out angry words demanding answers from the gods, demanding greater power. I raise my spear, stand, and hurl it. One of the warriors falls but there are three more. In a haze, I stab bodies, slice and cut them until they are on the ground moaning. I turn my dagger inside stomachs until warm liquid oozes thick over my arms. I move with a speed I never knew I had, and don't stop until their moans are no more.

Victorious, I thank the gods for the wrath they have given me this night, and pray they grant me more.

More wrath—more power—more focus. For I have more blood to spill, more battles to fight.

As I pass over the stilled bodies, the gods answer my prayer, sending me reason for the rage I sought.

Two of the bodies are old, elders of our enemies, and one is in royal garb.

The last body is a woman and when I recognise the fabric of her skirt—bloody like the corner of it we found by the stream this morning—I fall to my knees and moan as if I too have been stabbed.

In my craze, I did not see how close my enemies were bringing death to me. Last night, my wife tried to push it all away, predicting for me futures I did not want to see.

Now nothing can change what is to come. A kingdom of pain will be mine, for I prayed for more rage and have been granted my wish.

My daughter is dead at my hand. Now wrath will be mine for all eternity. It was always in my nature. I am the killer, I am death— now too a monster made.

About the Author:

Zena Shapter is a multi-award winning author of science fiction, fantasy, speculative and contemporary fiction, conjuring journeys into the beyond and unusual. Author of 'When Dark Roots Hunt' *(coming soon from MidnightSun),* 'Release of Eaglick' *(coming soon from Grimbold Books),* 'Towards White' *(IFWG 2017) and co-author of* 'Into Tordon' *(MidnightSun 2016), she's a 'writer with a need for adventure' (Midnight Echo magazine), writing 'dark fantasy at its blood-soaked finest' (Australasian Horror Writers' Association), who 'deserves your attention' (Lillian Csernica, Tangent Online).*

She loves movies, frogs, chocolate, potatoes, and living with her family on the beautiful Northern Beaches of Kuring-gai land, where she's also an inclusive creativity advocate, writing mentor and editor. Find her online via @ZenaShapter and zenashapter.com.

TAURUS
APRIL 20 - MAY 20

THE BULL OF HEAVEN

Leanbh Pearson

I woke to the trill of a blackbird. Weak sunlight struggled to push through dense cloud cover and the morning air was crisp. My dog lifted his head from the bed, opening a bleary eye to glare reproachfully toward the window. Lance was a rescue dog, the mystery of his canine parentage reflected in his disproportionately long ears and wiry brindle coat. The blackbird called again, and Lance sighed, jumped from the bed and trotted purposefully toward the back door. My yard was mostly wild and overgrown except for a small paved courtyard where Lance and the blackbird had an ongoing war over territory. Sighing with resignation, I climbed from the warm bed covers.

My bare feet scuffed across the chill slate tiles of the kitchen. Quickly I opened the sliding glass door, letting Lance into the yard before I turned away from the cold morning air, and flicked the switch of the coffee machine. While waiting for the coffee to brew, I twisted my long blond hair into a loose bun. I halted, catching sight of my reflection in the window glass. I barely recognised the thinner woman dressed in yesterday's wrinkled clothing. I thought for a moment of how my husband had never understood my obsession to detail, my compulsion for orderliness. He would not recognise you either, I thought, the memory of his death hit me again like a blow. Turning away from my reflection and painful memories, I focused on my tasks for the day.

I poured a cup of coffee, inhaling the familiar inviting aroma. I decided I would try taming part of the overgrown garden, a section extending beyond the confines of the small courtyard. I had recently moved to this small rural Australian village, several hundred kilometres from the nearest major city. This town was old, originally constructed at a crossroad of two intersecting thoroughfares between the main capital cities. But with the passage of time, new roads bypassed this once-vital artery and now the hamlet was almost empty, nature had already reclaimed what humans had constructed. In the decades this house had stood empty, the garden seemed somehow wilder than the surrounding forests, the vines easily consuming garden walls and veranda alike. If I were to make some semblance of a new life in this place, I needed to tame the garden.

I finished my coffee and rolled up my sleeves, ignoring the pulse of guilt that I had slept in yesterday's clothes. None of that matters, I told myself. None of it matters when he is dead. Gritting my teeth, I strode into the courtyard, sunlight beginning to pierce the morning fog and started clearing the ground in the garden where I would construct a new stone wall. Sitting on my heels, I manoeuvred the hand-trowel, mechanically scraping away detritus from the long-abandoned garden beds. Beside me, a pile of broken roofing tiles, fragments of charred timber and broken terracotta pots grew. Behind me, Lance bounded around the yard while I wiped the back of my dirt-smeared hand across my forehead. Midday was approaching and already the warmth of the day seemed to leach back into the cold earth. Winter clouds scudded across the brilliant blue sky and a breeze rattled bare branches like sabres.

Shivering, I scraped away another section of dark soil, revealing a sand-stained shard of pottery. The incongruous light-coloured clay fragment drew my attention, and I peered closer at the shard, amazed at how none of the surrounding moist soil clung to the pottery fragment nor how any was ingrained in the uneven texture of the clay surface. I smoothed a finger across the pottery, revealing some carved inscriptions. The palm-sized piece fitted neatly in my hand and was smooth on the sides as though time had caressed the sharpness from the edges.

I stood up; trowel forgotten beside the garden bed. Walking carefully to the small garden table, I cradled the pottery fragment in my hands. Squinting at the inscriptions, I realised they appeared deliberate, markings covering every available surface of the pottery piece. It was not a pattern, or if it was, I did not recognise it. I leaned back on the wrought iron chair, eyes closed, face tilted up to the midday sky. An inexplicable knowledge coalesced that this pottery was old, and, equally strange, the certainty that if I lifted the pottery closer, I would hear the hissing of desert winds.

A voice whispered close behind me. "Release the bull of heaven."

I stared at the inscription, gaze unfocused and frowned. I shook my head, half-twisting to stare at the empty space behind my left shoulder. Did I imagine a voice? Had it been real? I shivered at the implications of hallucinating but more fearful still was the unwanted intrusion into my usually orderly mind. Lance whined beside me, breaking the fugue of strangeness that engulfed me. I shook my head then stood so abruptly I nearly knocked the chair to the paving stones. Without hesitation, I moved inside the house, still holding the odd clay fragment in my hands. Although I walked purposefully, I could not ignore the uncomfortable awareness of a presence behind me.

Once in the kitchen, I placed the pottery fragment on the counter-top, the clink of the clay against the hard surface seemed to echo in the quiet house. My hand trembled as I reached for my phone. There was something I could not explain about the pottery, the inscriptions and the texture of the clay itself that jarred against reality. After uploading the photo I had taken, I searched for similar images online. Although I wanted to justify my instinct that this was some ancient and unusual pottery fragment, I equally wanted the comforting confirmation that my thoughts were ludicrous. Surely, I was just being over-imaginative?

Less than a few brief seconds later, I had the answers I sought. I stared at the screen, the rows of many small images, each showing a pottery piece similar to the one I had found. I scrolled through the images with growing consternation. If I had hoped for clarification and some closure, this did not achieve it. Many of the images contained brief descriptions, with the same word repeated throughout. The pottery pieces were known as cuneiform tablets and all were related to museum collections. What on earth was cuneiform? I frowned, reaching across the counter for my laptop. I needed to expand my search and find out what cuneiform was, whether it was as ancient as my instinct warned me it was. Most of all, I wanted to understand why a cuneiform tablet had been buried in my garden.

The answers provided by an online search seemed improbable. Every article explained that cuneiform script was an ancient proto-writing system that had developed in the Near East over six-thousand years ago. My frown deepened as I considered the implications. How did cuneiform tablets become buried in my garden? Australia was a long way from the ancient empires of Iraq. Was the tablet in my yard evidence from some illegal trading or forgery attempts? I shook my head slowly at my rational attempts to explain an impossible event.

I continued to read, realisation dawning on how unlikely my discovery had been. Cuneiform was the common writing system between the ancient kingdoms of Sumeria, Babylon, Assyria and Persia. Again, I felt a keen awareness of a presence behind me. Half-turning from the kitchen counter, I was almost expecting someone to be standing a foot behind me. There was no one. I shivered, returning my attention to the search results. It's an impossibility, I reminded myself. You've never studied ancient texts; you've never even travelled to Iraq. Cuneiform tablets simply don't just appear from thin air. This is madness.

Although it was ridiculous to think the pottery I had found was a genuine cuneiform tablet, I continued to learn the fascinating history of these small palm-sized tablets made by ancient cultures several millennia ago and half a world away.

Daylight faded outside and as afternoon stretched into twilight, I continued to read. Even as I considered quitting this strange obsession to learn more, my gaze fell on the title of a poem and it flared in my consciousness as though some brilliant beacon. The Epic of Gilgamesh; an ancient poem detailing the struggle between a Sumerian king and the powerful gods. The awareness behind me grew suddenly stronger, transforming from a presence to a prickling on my skin, as though long fingers danced across my back. I slapped at my shoulder, certain it was just a spider or another insect. My hands found no insect, but the prickling worsened, now feeling as if a chill breath touched the back of my neck. I wanted to move, to flee, but instead I glanced warily behind me, certain someone leaned close to me, almost touching my left shoulder. Again, there was no one.

"Get a grip," I muttered, trying to enforce calmness and rationality.

I returned my attention to the computer screen. The Epic of Gilgamesh was recorded in cuneiform, inscribed on similar palm-sized clay tablets as the one I had found. It told the deeds of the heroic Sumerian king Gilgamesh and how he overcame philosophical dilemmas during his battles against the ancient gods. I paused, suddenly unsure what had seemed so important to me about The Epic of Gilgamesh. I shook my head slightly and refocused on the page. One phrase seemed to illuminate amid the surrounding lines of text. The Bull of Heaven. Perspiration broke out across my skin and my heartbeat quickened. I had heard those words whispered to me in the garden. I had not imagined the hissing voice and now that same phrase was written down here. What was the Bull of Heaven? Whatever was happening to me it didn't seem like some mental breakdown or an odd delusion. This was more than that, a coincidence on a higher level I could not deny. I inhaled slowly and opened the link to another document, determined to learn whatever I could about the Bull of Heaven.

According to the myth, Gilgamesh angers the goddess Ishtar who sends the destructive Bull of Heaven to extract her vengeance. Gilgamesh, however, slays the mythical bull and dismembers it, casting the hindquarters into the sky to form the constellation synonymous with Taurus.

A strong but inexplicable fear and precognition shivered through me. I stopped reading, titling my head and straining my hearing. I thought I had heard a faint chuckle. Now there was only the silence of the evening and the distant ticking of a clock. I shrugged, returning my attention to the screen.

Before long, I discovered another account of the Gilgamesh story, a much older form where Ishtar had another, more ancient name: Inanna. The goddess Inanna was the daughter of the sun and moon deities and in vengeance for an unknown offence, Inanna sent the Bull of Heaven against Gilgamesh. In this poem, the Bull of Heaven was more than a mythic beast to be slain by a heroic king. Inanna had a much darker nature, the goddess of bounty was also the goddess of famine and when she unleashed the Bull of Heaven upon the world, it delivered Inanna's vengeance in famine, fire and destruction. Fortunately, Gilgamesh still slays the Bull of Heaven, and prevents the destruction Inanna had sought.

I finished reading, a cold fear settling over me as I stared at several depictions of the Bull of Heaven, the muscular form carved into stone on temple walls, inscribed into gold and silver, shaped into tiny statues and icons. In every representation, the bull was a formidable beast with horns lowered to charge, one hoof raised in challenge.

After dinner, I walked outside into the shadowed garden, following the meandering step-stone path. I halted and exhaled, my breath an icy cloud in the night. I tilted my face upward, staring at the bare winter branches silhouetted against the night sky. I searched the starry dome, seeking the constellation of Taurus, following the path of the Milky Way, noticing the brighter points of significant stars which were, nonetheless, still nameless and unfamiliar to me. The night sky was as peaceful as always and that familiar sensation seemed to absorb the dislocation threatening to engulf me. I smiled in the darkness, fascinated by the shimmer of stardust along the Milky Way and I felt complete again as I had not been since my husband's death.

When the cold became too much for even the most determined stargazer, I hurried back toward the house, hands stuffed into the pockets of my old dressing gown. I paused at the glass door, smiling back at the night and reached for the door handle. Perhaps it was because I wasn't paying attention, but my fingers slipped on the handle, falling instead to the empty earth of the window-box beside the door. The window-box was devoid of plants this early in winter and yet my fingertips touched textured surface that was not soil. I held myself still, heart pounding as I moved my fingers along the now-familiar clay surface, exploring the inscriptions that covered the uneven shape of the clay tablet.

"Bring forth Inanna's vengeance, let the world be reborn," a voice hissed behind me, tone like shifting sand against stone.

I shivered violently, fear rising and drenching me in sudden perspiration. I fled inside, my traitorous fingers grasping the clay-tablet in a reaction I could not explain.

Once inside, I pushed my back to the kitchen counter, breathing quickly, staring in surprise at the tablet I held. Incomprehension consumed me as I stared from the cuneiform tablet in my hands to the one on the counter-top. Wordless sobs tore from me and I slowly sunk to the kitchen floor. I cradled my head in my hands, trying to stifle the sounds breaking unbidden from my throat. Lance whined uncertainly from the doorway and approached, tail wagging as he climbed into my lap. The reality of the madness engulfing me seemed stark and I could no longer hide from it.

I woke in the early hours, slumped awkwardly on the kitchen floor. Morning was just beginning to blush across the eastern horizon, barely a smudge against the darkness of night. Lance was still curled in my lap, but I was bitterly cold. I uncurled my cramped limbs, urging Lance to get up so I could climb stiffly to my feet. I stole a quick glance at the two cuneiform tablets on the kitchen countertop before hastening toward the bedroom, hoping for the oblivion of sleep.

I was chilled and frightened as I stepped into my bedroom, filled with the horrible sensation that someone followed behind me. I halted near my bed, staring at the empty expanse, the space my husband used to occupy that would be forever vacant. I shivered in the cold predawn air and took a desperate step toward the bed.

My bare toes touched an object, half-hidden beneath the overhang of my bed covers. I sucked in a breath with a hiss. I wanted to recoil, to flee. This could not be another clay tablet. My world seemed to spin around me, the future balanced precariously on my next action. I slid my foot back and saw the now-familiar cuneiform script on the surface of the pottery. I stared in disbelief and felt the future shift toward a decisive moment. The constant presence behind me coalesced.

"With Inanna's vengeance slaked, all will grow anew from ashes and bones," the awful voice whispered, breath tickling my ear.

"Go away," I shouted, slapping ridiculously at my ears as if that could somehow silence the voice.

"You don't truly want me to leave," the voice mocked.

"What are you?" I demanded, aware it lingered behind me and half-expecting if I turned around, it would be visible in the doorway.

"I have many names," it hissed. "We have been known as jinn or demons, but we are neither."

"What do you want then?" I pleaded.

"What you desire most of all," the thing crooned.

My anguish was a sound that seemed to shatter the room, slivers of myself spinning in every direction, reflecting back images of my face contorted with terror, fingers raking at my cheeks.

I ran into the sunroom, knees finally buckling, dropping to the floor. Lance skidded to a halt beside me, hackles raised as he stared at the empty space near the window. I looked at the large window that covered the northern side of the room but could discern nothing but my own reflection. I stared at my pale face smeared with tears and gave a sharp cry of frustration, scrubbing roughly at my cheeks, trying to enforce some composure. The awful panic that had taken hold seemed to subside and I sat back on my heels, looking out the northern window as dawn light broke through the morning clouds. I sensed through some precognitive

149

awareness that this was the last dawn I would ever see. The dense cloud mass was already spreading like a blight across the sky, and soon not even the bright morning sunlight would stop it. Alongside that awful realisation came a sense of claustrophobia as though the air itself pressed upon me, as if it were a tangible, heavy weight.

"Release the bull of heaven." The jinn urged me again.

"Shut up!" I shouted into the silence.

The jinn only laughed, a deep horrible sound that reverberated through the room and sent tremors shuddering through me. I cried nonsensical objections, promised impossible threats, but that taunting voice continued to ripple with laughter. When finally my terror peaked, I scooted backward across the floor, slamming my right shoulder hard into the window ledge. I cried out in pain, echoed by a sharp clatter from behind me that sent another wave of uncontrollable trembling through my body. I turned my head slowly, expecting to see the jinn from the periphery of my vision. There was nothing there, like all the times before. This is a hallucination. There will never be anything there, I reminded myself. I slumped forward in exhaustion, relief rolling through me as I bent my head to my knees. That's when I noticed the fourth cuneiform tablet. It must have fallen when I hit the window ledge. I watched as though from outside myself as my fingers reached for the clay fragment. I lifted it, turning it over in my hand, marvelling at the unnatural heaviness of the small tablet.

"With Inanna's cry, the bull will stamp the earth to dust and vengeance be claimed in her name," the jinn pronounced with dreadful certainty.

Time passed, or perhaps it no longer existed. I sat in the shadows of the sunroom, cuneiform tablet gripped in my hands as a storm descended on the afternoon, the last of the sunlight cutting thin slivers through the black clouds. The room was suffocating, the sense of anticipation seeming to crush the oxygen from the air itself. I struggled to breathe, fought to master my panic that an unavoidable calamity approached. The rooms seemed too small, the temperature was stifling and outside, the sky was too dark. The storm had not broken but seemed to wait, tense and patient, swollen with unleashed rage. The jinn was a menacing presence filling my small house, taunts and cries flushed with exultation.

"Inanna?" I called, uncertain but pleading into the growing shadow of the storm.

The jinn suddenly halted its rapturous cries and listened, silence falling heavy around me.

"Inanna?" I called firmly, heart beating loudly as I lifted my face to the gloom outside my window. "Inanna!" I shouted, calling on the name of the goddess again, this time an invocation.

"Do you know who you seek, mortal child?" the jinn asked in a hushed whisper.

"Please stop this," I begged, burying my face in my hand, leaning heavily against the window frame.

"Ah," the jinn cooed. "Only Inanna can grant you that release you seek."

"Tell me how," I sobbed, clutching at my hair as though pulling it from my scalp would stop this madness.

Across the room, Lance growled and stood, legs apart with short hackles raised, but did not approach, just stared at the emptiness behind me. Again, I desperately wanted to twist away. I felt the icy prickle of fingertips brush on my cheek and I might have been frozen beneath that touch.

"Only you hold the power to grant Inanna's wish," the jinn said. "In granting her wish, your desire will be returned in kind."

"How?" I sobbed again, wanting to move away from the horrible being that seemed to lurk behind me. I forced myself to hold firm, to ignore the frigid breath on the back of my neck that burned like fire. I barely repressed a shudder as, around me, the pressure of the storm increased and with it, a throbbing pain blossomed in my skull.

"You know what to do," the jinn said.

My eyes focused on the cuneiform tablet beside my foot. I did not let myself think but focused my attention on the uneven edges of the pottery shard. Suddenly, I could see where it had been broken from a whole, where the other fragments had once fitted around it.

"Does it make a poem?" I asked, picking up the tablet. "Does it tell a story like Gilgamesh?"

The jinn howled in rage; the noise reverberated through the house like the screeching against stone. I clutched at my ears, trying to lessen the noise but it seemed to tear the air to shreds around it.

"Not a story of destruction like Gilgamesh," the jinn snarled.

"But it tells a story?" I asked, dizziness engulfing me as my vision spun.

"Yes," the jinn replied. "The false hero Gilgamesh is long buried beneath the sands of time, but these lands have never known the stamp of hoof. It is Inanna's greatest wish that such a power remind them of their faith."

I tried to consider the jinn's words but the pain inside my skull climbed to a crescendo, the throbbing of my eardrums nearly deafening but I still heard the rasping voice of the jinn behind me.

"Work quickly, mortal child," it advised.

I moved as swiftly as I could, my legs trembling as I gripped the clay tablet, blood dripping from my nostrils. I ran into the kitchen, quickly rearranging the clay fragments, guided by an unfathomable intuition. When I was finished, I stared at the arranged fragments, the centre still a dark and yawning void. Hastily, I wiped away more droplets of blood falling onto the counter-top, carefully manoeuvring the final piece of pottery into place. The final fragment was the most recent, the one that had fallen from the window-ledge in the sunroom. I stared at it, noticing that, unlike the other tablets, this one contained no cuneiform inscriptions but depicted the Bull of Heaven—horns lowered, muscular body tensed, and one hoof raised to crush an enemy beneath it.

I did not allow myself time to think. I ignored the pain in my fingers as the sharp edges of the clay sliced my skin. I moved with near reverence, carefully lowering the final fragment into place, the uneven margins smoothing away to reveal the tablet, whole and complete as though it had never been broken.

The pressure in the atmosphere dropped, the storm grew quiet and silence descended. I could hear nothing since the jinn had screamed at me. Now, in confusion, I turned to survey the windows of the sunroom. I looked down in bewilderment at the stain across my shirt, the blood still trickling from my nose. I lifted my eyes again to the windows and with a quickening of my heart, I walked towards them.

Outside, the massive storm clouds now swarmed across the sky, turning in a slow spiral, edged with flame.

"What have I done?" I whispered.

"What you desired," the jinn chuckled with apparent glee.

"Just tell me what I did!" I shouted.

The silence crackled, paused, before a roar of thunder split the sky. The wind burst into a gale, hurling debris and leaves across my garden, increasing in strength that shook the large windows of the sunroom. Cautiously, I stepped back from the glass panes, expecting them to shatter from the onslaught. Lance whined piteously from my bedroom doorway; ears flat as he glared toward me. No, I realised. Not at me but behind me.

"Inanna granted you the release you sought," the jinn explained. "And in kind, you released the Bull of Heaven."

"But what does that mean?" I roared against the tempest outside.

"Didn't you understand the summoning?" the jinn mocked. "The bull will bring these lands into subservience."

I remembered the poem from the cuneiform tablets, and all the jinn had quoted to me.

"Bring forth Inanna's vengeance and let the world be reborn. For only when Inanna's vengeance is slaked, will all grow anew from ashes and bones. With Inanna's cry, the bull will stamp the earth to dust and vengeance be claimed in her name. Release the bull of heaven."

"Exactly," the jinn said jovially. "The foolish mortals of these lands sought to challenge the might of the gods. Millennia may have passed, child, but this is the briefest of moments to the gods. Inanna now takes her vengeance for the defiance of mortal men."

I blinked in dumb confusion. "Inanna is punishing us now for the actions of Gilgamesh?" I asked. "Those actions committed thousands of years ago?"

"Yes," the jinn snapped with irritation. "Inanna does not discriminate between her children. You may think you acted as one, but his punishment befalls you all."

"How did I do this?" I asked, gesturing to the flame touched sky, ash now falling from the clouds like rain.

"How else?" the jinn asked. "If Gilgamesh was only one man who committed an injustice, why would it matter if one mortal restores the balance and delivers justice?"

"Justice?" I croaked, staring in horror at the fiery sky outside.

"To gods like Inanna, this is justice," the jinn explained. "It should not bother you, mortal. For now, you are free."

I stared in bitter wonder at the destruction I had unleashed. "Free from what?"

"From me," the jinn chuckled.

I turned then, noticing a sudden spray of sparks behind me. Dark tendrils of smoke spiralled upward, evaporating almost as quickly as the half-visible form of the grinning jinn, simply vanished. I felt the sudden departure of the jinn as though oxygen had been pulled from the air. I lurched forward, clutching the window frame for support. I pressed my face to the glass, unable to stand as my legs weakened. I leaned on the window frame for support, forcing myself to witness Inanna's merciless vengeance borne from my own actions.

I stood mute; a soundless scream caught in my throat as dark clouds edged with lightning coalesced into the massive form of a bull. I tasted bile as the Bull of Heaven lowered wicked horns crafted from lightning. The beast stamped a hoof, molten rain showering down on the earth below, birthing wildfires and flushing the sky an angry red. Tears left ashen tracks down my face as the Bull of Heaven moved across the sky and, where it briefly touched the earth, decimation lay in its wake. After moments that could have been eons, the Bull of Heaven raised its massive head and bellowed a challenge like thunder, hoof stamping and sending more fiery tornadoes across the barren earth below. A hollow silence echoed from the land around me and with a toss of its muscular head, I watched as Inanna's vengeance was finally slaked and the bull retreated.

For a long time I stood there, clutching the window frame of my small house, the landscape surrounding me now a wasteland of burnt forest and charred rock. Clouds of black smoke blew across the window, hiding the barren lands beyond. I did not think anyone could have survived the devastation I had unwittingly unleashed, but I had to save anyone I could. I walked unsteadily to my door and with one glance knew Inanna's vengeance for the destruction it was, for wherever the Bull of Heaven had stood, only ash and embers remained.

About the Author:

Leanbh Pearson lives on Ngunnawal Country in Canberra, Australia. An LGBTQIA & disability author of horror & dark fantasy, her fiction features in numerous anthologies. Always aided by her canine assistants, her writing is inspired by folklore, fairytales, archaeology & the environment. She has judged the Australian Shadows Awards, Aurealis Awards, received an AHWA mentorship, participates on convention panels & is a member of the HWA & SFWA. Leanbh's alter-ego is an academic in archaeology, evolution and prehistory.
Follow her at www.leanbh pearson.com.
Twitter, Facebook & Instagram @leanbhpearson.

MEET ME BY THE MOON WHEN I'M FLICKING THROUGH A CHEAP MAGAZINE TALKING ABOUT ASTROLOGY

Brianna Bullen

There is nothing more inconvenient than to love when one is fated to die. We attach ourselves to others at the worst of times, making kinships out of borrowed time and late-night whispered dirges, barely audible over the vacant hum of the ship and our laboured breathing. The air down here feels toxic through the nose. There is little oxygen here. Pressed up against each other, shoulder to shoulder, we consume each other's carbon dioxide as if it were food. In the lower rungs of the ship, we are allocated little in the way of air supply or comfort.

What we are given is hay. Hay, cruelty and—strangely—books. Little paperbacks to give us a 'moral education' and to mock us. Asterion, Asterion, Asterion. Borges' story repeated as mocking litany, again and again, pacing inside our heads. None of us are mindless monsters. With clipboards and a checklist, they monitor our progress and neural waves—are these creatures registering our words? How complex can we go? Dr Seuss or Tolstoy? Realism or the existential fantastic? Orwellian dystopic lives. How to measure them using theories of development if they cannot speak? A biped with the title scientist visits us every few rotations. I have given up measuring it through the release of food through the chutes above. The scientist comes at irregular intervals. It makes it harder to breathe, all of us tense, large lungs afraid to heave for fear of drawing attention at the wrong moment.

A new calf has been born. The biped has been down more regularly as of late to check on its progress. The creature is a runt; a mewling, baying thing with terrified eyes and flared nostrils. It stomps at the ground with the self-righteous audacity of a child, looking for an exit with nowhere to run. We were all born this way. The child will soon know it is not special, will be as still and silent as the rest of us.

His mother is an older cow with sad grey eyes, hunched over shoulders and a weak back. Her ear tag has a list of numbers that those with cerebral enhancements can read but do not tell her what they mean. If numbers are designations for humans, I refuse them. We refer to her as Mother, and before that, Key, as the pattern on her rump matches the adornments of our captors. There are many in our sad herd, but she is the cellmate placed by my side, and the one I am fondest of. The calf could be mine, or it could be one of any of the bulls. Extraction and insemination is entirely artificial. The touch we get is only from metal and the bruising rub of shoulders shoved too close together in not enough space.

I have a tag pierced through my own ear, a dandelion yellow. I only know of dandelions from a freak mix-up in the seeds meant for our food. I have not seen anything so beautiful nor delicate since they removed the few stowaway flowers. The number is not important, but the tag claps against my ear, I can feel its touch on my neck like a fly with every step I am privileged to make or every shake of the head. It is another sound effect I use to distract myself whenever the tension is too much. The other bovines call me "Lucky" in both their rudimentary human words and in their eyes. I was one of the few the neural operations worked well on. "Predisposition from the genetic modification of the parents," the scientist and his own flock once muttered, and it stuck with me. Stuck like the scars sealing over my head where they cut open my skull to prod needles, scalpels and tubes in my brain, hoping to "enhance and unlock potential" with brutality and quackery. Hacksaw through horn and bone.

Cud crawls up from stomach through throat and back into my mouth. I ruminate on it, chewing every now and again. My ears are pricked, anticipating the door to open at any moment. There's a drop of sweat running down my shoulder, stinging hot skin with chill. My hooves are pace-begging, but there is no room. Every nerve cell and hair on my body seems to be pulsing on end. My heartbeat barrels through its heavy-set chest—or am I hearing the anxiety of any number of my herd? Moments of terror mobilise empathy. A network connection, everyone attuned to the same frequency.

It is hard to measure days in a windowless room, no less a windowless room in the depths of space. Light is a luxury, even when it is dim and artificial. But I think it's a harvest day, one where the biped crew in the surrounding rooms feast on the flesh of one of our own. We are a resource kept not just for the idle fancy and experiments of bored scientists, but for the meals of the wealthiest crewmembers every few months. They needed to ensure we were living in "sustainable" amounts, rather than taking up too many resources, "human intelligence" or no.

I'd fear for my kin if I wasn't also relieved for whoever was chosen. The cud goes back down my throat as I swallow. Someone moos behind me, a forlorn sound. It is impossible to tell who began the cry as the dirge is soon added to from every angle. It bounces off the metal walls. At least twenty voices are calling out—loudly, screaming, crying and wanting to be recognised as suffering. I feel each soul through the ground, through my hooves. Even the calf stops its incessant suckling and halts all movement, as if caught in a tractor beam. Its innocence will end as soon as one of its companions is bolted through the head. I keep my eyes on its cheerful pair. It will know no better than these first few months.

I do not join the song of my peers; no sound can pass on what I fear.

We hear the scientist before we see them today. A cooing sound we now know is condescending but would previously have been soothed by. "Hello, my lovelies." They start humming a song which creeps beneath the door and into our bones. The door takes a while to unlock, but we can hear each bolt being moved with finality before the handle is turned with a dropping whine. Metal screams with regularity. The scientist pokes their head through, glasses fogged up by coffee steam but I can still see the laughter in their steel eyes. It's the one with the matted hair today. They've taken one step into the room and already they're tugging through dark hair, scratching at their scalp. Even cruel people seem to have habits they want to break.

Today, the scientist has several glasses and a torch balanced on their book. It's a thick textbook today, even though I can't make out the title. It's all in the shape, overstuffed with facts and definitions, with some glossy photos which make little darker lines in the pages' sides.

"Alright my bovine beauties, today we are going to be taking a page out of Piaget." They put down the book and holds the glasses behind their back. "Stomp your feet if the glass is still present."

There's a frenzied stamping from the herd. Many understand his words; the others know to follow the actions of those that react. The calf bleats in alarm as his mother stomps, eyes white. Following too slowly or not at all increases the risk of being on the chopping block. Our regular handler has also slipped through the door. From the bolt-gun at his side, we know he is bringing neither food or care. Luckily for the calf, no others bleed into the room from the gap in the door. It is strange, but it sometimes happens that they lead one of our number out into the foyer outside where a team is waiting to kill it and disassemble the body. Less stench and panic and bodies to manoeuvre through. Greater efficiency, minimal panic, less chance that the cow will escape than if they led it into wherever it is that they prepare food.

The scientist sometimes mocks us with our history, speaks of ramps and houses made for our slaughter, says that we're "a lucky bunch of fat cows" as if they've forgotten they've taught us how to listen to their words.

"So that's a resounding understanding of object permanence," the handler mutters as they check our water levels, drawing more for us with the switch of a high-up button. Had it been any lower, I know I would have been tempted to press against it. Waste more of their water from our allotment. But it would only have punished us.

"Hm, maybe Jo." the scientist slaps an older heifer on the shoulder, feels down its leg and manoeuvres it in a circle to check for movement. "Or herd mentality. One knows, the rest follow."

The handler scoffs. Pulls a face after the first sentence. I don't know why they do this.

The heifer gets praised by the scientist who then moves onto the next. "Do you mind filling that tall slim glass for me? Got to make sure they still understand conservation principles."

The handler grumbles but complies. "Don't know why you have to do this so much. They know. That's not going to change."

"Oh no, regression is entirely possible. Would be annoying after all this time—interesting and a new direction for study, but annoying."

"You ever going to get them to speak?" The handler scratches their neck. There are no flies in the ship, but the sweat-damp air creeps across the skin, stings the senses. Flies remain a story, told across generations. At least there aren't any flies, the old Earth-born cows had said. Annoying miniscule creatures that latched onto the side and stung.

The scientist titters.

The handler laughs. The sound is a cruel growl, loud and slightly awkward as if expecting discipline from the noise. "Stupid of me, I know. What would a cow even have to say? Nothing of any value, surely."

The scientist turns to them. I can't see their gaze or expression, but it causes the handler's to freeze and then drop.

"It'd be my dream to hear if they have anything to say. I only laugh in the face of the task as it seems momentous, too large for someone so simple. I'm just imagining the operations I'd need to do to get their larynxes and brain capable of the task—too traumatic. They would not want to speak to us after that kind of torture. No, it'd be enough if we could get them to understand us. To understand themselves."

The handler shakes their head. "Don't think there's much to understand there. Maybe just moo, shit, smelly, food, yum, water, drink, walk, danger. Might not even be able to understand danger if I'm honest."

The scientist pushes up their glasses. "Honest for what you know, not honest of the actual truth. Can't you see their nerves? Feel it in their sides, the tension in their backs, the snorting of their nostrils? They understand fear."

"Upper management know that?"

"Wouldn't let me keep a herd with our limited resources if they didn't."

It's strange. I hear these words. I know these words as individual units from the stories this person tells us. Can stitch them together to try and comprehend what they mean in the sequence spoken. But often I do not understand. I do not understand, because I do not understand these creatures, or this strange land of humming air and engines that we find ourselves in.

"Do you think any of this lot will ever touch down on Kep?"

"This lot? They'd be pushing it." The scientist walks over to the calf beside me. It shivers, buries itself beneath its mother as much as it can. Smart child. The scientist coos and rubs its mother's shivering side, trying to coax movement. "Next generation should, though. Just got to check your baby, sweetheart. Thata girl."

Their words of comfort trickle as poison, some chloroform or relaxant that forces your guard down however much you struggle against it. The shuddering calf peeks out, face still half-tucked away. It's reached for, and it flinches back.

"Relax little buddy," the handler came over to assist, coaxing the baby out. "The captain doesn't want veal tonight, you're safe."

I feel my hair stand on end. How dare they threaten a child who doesn't understand. The calf squeals and hides deeper underneath its mother. Smart kid. They laugh. Why are they laughing?

The lesson today is truncated. The humans clearly hunger. The calf's mother is sleepy-eyed, more milky than present. She falters on the mathematics tasks, reaction time slower and the amount of hoof beats off by one, which she slowly corrects after a deathly pause.

My own task when they get to me is literary. They hook me up to a machine, putting a cap with little spore-like buds against my scalp. They read to me. Measure my emotional responses on a handheld screen in the areas activated in my brain. It's a simpler story today, one of ill-fated friends on opposing sides in a war who meet under the cover of darkness. They play naughts and crosses in the dirt on the ground. Talk about what they'll do when the battle is over. Then one dies on the field, and the other returns to their hidden enclave and waits until morning with no response. Their marks on the ground have been dusted over in the wind. I don't understand any of it. Why bother befriending an enemy? Why risk being caught and shot? Why the mundane tasks? It's confusing, but they seem to like my responses. Apparently confusion is a sufficient emotional response when it comes to pondering humanity to allow me to live another few months.

It was the bull in the corner, the one who often shivered and snorted with barely concealed hate, that set himself up to die. Stubborn bastard refused to so much as face the scientist, turning his head to the corner of the room and presenting his backside with a kick of the hay beneath him. His tail flicks up as he shits on the ground. The scientist laughs nervously and looks at the handler who shrugs.

"Kinda like this one's personality. He's an utter dick."

The scientist chuckles harder at the comment, mutters in low tones, "so maybe veal tonight after all?"

The words rock through me, freeze me in place. My heart thunders regardless of my body's stillness, jackhammer in a rock. How dare they. How dare they.

I wasn't aware I had moved. Wasn't aware I had gored the handler. All I was aware of was my own mind and heart, clinging to the word "unfair, unfair, unfair.'

My body barrels as a bullet to the door, knocking down and trampling the scientist who had scrambled in fear to open it. The opening is there. I part it further as I birth myself into my new life as a bull on the run. I run, and run.

I leave my family by fate behind me. I can not look back. Do not look back. I do not hear them gain the courage to follow.

Panic. Sheer panic. My soul seems to run before me, carrying my breath, and my body lumbers after it. No door can stop me, and for the first few rooms, no door does. The human pair had left the latches unlocked, to save them the minimal effort on the way out of our first heavily locked room. The doors part under my weight, before I even have time to register them; I hear only the ghost of my impact in the echoing shudder of the doors. Before I know it, I am running down a vacant corridor. Steam hisses off the side, the walls seeming to sweat as I pass a generator. Only something integral to the ship could be so loud; I avoid hitting the walls or its protrusion at all costs, slowing my pace. Temperature gauges tremor on their side, maintaining a safe range of movement. Just a flicker, then back, not a huge swing. It is damp, dark. A room barely ventured to. Lit by manual lights.

There are flickers of sound—operational buzzes, engine whines—the barest hint of movement from some stowaway pest, but otherwise it is silent. All I can hear is the heaving gasps from my barrelling chest, and the occasional howling moo of my rage. I hit an end to one corridor, I turn into the next, then the next. I am running through the labyrinth, my echoing steps my only company. If I close my eyes, I can pretend I have a herd with me. I am running for a while before my first contact with the opulence of the human beings. The corridor lights up with me, as if anticipating my movement. A reverse shadow, light protruding out before me in incremental shifts. What creatures could summon light with their own steps, demand it light their way?

There is a pair of doors before me, so different to the metal that has surrounded me all of my life. It is carved, the handles glinting. But the material—it is wood; polished and deep as the brown of my own hide. The handles curl down, long and thick as human arms, until they meet at the centre of the door's opening, like two fists side-by-side. I do not stop. The door splinters open, but I meet heavy resistance, jagged pieces embedding in my face and sides.

There are sounds of beauty I have never heard before, which seem to screech to a stop as soon as they touch my ears. On the podium, humans sat and stood holding various tools and instruments—was this an operation? What were they operating on? Each other? The air? The silence? I connect the beautiful noise with their tools as one continues beyond the rest and only jerks to a stop when their elbow is touched by a member above.

I spin around, delirious from pain and exhaustion. The adrenaline is still pumping, but the lights and the noise and the people and the smells make everything spin, triggering senses and synapse from seemingly every angle. People, even those standing still, pass in a blur. Black and white static from all the tuxedos, interrupting the usual shades of grey and muted browns. Above my head there is an upside-down tree of glittering glass. Not only does each lens catch the light, but it seems to create it. Pulse with it. Little crystal hearts. It makes me dizzier; vision flashing, melding shadow and light. The humans are eating from a trough, only it seems to be upside down with the food on top. A table? It matches the books' descriptions. Mushy peas. Carrots. Jellied cubes of protein. A banquet for those living off the essentials, with a ludicrous fountain of liquid in the centre to keep morale up. A hairless man is ladling it into his glass but it spills over as we make eye contact. Laughter bleeds into confused whispers, morphs into delighted squeals.

A real-life animal from the decks below! What luxury was this?

I bolt through the gathering circle, splitting the shape through the centre. People leap to the ground to avoid me, while others merely side-step. My hooves click on a lacquered floor, flat feet nearly slip on the smooth stickiness as I search for a door to another room.

There is no exit.

But I am not met with a wall.

Outside is a sea of stars. Little flashing pixels. Light trying to be seen, from thousands of years away. Already dead ghosts, most of them. No less pretty. I do nothing but stare. I have never seen the sky before, but my soul and the sublime awe of stories tell me that this is such. A deeper sky, dark as oil, thick as blood. I let myself still, knowing my journey is over.

Nowhere to hide in a spaceship. My breath fogs up the window's glass, and spreads its own stars from the ghost of my lungs.

About the Author:

Brianna Bullen lives just west of Melbourne on Wathaurong and Wurundjeri Woi Wurrung land. She writes science fiction short stories and poetry. Her poetry chapbook 'Unicorn with Unibrows' *was published by Puncher & Wattmann, with a second chapbook* 'Omelettes for Night Owls' *forthcoming with Dancing Girl Press.*

GEMINI
MAY 21 - JUNE 20

WELCOME HOME

Belinda Brady

My twin sister, Freya, is waiting for me in the hallway as I enter our home. Her face is one of shock as she grabs me by the shoulders and moves in close. "Whatever you do," she whispers in my ear, her voice panicked, "don't let him know you know. As far as you're concerned, it's really him."

"Who?" I whisper back, confused.

Before she can answer, he appears behind her.

I pull back from my sister and inhale sharply. It takes all my strength to stay standing, to smile back at him, when all I want to do is turn and run.

"Welcome home, Alice! We've missed you!" Dad beams at me.

Freya is gaping at me, her eyes reflecting the horror I feel. I stare back at her, forcing my face to stay neutral.

My gaze shifts back to my father. The same father who raised us alone for ten years after our mother walked out when we were just eight years old. The same father who read us bedtime stories, taught us how to drive and was our shoulder to cry on when we experienced our first heartbreak. The same father who is now coming towards me with huge smile on his face, his arms outstretched for a hug.

The same father we buried over a year ago after he was killed in a car accident.

"Dad," I finally manage, as he wraps his arms around me. "It's so good to see you. I've missed you too."

He's exactly the same: he smells the same; he feels the same; he hugs the same. But it's not him. I know it.

"I've missed you so much, Alice. You and your sister." He smiles, his fingers gripping my forearms as we pull away from our embrace.

"It's been a while . . ." I look over to Freya, who remains glued to her spot.

"And that's why I'm here!" Dad exclaims. "To be with my girls, to be with my beautiful twins."

"Well, I'm really glad you're here." I smile back, my heart racing.

"I'm making us our favourite dinner—a roast with all the trimmings. I'm sure you can smell it. My famous gravy is simmering away on the stove and I'd hate to burn it, so come, follow me to the kitchen." He drops my arms and looks from my sister to me, grinning at us both.

"C'mon girls, don't just stand there. Your feast is waiting for you," he repeats and it's then that I see it—a flash. A blink-and-you'd-miss-it flash that fills his eyes with the purest of black. Every hair on my body stands on end.

"Oops! Nearly forgot!" he exclaims suddenly, his eyes widening. He barges between Freya and I, marches to the front door, and locks it with a key that has magically appeared in his hand. "I have Freya's key. I'll have yours now." He turns to me, hand outstretched.

Freya bows her head in silence. I open my mouth to ask why he has locked the front door, when he narrows his eyes at me.

"Now, Alice," he demands.

I bite my lip and hand him my key.

He places the two of them in the top pocket of his shirt, patting them in place. "Just to be safe. We don't want anyone interrupting out little reunion." He winks before he turns and walks down the hallway toward the kitchen.

Freya is by my side in an instant, grabbing my hand. "Did you see that?" she asks, her voice quivering.

"I did." I nod, trying to keep composed. If I lose it, she'll lose it, and that can't happen. To get out of this house, we need to keep it together. *I* need to keep it together. "Tell me everything from the beginning."

"I came home from school early, my science teacher was sick or something so our class was cancelled and there he was in the kitchen, cooking dinner. I nearly died from shock. He told me he missed us, he wanted to see us again, so he thought he'd drop in, cook us a meal just like he used to," Freya blurts out, her eyes darting to the hallway. "I know it's not him, I *know* it. I was so afraid of what to do, what to say, so I just went along with it. He was talking like nothing had happened—asking how school was, asking when you were getting home. I tried to get to the front door to get out, but he was in front of me in a flash, blocking my way, wanting to know what I was doing, demanding my house key . . . Jesus, Alice. What the hell is going on?"

"I don't know," I answer, "but one thing is certain. Whoever that is, it's not our Dad. We need to stick together on this. Don't let on we know, don't show him we know. We just need to keep our cool until we can work out how to get out of here."

Freya nods, tears spilling from her glassy eyes.

I pull her into a hug. "Just follow my lead. We're going to get out of this, okay?"

Dad sticks his head around the corner. "Are you girls coming? I can't wait for you to see what I've got prepared for you!"

"We're coming," I reply, releasing my sister from my arms, forcing a smile as he looks at me expectantly. "And we can't wait to see what you've got for us."

We walk into the kitchen to find it bustling with activity. Saucepans are bubbling noisily on the stove. The oven is on, our dinner cooking, emitting warmth and delicious aromas. My father returns to the stove stirring his gravy. I stand in the entrance and stare at the scene before me, not sure what to do next.

"I know how much you two enjoyed my roasts, so I thought I'd whip one up for you. A welcome home meal if you like. A welcome home meal for my girls and I . . . my beautiful twins," he says, keeping his back turned as he stirs. "My girls who couldn't be any more different if they tried. Isn't that right, Freya?"

He turns to look at Freya, who is leaning against the bench near the sink, nodding her head in a zombie-like trance. "Well, Freya? Cat got your tongue? Speak!" he snaps, his tone taking a dark turn.

"Sorry . . . yes, we are different, Alice and I. Typical twins, typical Geminis. I'm the impulsive, superficial, emotionally detached one, while sis here is the intelligent, outgoing, yet more anxious, twin. I tend to do things without thinking, while she is frustratingly indecisive and takes forever to make a decision. It takes her a week to decide what she wants for lunch." Freya laughs, a sudden and unexpected confidence to her voice.

Dad smiles at Freya and something passes between them—a look, a knowing look.

My breath catches in my throat and my stomach drops as I realise my sister knows something I don't. Dread crawls up my chest as Dad turns back to the stove and Freya stays by the bench, staring at the back of him. She won't make eye contact with me. I fight to keep my breathing steady as my mind races, trying to think of a way to make it out of this house safely and away from them both.

"Oh damn it!" the man who looks like my father exclaims, turning around with an empty salt bottle in his hands. "I'm out of salt, and this gravy is nothing without it. Do you reckon there's some in the back shed?"

"I'll go look!" I offer, jumping at my chance to flee. I turn and make a beeline for the back door, fighting the urge to run as I make my way through the back of the house. Reaching the door, I turn the knob and pull it open with a violent yank, as though my life depends on it.

Because it does.

Stale afternoon air hits my face as I exit the house and make my way to the shed, still not running, but not far off it. The shed is home to a variety of weird and wonderful tools—it's also where we store any excess groceries. It stands just behind the house, separated by a small footpath, its only door facing our huge backyard. Opposite it, built into the fence, is a gate that leads to a back laneway—and my escape. The shed door is a noisy, creaky thing and there's no mistaking the sound when it's being opened. I know they'll be waiting for that creak of the door; the flicker of the light as it's switched on. I have to go inside for just a second, make them think I'm looking for the salt, when I've really snuck through the gate to my freedom. It's risky, but it's my only chance. I have to get out. I *have* to try . . .

Hands shaking, I open the door and wait for the dust to clear before I step inside, swatting away a few flies that buzz past my face. I turn on the light and scream.

In the corner, propped up like a doll, is the body of Freya. It is bloated and pasty, dried vomit crusted to the side of her face and down her neck, her dead eyes staring back at me in silence. Lying next to her is the body of my father, which I had not seen since his funeral. He was broken and bruised then, and still is now, only decomposition had well and truly taken over. I fight the urge to vomit as maggots and flies crawled in and out of his mouth. Before them lies an altar, a pentagram filled with black candles, glass jars filled to the brim with items of various sizes and colours, and several family photos of the three of us, smiling happily for the camera. I turn to run, but Freya and my father are behind me, blocking the doorway. Their skin is pale, almost translucent, their eyes jet black, the same happy smiles from the family photos plastered across their faces.

"What? What happened . . . I don't . . ." I gasp as I grab the wall for support, my legs threatening to collapse at any moment.

"You know I wasn't coping with the death of Dad," Freya starts, her voice higher than usual. "We lost him too soon, too young. It was so unfair."

Dad nods in response, his eyes on me, his face giving nothing away.

"I just couldn't get over it. I couldn't. I was so grief-stricken that I didn't see the point of carrying on, so I contemplated ending it all. But then I had a thought— 'what if I can get him back and things can go back to how they were before he died?'" Freya takes a step toward me. "So after a bit of searching on the dark web, I found a way. I found a spell. Not one that could bring back the dead, but one that could return things to how they were . . . before. It was one that can transport you back to that life before death, before loss. We could have our old lives back, the only catch being at least two of the parties involved in the spell couldn't be alive for it to work, we *had* to be dead, which was fine by me. I mean, Dad was already taken care of, so all I had to do was take care of myself, right? Then we could live our lives again. Not as spirits per se, but as the dead living their old lives in a perfect, unbreakable bubble. To the outside world, we didn't exist and never did. Our lives and memories would be completely wiped and we could just live our lives as they were without interruption. It was exactly what I wanted."

It's at that moment I notice the weather. *Really* notice it. It's June, our birthday month, the beginning of winter, and the air should be brisk and cold, but all I can feel, all I can smell, is warm air and fresh cut grass. Looking past them to the backyard, I see the trees are in full bloom, their foliage an explosion of green. The sun is high in the late afternoon sky, and a pair of swimmers are on the clothesline, dripping water on the grass below as they dry, fresh from a swim at the beach. A typical summer's day.

"What's the date?" I stutter, already knowing the answer.

"It's the twentieth of January," my dad replies solemnly.

The day he died.

"The day he died," Freya states, reading my mind. "I'm sure you remember, Alice. You had just come home from the beach and Dad was cooking dinner, his famous roast, when he was called into work. An elevator had malfunctioned at the local shopping centre and he had to go and repair it. Dad promised he'd be back in time to make his gravy, but never did. He was involved in an accident, a head-on collision, and died instantly. That was the day it all turned to shit."

"I was just as upset about dying as you and Freya were, Alice," Dad continues, moving next to Freya, "I had such *anger* attached to my death, but lucky for us—*all* of us—your sister here found a way to get us all back to that afternoon before I was killed, before I left for work. She found a way to get us back to that life, that safe, happy life and now it will be our new existence. It will be our *only* existence."

"My god, Freya, what have you done?" I murmur, hot tears wetting my cheeks.

"It took me a while to get what I needed, of course," Freya continues, ignoring my question. "Some things were super hard to come by, such as goat embryos and cow's blood, but I got them, and I got them past you. Remember all those parcels that were being delivered? The ones I told you were clothes I'd bought on sale?"

I nod slightly, remembering the influx of plain packaged parcels Freya had been getting almost daily a few weeks back. She had told me her favourite online clothing store was having a 'huge, once-in-a-lifetime sale', when I questioned her spending and naively didn't think to push it.

She turns her head and looks at Dad, a satisfied smirk on her face. "But where there's a will there's a way, and I got every damn item the spell required. I knew you'd never go for it, you and your anxious little mind, so I kept it to myself. After all, I didn't want to spoil the surprise."

She inches closer, Dad right behind her.

"I dug Dad up that weekend you went away with your friends, stashed him away in here. Boy, what an effort that was. I had to wait till after midnight to go to the cemetery, dig him up, lug his heavy body back to the car and then fix up his grave. The cemetery never noticed of course—I made sure his grave was in pristine condition when I left. But it had to be done—he was a pivotal part of the magic. I needed to end my life right after I cast the spell, but I had no objections. If it worked, bonus, if not . . . bonus. The overdose was messier than I had anticipated. Funny that." She looks over my shoulder to her vomit-soaked body and laughs. "But it was worth it. We are back here, back to this day, back to this moment before Dad leaves the house. We are back to that moment when he is here; preparing dinner and everything is just so freaking perfect. We just need to finish the spell now and this will be how it is forever—Dad and his twin girls living this day, living this life on repeat."

Freya's face hardens as her black eyes meet mine, her arms moving to the front of her body, revealing a hammer in her curled hand. "It's time to finish the spell, Alice."

Dad lunges from the doorway and is behind me before I can blink. He grabs at my arms, trying to hold them against my sides, but I break free, pushing him away as I make a desperate dash for the door. I charge at Freya, knocking her to the floor, her screams muffled as the blood rushes in my ears and I burst into our backyard. My adrenaline is pumping as I run, gasping for air, grass crunching under my feet, as the gate to the laneway gets closer.

There's movement and shouting behind me and everything slows down. I'm still running but I'm moving in slow motion, the gate sliding away from me, as though imaginary strings are pulling it back.

I hear a whooshing sound and turn to see the hammer coming straight for me, flying through the air with a guided grace. Freya is in front of the shed, her left arm mid-pitch, her face twisted in rage as she chants words I don't understand. Dad is next to her, arms crossed, his face creased into an impatient scowl. The hammer connects with my temple, the sound of cracking bone loud and sickening, the pain instant and breathtaking. I hear laughter; the loud and hysterical laughter of my sister as I collapse in a heap, blood gushing from my broken skull, soaking the grass underneath me as my life slips away. The last thing I hear before I take my last breath, before I join my dead family in their unearthly new world, is Freya's singsong voice calling out from the circling darkness.

"Welcome home, Alice."

About the Author:

A bookworm since childhood, Belinda is passionate about stories and has turned her hand to writing them, with several stories published in a variety of publications. Belinda lives in Australia with her family, two moody, yet oh so loveable, cats and two super cute miniature dachshunds who love annoying said cats and each other. Belinda adores all things spooky, music and travel.

ETHAN

Talien Jae

"Ethan!" Sophie's voice needled into his ears as Ethan moved down the stairs, sluggish and tired. It was nearly noon, but morning nonetheless for the malcontent.

"What?" He stepped off the landing and turned the corner into the kitchen, reaching for his cigarettes on the bench as soon as he did.

She held out a purple envelope, smiling gently at him. "You've got mail."

Ethan waved it away and moved toward the kitchen door to head outside. "Probably a bill, put it in the bin."

Sophie sighed. "Ethan, it's from the Dioscuri."

Ethan stopped, his hand still on the door handle. "Bin it."

Outside, the air was chilled and fresh, and Ethan clasped his robe as he pulled a cigarette from the deck and lit it.

"Morning." Dana sat at the outside table, a blanket over her legs, a laptop and a still-steaming coffee in front of her.

The door banged shut as Sophie exited the house, purple envelope in hand. "You can't ignore it, they'll know."

"What's going on?" Dana picked up her coffee, wrapped her fingers around it and sat back, looking up from her laptop, forgetting it for a rare moment. She spent her time studying, for the most part. So far she had four bachelor degrees, each one vastly different to the next. Geology, psychology, liberal arts, and anthropology. She liked to keep her mind 'busy'—so she said.

"Ethan's got a letter from the Dioscuri, but he won't even open it."

"Since when do they send snail mail?"

Ethan snorted. "Right?" He sat down opposite Dana. "I'm surprised they sent anything at all, considering one of them is 'busy' all the time and the other one seems to be nothing more than a stoner."

"You can't say that!" Sophie said, looking around nervously.

Ethan shook his head. It wasn't like they were watching, but Sophie was always one for dramatics. "Pollux is high *all* the time."

"It's true, he is," Dana said. Her gaze flicked from Ethan to Sophie, their mouths open. "What? I had to meet with them last week."

"How often do you meet with the Dioscuri?" Sophie asked.

"First time in two centuries."

"Why *you*? You're a Sag, there's no reason for them to want to talk to you," Ethan said, suspicious.

Dana rolled her eyes. "What do you *think* they wanted to talk about?"

"Why their sudden interest in me? I've not done anything, not that I know of."

Sophie held out the envelope again. "Maybe that's the problem? But you won't know until you open it, will you?" She waited a moment before stamping her foot. "Take the damn envelope, Ethan, I want to see what it says!"

Ethan took the envelope. He didn't want to read it, and particularly not in front of anyone else. If the Dioscuri had decided to summon him, then things weren't looking good for his future. If it was a simple assignment, then he should be fine, but assignments usually came through email—had for years. Right now, he didn't want to know either way. They would know he had the envelope now, just as they would know when he opened it. It was who they were. They knew everything. Well, everything to do with their representatives. They would know he hadn't completed any assignments recently. The last decade at least. He'd been busy—and avoiding it, if he were honest with himself. Representatives only dealt with babies due to be born on the cusp of a zodiac. That was their job. Go to the house or hospital, find the mother. If the baby's future showed certain traits, it would be assigned a zodiac, determining their dominant sign. If not, the job went to the opposing sign's representative. Those not born on the cusp were left to the sign they were born under, but cusp babies were complicated, their destinies woven with positive and negative energies. The wrong sign assigned to a cusp baby could spell disaster.

He put out his cigarette in the ashtray. "I need coffee. And food." He stood and tucked the envelope in his dressing-gown pocket.

Dana leant forward, her eyes focusing on her laptop screen again. "Put enough water in for me, will you?"

Ethan nodded and went inside, escaping Sophie's glare. She didn't follow him. He put the kettle on, then went upstairs to his room, closed the door and sat on his bed.

He ripped the envelope open and pulled out the stark white paper inside.

An address and a date and time. Nothing more. *42 Wickenbrook Crescent, 20th of June. 8:54pm.*

"Well, that's not specific at all," he mumbled to himself. Dead-centre of the cusp. Normally, when he was assigned babies, he had at least a month before they were born to deal them their zodiac, not this late in the cycle. It was already the seventeenth, and the cusp was due to begin that night. It was on the outskirts of his zone, too.

Why this baby? After all this time, why send him an assignment? He'd not completed a job in ten years or more; not that it mattered much, there was another Gemini in the area, had been for about six years. They'd not spoken. Geminis didn't blend well. He placed the letter in his pocket but left the envelope on the bed. No doubt Sophie would come looking for it—probably shift into a mouse or something, he thought. She had a problem with boundaries even at the best of times.

Downstairs, the kettle had boiled. Ethan prepared Dana a cup first. Knowing she liked her coffee strong, he poured the instant into the cup rather than use a spoon. He filled it up with hot water and set the kettle aside. He placed some bread in the toaster and retrieved the margarine from the fridge. The vegemite lived on the bench, mostly because Sophie never put it away. He unscrewed the lid in anticipation.

"Morning."

Ethan didn't turn around. "Morning, James." He pulled the letter from his pocket and passed it over. James unfolded it as he reached into the cupboard to pull out two teabags—he always had two, even if the teabag was listed as extra strong. James refolded the letter and passed it back.

"You're going to have to go, you know that, so why fight it?"

"They'll send someone else," Ethan said, placing his toast on the cutting board. James, a representative for Aquarius, was probably the truest to his sign than anyone else in the house. Aloof? Check. Progressive? Also check. Lack of emotional expression? Triple check.

"No, they won't. They've chosen you to deal this child their zodiac, which means they'll make sure it's you who does it." He paused, watching Ethan closely. "You remember what happened to the last Scorpio who lived here."

"De-deified, probably." It was rare, but it happened. A representative could be stripped of their immortality, their gifts

191

taken away in an instant. It didn't seem like something the Dioscuri would do, though, even if they were angry.

"Not *probably*. She was left with nothing. No memories. No family."

"She was a bit unbalanced though."

"She was certifiable." James stopped dunking his teabags, and Ethan frowned—there was no water left in the kettle. "Will you go tonight?" James asked.

"No." Ethan left the kitchen, taking his toast with him to the lounge room, not bothering with a plate.

Ethan spent the next two days in his dressing gown, headset on, ignoring the world around him. It was James who came in to draw him from his makeshift nest on the couch.

"You need to get dressed and get moving," James said, absentmindedly watching the TV screen.

Ethan pulled his headset down. "I've got time."

"Not if there are delays on the train line."

Ethan groaned. James was right. He was always right. He put his controller on the coffee table, shifting the mix of dirty plates, glasses and mugs to make space for it.

"If you don't go, the Dioscuri won't take it lightly." James looked over at him. "I haven't known them to keep tabs on a rep for decades, and they've had both Dana *and* Soph in already."

Ethan looked up. "Both of them?"

"Both." James sighed gently. "You know you're going to go, so perhaps stop delaying." He turned and left the room without another word.

After showering and dressing, Ethan left the house. He did not own a car, so he had to leave early; trips across town took much longer than they were supposed to, the public transport in the area usually being delayed either by roadworks, rail works, or just *because*. That, and he hadn't caught transport since his last job interview two years ago.

It wasn't that he didn't want a job, he thought, looking at the overhead timetable. Five minutes until the next train. He just couldn't be bothered searching for one. Was there any point? Really? The Dioscuri paid for the house they lived in, along with the other heads, Leo, Sagittarius, and Aquarius. The representatives of each sign usually lived together, though not all in the same house. The houses were nice enough though; no mould, plenty of space, working plumbing. It was free, after all. The food wasn't, though. He'd been happily living off James, much as Dana did. James was a corporate lawyer, so it wasn't like he didn't have the money to burn.

It took three hours to get to his stop, but he still had six streets to traverse before he got to the house. He started walking and his phone rang.

"Ethan, it's Sophie." Her voice was hurried, frantic.

"What's wrong now?" The last time she had called him it was to yell at him for something. Leaving a plate on the table? No, that wasn't it. Ah, hair in the sink. That was it.

"The Dioscuri want to see you."

He stopped in his tracks. "What, now? I'm nearly there!"

"They came here first, thinking you were still at home. I told them you'd gone, but the herald didn't care. Said he had been told to get you and that was what he'd do."

"Hi."

Ethan turned, startled. Beside him stood a tall man dressed in a neat suit.

"Soph, I gotta go."

"But—"

He hung up on her. "I'll be late," he said.

"Not my issue, mate." The man reached out a hand and placed it on Ethan's shoulder. The dizziness came first, as it always did, and Ethan stumbled as they appeared at the Dioscuri's headquarters.

The Twins—the Dioscuri as they had been known for millennia—certainly had a taste for the ostentatious. It had been a long time since Ethan had been here, and last time their headquarters had been in a much smaller house. This was an enormous building, or so he could see from the window. How high up were they? Thirty floors? Forty? Not that it mattered, there was no escape from here. He moved to one of the high-backed leather chairs and sat down, glad to be off his feet.

"Ethan?"

He looked up. A receptionist dressed in a smart pantsuit smiled gently at him.

"They are ready for you."

Hmph. Last time they had kept him waiting for over an hour.

Inside the office, Castor sat behind a desk in an impeccable suit, while Pollux sat on the couch, dressed much the same but without a suit jacket. He was also missing a tie, and his wrinkled shirt was unbuttoned and untucked. Despite his appearance, he looked unusually sober. Ethan said nothing but stood in front of the desk, waiting for Castor to look up.

"Sit."

Ethan moved to the chair and sat down, sitting nervously on the edge.

Castor looked up. "It is good to see you again, Ethan."

"Same," Ethan said.

Pollux laughed. "Bullshit," he said. "You hate being here."

"It's true, you can't lie here, Ethan." Castor rose from his chair and rounded the desk, leaning back to sit on its edge. "We know you don't want to be here."

"Or anywhere," Pollux said.

Castor gave his brother a look, sending him to silence. "Indeed. Now, you have no job, is that right?" he said, looking at the sheet of paper in his hands.

How much had Dana told them? "Er, yeah."

"And you currently undertake no studies."

"I don't."

"What do you do with your time?"

Ethan shifted uncomfortably. "I play games, I guess."

"Good." Castor returned to his chair and sat. "We have a new assignment for you." He tapped at his computer and spun the screen. "This is Mary, she is due to have her baby very soon, and we want you to guide the child."

"Guide the—What about the kid I'm supposed to be assigning?"

"Same child. More information has come to our attention. The Cancer representative has already inspected the child and it will be a Gemini. I still want you to confirm that, though. If the child is to be a Gemini, it will need a strong guiding figure in their life. That figure will be you."

"I haven't been a guide in centuries, and last time . . . well, last time it didn't work out so well."

"No shit. Right screwed that up, didn't ya?" Pollux said, standing. He wandered over to a drinks station and pulled the cork on a bottle of wine. In moments Ethan and Pollux each had a glass in hand. Ethan hated wine.

Castor frowned momentarily. "We're not asking, not this time. We know last time didn't end as desired, but that happens sometimes. Your lack of direction since has been problematic, but lately you've stopped working assignments and we cannot have that. It's important to us that each representative have *something* to busy themselves with, otherwise"—he looked to his brother briefly, who was once again sitting on the couch—"they fall to addiction, or they become listless, much as you have. When that happens, our options are limited."

"De-deification."

Pollux grinned, leaning back into the cushions. "Yup. See? He's not as dense as I thought he was. He gets it."

Ethan's heart thumped in his chest. Surely they wouldn't do that for so small a transgression?

"Relax," Castor said, feeling his tension. "Provided you guide the child all will be fine. It's a long commitment, but you of all representatives are well suited to this particular child."

"How so?"

"You are ruled by curiosity, it's one of the reasons you were originally selected as a Dioscuri representative."

Night had fallen by the time Ethan was returned to his assignment. While he hadn't had to stay long with the Dioscuri, he'd had to wait for a trip back. 42 Wickenbrook Crescent was a small house; the yard was untended, but the house seemed in good order. The lights were on inside. Ethan grumbled to himself. He could shift form, of course, or he could phase. He'd not shifted in a long time—last time he had been a cat and he'd gotten hit by a car. James had picked him up from a bunch of bushes at a nearby park. It hadn't been glamorous.

Ethan phased before he walked into the yard. The sturdy front door was no obstacle. He always loved seeing other people's homes. Some were clean, so clean it was as if no one had ever lived in them. Not this one. It wasn't messy, but it was lived in. He wandered through the rooms unseen. In the lounge room, a man snored on a desk chair in front of his computer. The TV lit the room—advertisements for the most part. Mary wasn't in here, nor was she in the adjoining kitchen. He eventually found her in the bedroom; half dressed, and half asleep on the queen-size bed. The room was a bit of a mess, but no worse than his own. Clothes had been dumped on the floor, there were baskets of washing in the corner—clean or dirty he couldn't tell—and a damp towel hung on the door.

The alarm clock on the bedside table read 8:52pm. Ethan pulled the note from his pocket. He wouldn't do anything until 8:54pm. The time given by the Dioscuri was the best time to see its zodiac, and this baby was, apparently, difficult. Cancer might have checked the baby early—the zodiac was always given early—but at this stage of the cusp, the baby would be here soon; a day, a day and a half at most. *I have to be certain.*

Mary would go in to labour soon, and already the baby inside pulled at Ethan, demanding its zodiac; demanding that a choice be made. Ethan moved closer. Mary's eyes fluttered briefly before closing, she was exhausted and uncomfortable, and he was once again glad he would never have to bear a child. She rolled to her side, an effort in her state.

8:53pm. Ethan moved forward. It was never easy to touch a person while they were sleeping, it felt a little creepy, but they couldn't feel it as anything more than a slight churning in their bellies. He leant across the bed and gently placed his hands on her side. Immediately the baby kicked his palm and Mary shifted in her sleep. Ethan repositioned.

8:54pm. Ethan closed his eyes and felt his power surge. It had been so long since he'd used it and he relished the feeling of lightness, his negative energy dissipating until there was nothing but a steady calm. The baby squirmed, impatient. Ethan searched for its future, for the traits that would guide him in his decision. *Duality.* Similar to the last child he had acted as a guide for. Except this child was *pure* duality, there was no lean to either side. The last had leant slightly to the side of Cancer, but not enough to be a true Cancer. Everything about this child was Gemini. As true a Gemini as Castor or Pollux; maybe more so, as their duality was split. There was something special about this child, unseen. There was nothing more, just an intensity that Ethan had not felt before. Things could be wonderous for this little human. They would bring immense change, but for good or for bad Ethan couldn't tell. The last child had fallen, fallen to the wrong side. Fallen to a darkness Ethan hadn't been able to pull him out of, and the boy had done much damage to humanity. It was Ethan's biggest failing.

But this child . . . Ethan's curiosity bloomed. This child could go either way. The little girl stood on a razor's edge, neither here nor there, each potential future as beautiful and as terrible as the next. He knew he would stay with her until the end, even just to see where the adventure would take them.

About the Author:

Talien works in the publishing industry and Ethan is her first foray into publishing her own work. She lives in western Victoria with her family, writes whenever she gets the chance, and lives and breathes speculative fiction.

CANCER
JUNE 21 - JULY 22

PHOENIX PHARMACEUTICALS

Jessica Nelson-Tyers

It was hard to connect the scarred, part-plucked chicken of a bird before me with the mighty phoenix of legend. It was small, for one thing. About the size of a bantam hen. Its gender was one of many unknowns about it—every scan they tried was a mess of noise, and its DNA defied analysis. They weren't going to risk vivisection, thank god. It was their only sample, so they didn't want to lose it. That'd be like gutting the goose that laid the golden eggs.

The bird—we'd been told not to give it a name, even in private—began a fine tremor at the sight of me. I opened three pieces of mint gum and popped them into my mouth, chewing hard to get the fresh flavour going. The wrappers fell like autumn leaves to the concrete floor. Nausea had been a problem for me at first, but Mac suggested chewing gum and it helped, it really helped. It seems crazy now that the bastard thought I could fight off my conscience with the taste of toothpaste. Crazier that it worked.

I ran my hand over the lab tools, slow as a snake in winter. The suspense added to the psychological trauma I had to produce. My fingers touched lightly on a scalpel and a ball-peen hammer before curling round the pliers.

The phoenix had long tail feathers once, bright as sunset and soft as blossom. They made it look like something special, but the pliers took them, and for some reason they never grew back.

I was the one who worked out the most effective way to get the tears flowing. It was the way it responded, like it knew what was going on. It was clever, brainier than a bin chicken or a statue-shitter pigeon. Watching the security cameras and the electric doors. Holding out as long as it could each time, denying us those precious droplets as though it resented us.

So one day, instead of cutting it, I sat down and told it my sob story. How Glenn and I found each other, how we got married and thought we'd be together forever. Then the cancer, eating him alive from inside, chewing his lungs, his throat and his stomach to pieces, seeding its way into his brain.

I told it Glenn was on the verge of death, how I didn't like causing pain, but I didn't want the love of my life to die. How I was being eaten up too, with everything that made me human being devoured. I'd have held myself together a little if I could—I was at work and on video after all—but the more I spoke, the more my nose and eyes dripped, adding fresh marks to my already stained lab coat. When I spotted the tear sliding over the phoenix's beak, I gestured to the lab techs to get over with a pipette and a beaker, quick.

Sara tried to follow my lead. She'd been cured a way back, but she laid it on thick, showing pictures of some random kids, pretending they were hers. Crying because they'd be orphaned. Poor ickle things. The phoenix cocked its head to the side and made a squawk-squawk, like the first two notes of a kookaburra's laugh. It stayed dry the whole morning with Sara wheedling at it, until she grabbed the screws and crushed a toe. It was laughing on the other side of its beak then.

Turns out it could tell when someone was lying, which had all kinds of potential. Pity it couldn't talk.

There's an animal, a sort of bearcat, native to the forests of Southeast Asia. I saw it in a zoo once. Its biggest claim to fame is that it smells like popcorn. It does, too. Its scent, as it paced in its cage, was just like the movies—buttered popcorn with a hint of sweat.

Know what a frightened Phoenix smells of?

Fireworks. Close your eyes and you're in a crowd on a summer evening, watching something dangerous and beautiful. Open them again and you're back in hell, holding the pitchfork.

The reality of medical science meant the first tears were wasted on rabbits. Goddamn rabbits. The pharmacologists cured their cancers (induced, of course), wrote up the studies, then euthanised the poor beasts anyway.

This might have gone on for years, the testing, the waiting—but when Prime Minister Bob Bronner got sick, it all went out the window. He denied it, but he was dying. Every doctor, scientist and snake oil salesman in the country lined up to give their two cents, but the consensus was that nothing could be done. When Phoenix Pharmaceuticals stepped in, it caused an uproar.

One day he was wasting away on national television, clinging onto office despite his jaundiced skin and withered physique. Answering press questions with his usual wit, but slowly and with dead eyes. If he hadn't yet been ousted by his party, it was only because they didn't want to look cruel to the public eye. He was a problem that would go away on its own. The sharks were circling.

Next day, he strode out onto the platform, announced his cure to the world. The miracle had come, the answer to his prayers, in the form of a medical breakthrough from Phoenix Pharmaceuticals. That Friday he took first place in the City to-Surf marathon. No kidding.

Now the only things standing between people and the elixir of life were money and conscience.

Guess which won out?

The big payday for Phoenix Pharmaceuticals came when they found they could dilute a tear to a one-hundredth part and it'd still be effective. There are only so many sick billionaires in the world to milk for all they've got. This revelation opened the cure

to the millionaires, plus a few lucky workers who'd do anything
for a drop. Anything.

On my own big payday, I drove to work with a flutter that flowed
from my heart to my hands. I'd been working in pharmaceutics
for three months. It had been a hell of a probation period.
Things were getting hairy for Glenn: the doctors said it wouldn't
be much longer. His hands were so thin I could see the skeleton
underneath. It reminded me how we're all just meat over a
frame, and there's nothing to stop us winking out like a dying
star.

The company makes a big deal about its philanthropy for its
workers. Sara got in early, did alright, but Sammy, he got too sick
to work and died before his payday.

That scenario played out in my head, drowning out the yells
of the protesters as I drove in. I imagined arriving at the hospital
with the cure that night and finding an empty bed.

The razor wire closed me in with the bird. Featherless now.
Looked like a cockatoo with beak and feather disease. If I'd been
able to name it, I'd have called it Lady Godiva.

It was getting harder to make it cry. How many tears could it
possibly have left in it? It had stopped drinking long ago, but they
hooked it up with a feeding tube and restrained its head and claws
so it wouldn't be able to pull it out. Still, what if they didn't work

like us, on hydration and misery alone? What if there's a wellspring in them that can dry up, and once it's gone, it's gone?

That day I brought in my tablet. Trying to ignore the cameras, I took a deep breath to get into the zone. I plastered concern on my face and showed it a video of a sun bear in a bile extraction facility. Got liquid in record time.

Mac called me into his office at closing time. A little amber bottle glittered on his side of the desk. He drew my hand into his own. Cold, smooth and manicured. I hadn't cut my own nails in weeks.

"How is Glenn?" he whispered. Mac almost always spoke in a whisper. Perhaps he was a butler in another life, trained not to raise his voice.

I swallowed. "Not good." My voice cracked, so I stopped speaking. My hands itched to slap him. This man could have cured Glenn months ago if he hadn't wanted leverage over me.

He didn't make a move to pass me the bottle. I'd have snatched it from the table and run if I could.

"I do hope you'll continue with us once he's cured. We need workers with your imagination and finesse." Mac pushed a contract across the table towards me.

My breath came shallower. He was corralling me before I'd even had a chance to say I was leaving. I wouldn't put that cure in jeopardy.

The contract specified a year, strict confidence and a salary in the hundreds of thousands. The bottle glinted.

I signed.

As always, a moron ruined everything. Leon bloody Carter. He made the empire fall. Anyone with a smattering of mythological comprehension knows phoenixes are flammable. This guy was illiterate. Probably not even sick like the rest of the crew—or sick in a different way. A bit too keen to get results, if you know what I mean. Probably practised on puppies as a kid. Anyway, this psychopath had the bright idea to use fire.

The security footage shows him pulling a lighter from his pocket and applying it to the underside of the phoenix's claw. He was probably expecting to hear it squawk, get the tears coming really thick and fast. Instead the flame licked up the bird's leg like a wick. You can see Carter jump back, for all the good it did him. The video cuts to static there. It delighted news corporations around the world before the end of the day.

The aftermath showed the bird had detonated like a miniature nuke, leaving blast shadows on the walls where the techs had been standing. Those poor saps were left as charred husks, and as far as I know nobody ever found what was left of Leon.

In stories, the phoenix is reborn from the ashes, but although they left the room intact for weeks (cremated staff included), the legends proved wrong.

That was it. A relief, really, except for the thought of all the people who'd never get their cure. Glenn had been given the all-clear a month prior, so I was looking for an out. The redundancy package was generous enough to allow me some time off—maybe six months or a year to relax with Glenn, drinking home-made martinis on the back porch, finally getting the veggie garden under control.

I won't say I never had trouble sleeping. Sometimes when I hit the hay too early, I saw blood and feathers and tears. Other times I thought too much about the stories I told the phoenix, and how they were all true, and this world is a hellish place. Then Glenn would hop into bed and curl up around me, and that was all the world I needed, right there.

The round lump on the scan made me scream like a rabbit caught in a trap. It was a mass the size of a golf ball, nestled deep in the folds and crevasses of Glenn's brain.

"It's inoperable," the GP murmured. She explained they'd have to cut through too much to reach it. There were some anomalies on the scan and she'd arrange for a specialist, but given Glenn's history there was a high likelihood that it was a return of the cancer. It had caused the onset of his seizures and other symptoms, of course. As the doctor outlined Glenn's options, I considered smashing her computer from her desk, ripping her framed degrees and kid's paintings from the wall. In the end I just sat there, tearing a pamphlet to bits.

He sagged onto me in our car afterwards. I stroked my hands through his hair again and again. The smell of car fresheners still brings me back there. Fresh with an undertone of death, like a corpse in a pine forest.

"How could this happen?" Glenn whispered into my shoulder. "Phoenix tears are meant to cure everything. We were meant to grow old together."

It was clear what had happened. Mac, that sonovabitch. He must've diluted it too much, till it was only an interim cure, as shitful and as weak as he was.

That night I dreamed of work. I dreamed of cutting and twisting. I dreamed that even tears didn't stop me. I dreamed of using the pliers to yank out teeth, and woke when Mac drowned in his own blood.

We both rose with the sun and snapped on the TV for a reprieve from our own thoughts. The whirr of the coffee machine made things feel normal. Maybe it would wake us enough to emerge from our nightmare.

Glenn gestured to the telly. Prime Minister Bronner, smiling and slick, was the centre of a crowd of workers who should have known better, really. He was wearing a hard hat and a fluro vest, looking like a kid in dress-ups.

"How come he gets the happy ending?" asked Glenn. "He breezes through life, screws the country, and gets to cheat death, too."

What could I say?

We stared at Bronner, who sold his sympathy for the cause, his empathy for hard-up workers with a slick car-dealer's demeanour. He faltered mid-speech and lost his croc's grin. He tore off his vest and the work shirt underneath. An aide leaned in close to him to whisper, probably scoping out what the issue was—a spider in his shirt, perhaps? He leapt away as smoke and blood blossomed from Bronner's abdomen, just below the ribs. Bronner sagged to the ground like a scarecrow off its stick.

I set down my coffee and turned up the volume.

The camera jolted then tracked back to the action. There were screams about snipers and bombs; workers and reporters running for cover. Then movement at Bronner's body.

A beak poked through the open wound, followed by a head and smoking wings. The chick flopped onto the ground, feathers fully formed, bloody and bright as a fiery dawn. It sped across the grass, flapping its wings and jumping like a chicken on the run. It left a trail of smouldering entrails as it went.

It struggled to make it off the ground at first, but it launched itself like a drunk chook and somehow made it to the top of a nearby lamppost, where it sat carolling. It sounded like a cross between a magpie and an angel. All I could think was that the phoenix I knew never made those sounds.

A cop took potshots at the thing, but it flew, and hey—who knows—maybe it made it.

Glenn realised what it meant first. His coffee mug smashed all over the floor as he dropped it to claw at his head. I didn't know what he was on about until he started screaming.

"It's not a tumour. It's not a tumour, it's an egg. Get it out of me! Get it out!"

About the Author:

Jessica Nelson-Tyers has previously had stories published in magazines and anthologies ranging from children's fiction to the darkest horror. She tries not to get confused about where she is submitting. Jessica has a Graduate Diploma in Professional Writing and is part of the Andromeda Spaceways Publishing team.

She lives with her family on a bush property on the coast, which provides her with all kinds of weird inspiration. You can find her at jessicanelsontyers.com or follow her tweets @JessNelsonTyers.

KLARIA'S BATTLE

Heather Ewings

Klaria watched as Pedro heaved the canvas sack onto his back.

"Will ye come to town this time?" he asked, as he always did.

Klaria shook her head, as she always did. "My bleeding time has come." She hadn't bled for years, but Pedro never seemed to notice she no longer hung her rags out to dry.

"No wee ones then?" Pedro's face fell.

"Sorry, love."

Pedro heaved the door of the bothy open, and headed out into the cool spring day.

Klaria followed him to the doorway, watching until he disappeared out of sight down the slight incline of the meadow.

Klaria avoided town. It was too close to the ocean. She couldn't control herself near the sea, the urge to take to the waves too strong. She'd already scared herself once by nearly drowning.

It turned out she wanted life more than she wanted to go home.

She went back to the house. Pedro had packed the butter and eggs for the market, but he'd left her a fish caught fresh from the river this morning, still splashing in the bucket in the shade of the verandah. Klaria retrieved her basket and headed out to the garden. Fresh fish with salad greens would make a good dinner, and there'd be enough to leave in the meat safe for a cold breakfast the next morning.

The day passed slowly without company.

Klaria weeded the garden and gathered the eggs, the murmur of the chickens a comfort in the quiet. She swept out the single room of their small house, and spread the blankets across the line to beat out the dust. As the day drew to a close she returned to the house, to gut and cook the fish before dark.

For the most part, Klaria was pleased she and Pedro had not had children. She'd determined it, after all, drinking the tea recommended by the wise woman to stop babies coming, certain one day she'd find her shell and be gone, and not wanting to abandon an infant with a bereft father.

But days like this she wished she'd not been so certain of that future. It would've been nice to have a handful of children to fill the silence of the days when Pedro went to town.

She'd never found her shell. She'd scoured every inch of the property, outside and in, probing hollow tree trunks and abandoned animal burrows, searching in the wall cavities of the house and shed, and under all the loose floorboards. Even under the ones securely nailed in place. Wherever Pedro had hidden it, it certainly wasn't here.

Dinner cooked, Klaria took her plate down to the river's edge.

The moon would be full, and she wanted to sit where its light would fall upon her as it first rose.

She could escape the sea, its pull not so strong here in the mountains. But she could not escape the moon, and the pull it exerted on her was far stronger.

Though she kept her gaze on her meal, her skin tingled when the moon first peered above the horizon. She held off from looking as long as she could, resisting the pull until she couldn't and she gazed up at the full round moon, her vision blurring with tears.

Once she'd gathered with the other crab-folk, and they'd shed their shells and danced upon the sand, frolicking under the moons rays.

Did they still do that, after all this time? Or had the human presence grown so large it was too dangerous?

She closed her eyes, letting two great drops roll down her cheeks.

If only she could see her family again.

As if in answer there was a scuffling at the water's edge, and she opened her eyes as a large rock emerged from the river and scuttled up the bank.

Klaria stared. She knew what it must be, and yet it was too unlikely to be possible.

She'd never known a crab to come upstream. They didn't like the fresh water, weren't strong enough to swim against the downward current.

Still, two beady eyes emerged from one end of the rock, and it paused, the eyes scanning the surrounds, coming to rest on Klaria. It sidestepped towards her on the stony bank.

She held her breath as it approached. Sure enough, before it reached her, it propped itself up on its four back legs, claws and two front legs waving in the air.

There was a distinct crack as the soft centre line of the undershell pulled apart, followed by much wriggling and squirming as a young, wet woman emerged from within.

At first she was small, child-sized to a human, but as she unfolded she stretched limbs and torso until she was almost as tall as Klaria.

She pulled herself to a sitting position, blinking a couple of times before her gaze landed on Klaria, and a beaming smile broke across her face.

"Aunt Klaria. I found you!"

Klaria's heart pounded, and she blinked several times herself, an attempt to clear her vision from this unexpected sight. Twenty-five years had passed since she'd seen another of her people. Twenty-five years of settling into the certainty she'd never see them again.

"We need your help," the woman said.

"Who are you?"

"I'm Anabelle, Ninian's daughter."

"Ninian?" A lump formed in Klaria's throat at the sound of her younger sister's name. "Is she . . ?"

Anabelle shook her head. "She's fine. Scared, like we all are, but fine."

"Scared?" Klaria's heart increased its pounding. "Why are you scared?"

"The townsfolk are hunting us. We need you to come, to help us."

Klaria shook her head and pushed herself to her feet.

"I can't help you." She took a step backwards. "There's nothing I can do."

"You know the human's ways," Anabelle insisted. "You've lived with them for two dozen years. You can teach us what you know."

"I don't know anything. I've been living in the mountains, I only see my husband, and the few friends who drop in."

"He must talk," Anabelle said. "You would hear things."

"I don't have my shell." Klaria looked away, back at the house. Could she lock herself in?

She couldn't stand against the humans. She was weak, soft. Old. How could her people expect her to do anything?

Anabelle shook her head. "You don't need your shell to teach us what you know."

Klaria imagined the pitying looks of her kin if she returned in her soft human form, and her chest constricted. "I can't come back without my shell!"

"Please, Aunt. You must come."

"I can't."

"They're killing us, Klaria. No one believes in the crab-folk anymore. They forget we are human inside, as they are, and they hunt us." She reached out to grab Klaria's hand, forcing Klaria to meet her gaze. "They *eat* us."

Klaria swallowed against the lurching in her stomach. "What about the other crab-women in town?"

Anabelle's eyes grew wide, and she shook her head. "They're all dead. They pined away for the sea to the point where they died of heart break. You're the last still alive."

Klaria dropped back onto the bank, the breath knocked out of her.

"Seysill, Aine, Ena? Dead?"

Anabelle nodded. She squeezed Klaria's hand, and Klaria realised her niece was shivering.

She forced herself to stand. "You're so cold! Come inside. Let me find you a blanket."

Klaria lifted Anabelle's shell. It was large and cumbersome, awkward to wrap her arms around, and by the time they reached Pedro's hut her muscles ached.

Inside the fire was still burning low, and Klaria added a few extra branches, pulling the blanket from her bed to wrap around Anabelle.

"I never knew it would be so cold in the mountains." Anabelle pulled the blanket tight around her shoulders. "I can barely feel my limbs."

Klaria reached out and rubbed some colour back into Anabelle's arms. "I'll get you some tea, and you can tell me what's happening."

Anabelle's story lasted well into the night.

The human population had tripled in the twenty-five years since Klaria was first taken, their settlement spreading out along the shore, their buildings popping up in all the sheltered coves where the crab-folk had once gathered for their ceremonies. The humans hadn't liked to see the crab-folk dancing naked under the moon, and had chased them away, so now Klaria's people no longer gathered on the sandy shore, but on the rocky islands dotted off the coast, which were too sharp for the crab folk's soft human feet.

Where Klaria's childhood had been one of a truce between human and crab, Anabelle's early years involved a continuing cycle of loss. Family and friends were killed, at first while they danced upon the shore, and in later years in crab form, taken from the sea.

Klaria's stomach churned at the images Anabelle painted in her mind, her bile burning as it rose up in her throat, even as her cheeks were cooled with tears.

"You have to help us," Anabelle urged again. "You have to teach us what you know."

"I don't belong without my shell." Klaria shook her head.

"We found your shell," Anabelle said.

Klaria couldn't believe it. "How?"

"Your husband has it hidden in the inn where he sleeps when he visits town. My mother took human form, she—" Anabelle's eyes flicked away, but then her jaw set and she met Klaria's gaze again. "You should know. My mother seduced your husband. He told her how he loved you, as he made love to her, and when he left to go to the bathroom she searched the room. She said she felt it, as though you yourself were in the room with her. But your husband returned before she could retrieve it."

Conflicting emotions swirled, so many Klaria didn't know which one to grab onto. Her sister seduced her husband, and he gave in to it, though he swore he'd never lay with another woman. Why did she hurt so much about the infidelity of a man she tolerated, a man who'd kidnapped her in the first place? She shook those feelings aside. All the more reason to escape.

If she had her shell she would be free. She could escape the man, and the mountain, and return home.

"Can't she try again?" she asked Anabelle.

Anabelle shook her head. "It's too dangerous. We're not taking human form again, not until we know how to fight them."

A strange sense of calm swept through Klaria's body. Her shell had been found. With her shell, she could do anything. She could help Ninian, and Anabelle, and the rest of her people. She could lead them against the humans.

She looked at Anabelle. "Next full moon, Pedro will return to market. I will come with him. Gather everyone. I will find my shell, and I will return."

"You'll help us?" Anabella's whole face lit up.

Klaria nodded. "I'll help."

The month passed painfully.

Klaria wanted nothing more than to confront her husband with what she'd learnt, but what good would it do? He knew she never had visitors. He'd deny it, accuse her of paranoia. He might even refuse to allow her to join him the following moon.

Her days were spent arguing with herself, angry at her husband for laying with another woman, angry that the other woman was her sister, angry that Pedro had taken her shell from her in the first place.

But she was hurt too, and that baffled her the most. He was a foolish human who couldn't get a wife by any other means, and yet she'd grown fond of him, of all the thoughtful little things he did to make her life as comfortable as possible.

Everything except return my shell.

Finally the time came. Pedro heaved the sack up onto his back, and Klaria waited for him to invite her along.

He approached her, kissed her forehead, and turned to leave.

"I, uh—" Klaria began.

"Yes?" He turned. "Is everything all right?"

Klaria wrung her hands together. "I thought I might come with you, this time."

"You're not bleeding?"

Klaria shook her head. "Not today."

His eyes lit up. "Do you think there's a wee one on the way?"

Klaria licked her lips. Could she lie to him? She shook her head. "It's too early to tell."

He nodded, but still his eyes shone in a way they hadn't for years. "A son," he said. "To carry my name." He glanced at her. "And now your barreness has lifted, he will soon be followed by a daughter to carry yours."

He beamed, and Klaria forced a smile. Better to allow their last days together to be happy ones.

Pedro was not often talkative, but now his spirits were up he filled the walk to town dreaming about the future, about the rooms he would build onto the house, about how he would teach his child to fish, and garden, and hunt.

"They'll be self-sufficient like we are," he announced. "Not like the young folk in town, growing up with no idea how to care for themselves, nor what their place is in the world. That's what's causing all the problems in the world today. One day it'll all crash down around them, and then where will they be? Starving, that's where." He shook his head. "I'll have no children of mine in that position."

Klaria listened, nodding whenever he looked her way, making small noises of agreeance now and again, so he felt she was listening.

They reached town by nightfall, the moon fat and round on the horizon.

It called to her, as it always did, but now something else pulled her, too. Lapping at the edges of her senses were rivulets of energy, calling her home.

A strange longing overpowered her as they approached the inn, a pull that led her feet to the very place Pedro wanted to go.

The inn keeper gave her a strange look, but Pedro introduced her as his wife, and the innkeeper nodded.

It was all Klaria could do not to run to the room, and once in the room, not to seek out the hiding place where he'd hidden her shell.

Pedro set their bags down and knelt before the empty fireplace, scrunching up bits of bark into a ball and placing it in the grate.

"What can I do?" Klaria asked.

"Help me with the fire." He gestured to the basket of kindling. "It gets cold here at night. The chill wind whips off the water and sneaks in through the gaps, and these days my bones ache when it's too cold."

Klaria did as he asked.

Once the fire was burning brightly, she asked if she might go for a walk.

He grunted a reply, commenting that she could do whatever she wanted.

Outside the night air felt crisp against her face. Klaria pulled her shawl tighter around her shoulders and followed the narrow path to the shore.

With every step she fought the pull to turn back, to retrieve her shell. There was no point. She couldn't do it now, not with Pedro in the room.

She'd hoped to find the beach empty at this time of night, but there were people scattered all along the shore. Fishermen strode into the sea with long nets, muttering to each other. Further along a man paced, and when Klaria drew closer she saw he was holding a baby, patting its back in time with his steps.

He glanced at Klaria as she walked past, his eyes drawn.

She offered him a weak smile.

"Do you know how to get a baby to sleep?" he asked.

Klaria shook her head and kept walking.

There was a young couple further up, hand in hand as they strolled along the sea's edge, the waves lapping at their ankles. And further, around a curve in the coast, a group of young men loitering on the sand, the scent of ale carried on the breeze.

Was there nowhere where the crab-folk could come ashore in safety?

Klaria came to a stand of rocks, jutting out into the sea. The points were hard on her feet, but she followed them as far out as she could, until the sea splashed around her ankles and sent her feet slipping.

She flung out her arms, her heart racing as she steadied herself. It would do no good to fall into the water in her heavy skirts. Pedro would be angry, *if* she managed to pull herself out of the sea, and she couldn't help her people if she were dead.

She took a few steps back and sat down.

"Ninian," she called, her voice soft. "Ninian!"

It would take time for her call to be heard under the waves, time she wasn't sure she had.

Would Pedro be asleep? Or was he wondering where his wife was, and what she was up to?

Could he be suspicious of her sudden desire to join him in town, or did he truly believe she carried his child, that the connection would be enough to make her stay?

The moon was high in the sky now. The wash of the waves made Klaria want to dance, but if she did the human-folk would know by her movements she was truly crab and then there'd be trouble.

She wondered how her family coped below the waves, feeling the moon's presence, and yet unable to come to the shore.

The waves washed again, in and out. Was no one coming? She was about to stand when a crab scuttled up the rock.

Its eyes peered at her.

"Ninian?"

The eyes swayed ever so slightly, and Klaria felt a surge of panic that she had forgotten what her sister looked like.

"Is that you?"

One claw raised and snapped. Yes.

"Can you not change, for a moment?"

The eyes watched her for a moment, before the two claws raised and snapped together. No.

Klaria glanced around, realising the group of young men on the beach were on their feet, watching her. "I know where my shell is," Klaria said. "I'll find a way to get it. When I do, I'll be back."

Ninian's claws clacked together, two, three, four times, in quick succession.

Klaria nodded. "I'll be as quick as I can."

Back at the room, Pedro snored soundly. Klaria took a moment to peer under the bed, but the fire was nothing more than hot coals, and gave out little light. She pressed her fingertips against the floorboards, feeling for gaps or loose, wobbly boards.

Nothing.

Then she realised that the nails had been removed from the board directly beneath the bed's leg

Her breath caught.

It must be there.

She couldn't grab her shell now, but if she waited until Pedro went to market the next morning . . .

Klaria undressed and climbed into bed. Pedro snorted, and rolled over, a heavy arm crossing her shoulders. She forced her breathing into a slow even rhythm. Her shell was in her grasp.

Morning couldn't come fast enough.

Klaria tossed and turned, disturbing Pedro enough that he snapped at her in the early hours of the morning, taking most of the blanket with him as he rolled away from her, the bed rocking from his movement.

Klaria waited until his snores started up again, and then sidled up close, careful to lay extra still under the tiny portion of blanket available to her.

She didn't sleep.

When Pedro woke the next morning she slowed her breathing, listening as he climbed out of bed and pulled on his shirt and trousers.

There was silence for a moment, and then his lips pressed against her forehead, and she heard him add another log to the fire, before the door clicked as he left the room.

Klaria waited a moment longer. When there was no other movement she opened her eyes.

The room was empty.

She took a deep breath.

After all this time. If only she'd accompanied Pedro on his trips to market from the beginning! But she'd been so scared after that first time, when she'd nearly drowned trying to return to her home. When she couldn't find her shell at his home, she'd assumed he'd hidden it somewhere along the path to town, or else higher in the mountains. The task of searching such an area had seemed impossible, and she'd given up, too easily. She'd never imagined for a moment he'd leave it behind in the town itself.

She shook her head, and slid out of bed.

The bed was made of solid wood, bulky and heavy. Klaria pushed against it, satisfied to feel it shift under her effort. But it bumped against something and wouldn't budge any further.

She knelt by the bed to try to manouvre the floorboard, but the bed hadn't moved far enough to move it, so she lifted the bed again, her muscles straining against the effort. Something seemed to be stopping the bed from moving.

She moved around to the other side of the bed.

There was a nail jutting from the floor, preventing the leg on this side from sliding any further.

Klaria bit her lip. She didn't have any tools to remove the nail, so instead she lifted the bed, heaving it towards her.

Sweat dripped into her eye, stinging. The fire flared, and she wished Pedro hadn't bothered to stoke it before he left.

Finally the bed slid easily, and Klaria slipped and fell, dropping the bed with a thud.

She froze, straining her ears but couldn't hear anything over the pounding of her heart.

When there was no movement in the hallway, she stood, taking a drink of water from the jug on the mantlepiece, forcing her breath to slow enough so she could hear over the beating of her heart.

All was still quiet out in the hallway, so she knelt by the odd floorboard. She could *feel* her shell through the thin strip of wood, reaching out to her just as much as she reached out to it.

There was no indent to fit her finger, but Klaria pushed on one end and the whole floorboard tipped upwards.

A waft of salty sea air reached her nose, and then Klaria saw it, the brilliant blue of her shell, visible under years of dust. She set the floorboard to one side and reached in, a current of energy zapping along her fingertips as she touched the hard surface, tears rolling down her face, creating shiny trails on the shell where they washed away the dust.

She had to press the underside of the shell up into the indentation of the back to get it up through the narrow gap, the legs and claws clattering against the wood as they came through.

"I never thought I'd find you again," Klaria whispered, her breath catching at just how her shell gleamed even after all this time.

"What have you done?"

The voice boomed. Klaria looked up to see Pedro crossing the room, his face red, the veins in his neck bulging. She hugged the shell as she stood, stepping away from Pedro's anger.

"I—"

He crossed the room in two strides, grabbing the legs of her shell and ripping it from her hands.

"No!" Her voice was a howl. "Please."

"I've kept you safe, all this time." He waved her shell in the air. "You're going to leave? Now you're with child? Is that why you stayed so long?"

It took Klaria a moment to understand what he was talking about.

She clenched her fists. "There is no child. There's been no bleeding for years, though you don't care enough to notice. I never stayed because I wanted to, I stayed because I had no choice." Her eyes darted from Pedro's face to her precious shell. "But now . . ." She lunged for her shell, and in the same movement he swung it back, flinging it into the fire.

Everything moved in slow motion.

Klaria's fingertips brushed a claw as she fell through the air, pain jolting up her body as her knees crashed against the floor.

The shell spun, round, and again, and once more, before it landed with a puff of ash and smoke among the flames.

Neither Pedro or Klaria moved for a moment, and then pain shot up Klaria's right side and across her back as flames licked the underside of the shell.

"No!" She pulled at her clothes a moment too long before she realised it was not her clothes that were burning.

"Save it. Save it!" She screamed at Pedro, who watched her wide eyed as she clawed at the pain now shooting across her face.

Finally he jerked into action, grabbing the poker to knock the blackened shell from the fire.

Klaria collapsed on the floor, her chest heaving.

"Love. I'm sorry. I didn't know." He was by her side in an instant, brushing hair from her face. "I didn't realise the stories were true."

He pulled on her shoulder. Klaria tried to push his hand away, but he was too strong and he rolled her over.

His hand covered his mouth as he recoiled. "Oh, Love. What have I done?"

Klaria brought her hands to her face. She flinched as her fingers brushed her cheek, the pain still raw though the burning sensation had stopped.

When she gingerly touched her cheek again there were bumps and valleys, her skin puckered from the heat.

Tears filled her eyes, and she scrambled for her shell.

Pedro just watched as she picked it up, examining the charred crack that almost split the shell in two, the crisp underside that had been soft and pliable moments before.

"What have you done?" she asked him, tearing off her blouse to swing the shell up and over her shoulders.

She waited for the sense of suction, pulling her back into her true form, but the hard edges of the shell just poked into her skin.

"What have you done!" She wailed, trying to somehow push herself inside the shell that wouldn't take her.

"What have you done?" She sank to the floor.

Her stomach churned, and she sucked in deep breaths of air that never seemed to reach her lungs.

"Love. I'm sorry. I didn't know." Pedro's gaze was pitiful.

Rage burned in the pit of her stomach and she pushed herself to her feet.

"You ruined me." She waved her shell at him. "You ruined my life. But I won't let you and yours ruin the lives of my people."

Pedro flinched, and Klaria stormed out, ignoring the stares of those she passed, peering out of their rooms. She strode to the beach, grabbing the first dinghy she could find. Throwing her damaged shell inside, she pushed it out into the waves.

Somewhere there must be a quiet space for the crab-folk to come ashore.

Klaria just had to find it.

There was nowhere.

Klaria rowed until her arms shook under the strain, but everywhere there were signs of human habitation. Small coves were watched by lonely cottages, while on the shores of larger bays houses snuggled together as though for safety.

How was she supposed to protect her people from humans, when the creatures were everywhere?

The oars slipped from her hands, and Klaria watched them float away before laying down in the boat, her gaze on the clouds above.

She was not human. But now, she was also not crab.

The sun beat down on her from above, the heat searing her skin. She welcomed the pain, which matched the intensity in her chest, the burning in her lungs as she sucked in each breath, and tearing in her heart as Pedro's act replayed again and again in her mind.

Who knew her shell could be damaged so badly, and she could still live?

She must have dozed, for she woke to the boat bumping against something solid.

The sun was even higher in the sky, her skin red from its rays. Her throat hurt, and her lips were dry.

She pushed herself up, blinking at her surroundings.

Across the waves she could see the coast, houses dotted all the way along. When she turned, she found herself at a rocky island, barely more than two dozen steps across. She climbed out on unsteady feet, leaving the boat to the current.

Movement in her periphery caused her to turn.

A crab scuttled along the shore towards her, then another lifted its beady eyes above the water, and it too emerged from the shallows. Soon she was surrounded.

"I failed," she told her family, showing them her damaged shell. "I can't help you."

A crab came close, grabbed the edge of her trousers with a claw, and pulled.

"I'm coming."

The crab released her, and scuttled towards the centre of the island, where the rocks were higher. Here Klaria found a rock pool, seawater and rain-water mixing and she lowered her mouth to drink great soothing gulps.

When she was done she sat in the semi-shade provided by the rocks, holding tight to her shell.

All around, more and more crabs gathered.

Klaria must have dozed again, for she woke to the sound of a hundred shells cracking.

All around her the crab-folk were emerging. They came to her, and held her in their arms, and they cried together for the loss of her shell, and for the loss of their people, and for the loss of their cove.

"Tell us about the humans," Ninian said. "Tell us how we can defeat them."

"We cannot defeat them in human form," Klaria said. "We're too vulnerable. Our shells are our armour. But we can only defeat them if we all stand up to them. If we all storm the beach together they will be afraid, and they will flee, and then we'll get our cove back."

"Can you lead us?"

Klaria's heart dropped and she shook her head. "My shell is broken beyond repair. I can't help anyone now."

An older woman stepped forward and took hold of Klaria's shell. "You would not still live if your shell was destroyed beyond repair," she said. "There are salves that can help a damaged shell." She turned Klaria's shell over in her hands. "I don't know how much we can help this one, but we can try." She called over several of the younger women who retrieved their shells and, in crab form, disappeared into the sea.

"While Isla seeks to mend your shell, we must make plans," Ninian said. "You must tell us the weapons of the humans."

Klaria nodded and thought of all the things that could be used as weapons. Of what she would use for a weapon, if she needed to. "They have bows and arrows, and spears for hunting fish, and nets to tangle their prey. If they come from their gardens they have forks and spades and hoes and axes. There are rolling pins, and heavy pans."

Anabelle shook her head. "What are all those things? What do you mean?"

Klaria explained in detail, the size and shape and sharpness or bluntness of the item. "Their heavy items could crack shells, but their sharp items may be deflected."

She looked at the group around her. "They are superstitious. If we gathered the crab-folk from all along the coast and swarmed the beach together we might scare them so that they ran at first sight and we did not have to fight."

The other crab-folk nodded, taking in Klaria's words.

"Then that is what we will do." Ninian turned to face the gathered crowd. "We will wait until Isla returns with her salve, and we will see if Klaria can be healed. And then we will storm our cove, and reclaim our space!"

A cheer went up through the crab-folk.

That night Klaria ate the food of her people; limpets, and seaweed, and tiny shrimp. The salty freshness brought tears to her eyes, as she realised how many years had passed since last she'd eaten food that she truly loved.

They sat on their shells and spoke of the passing years, and their different experiences, and in the early light of dawn Isla and her assistants returned. Isla held a clam shell, shut fast, and passed this to Ninian before she removed her shell.

In human form she turned to Klaria. "I do not know how well this will work. I've never seen a shell so badly burnt, where the wearer was still alive. It may be too far gone."

Klaria closed her eyes as Isla smoothed the salve over the shell first, and then over Klaria's burns.

"Face the moon before it sets completely," Isla instructed, and Klaria did so, aware of the growing light behind her as the dark ahead began to fade.

Her burns tingled, the puckered skin on her face stinging as the salve did its work.

She didn't dare look at her shell.

As the moon dropped below the horizon, Isla massaged Klaria's back. "Shall we try it now?"

Klaria swallowed the lump in her throat, trying to ignore the swirling in her stomach. She held her shell. The top side was still cracked, the softer underside still hard. "Will it work? Would it be better to give it longer?"

"If it does not work now, it will never work."

Klaria nodded, and squeezed her eyes shut tight as Isla lifted the shell and placed it across Klaria's shoulders.

Klaria held her breath.

Across her back she felt the tiny tendrils of the two parts of her body reach out to each other, and connect. Her eyes flew open. "It's working," she whispered.

But then it stopped.

The shell fused with Klaria's shoulders, but Klaria's body was not pulled inside.

Klaria's heart pounded as she tried to fold herself into her shell, tried to pull the now-hardened underside of the shell around her chest, but nothing took hold. "Argh!" She spun around, screaming her frustration at the sky. "I'm ruined."

She felt a light touch through her shell, and glanced to see Isla examining her.

"You're not ruined," Isla said. "You're merging just isn't complete."

Isla bent down to tear long strands of seaweed from the rocks at their feet, and strapped the now-brittle under-shell together across Klaria's chest. "Let's see," she said, lifting her own shell. "Come into the water with me. Let's see if you can breathe and swim. You might still be able to lead us. You might be stronger than you were before."

Klaria doubted it, but still she followed Isla's crab form into the water, her shell an extra weight on her shoulders, her six crab legs waving about uselessly.

Her heart sank in her chest as the water rose about her, covering her knees, her thighs, her hips. How could she possibly be of any use to anyone like this?

She hoped for nothing more but that the weight of her shell would send her to the bottom, where she could leave the pain of this life behind.

But as the water covered her shoulders Klaria felt lifted by sea. She took a deep breath, closed her eyes, and submerged herself beneath the surface.

Strange grey swirls swam before her eyes, and it took her a moment to work out that she was seeing through her crab eyes.

She released the breath in her lungs, only to find her lungs had merged into gills and she could breathe.

Isla's claws clattered together in front of Klaria's face, expressing joy in Klaria's strange new form.

All of a sudden, the clicking noises around her became clear as speech, and Klaria understood that all her people had gathered around to offer support and share their joy that she was with them again.

"We will face the humans tonight," Isla said. "We will storm our cove, and reclaim it for our people."

"I am deformed," Klaria said.

"You are you, and you are back, and together we are all stronger."

Klaria forced a smile, though inside her stomach churned. Her people needed her. They could not continue to live as they were. Perhaps feigning confidence would be enough?

The crab folk gathered in the deep of the cove, and spent the day feasting on clams and snails and algae. Above the waves the afternoon wore on, as below they told stories of the times when they were free to shed their shells and take human-form, and sing and dance in ways they could not under the sea.

As the light filtering through the water faded, the crab-folk began their scuttle over the sea bed, determination bouying their spirits.

By the time they reached the shallows, the moon was visible just above the horizon.

Klaria, Isla, and Ninian approached the surface, their crab-eyes extended above the water.

As Klaria had seen on her first night in the town, fisherman were gathered along the shore, great nets spread out. People walked the shoreline, couples, friendship groups, singles.

Klaria held her breath. Was Pedro there, somewhere? Was he searching for her, or had he returned to their empty mountain home? Did he feel as lost as she had felt, when he first took her shell and hid it away?

All around her the crab's shells clattered together as they tried to settle. Her heart seemed to beat just as loudly. Couldn't the humans hear it?

Klaria saw no indication from those on the shore.

She took a deep breath, exhaling forcefully as though doing so could expel the tiny fish darting about in her stomach, and clicked her claws twice in the sign to charge.

All around her, crabs surged up the beach.

Klaria watched as the humans turned, shouted and stared.

They didn't run.

Why didn't they run?

"Fresh crab tonight fellas!" one fisherman called, gathering one end of his large net. The others followed suit, and soon nets stretched across the length of the beach, several men on each end as they walked back towards the water, scooping up crabs in their wake who ended up upside down and sideways as the nets caught them up and they were tumbled over each other.

"No." Klaria stood, but in the chaos the men paid no attention, and they came around behind and then pulled on the net, scooping up all the crab-folk and dragging them up the shore.

Klaria was face down in the sand, her arms and legs tangled up the net, almost smothered by crab-folk.

That's when the killing started.

Thuds and thwacks from the human's clubs filled the air. The cracks and crunching of shell, and the cries of her people, mingled with the excitement of the humans at such a feast.

"No!" Klaria twisted her head, spitting out sand. "Help."

"Wait," a voice called in the darkness. "There's a woman in there."

"I'll save her."

Men walked across the net, their heavy boots cracking open the shells of those they stepped on.

Klaria's stomach lurched at the sound. "Stop, please."

The net around her was cut away, the crabs picked up and thrown.

Klaria felt a hand on her shell, felt it being lifted, then dropped.

"The crab's trying to eat her!"

From the corner of her eye Klaria saw the man lift his club. "No, please."

Down it came, pain shooting down her spine as she screamed out for help.

"We'll get it off you, don't worry."

Another thwack across her shoulders. Klaria bit her tongue, a sharp tang filling her mouth.

"Stop." Klaria's cry was strangled.

"Help me with this, will you?"

Four hands this time, on either edge of her shell.

She was lifted for the briefest time, and then dropped again, her head thumping on the hard sand beneath her.

"What the—"

"What is she?"

This time a hand came under Klaria's shell, and pulled her over onto her back.

Two faces looked at her in disgust.

"She's one of those crab people. From the stories." A young man spoke, his eyes wide.

"Don't be stupid," his companion laughed. "That's just a myth."

"Look at her." An older man stepped into Klaria's view, nudging her shell with his foot. "She's a crab person all right."

The second young man grimaced. "Monster!" he shouted, raising his club in the air.

"Wait!" Another voice, a familiar voice, and as Klaria blinked in a losing battle for her vision, Pedro's face swam into view.

"I'm sorry, love," he said.

Then the world went black.

When Klaria woke, all was quiet.

She was still on the beach, but had been moved up to where the sand was softer. Towards the sea, human figures lifting things from the sand and carrying them down to the ocean.

Crabs. Humans were carrying crabs, which hung limply in their arms.

She'd failed.

She'd brought destruction on her people, not salvation. Now they not only had no cove in which to safely change form, their entire community had been slaughtered.

"You're awake."

Klaria saw Anabelle was watching over her. "Anabelle. You're alive?"

Anabelle smiled. "Of course I'm alive. And Ninian, and Isla. They're down there with the others, helping to heal the wounds of the injured."

"The injured?" Klaria frowned and glanced back across the beach.

Now she realised that none of the human figures wore any clothing, that they all carried the crumpled crabs carefully as they carried them to the sea.

To the sea, Klaria realised. Not to their village, to a cooking pot or fire.

These weren't humans, they were crab-folk in human form.

"What happened?" She glanced back at Anabelle.

"You don't remember?"

Klaria shook her head.

"Your husband came. He cried over you. He kept saying he was sorry for having stolen so much of your life, and for the damage he did to your shell. He told the other humans to stop. He said it wasn't worth it, he asked who the real monsters were, those being killed, or those doing the killing. He said they must give us back this cove, that no human must step foot here again. Look." Anabelle pointed up to the hilltops all around, where Klaria could see men, hammering at stakes in the ground.

"They are fencing the area off, so that no humans will come again. You won us the battle, Klaria. You returned to us our cove."

Klaria couldn't believe it. "Is it real?"

Isla approached. "The sea is healing our injuries," she said. "And the humans have left. It's real."

Klaria pushed herself to a sitting position, suddenly aware her shell was no longer attached to her shoulders. "The sea can't heal me," she said.

Isla shook her head. "No. But we can visit you now, as we couldn't before, and you can wear your shell and visit with us under the waves, in your new form."

Klaria swallowed back the lump in her throat. She could not return home, not properly, but she was alive, and she was back with her people.

As the days passed the crab-folk brought driftwood and built Klaria a home on the shoreline. She kept her shell on the wall above the mantle, taking it down whenever she needed to be submerged under the waves, and when the moon was full joined her people in human form to dance and sing and celebrate as they always had.

And the humans kept their word, and the crab-folk never had to fear them again.

About the Author:

Heather Ewings lives and writes on Pallittorre land in Northern Trowunna. With a Masters in History and a fascination with myth and folklore, Heather's stories often explore the world through the lens of the magical.

With a tendency to write in shorter forms Heather's micro and flash fiction has been published by Microcosm, The Lark, and Black Hare Press, and her debut novella 'What the Tide Brings' was released in the midst of lockdown in April 2020. Her most recent (unpublished) novella 'Fixing Kendra' received an Honourable Mention in the Stillhouse Press 2022 Novella Competition.

More information about Heather and her work can be found on her website: www.heatherewings.com.au.

LEO
JULY 23 - AUGUST 22

FIRESTORM

Emilie Morscheck

Ella saw the smoke first. Heavy grey puffs spreading across an otherwise cloudless sky. A gust of wind brought the tang of eucalyptus oil burning. She was not concerned. The rural fire service hadn't issued any warnings. Ella gathered the rest of the washing off the line, folding each item of clothing and setting it down neatly in the basket.

Her children, Sophie and Henry, chased each other around the yard, oblivious to the changing horizon. Ella heaved the basket onto her hip, dodged her children, and walked down the cracked concrete path to the rear veranda. The wood varnish was sticky in the heat, Ella's shoes leaving dusty imprints.

She slid the glass door open, quickly entering and shutting it to trap the cold air inside. The evaporative cooling had made the floor damp and Ella was careful to maintain her balance as she headed towards the children's bedrooms.

In Henry's room, Lego was scattered across the floor. His cupboard, however, was tidy. Ella returned all his fresh clothes to the drawers, her hands pressing on the torn shirt that he refused to let her throw away, the school socks that were stained brown and his uniform for next week.

Sophie was much tidier than her younger brother. She had her toys stacked in the corner under the window. Ella hung up the school dresses, remembering each stitch that she plunged into the checked fabric. Ella had offered her any variation of uniform that Sophie wanted, but the girl had insisted on having a dress like the rest of her friends. That desire wouldn't last long.

The back door slammed, and Ella proceeded to her own room, taking care to restore all items to their usual place. The television turned on to the Saturday cartoons. Much louder than necessary.

With the morning's chores done Ella picked up her novel and settled into her reading chair in the study.

If it weren't for the children, Ella wouldn't have realized the power had gone out. The television had shut off, leaving them to come annoy their mother. Ella left her book on the reading chair and left to find them some lunch.

Through the kitchen windows, the sky had darkened, with the smoke reaching towards her home. No warning text had come about the fire. She'd left her phone charging on the kitchen bench with the volume turned up on full. Ella unplugged the phone and slipped it into her pocket. She prepared food for the children, keeping her tone calm and her voice gentle. And then she began to pack.

A few sets of clothes for each of them. Family photos. The box with her mother's jewellery. The envelope of money she had shoved into the back of the bedside cabinet.

Ella put them all into the boot of her car. The ashy smell had permeated the garage and was leeching into the rest of the house.

Once the children had eaten, Ella strapped them into the car, Henry secured in his booster seat. Sophie looked confused but did as her mother asked. The engine was running, recycling the cool smoke-free air into the cabin.

Ella had one last look around her home, in case there was anything she'd missed. Everything was perfectly in place. The floor which had been clean that morning now had a coating of grey dust. She pressed her fingers into her palm, knowing every moment she stood there the fire could be getting closer.

She drove as quickly as she felt comfortable away from her home. The smoke was getting denser, obscuring the blue above. Down the street and onto the side road. The highway was half an hour away.

The bush alongside the road glowed, the fire deep within. The heat licked Ella through the windows. Every surface in the car began to heat up. The children were complaining, uncomfortable, but Ella had to ignore them. Her foot pressed onto the accelerator.

The engine groaned. Warning lights flickering on the dashboard. Everything was too hot, and getting hotter. Ella wiped her face. Why hadn't she left sooner when she'd seen the oncoming rage and heat? When she'd smelt the crumbling bush?

She turned a steep bend on the road, the boxes in the boot tumbling and crashing. Henry was crying. Sophie was silent.

Fire leapt across the road through the canopy of the trees as sudden as a flighty kangaroo. Ella slammed the brakes as a branch crashed down, sparks flickering. How had it come so close so quickly? In the flames, a shape emerged. Humanoid and growing. Reaching for the car.

Ella put the car in reverse, her mind searching for escape routes. Her driveway at the end of the street, was no doubt already in flames. Her downhill neighbour halfway down the street was her only option, all other exits choked.

The fiery figure crawled into the bush, alighting a shrub and gripping onto a trunk of a tree. It pulled itself up and then began to race through the vegetation, an angry red monster chasing Ella down.

The children were screaming now. Ella couldn't scream. All she could do was drive.

She stopped in front of the neighbour's driveway, throwing the car back into drive, and crashed through the latched gate, the tires struggling to grip the gravel. Maybe the dam had water in it. Maybe.

The fire rushed along the street as if in pursuit, struggling to slow down to make the bend. Ella could see in the rear-view mirror the open hungry mouth and the hands that consumed all.

The dam was at the bottom of the hill. The summer had been dry, as usual, and the dam was muddy and shallow. But it was all Ella had left.

She stopped the car by the edge and grabbed her children. They'd stopped screaming, the image of the fire stuck in their eyes, mouths open. They all coughed out smoke.

Even though the children were better swimmers than her, Ella made Henry cling to her front and Sophie to her back as she waded into the dam. She went as far as she could stand with their heads above the water. It was dark and cold against her burning muscles. Henry's teeth chattered.

The fire caught up. The figure was larger than before.

Ella watched as it danced around the edge of the dam leaving behind glowing embers and ash. The car glowed white, the metal twisting and collapsing into a melted mass. The fuel tank exploded, spitting sparks.

She didn't know how long they were there in the water, waiting for the fire to die. It only got hungrier, burned hotter, desired more. Oxygen was sucked out of the air. Would there be enough to breathe? The surface of the dam appeared small compared to the fire.

In vain it tried to stretch out across the water towards the family. Ella hugged Henry, water slipping into her mouth as she stepped backwards. She was tied, stuck between the extremes of hot and cold, Sophie's grip slipping. Ella called to her, told her to hang on.

For the monster would have to die. There was nothing left to burn.

In a surge of heat, it burst, collapsing in on itself. The world was dark. Smoke blanketed the world. And everything was gone.

About the Author:

Emilie Morscheck lives and works on Ngunnawal land. She is an author of YA speculative fiction. In 2019 Emilie received an artsACT grant to edit her YA fantasy novel 'These Cursed Waters'. *She was a 2020 Anne Edgeworth Fellow, receiving support to develop her second novel* 'The Selkie Curse'. *Emilie was shortlisted for the 2021 Text Prize and an inaugural recipient of the Steph Bowe Mentorship for her novel* 'These Cursed Waters'. *She is a fan of kelpies, selkies and watery graves.*

NIGHT OF THE LION

Deeanna West

Golden rays split the still dark sky creating a silhouette of everything in the foreground. The soaring branches of the boabs lining the ridge were the dark smudges of an oil painting. I squinted, forcing my eyes to focus. There. Movement. I raised my arm to point, directing everyone's attention between the trees. They tittered, whispering to each other that they couldn't see, that there was nothing there, but I ignored them. They'd see what I had seen, and soon.

The sharp intake of five sets of tourists' breaths announced the second they saw them. The lions. It was a small pride, but they were reliable. Every morning at daybreak they rose, meandering down to the waterhole without a care in the world. They were used to the jeeps, used to the staring of safari-goers desperate to tick lion off their big five lists.

"Nick, can we get closer?" one of the tourists whispered.

I glanced to her. Blonde hair hacked off around her ears and eyes hidden behind sunglasses too big for her face. I was terrible with names. There were too many people passing through and as head ranger I didn't usually run tours or interact with the guests all that much. The only reason I was running this one was because

Larkin was sick. As it was, I'd just get the hang of a group and then they'd be gone again. Their spots filled with fresh faces I had to learn all over again. It was odd for me to remember hers so clearly. Bridgette. When Griggs had announced he was taking on a vet student we'd all been shocked. He was a cranky bastard and was more likely to make a student cry than teach them anything. If she survived him, she'd be a great vet.

"Just wait," I replied to Bridgette's question.

As if summoned by my words, he approached. Abioye. He stalked towards our jeep with all the arrogance of a creature that knew he was king. He left the females to stand before us, glaring at us, pretending that he may pounce at any moment. He wouldn't of course. I met his eye. My green to his deep golden. We understood each other, he and I. Seven years he'd ruled this area. For seven years I'd watched him grow into the magnificent specimen that commanded the attention of all.

"He's stunning," Bridgette gushed, camera forgotten in her grasp. "What is he, one hundred, two hundred kilos?"

"About a hundred and ninety, yeah."

She nodded to herself and I wondered what she was thinking. I almost asked but her attention had already returned to Abioye so I turned back to the staring tourists.

"Every morning Abioye and his pride make this trek to the waterhole. It's the best time to get close to them. For those that are interested, there's a hide by the water's edge. Three people can go at daybreak tomorrow and get a close view of the pride. You'll most likely see some wildebeest and gazelle as well."

"Oh yes, I want to do that! Mum, can we do that?" The youngest of the tourists asked. Just turned sixteen, she and her mother had booked this safari to celebrate. Abbi. That was it. Why could I remember their stories so much easier than their names?

Her mother nodded. "If you can drag yourself out of bed early enough, then we can."

"Ugh mum, come on."

Smiling, I restarted the jeep. "Come on troops, it's time for breakfast."

Bridgette smiled at me across the table, plate loaded with bacon and coffee balancing precariously as she dragged a chair across with a foot.

I raised an eyebrow at her. "I would have thought a vet student would be all about the veggies."

"Oh, heaps of girls in my class are vegetarian, but I'm not one of them. I mean, what kind of psycho can turn their nose up at bacon?" She accentuated her words by taking a huge bite and smiling as egg yolk dripped down her chin.

A laugh escaped me. "You're an animal."

"I'll fit right in here then."

She wasn't wrong. It could get pretty wild here sometimes. Between the morning rounds of the park and the tourist parties that went late and kept everyone awake, there were some days I only got a few hours sleep. "So how long is your placement?"

"Three weeks."

I whistled. "Three weeks with Griggs. You're a brave woman."

"He's been great so far. He's like a superstar of wildlife medicine. There's so much I can learn from him and his reference for internships is like a golden ticket."

"I don't doubt that there's a lot he can teach you. Just don't take his crap personally, okay?"

She frowned. "What do you mean."

"Griggs can be a little, grumpy is all."

"I see. Well I think I can handle myself, so don't you worry."

My eyes drifted down to my empty plate. I'd come in early to avoid the rush for the buffet having learnt the hard way not to get between someone's great aunt and the chocolate chip pancakes. I watched Bridgette eat, I had no reason to hang around, but wanted to stay and talk with her. Time had caught up with me, I needed to go and she was probably expected at the clinic.

As if she was reading my mind Bridgette spoke around her food. "So, Nick, can I count on you being here for dinner?"

I nodded. "Can't wait."

Unease settled hot in my gut and I frowned as the lionesses paced through the grass.

"Something disturbs them," Jaafan stated.

"But what?"

Jaafan had spotted them on his return from the tree tents and found me at once. As head ranger all the staff knew to find me if they noted anything out of the usual with the animals. His main job was to transport the tourists to and from the tree tents, and Jaafan was always watching out for the park as he drove. Since the park was so small, everyone helped out where they could, and everyone had some basic training with firearms. The last time the pride was this distressed, poachers had cut through the fences, so I appreciated Jaafan coming with me now. An extra set of eyes to keep watch could be invaluable.

At this time of day, the pride sought shelter from the noon heat beneath the acacia on the edge of the reserve. To see them milling around now was concerning.

"You think poachers again?" Jaafan's black skin seemed flushed from the heat and worry marred his usually cheerful face.

"I don't think so," I replied. "The guys didn't report any problems this morning after their rounds. No cut fences or campfires. No, something else is going on."

Frowning, Jaafan inched the rover closer. The lionesses eyed us but didn't move away.

"Where's Abioye?"

Jaafan shook his head. "I haven't seen him since yesterday."

"He was around earlier when I took the group out for Larkin." As I spoke, I turned and fished the binoculars off the back seat. I scanned the pride, but the big male was nowhere to be seen.

"I don't think he's—" I bit off my words as I spotted on a tan shape lying still in the grass. "There!"

Jaafan drove where I indicated, beeping the horn in an effort to drive the lionesses away. Leaving Jaafan to keep watch and handing him my rifle, I approached the body. Abioye didn't move and for a moment I worried he was already dead. His chest rose in a ragged breath and hope replaced the dread I'd been feeling.

"He's still alive! Call the other rangers and Griggs."

Jaafan leapt to obey, shouting down the two-way that we needed a transport vehicle and Griggs. Even with Abioye unconscious it wasn't safe to try and move him without more hands and sedatives.

"Hang in there buddy," I whispered. "We got you."

It took four of us to stretcher Abioye into the small veterinary clinic beside the resort. The moment we heaved him onto the treatment table, Griggs started yelling, causing the others to flee the room.

"Get a catheter in!" Griggs snapped at a nurse. His hands were already busy, drawing blood from Abioye's jugular as a second nurse fought to keep his head raised.

She was struggling, Abioye's head was a dead weight and she was a petite thing. I hadn't been told to leave so I stepped into the room to help her. The nurse—Izzy, I think—nodded her thanks and hurried to press an oxygen mask to the big cat's face.

"Catheter's in."

"Good. Run this blood." Griggs shoved the tubes to Bridgette. "Full health profile and bring in the results as soon as they're ready."

As Bridgette leapt to obey, Griggs drew a clear liquid from a small glass vial. He flicked the bubbles out before injecting the liquid into the catheter. "Hold his head up again."

I obeyed, hefting Abioye's head up by the scruff and a lip, watching in awe as Griggs shoved a tube down his throat. I'd watched Griggs work before of course. Seen his clean sutures on Hamlet, the cook's dog, after it had tried to chase a baboon away from the bins. But seeing him working now, a solid block of calm amidst the chaos of the emergency room was a whole other thing. Even though he was a stuck up prick any other time, I couldn't help but be impressed.

Bridgette raced back in and handed Griggs some papers. His eyes scanned the document, lips moving as he read.

"What's wrong with him?" I asked, unable to stop myself.

Griggs sighed and looked straight at me. "His white cell count is almost non-existent, he's anaemic and his globulins are tanked. Fluid in his abdomen. I'd have to send bloods to the lab to be one hundred per cent sure, but I'd put money on this being FIP."

It wasn't a disease I'd heard of before. We'd had reports of Distemper and Babisiosis killing lions but there'd been no sign of that here.

Griggs must have seen the confusion on my face. "Feline Infectious Peritonitis. Nasty disease. Abioye doesn't fit the

261

textbook case but I'm pretty sure. He has all the indicators." A brief pause as he connected a fluid line. "I'll do my best to support him, maybe even get him up and going again. But Nick, it's a band aid, this will catch up to him eventually. And that's *if* he survives the night."

I nodded, throat tight. Abioye wasn't a pet, he didn't belong to me, yet seven years watching him rule his pride had created a bond. Swallowing hard, I tried to be practical. "Do what you can but we can't let him suffer. Better to put him to sleep than let him suffer and die out there on the plains."

"That's a good way to look at it," Griggs agreed. "Now get out of my surgery and let me do my job."

I obeyed, pausing as Bridgette placed a hand on my arm.

Her eyes were sympathetic. She'd almost certainly seen this before as a student, seen the grieving owner receiving the news that there was no hope.

I tried to smile. This was Africa after all, I'd seen death before and would again.

The sound of flesh hitting stainless steel drew our attention before I could leave.

"Shit!"

The expletive broke through Griggs' cool demeanour as he lunged for the vials of medications on the shelf above the table.

Abioye's body thrashed, held down by the nurses leaning on him. Legs kicked despite the drugs Griggs had administered.

I couldn't move, rooted to the spot as the shit hit the fan. It was for the best though, I'd just get in the way. Everything moved in fast forward, everyone fighting to regain control until, with a strained silence, it all just stopped. Abioye's body fell still, no residual tremors or rise of the chest to mark his life.

Griggs pressed his stethoscope to his chest but almost straight away shook his head. "He's gone."

I nodded, but was unable to speak past the lump in my throat.

"I'll take care of his body," Griggs offered.

He understood and it was a god send.

Bridgette caught up as I escaped down the hall. "Hey, are you ok?"

I just stared at her.

"Right, silly question. He was a magnificent animal, I'm so sorry he died." She paused and laid a hand on my arm. "Do you want to go see if there's any ice cream? Or Bacon? Something tasty might make you feel a little better?"

My mouth twitched. Almost a smile, this woman was special. "I'm ok without the food. Thanks for the offer though. I was thinking that I need to go on patrol, check the rest of the pride, make sure none of the others are sick. Usually Griggs would come but maybe he'd be happy for you to instead?"

"Right, good thinking. Give me two seconds to check with Griggs and then I'll come with you."

I waited as she disappeared around the corner, not really believing that Griggs would let her come. She bounced back again and this time I let myself smile. Griggs must think highly of her if he was letting her come instead of himself.

We walked in silence until we got out to the rover. Jaafan was leaning against it, arms crossed and chewing jerky. He snapped to attention as we approached, waiting for an update. I shook my head. "He didn't make it."

Swearing under his breath, Jaafan kicked at the dirt. "So what do we do now?"

"We're heading out to check the girls. Make sure none of them are sick."

"Call me if there's something?"

"Of course." I agreed.

Tyres spun on the dirt road as I tried not to shower him in dust as we left. Within the clinic it had felt like mere minutes had passed but the outside world had continued as scheduled. The afternoon sun blurred the horizon, but I was used to it. Used to the way you had to squint to focus. The lionesses hadn't moved from where they had found Abioye. Their pacing had stopped but they still seemed watchful.

"They look well enough," Bridgette whispered. She had the binoculars pressed so tight against her face an indent was forming.

"They do. But so did Abioye this morning."

We watched until the sun had begun to set, and the chill had me pulling on a jacket.

"We'll keep checking them but for now they seem ok. Let's head back." I said as I started the car.

Bridgette just nodded. There was nothing else we could do.

I didn't need to walk Bridgette back to the clinic, but it seemed like the polite thing to do. She had come with me to check the lionesses because she knew I was sad, after all. Shadows extended across the path as the sun set. Bridgette didn't know her way around well yet, so I directed her as the solar powered lanterns lining the paths gradually switched on.

"Do you still want to meet up for dinner?" she asked.

"I can just wait for you and we can go now." The sun had set on our way home and—despite everything—my stomach was making its hunger known.

Bridgette nodded. "Just let me get my jacket."

She disappeared into the clinic and I leant against a wall to wait. Shadows flickered at the end of the corridor where a light had blown and I briefly wondered if maintenance had been called.

A piercing scream snapped my attention from the busted light. I stormed into the clinic ready to fight a monster, or a poacher. Instead, I found Bridgette collapsed on the floor, hands pressed tight against her mouth. Blood oozed from a pile of flesh in front of her. Flesh that had been torn to pieces. The scent of the blood made me gag. The scattered scraps of blue fabric were all too familiar. Griggs.

I fought to swallow the bile threatening to rise in my throat, I leant in closer. An arm had vicious claw marks extending down the forearm. Instruments were strewn across the floor and Abioye's body was nowhere to be seen. We'd been gone for a while, but still Abioye should still be there. Griggs was going to perform a necropsy on him.

"I think Abioye did this." My voice sounded strained to my ears, and dragged Bridgette's attention away from Griggs' body.

She shook her head. "The scratches look like they're from a lion, but this violence. It's like a frenzied attack. A lion wouldn't do this."

"There's no other explanation," I argued. "Look, I don't want to believe it either. Maybe the illness made him act irrationally? I don't know."

"What do we do?" Bridgette asked, regaining her feet.

"We have to make sure everyone is safe. Get the tourists back to their rooms. Then we find Abioye."

As a rule, we didn't carry our rifles around the villas. But I hadn't had a chance to stash the gun in my room since we got back. For once I was grateful for its weight slung across my back. I drew it as we headed out. I was loathe to shoot Abioye but if he had killed Griggs. Panic at being trapped in a small room and illness may have disoriented him, but it meant nothing. I wouldn't have any more lives lost today. If I could, I'd force Abioye back out into the park but if it came to it, I'd shoot.

We inched through the building, making our way towards the sleeping quarters. Most people would have headed to the tree tents at this time of the evening. But anyone here would be in the dining hall. Still, the bedrooms were closer.

"Mum, are you out here?" Abbi stepped out of a room as we rounded the corner. I started to order her back inside when he appeared.

Abioye stared at us, eyes unblinking and clouded. He didn't move, no muscle twitches or the rise and fall of his chest as he breathed.

"Abbi," I hissed. "Get back in your room."

She whirled to obey, but Abioye was faster.

He lunged with claws outstretched and mouth open wide. Fangs sunk into Abbi's neck as his jaw snapped shut. Red sprayed against the wall and her scream became a gurgle. With practiced efficiency the lion shook his head and Abbi went limp.

I didn't scream. Shock had driven the air from my lungs.

Abioye tore into Abbi's lifeless body, not feeding, just ripping her to shreds.

"Nick, the gun."

Now was our chance to put him down. At this close a range I wouldn't miss. Since his head was turned away, I aimed for his heart. Cracks split the air as I fired three times in quick succession, and the scent of gunpowder burnt acrid. The bullets sunk deep into Abioye's chest, decimating muscle and lung tissue to leave gaping holes in their wake. Undeterred the big lion continued to work, unconcerned by the kill shot I'd just delivered.

"Oh lord help us. The wounds, they aren't bleeding."

Those bullets would have torn through so many vital structures Abioye should be gasping on the floor, not turning to face us.

"Run!" Bridgette shrieked but I needed no prompting.

I'd never run so fast in my life. My lungs screamed in protest, but I just kept pumping my legs.

Bridgette's lithe form had already reached an open room.

The clinking of Abioye's claws as they scrambled to find purchase on the tiles drove me forward. The thought of those nails tearing through flesh made me cringe.

As he rounded the corner, legs sliding out from under him, his great bulk slammed into the wall. In an instant, he rebounded and continued his charge towards us.

Bridgette threw the door shut behind me. The wood bucked as Abioye collided with it. Somehow the lock held, but I doubted it would survive more hits like that.

Scraping filled the room as Bridgette pushed a bookshelf across to reinforce the door. She was struggling, but fear kept me rooted in place--what if my weight was helping the door not give in?

She got the shelf close enough for me to help wedge it into position before we collapsed in front of it.

"What the hell is going on?" I hissed.

"I have a theory." She was hesitant, whispering to the floor without looking at me. Whatever she was about to say scared her. "Those bullets should have killed him. But did you see it? There was no blood. And I don't think he was breathing either. We saw him die in the clinic."

"Griggs must have saved him after all," I interrupted.

"I don't think so. I think he's still dead." She took a deep breath. "Look I know this is going to sound crazy, but I think Abioye is a zombie. The walking dead. Hungry for brains. Whatever you like, but it explains the lack of blood and the change in behaviour."

I couldn't help it. I laughed. "You watch too much telly."

She frowned at me. "No, seriously, think about it. We watched him die. Now he's back killing everything he sees in a most un-lion way, doesn't breathe, doesn't bleed. This is the truth. The FIP must have mutated somehow."

The word seemed to echo around the room. Zombie. It was ridiculous, insane and yet now that it had been put forward, it made sense.

"Ok, let's say he's a zombie lion."

"He is," Bridgette asserted.

"So, we have a zombie lion roaming through a safari park. Most of the tourists are at the tree tents with Jaafan. They're safe. But there are a few still here. Abbi's mum, Lorraine."

Bridgette frowned. "And the Clines."

"And Frank, Livia and Bisa. All the rest of the staff live off-site so they'll be ok."

"We have to trap him. Stop him hurting anyone else and stop him escaping," Bridgette said.

"We're going to need help."

I nodded then pressed my ear against the wall. Silence. There was no way to be sure, but we had to get out of this room. Hopefully the quiet was real and Abioye had moved on. Heart pounding, I pushed the bookshelf aside and opened the door a crack. The hallway was empty.

"Where do you think he went?" Bridgette whispered.

Abioye had only hit the door twice in his attempt to get to us.

"I know what you know," I replied. "Chances are he's lurking just around a corner."

"That's a pleasant thought."

"Somehow we have a zombie lion. I think pleasant is long gone."

She nodded and started walking down the hall. Or maybe creeping would be more accurate. I felt like I was inching my way along the hall rather than walking. On a normal day, the gun slung over a shoulder was enough to make me feel safe. Just the sound of it discharging was enough to scare most predators away. Yet now the weapon was useless to me.

The smell hit us first. Metallic. We both recognised it as we approached a t-section in the corridor. Blood seeped across the floor to our left. Abioye was nowhere to be seen but the mess he'd left behind was fresh. Limbs lay strewn separate from the body and one blank eye stared up at me, the other mutilated with scratches. I couldn't stop it this time. My stomach clenched and purged itself. Embarrassed, I wiped my mouth with my sleeve. "Sorry," I apologised to Bridgette.

She hadn't noticed, eyes fixated on the body. "Who is she?"

"Livia. The housekeeper"

"I'm so sorry, Livia," Bridgette whispered before turning to me. "We need to keep going."

I followed her down the right corridor, towards the dining hall. The faint thrum of chatter greeted us, but it was quieter than usual with everyone at the tree tents. As soon as we entered, I called for attention. I had no idea what I was going to say. How did you explain a zombie lion was terrorising the villa without sounding insane?

"This is going to sound crazy, but I need you all to listen to me," I started. "One of the lions has contracted a serious illness. He passed away, but somehow, he's come back. I shot him but it had no effect. Now I know what I'm about to ask is going to be hard, but I need your help. Our best option is to trap Abioye in the walk-in freezer. Its large and strong enough to contain him."

The Clines nodded without hesitation. From memory they were an action-seeking couple on their anniversary. They'd spent the last one climbing mount Everest. I indicated they should follow me, leaving Bridgette to speak with Lorraine, Abbi's mum.

I ran through the plan with the others but couldn't help watching Bridgette. She spoke too softly for me to hear. How did you even tell a mother that her daughter had been murdered by a lion? Lorraine's face went pale in an instant and her eyes

271

widened. She sank down in her chair, her hand clasped over her mouth. Bridgette wrapped her arms around her, holding her. Truth be told I'd expected screaming, but it seemed Lorraine's grief was the silent type of streaming tears and withdrawing from the world. My heart ached for her.

"Wait here," I told the Clines, turning my attention away from the mother's pain.

They obeyed and I slipped into the kitchens. As expected, Frank and Bisa were huddled in the back over a small fold-out table. Cards lay strewn, in the middle of a game. They started as I approached. Harvey the chef hated them gambling in the kitchens. They'd been on the receiving end of his rants more than once. It was unusual for them to take the risk so soon after dinner. Harvey could return any moment.

"It's ok, just me."

"Nick, nice to see you. What is happening?" Greeted Bisa.

I started to fill them in when the radio crackled.

"This is Jaafan. We require immediate assistance at tree camp, over."

"Jaafan its Nick. What's going on."

"Nick, it's the lionesses, they've gone crazy. They killed Harvey. He came to deliver more dessert and they killed him. Oh lord they killed him."

Jaafan's sobs were clear. I longed to help him but there was nothing I could say that would make this better.

"Listen to me, Jaafan. The same thing's happening to Abioye. Guns don't work. You have to stay in the trees."

The crackle of the radio was my only reply. "Jaafan? Jaafan? What's happening?"

Nothing. Shit.

I couldn't dwell on whatever was happening at tree camp, could only hope everyone would stay safe within the branches. Saving the people here had to happen first.

"Is everyone in place?" I asked.

A chorus of 'yes' and a 'roger that' from Frank was my reply. I took a deep breath, trying to quell the shaking in my hands. Chances were, I would die in about a minute. Right. Well, no point in delaying.

The freezer doors stood wide, sheltering everyone behind them. A pile of microwaved meat lay in a steaming heap in the centre of the room. The bait. Well, the second lot of bait that I hoped would command Abioye's attention once he was in the freezer. I turned my attention to the large ornate double doors of the dining room. We'd created a path from those doors, through the kitchen to the freezer. Our trap.

Not a squeak announced the opening of the doors. Not what I needed. I took a deep breath then screamed. Loud and long I kept screaming. Hopefully, I sounded like a wounded animal. Like prey.

I heard him coming. The heavy pad of his paws as he moved towards me. The second he rounded the corner and spotted me, I ran.

Abioye followed.

At the freezer door I turned to face my killer. This was it. Abioye leapt, a solid wall of muscle and teeth. I collapsed onto the floor letting the momentum of his pounce carry him into the freezer. Pain seared across my shoulder and then I was moving. Yanked sideways by Bisa as planned. Our timing was perfect. As soon as I was clear everyone set shoulders against their door, heaving them shut. The gap closed as Abioye eyed the meat we had left him. How was I alive?

Our meat bribe wasn't enough.

"Push!"

I leapt forward to help, but we were too slow. The closing doors jerked to a stop as Abioye forced his shoulder and arm through the gap. His body trapped within the freezer he clawed at the metal, trying to pull the rest of his bulk through the door. I grunted, white fire burning down my side where his claws must have cut me, but I couldn't stop. If he got out. No.

"Keep pushing!"

We strained and someone cried. Abioye's claws scrambled for enough purchase to push his way free. The doors gave and Abioye launched into the room.

Frank screamed as a swipe of Abioye's paw opened his abdomen to spill intestines on the floor. Glistening coils covered in blood that held my gaze despite Mr Cline crumbling beneath the lion in my peripheral.

"Come on, come on!" Bridgette screamed as she grabbed at my arm. The panic in her voice snapped me back to attention.

Mrs Cline went down trying to save her husband as we fled, Bridgette towing Lorraine with me and Bisa following behind.

"Which way?" Bridgette asked, letting me take the lead.

"The cars," I replied.

A crash drove us faster. We could hear him, upending tables in his pursuit.

"He's coming," sobbed Lorraine, over and over again. She provided the soundtrack to our panic.

Bursting into the night and seeing the cars parked before us brought tears to my eyes. "Get Lorraine in the rover," I yelled to Bridgette.

She didn't break stride, just veered towards the vehicle as I ran towards the lockbox for the keys.

Keys in hand, I turned back. Abioye loomed in the doorway, clearly lit within the golden pool of light spilling across the threshold.

Hearing the lion, Bisa turned, with terror written upon on his face. The movement unbalanced him, feet twisting as he fell. He hit the ground hard, crying out in pain and then horror as Abioye descended on him. Blood sprayed, collecting in Abioye's coat.

The car. I had to get to the car. I covered the ground in a few strides and vaulted into the vehicle. It started the first time and the relief had me sobbing. The tyres skidded on the road, but I didn't care. It didn't matter, we were alive.

"He's gone," Bridgette stated. She was twisted in her seat, looking back on the villa, one hand still clutching Lorraine's as she sobbed.

I just nodded. There was nothing there to keep him. Everyone was dead.

"What's going to happen now?" Bridgette asked.

"I don't know," I replied.

As we lapsed into a tense silence a roar exploded in the night around us. Though we sped away it felt like it was right outside. Another roar sounded in reply, further away but no less powerful. Fear tightened my knuckles on the steering wheel. Fuck. I reached for the radio, praying Jaafan's earlier unresponsiveness had just been radio error.

"Jaafan, it's Nick. Are you safe?"

The radio crackled but no voice answered my call. The sound echoed around the car and my stomach clenched. There would be no help there.

About the Author:

Deeanna West is a fantasy author writing from sunny north Queensland. If a book has magic, strange and amazing creatures or a world completely different to our own, then she's sold. When not holed up writing, she can be found playing games on the Xbox or out riding her horse.

VIRGO
AUGUST 23 - SEPTEMBER 22

MARY MARY

Eva Leppard

It's often very difficult to discern whether any given day is going to be the average, run of the mill kind, or whether it's going to be the awe-inspiring, magical, and life-changing kind. Given that the former tends to outweigh the latter by one thousand to one, it's usually the case that you're rather underdressed when one of the spectacular occasions does present itself.

That's assuming you're without the benefit of knowing the future, and given the irritating intricacies of time travel, it's a better bet to just wear a nice frock and good shoes every day and hope for the best.

But Mary didn't know any of these things then. She did know, however, know that if you nip down to the supermarket without any make up and in a paint-spattered flannelette shirt on a Saturday then you will see anywhere between one and twenty-five of your exes, and so she had tidied herself up just a little to ensure that she would see no one that she knew. She was going through a vintage stage, so she threw on a floor-length white dress and a hooded blue cape. She weighed up the pros and cons between a pair of heels and some flat strappy sandals and decided that you could take this dressy thing too far, so chose comfort over height. As an artist, she felt it her duty to look eccentric.

She had remembered to grab her shopping bags (outstanding), and she even had a list which, she decided, was a personal highpoint in her adulting life. Therefore she was miffed when she got to the shopping centre and found that it was closed.

Checking her phone, she noted it was 4:20pm. Closing time wasn't until 10pm on Saturdays. She peered through some darkened windows and could see no movement within, so she readjusted her cape, wriggled her toes in her sandals, and returned to her car.

It wasn't hard to find her car in the car park. It was the only one there. Two hundred empty spaces stretched out around her as she turned in a circle, squinting at her surrounds.

No cars.

No people.

At all.

Had there been anyone around when she had got here? There would have been. She would be the first to admit she spent a lot of time in her own head but an empty shopping centre on a Saturday afternoon in Melbourne was something even she would be alert to.

Well, if there had been people when she arrived, they weren't here now. There was no one about at all.

She cocked her head—a movement she could swear she had never done before—and listened for something. Anything.

But there was nothing.

Nothing at all. In the middle of this vast, burbling city, she could hear no sound.

While she had dressed to avoid people, she certainly hadn't pictured this scenario.

She unlocked her car and almost threw herself into her seat, so eager to get out of the vast swathe of nothingness that surrounded her. Everything felt wrong, as if she was no longer in her own, familiar space at all, as if she was occupying somewhere else. She grabbed the steering wheel in both hands, as much to steady herself as anything. She had no intention of starting the engine; making any noise at all in this void seemed like a foolhardy thing to do.

Mary closed her eyes. Right. Maybe everyone had just popped off to do something important. Was it Grand Final day? Maybe there had been a bomb scare or a terrorist alert or . . .

A tap tapping was coming towards her, across the car park.

Tappa-tappa tap. Tappa-tappa tap.

She opened her eyes to see the face of an elderly woman peering in the window, a worried expression on her face. She broke out into a wide grin and motioned that Mary should wind down the window.

"Hello dear," the woman said. "I'm ToriBlan. So sorry I'm late, got the times mixed up you see. Got caught in a meeting on the Upper Realms and it quite got away from me. By the time I realised we had activated your summoning, things had already got quite weird for you, I expect?"

Mary nodded and confirmed that yes, things were quite weird for her.

"So, if you'd like to just pop out of the vehicle, we can get started."

Mary stared at her. She could feel her mouth hanging open but seemed powerless to close it. "I—"

"Come on dear, chop chop." ToriBlan clapped her hands together, the sound muffled and dull in the staling air. "I'm keen to get out of here as soon as possible. Staying in Time Past gives me the willies, to be honest, so the sooner we get out of here the better."

Mary continued to stare.

"Wait." The woman, who was bending over to see through the window, put one wrinkled finger to her mouth and pursed her lips. "Wait." She peered off into the distance for a moment, and then crouched down so her head was almost inside the window of the car. "Do you know what I'm talking about?"

Mary shook her head.

"Damn." The woman stood up again, walked a few steps away from the car, and waved her hands about in the air.

Mary couldn't make out who or what the woman was speaking to, but Mary thought that she could make out 'ignorant', 'urgent' and 'fucking substandard behaviour', and she hoped that she was not the target of any of them.

"Okay dear." ToriBlan had turned back and was now addressing her. "There seems to have been a frightful cock up, of which I most humbly apologise, but this is becoming quite urgent now so I'm going to have to ask you to exit your car and come with me, before we both end up being obliterated and sent to the Great Abyss."

She reached the car, pulled the door open and grabbed Mary's arm. "We need to go," she said. Her eyes looked over the car, towards the distant skyline where an oppressive black mass tinged with red was rolling towards them, covering everything as it spilled forwards.

"We need to go now."

And at that moment, Mary believed her.

Taking her hand, ToriBlan pulled Mary forwards, to one of the empty car spaces. "Okay, let's go."

Before Mary had a chance to tell her that a) it was an empty car parking space and b) she was quite mad, they had both stepped forwards and found themselves in another world, at which point Mary fainted.

ToriBlan told her that it was quite normal, and she shouldn't be embarrassed or feel as if she was putting anyone out. This wasn't something that Mary had considered, but given there were people running around finding pillows and drinks and cold compresses for her head, she realised that it was quite possibly what everyone was thinking, as a matter of fact.

"People often faint when they step through the Vector Segmentor for the first time," ToriBlan explained. "It's because of the temporal manipulation or some such thing, I've never taken much notice, but it works a treat when you want to step from one vector into another."

They were in a large room, bustling with activity. A variety of people were moving around, attending to what must have been frightfully important matters, and after the initial flurry of drama that she caused, people had drifted away from her to continue with whatever it was that they were doing.

"Right." ToriBlan sat down next to her, a concerned look on her face. "We need to get jogging along with things, now that you're here, but before I start, can I just clarify what you do, and what you do not, know."

Mary took a deep breath. "I think it's safe to assume that I know nothing. I went to the supermarket to buy ingredients to make Pad Thai, and" —she gestured around her— "here I am. I have no idea what's going on." She closed her eyes and wished she was back at home. She knew that shopping to make her own dinner had been a terrible decision.

ToriBlan looked at her with a degree of scepticism. "Are you sure you didn't know that you were coming here? Because you seem to be dressed the part."

Mary glanced down at her long dress and blue cape. "What?"

ToriBlan sighed. "I don't know if this is the right place to talk, but I don't want to risk you falling down again. You see, you've been summoned here because there's a very important job you have been working towards your whole life, and now it's time for your Creation."

As far as Mary was concerned, this confirmed that the old woman was quite mad.

"Haven't you felt, all your life, that there was something else waiting for you?"

Mary shook her head.

"A certain emptiness, a certain lack of purpose and meaning?"

"I'm really happy," protested Mary. "Really happy. I promise. I like my life, I paint. I don't have much money, but I cope."

"And that fact that you're a virgin means that—"

Mary started coughing and wasn't able to stop until a man brought her a nice big glass of water with ice.

ToriBlan looked at her with a sense of impending doom on her face.

"I'm not a virgin," said Mary.

"Are you sure?"

"I think I would have noticed."

"Bugger. There has been an enormous cock up somewhere along the line."

"Who do you think that I am, then?"

ToriBlan ran her fingers through her hair and sighed. She rubbed her eyes and Mary realised for the first time how tired she looked. "I shouldn't tell you too much, given the circumstances. If you're not actually—"

"Not what?"

"Not the Virgin Mary number 134."

"I beg your pardon?" said Mary.

"We rotate through deities up here," she said, gesturing around. "Being in charge of all the faith systems of your planet is a very big job. There are a lot of religions, you know," she said, almost aggressively. "Your lot just can't pick one lane and stick with it, if you hadn't noticed."

Mary raised her hands in mock submission. "Don't look at me. I'm an atheist."

"Well, yes, that would make things much easier. Anyway, we have to keep every faith system alive and kicking, as you say, and so we find it's not fair to just saddle one god or saint or deity or whatever with the job. We like to share it around."

Mary racked her brains, dredging up some early childhood catholic memories. "So, let me get this straight. There are a bunch of . . . Virgin Marys?"

ToriBlan nodded. "And Thors and Allahs and Cerridwens and Dianas. The list goes on. We keep all the stories alive, you see. For when they come back into fashion."

"And I am supposed to be—"

"In theory, you're supposed to be Virgin Mary number 134 but from what I can tell, you're not her."

Mary felt a moment of disappointment.

"Could I give it a go?"

ToriBlan looked at her, scepticism clear on her face. "I don't think you understand. The woman who will be stepping into the role next has been chosen and cultivated her whole life. She has led a life of chastity; she is a true maiden. She is pure; barely of this world at all."

"Yeah that doesn't sound quite like me."

"See what I mean?"

"It seems a waste though, doesn't it? Now that I'm here and all? Now that you've gone to all the effort of putting me in the vectoral thingy and suspending time or whatever it was you did down there."

"We didn't suspend time," explained ToriBlan. "We just stepped out of it for a moment."

"Well, that then. It sounds like an effort, is my point. Maybe there's another role I could step into, one that has needed less . . . grooming? Some old goddess that no one even knows about anymore."

"But you just told me you were happy with your life."

"Before," said Mary. "That was before I found out about all of this! Do you think I can just go back to all of that now I know all *this*?"

"Hmmmm." ToriBlan thought for a moment. "That is a good point. We would have to wipe your memory and I still feel bad about the last person I tried that on. Took the last five years of their Earth life as well. I got an official caution about that one." She stood up. "All right, what are your interests? What kind of things are you into? Because whatever we choose, you'd have to do a lot of it."

"Well, I'm an artist. I paint and I'm a sculptor."

ToriBlan walked over to a desk and flicked through a file. "How about Saraswati? She's the Hindu goddess of art and wisdom and she's due to be replaced in" —she looked forwards through the papers for a moment— "just a few months. How about that one?"

Mary frowned "I don't know about that one. I'm not Hindu. Or Indian."

"So?"

"Cultural appropriation," replied Mary in hushed tones. "That kind of thing just isn't ok."

The woman rolled her eyes. "All right, then what is your cultural heritage?"

She thought for a moment. "Dads dads dad was Scandinavian of some sort. Any Norse gods going begging at the moment?"

Another check of the file. "Well there's Bragi. He's a male, but it *is* the year twenty-twenty, we don't want to be constrained by the gender ideology of the past, do we? And he's more of a poet, to be fair, but I'm sure you could throw some painting in there somewhere."

Mary clapped her hands in agreement. "Yes! Let's try that one! It's ok if I rewrite things a bit, isn't it?"

ToriBlan made a face as she looked at the file. "Shit. There's been no one doing this for two hundred years. That's a bit of a bloody oversight."

"Has anyone noticed?"

"Not the point." ToriBlan closed the file with a snap. "But no, as a matter of fact. So, as it turns out I'd be very grateful if you'd take on this role. When can you start?"

Mary stood up and smoothed down her dress. "No time like the present!"

"Fantastic!" ToriBlan gestured to some people who were huddling around a touch screen at the other end of the room. "These gentlemen will show you to your offices and get you set up with everything you need. You don't need anything from down on Earth, do you? Because we could organise it, but it would be tricky—"

Mary shrugged. "No. Might as well start fresh. I can do art all day, did you say?"

"That's right. Art, answering anyone who prays to you, but to be honest I'd say prayers to you would be fairly thin on the ground these days, and just occupying that specific vector in the rich pantheon of the human race's tapestry of gods, goddesses, deities."

As she left the room and stepped out into the multitude of realities that stretched out before her, Mary decided that this was a better option than applying for endless grants as a struggling artist.

Although she did wonder what had become of the woman who was supposed to take the place of the Virgin Mary.

About the Author:

Eva Leppard lives in lutruwita (Tasmania) with an elegantly sufficient amount of children and a disturbingly large number of rescue animals, all of which she raised by hand whether they liked it or not.

She writes fantasy and occasionally science fiction (usually by accident), and her debut novel 'The Pitfalls of Being a Goddess' will be published by Between the Lines Publishing in late 2022.

For updates, head to https://justevastories.com/.

MAIDEN VOYAGE

Maddie Jensen

The Lifeboats were the last hope of a dying planet. Earth was a scarred mess of waste and toxic emissions. It had been declared that the planet had a scant twenty more years before it became uninhabitable. The air was poisoned with toxic emissions. People were getting sick and dying by the thousands. A mutated virus had wiped out billions a decade before the Lifeboats had begun departing.

Astrea was the final Lifeboat, one of twelve. When the first of the Lifeboats had left, Earth's population became desperate, determined to save the planet they had destroyed. Yet it was far too late, the Lifeboats were the option for the survival of humanity. Each lifeboat only had room for a fraction of Earth's population. When the news spread, the riots lasted for weeks. Billions would be left on Earth, stranded and left to whatever fate their unforgiving planet dealt them.

The year was 2122, and it was mere days before *Astrea* left Earth for their destination. The new planet was called Beauterra, and although none of the Lifeboats had reached it yet, the images and scans from the probes showed just how beautiful it was. It would take over three hundred years for the generation ships to reach their new home.

Perhaps that was why Captain Stella Haynes felt such intense anxiety settling in, a heavy weight upon her chest that refused to shift. She had called Earth home for 28 years, and now she would be leaving it, never to set foot on soil again. It was a terrifying thought, especially as she had no idea what awaited her.

Stella and her crew were the first of three teams that would rotate throughout the ship's journey to its new home. The other two teams had already gone into cryosleep until it was their time to wake.

She would spend the remainder of her days in space, whether it be awake or in cryo. She would die in space, long before *Astrea* ever reached Beauterra. She believed in their mission, and yet . . . she couldn't help the doubts in the dark corners of her mind.

"Check." Leilani Mahoe, *Astrea*'s mechanics and engineering specialist, smirked as she moved her queen into position. On the other side of the chess board, pilot and navigator Arlo Hernandez raked a hand through his hair as his dark eyes swept over the pieces, searching for a way out.

"Ah, shit."

"You've gone real quiet, Cap." Cain Burgess, the ship's medical specialist, observed Stella as she sat in front of the controls. Boarding would commence today, and *Astrea* would depart hours after. It was settling in and beginning to feel real. The crew had already said their goodbyes—they were required to

292

be on board the Lifeboat for final preparations just before launch. To ensure a smooth transition to space with minimal complications, the launch was pre-programmed—not even Stella could override it.

"Just thinking."

"It'll be fine, kid." Jude O'Reilly strode past, ruffling Stella's auburn hair on his way over to Leilani and Arlo. He was their physics and astronomy specialist, and the oldest of the crew at forty-two. Stella sometimes wondered how many of them resented her for being the captain, despite being the youngest.

Stella's father was a billionaire, one of the main innovators and sponsors of the Lifeboat Project. He had gained passage due to his contribution, and Stella was uncomfortable with the fact that despite her intensive training, it was how she had gained the rank of captain at such a young age. There was no doubt it had crossed the minds of her crew before, but they'd had the tact to never mention it.

Eloise Petrova, biologist and botanist, looked up and gave Stella an encouraging smile. She was hunched over another table, playing a quiet game of cards with Warren Rowe, technician and communications officer. That was part of the problem—the boredom. Leading up to the launch, there was little for the crew to do aside from completing their routine checks on *Astrea*.

Lights flashed through the spacious cockpit, and an alarm blared throughout the ship. Everyone was on their feet and at attention. It could just be some kind of drill—or it could be something more sinister.

"*Astrea*, status report," Stella commanded. "Warning: ship malfunction." The ship's deep voice rumbled through the speakers. "If the malfunction is not fixed, *Astrea* will not be ready for pre-scheduled launch."

"What malfunction?" Arlo frowned.

"Gardens in the biology department failing," *Astrea* responded in that same calm tone. "Recommend doing a system check."

All eyes turned on Eloise, who was responsible for the ship's self-sustaining garden, essential for the survival of the crew and passengers during the three hundred-year trip. Over the years in space and with Eloise's care, many of the plants would flourish and create natural oxygen levels throughout the ship. With a problem in the botany department, the garden was put at risk.

Eloise's eyes were wide. "Failing? What does that even mean?"

"Why don't we go check?" Leilani suggested, before accusations started flying.

Stella was relieved at her intervention and nodded. "Yes, that's a good idea."

The crew marched out of the cockpit and through the pristine corridors toward the oxygen garden. None of them spoke, an indication of the situation's severity. The crew had trained together for months, they were family. The silence said more than words ever could.

"Well, everything looks fine," Eloise murmured as they stepped into the ship's vast oxygen garden. It pained Stella to look at the trees. The last of Earth's healthy forests would disappear long with Astrea. The lush forest filled her with awe, though today she panicked that all could be lost.

Eloise prowled through the rows of plants and trees, searching for the root of the problem.

"I'll need to look into this further," she said, approaching one of the botany department monitor systems. She tapped at the screen and her frown deepened. "The system's completely offline. But . . . that makes no sense."

"*Astrea*, turn on the biology department system," Stella called.

"Negative," the ship responded, but gave no further explanation for why.

Eloise kneeled to check the wiring to the monitor systems.

As far as Stella could tell, everything appeared to be fine. So why was the system offline? She raked her fingers through her hair, frustration bordering on panic. "Turn system online."

"Negative. System malfunction."

Without the oxygen system online, they were only functioning on the reserves. Once what was in the tanks ran out, the garden would die and so would everyone on board the ship. This was more than a minor malfunction. This was life-threatening.

Taking a deep breath, she tried again. "Explain, *Astrea*."

"System malfunction," the ship repeated, which did nothing but grate on Stella's nerves. Her attention turned upon Eloise, who was the one responsible for the ship's biology functions. She didn't want to believe that a member of her crew could have done this . . . but something had happened. They'd triple-checked the systems when they'd first come aboard. What could have happened since?

Eloise's expression was grim. "I think we need to have an emergency crew meeting."

"It's an outsider job." Jude leaned across the table. "We all know people were pissed about the lotto, about the entire Lifeboat Project. So someone sneaks aboard the ship and disables the system."

"Oh, come on." Leilani pulled a face at the conspiracy theories.

Stella had to admit that Jude had a point—with the final Lifeboat about to leave Earth, there had been chaos. Riots in the streets, shops being looted, buildings destroyed. The lotto's were the system that worked out, but even then people still claimed that it was rigged. There wasn't a quick fix that appeased everyone. It made sense that those left on a dying planet might want to take it out on those who had the chance to leave.

"What?" Jude leaned back, fingers turning his crucifix necklace over and over. "You don't think that one of us would do it, do you?"

Leilani didn't answer, but Warren did, his voice soft and thoughtful.

"Whoever caused the sabotage had inside knowledge of the ship. They picked on something that would take a long time to fix. Something that would be difficult to get done on a limited timeframe. You really want to blame an anti-Lifeboat group for that?"

An uncomfortable silence crept over them. Eloise wrapped her arms around herself, remaining silent. She looked self-conscious about the event, as she was responsible for the department that had failed. Had Eloise sabotaged the system? She hadn't said anything to defend herself, or anything at all for that matter.

"It has to be a member of the crew," Warren pressed, twisting the knife in the stinging wound of everyone's suspicions.

"Come on, that's bullshit." Arlo shook his head, dark eyes narrowing. "None of us would do that. Not with so much at stake."

"Are you willing to bet our lives on that?" Warren asked.

Shivers ran up Stella's spine. She wasn't going to be risking anyone's lives, especially not that of her crew. The idea that someone could be sitting here, knowing that they'd sabotaged the ship and unwilling to speak up . . . it was a dangerous thought. It was like a ticking time bomb waiting to go off. What would that person do, Stella wondered, when their sabotage was exposed?

"It isn't a department fault," Eloise piped up, finding her voice at last. She wrapped her arms even more around herself when she drew everyone's focus. "If it was, I would be able to fix it from the computers there. A system error indicates this is a bigger issue."

"Look, if it's not a fault within the biology department, then it has to be an engineering or mechanical override," Cain interjected. He didn't look at anyone in particular, but there was no doubt where his finger was pointing.

"Seriously?" Leilani scowled at everyone's curious eyes now on her. She pushed herself to her feet. "Alright. If you all seem to think I've done something, I'll go check on the engine room now. Does anyone want to accompany me so I don't fuck anything up on my way down?"

"Leilani . . ." Stella pinched the bridge of her nose at the volatility in Leilani's tone. She felt exhausted, as though she hadn't slept in days. "No one is accusing you of anything. Right now, we're just trying to pinpoint the problem."

Leilani didn't respond, marching out of the room without a backwards glance. They could hear her boots stomping down the corridors as she departed. Stella exhaled, knowing that there was a lot of tension amongst the crew.

"What are we going to do?" Arlo asked, leaning forward in his chair to examine the captain.

"Commence boarding of the lower decks." Stella's shoulders were stiff. "We can't let panic run rife among the passengers. We need to proceed on schedule."

Keeping everything on schedule was what mattered. If they caused unrest among the passengers, *Astrea* would be lost. They had to pretend as though everything was alright. They had enough issues without a potential riot from boarding passengers.

Arlo nodded and began tapping away into the ship's main computer to alert the boarding department to proceed. An uneasy silence descended among the crew. Everyone was suspicious, and the trust that they'd built over their months of training was fraying.

After a few minutes, Leilani returned, a grim expression on her face. Whatever she had discovered in the engine room hadn't been good.

"Leilani?" Stella prompted as the dark-haired engineer swung herself into a chair.

"I couldn't get into the control hub." Leilani folded her arms over her chest. "My access has been revoked."

An uncomfortable silence filled the bridge as they took in Leilani's words. This would mean it couldn't be an outsider job—only another crew member would be able to retract her access. Stella's eyes roved over the others, wondering who the culprit had been. Someone here was lying. Someone here didn't want *Astrea* to leave Earth.

"I'm not flying the ship if we've got a saboteur on board." Arlo shook his head, dark eyes wide with trepidation as his chair swivelled back around so he could face the others. "There are so many things that could go wrong."

"We'll have it fixed, Arlo," Eloise tried to assure him.

"I've got a mum and a sister back down there." Arlo jabbed a finger downwards. His eyes shone and a single tear slipped down his cheek before he wiped it away. "I signed up for this because I thought it would be worth something. If we aren't going anywhere, what's the point? Everything I worked for would be for nothing."

His eyes were wild and his chest heaved with ragged breaths. It looked as though he was hyperventilating. Eloise rested a comforting hand on his shoulder, but Arlo tore away from her, shaking. Stella didn't think she had ever seen him so freaked out. Arlo was always the cool, calm one. He was always there with a ready smile and a crude joke.

"Arlo." Stella raised her hand. "Go to the med bay. Cain, get him something to calm him down, please."

Cain nodded and eased himself up. Arlo followed, his steps slow and uncertain. He was on the verge of panicking, and Stella couldn't afford to let that kind of mindset infect the crew like a disease. Everyone was already tense enough as it was. They didn't need to think about what they were leaving behind, who was still on the ground.

"I don't want to cause alarm," Jude said, clasping his hands together, "But perhaps we've found the person responsible for our current dilemma."

"He's just scared," Stella said, shaking her head. "I don't think Arlo would have sabotaged the mission."

"I agree with Jude." Warren raked a hand through his hair. "I like Arlo. I think he's a great guy. But he's afraid, and sometimes scared people are the ones who do dangerous things."

Stella didn't want to think Arlo could be responsible for something of this nature. She didn't want to believe that whatever had happened to *Astrea* was fuelled by fear. She said nothing, unwilling to condemn Arlo but afraid she could be wrong if she continued to defend him.

Warren headed over to the mainframe computer and started tinkering away. Stella didn't stop him—he was good at his job, and he'd managed to fix all the minor technical glitches they'd experienced so far. This sabotage might be a larger issue, but she believed in his abilities. She believed in everyone's abilities. She just wasn't certain that she trusted their intentions anymore. They didn't have long now until the countdown reached zero, and then the *Astrea* would launch itself to the stars.

"I've managed to restore access to the control hub." Warren declared after about two hours of hard work. The crew had been in various states of unease. Leilani was playing chess with Eloise, a stark contrast to her enthusiastic game with Arlo only a few hours before. How could so much change in such a short space of time? They'd been friends, comrades. Now what were they all?

Stella glanced at Leilani, whose fingers were clasped around her rook. "Alright. Time to fix this."

"I'll come," Eloise offered, which Stella found odd. Why was she insistent upon accompanying Leilani, when the issue wasn't something Eloise could fix? Stella couldn't help but wonder, in a deep dark part of her, whether Eloise intended to confront Leilani alone. Could she be responsible for what had happened after all?

"I think there's only one person who could revoke access at that level." Leilani's voice was soft, but the implications were clear when she turned her accusatory gaze upon Stella. Her hands were balled into fists, and Stella went cold as the realisation of what Leilani was saying dawned on her.

"Are you kidding me?" Stella demanded, planting her hands on her hips. "Why would I do that?"

"Why would anyone?" Leilani shrugged her shoulders, but her eyes were fierce. "Like I said, you're the only one who has the clearance to do that."

Stella's temper burned like fire through her veins. She couldn't afford to lose control. She couldn't yell at Leilani and tell her that she was wrong, no matter how much she wanted to. The more Stella lost her calm, the more the others might believe Leilani.

"Just go fix the fucking problem," Stella snapped, refusing to have an argument on the matter.

Leilani's eyes narrowed, but she was a woman of duty, and she marched away with Eloise in tow.

Stella's mind was whirring with possibilities. She couldn't let this ship leave the ground without figuring out who was responsible for the sabotage, but neither could she cause panic by delaying take-off. Leilani would be able to fix the problem—though that was no longer the issue that concerned Stella.

When she looked around the bridge, Jude was sitting at one of the tables in the corner with a bottle of honey-coloured whisky and a clear glass half-full of it. He wasn't one to drink on the job, but she wasn't about to pass judgement. Right now, everyone was stressed. If alcohol was how Jude chose to cope, that was his business. It didn't stop her commenting.

"You're drinking now?" Stella raised her eyebrows.

Jude's smile was grim. "Just one to ease the nerves."

Stella slipped into the seat across from him.

Jude offered her the glass, and she took a tentative sip. The whisky burned down her throat like liquid fire. She grimaced, unable to say she liked the taste. She didn't think Jude was drinking it because he thought it tasted good, though.

"Who are you leaving behind?" Stella asked. She'd seen the background checks for the rest of the crew, just as they'd seen hers. Utter transparency—until now, when one of them was hiding a dark secret.

Jude shrugged his shoulders, running a finger around the rim of the glass. "Wife. Kids. My parents, but they're getting old now."

A wave of sympathy cut through Stella for him, despite his matter-of-fact tone. He betrayed no emotion. Either he was good at acting, or he'd detached himself from the idea that he'd have to leave his family behind on Earth. Nonetheless, Jude was not without flaws. He had been one of the first to point fingers when things had gone.

"You've been quick to blame people," Stella said.

He looked up and realised what she was saying. His smile was rueful and sad, as if he was disappointed that she would think to blame him.

"Come on, Captain. What do I know about locking people's access?" Jude shook his head, taking another sip of whiskey.

What do I know about locking people's access? The words caught Stella off-guard. It was true that she was the only one with the clearance to lock people's access. However, another person was on board with the ability to do it, and she couldn't believe she hadn't put the pieces of the puzzle together sooner.

"Where's Warren?" She asked, looking around the bridge to find he was no longer there. When Jude looked at her, brows furrowed, she repeated the question with more urgency. "Where's Warren?!"

"Stella!" Leilani's voice, laced with alarm, crackled through her comm. "I need help."

"Leilani?" Stella fumbled with the comm as she responded. "What's happened?"

"It's Warren." She was crying. Stella's stomach lurched. "It's him, Stella. He's insane. He killed Eloise and I got away from him. I can't go back there. He stabbed me, and . . ."

"Leilani, get to the bridge now. That's an order."

Jude's eyes widened with alarm. He put down his glass and got to his feet. "Should I go and find her?"

"No." Stella shook her head. "If Warren is resorting to attacking people, I want everyone here."

Stella's hands were shaking, her legs trembling as terror rose within her. Whatever she had anticipated, it hadn't been something quite so terrible.

Leilani stumbled in, her hands pressed over her stomach. Eloise's absence was noted. There were tears streaming down Leilani's cheeks, and her fingers were stained red.

Cain launched to his feet and rushed over to her, supporting her as she gripped his arm to keep herself standing upright.

Leilani had gashes across her torso, but nothing that appeared fatal. Nonetheless, there was no way she would be able to fix the malfunction in her condition.

"Cain, get her to medical." Stella raked her fingers through her hair. "Fix her up. Seal yourselves in if you have to."

"Someone needs to fix it." Leilani tried to brush off Cain's arm. "It has to be done."

"I know." Stella took a deep breath. "I'm going to do it."

There was a moment of tense silence as they all realised what that could mean. None of them knew where Warren was. Stella was putting herself at risk to fix the malfunction. There was a loud beeping throughout the bridge, and Stella looked up to see that the countdown was complete. Nausea roiled in her stomach, but she ignored it, forcing herself to focus. Boarding was complete, and it was time to finish what they started.

"Arlo, begin the launch."

"But, Captain . . ."

She fixed him with a firm look, and Arlo knew better than to argue.

He busied himself at the controls as Stella examined the remainder of the crew, wondering if this would be the last time she saw them.

"Once the ship takes off, we are going to need a new technician and a new biologist." She paused, letting the truth sink in. "Maybe even a new captain. There should be those among the civilians with qualifications that fit the bill."

"Stella . . ." Jude murmured, hurt flashing through his eyes at the idea that she might not make it back from this.

She ignored him, turning to face Leilani. "Tell me what I have to do to complete the manual override and get the systems online."

Stella didn't mention to the crew that she had taken the biggest knife from the kitchen when she headed to the control hub. She didn't want any of them to think she intended to kill Warren—but what else was she supposed to do? She didn't want blood on her hands, though she might have no choice.

Outside the control hub, Stella found what she had been dreading, and pressed a hand over her mouth to stifle a scream. Eloise's blue eyes stared upwards, and there was a blood-red gash carved like a gory smile across her throat. Stella had known Warren murdered Eloise, but it was different to see it for herself.

Stella found it hard to breathe. She kneeled down to close Eloise's eyes, her entire body trembling as panic overwhelmed her. If Warren had managed to ambush the two women, what chance did she have? Taking several deep inhalations to fight off an impending panic attack, she gripped the knife and pushed herself to her feet, entering in the code to access the control hub.

Once inside, Stella followed Leilani's instructions. She didn't rush despite the fact that she was terrified. If she did this wrong, she may as well not have done it at all. When she input the final sequence, the door hissed open and Warren walked in. Stella lurched away from the controls.

"Stella." Warren's eyes were wild, his face stained with blood that wasn't his. "I didn't think it would be you."

"Were you hoping you could finish Leilani off?" Stella's eyes narrowed. The knife was hidden up her sleeve. It pricked her skin, reminding her of its presence. "It's over, Warren. I don't know why you sabotaged the mission, but . . ."

"How do we choose who lives and who dies?" Warren demanded, his voice hoarse and a terrible rawness to his words. "Why are we playing god?"

"We aren't, Warren." Stella's voice shook. If only Warren had expressed his doubts sooner, then this could have ended in something other than violence and death. "We're working with the hand we've been dealt. There was a lotto. It was fair."

"No." Warren's eyes glimmered with unshed tears. "There are billions of people we're leaving on a dying planet. There is *nothing* fair about it."

"So you try and ruin the mission?" Stella asked, her voice breaking. "You killed Eloise. You tried to kill Leilani."

"I didn't want to." Regret flashed across his face. "I didn't want to hurt anyone, but I knew they would find out what I'd done. I thought stopping them would buy me time."

"Where could you go?" Stella walked toward him, one steady foot in front of the other. "There's nowhere to run from what you've done, Warren."

"I know." Warren swallowed hard. "I'm so sorry. I know you won't believe me, but I am."

He lunged at her, but Stella had been anticipating it, waiting for the moment that he would attack. She drove the knife forward, and at the awful sound it made as it pushed into Warren's flesh. Tears blurred her vision, but Stella withdrew the knife and stabbed him again. Once, twice, three times. She had to make sure. She couldn't make the same mistakes that Eloise and Leilani had. Warren couldn't live.

Warren stared down at the crimson stain slowly spreading across his uniform. His eyes were wide and horrified. He hadn't expected her to be here, and he definitely hadn't expected her to kill him. It was Stella's moment of hesitation, born of guilt for what she had done, that turned the tables.

Warren grabbed the blood slick knife from Stella's hand and stabbed her in the chest. It was only once, but it was enough. Stella screamed as pain burned through her, staggering back with the knife still in her. She knew what removing it would do—and she had a job to finish. Stumbling over to the controls, her trembling fingers finished the job she had started.

She thought Warren would have wrenched her away or tried to stop her. But stabbing Stella had been his last act—when she whirled around to face her enemy, he was lying on his side, blood dripping down from his multiple stab wounds. His breathing was shallow and his eyes were closed.

Stella collapsed, and the world shuddered around her. *Astrea* was taking off. A faint smile crossed her lips. The agony had stopped and in its place, there was a blissful numbness. As the life bled from her, Stella felt nothing but joy.

We're going to the stars.

About the Author:

Maddie Jensen lives west of Sydney on Dharug land. She is the author of 'Blood of Queens' *and* 'Heir of Kings', *the first two books in the Legacy of the Lost trilogy. She has been reading and writing from a very young age, and is particularly invested in complex characters, healthy relationships, and well-written female protagonists.*

LIBRA

SEPTEBER 23 - OCTOBER 22

THE SECRETS SHE EATS

Nikky Lee

Not all secrets are given willingly. Sometimes I have to hunt them from street to street, town to town. They run, scramble, try to weasel their way out of my grip, slippery things that they are. Often they beg, sometimes they cry. And sometimes, once they're cornered and at a dead end, they simply stand there, resigned and waiting for my final reckoning.

I blow into town like a tumbleweed on the wind. A woman in black, cloaked and hooded. Knife in my belt, pistol on my hip and boots crusted with mud. The villagers don't see my face, not straight away, but they are not fooled.

"Eater." The whisper announces my arrival, rushing ahead of me in undertones. Along the dusty main street it goes, passing through blacksmith and tailor's shops, into the saloon. In an hour it will have reached the plains; a day later, the plateau beyond.

They know what I am. And yet, there's something in my step that makes them turn; in the 'swish-click' of my boots that mesmerises. Something in my scent that draws the villagers in, like moths to a flame.

The first one staggers out of the saloon and finds me there in the street. There's distilled spirits on his breath and a pink flush on his dusty cheeks. He's young, pretty-like; soft brown curls grace his brow.

"I love Josie Fisher," he tells me.

The words roll over me like a sprinkling of sweet breadcrumbs. I lick them up, savouring each one. Barely a snack, but I'll take it. I nod and he turns away, his shoulders relaxing, an ecstasy of relief on his face.

"I love Josie Fisher," he says again, walking away in a daze.

An innocent secret. A smile twitches my lips. They're not particularly filling, but they are sweet. A footstep crunches at my back and I turn. An older woman is there, a hessian bag of groceries abandoned in the dirt. She trembles as she approaches. Her blue eyes dart to my hood, then away again, even as her mouth opens, revealing yellowed teeth. "I stole my husband's best horse to buy milk of the poppy," she murmurs.

Ah, a secret with a little more meat. The weight of it eases into my belly, a tasty morsel. But there's more, I can smell it as sure as I smell the horse shit swept into the gutters. I peel back my hood and the woman's eyes lock with mine. She quivers like a marmot caught in the glare of a snake.

"And?" I prompt.

She hugs her arms about herself. "I told him vagabonds did it. He went out searching for them and came back with fever. It's bad this year, you know? Real bad. Young Sally it took. And the Miller's wife."

Her words are like tiny steaks on my tongue. Juicy. Succulent. I breathe them in, relishing their taste. I nod again and a gasp whistles out of her. She sinks to her knees and releases a sob: her burden suddenly dissolved. I step away and she frowns as she finds herself slumped in the middle of the street. She picks herself up. With deft strokes, she beats the dust out of her skirts, picks up her shopping and walks off.

Perhaps now she'll have the courage to make it right. If not, well, I'll get another meal later.

I set up shop in the saloon. Soon they come, sweet and tender alike. They can't help themselves. A line forms out the door. Clearly it's been many a year since one of us has come through these parts. One by one, they sit down at my table and lean in to whisper their guilt.

"I stole a drunkard's shoes last winter." This from a girl in a woollen sweater patched over and over at the elbows.

"I put salt on May Cole's cake at last year's cake competition," a busty woman admits, wringing her gloves.

A sheepish grin from a grey-haired man. "I have a mistress. Every Thursday." That one barely touches the sides as it goes down. He'll come back later for sure.

"I wagered my father's fortune in cards and lost." From a gaunt young man in a fine cloak and polished shoes.

"I hate my children."

"When customers piss me off, I spit in their soup."

"I fucked a cow once." That one made me blink twice.

On and on. Bit by bit, their secrets fill me. Albeit briefly. When the afternoon shadows lengthen, Vander the barkeep lights the hearth and a slow heat creeps into the emptying saloon. The line waiting on me thins and clears with the coming of night. Fear of the dark overrides their instinct to spill their burdens. I curse under my breath. My mouth craves that big something I'd followed into town. Big and thick and heavy. Like wild bison roasting on a spit. It's here somewhere. I know it. Something I could sink my teeth into one hundred times over.

A throat clears next to me. My gaze swings back to the thin, dark haired man—a boy really—sat in the opposite chair, waiting. I'd scarcely noticed him.

"Yes, yes," I say absently, and reach for my drink. Alcohol doesn't sate me the way a good secret might, but it dampens the craving. Then I get a whiff of him; of his secret. I freeze, scenting the air between us. Not quite the same *big* I'd been hunting, but there's a kinship there. Something . . . important.

The boy shifts uncomfortably in the seat, straightens his too-big, probably hand-me-down, vest. His nails are bitten to the quick.

"I'm listening," I say.

"I, um . . ." His fingers twist and writhe, nimble-like, a tailor's apprentice perhaps or a jeweller's. They clench together as he clears his throat. "I saw something the other night." A gulp. "Something strange."

The magic rises in my belly, but I hold it at bay. The boy is twitchy, like a rabbit ready to duck back into his burrow if I push him too hard. This is a secret that needs teasing out. I sip my drink, trying not to let my interest show too much. "Go on."

"I was coming home late two nights ago," he begins. "Closed up shop like Mr. Cole asked and cut across Roper's field. I know I shouldn't but it was late, you know, and Da was waiting at home; he gets anxious when I'm out past tea. Roper's field is just grazing for his horses, and they're all trained gentle-like, wouldn't kick a gnat if it landed on them wrong, so I figured no harm done. I've taken that way plenty of times before."

He pauses as Vander arrives and places an ale on the table before him—and lingers. "Any dinner, ma'am?"

"No, thank you."

Vander is still for a long moment, before slowly turning for the kitchens. I sigh. I knew his type; clever like a vulture and ready to wring every coin he can.

The boy furrows his brow at the drink, then reaches for his pocket.

"It's on me," I say and wave my hand. "Continue."

"Well, two nights ago, I took the short cut, like always. But halfway through I heard a grinding sound," his lips purse, evidently trying to think of a way to describe it. "A pestle on mortar sound. Then cracking a few steps later, like sticks breaking. I froze, thinking it was perhaps a horse having a roll in the grass, or rubbing his back on a fence post, but then I saw sparks from a flint . . ." He shifts back in his seat as I lean in. Then realises what he's done and flushes.

"And?" I ask, unperturbed.

"I rushed at it. Think I even shouted, 'Hey, what're you doing?' Or maybe I thought it. Either way, lighting a fire in a grass field was asking for it to go up like a tinderbox. I wasn't raised a farmer, but even I know that." His eyes go distant, and he shivers, then takes a pull of his ale. "What I found, well; it was a fire, trapped in a stone circle, but the . . . *thing* next to it. I don't know what it was. But it wasn't human—I'm sure of that."

"What did it look like?"

The boy stares into his mug. "Ugly. Wrinkles all about the face." He traces a finger along his cheeks and jowls. "Snout for a nose. And small, squat. Like someone sat on it."

"And what did it say?" I ask.

The boy is silent for a long moment. "Nothing," he says at last into his ale. A deeper flush creeps up his throat and into his ears. "I screamed and ran away."

I nod, running a light finger over my empty glass. "Wise move," I muse, wishing he'd paid more attention to its appearance; I can name a hundred fey clans the creature might belong to. But a lead is a lead, and I yearn for something juicy. I stand. "Show me."

Aben, for I've learned that is his name, rests a hand on the fence paling. "In there," he says, pointing into the dark field. And it is truly dark, no kerosene lamps this part of town and there's little light beyond what our lantern provides—even to my eyes. Not that my eyes are much to brag about. I'm not fae-sighted like my father. I have my mother's eyes. Mortal eyes.

And a fae's hunger.

I set the oil lamp down on the post and listen. Grass stalks chitter in the breeze. The fence creaks ever so slight. I frown.

"What is it?" Aben asks.

"No insects."

"Tucked in for the night?" he suggests, the edge of a coy smile quirking his mouth. When I don't respond, he coughs and looks down at his shoes. They're well made, shiny iron buckles polished to a gleam. A shoemaker's apprentice then.

I sigh, set a foot on the bottom rung of the fence and swing a leg over.

Aben swings his leg over too.

"What are you doing?"

He stares at me dumbly, as if the answer is obvious. "Coming with you of course."

I snort. "No, you're not."

His eyebrows bunch. "I can't let a lady go out there on her own."

"Do I look like I need your protection?" I raise an eyebrow in return.

He considers me a moment there, straddled on the fence, gaze travelling to my calloused hands, the knife on my hip and the pistol holstered under my cloak. "No," he admits and shrinks into himself, looking more boyish than ever. "But I want to show people I'm not a coward. I can do more than run away."

The words hit me like a sucker punch. A memory rises up: my mother dabbing a rag on my torn lip and me, ten years old, saying *"I'm not a monster. I want to show them."*

"You will," my mother says in the same, tired tone of a parent listening to a conversation so old it's worn holes in its sleeves. *"Give them time."*

My fists clench. *"I want to show them now!"*

And mother's patient words, *"Give them time."*

Atop the fence, I roll my eyes. "Stay behind me."

Aben beams and scrambles over the pilings.

We creep through the field, lantern held high, dry grass scratching our legs. Halfway in, we stumble into a clearing where the grass is flattened—not trampled but carefully squashed down so that in another day or two it might spring back. A small stone circle lies in the middle, ashes cold.

"This was it," Aben says, there's an edge to his voice as he turns in a circle and squints into the dark. He stands so close his back brushes mine. The lantern in his hand quivers and the sphere of light around us wobbles.

"Relax," I tell him. Taking the lantern, I bend down to examine the ashes. "There's nothing here." I crunch a piece of charcoal in my hand and sniff. And there, underneath the smoke and soot birch, lavender and rosemary.

"Were you always a secret eater?" Aben asks from over my shoulder. His voice is stronger now, more confident.

"Always."

Aben's forehead rumples into a frown. "And you've been doing this all your life? Journeying from town to town, relieving people of their secrets." He pauses. "Why don't I feel your power pulling at me anymore?"

"What's to say you're not?" I dust my hands off, catch a glimpse of his face and laugh. As a rule, I don't pray on people's insecurities once they fess whatever is on their mind—that's a sure way to get run out of town, but his shock catches me off guard. "It doesn't work like that."

"It doesn't?"

"I can't force you to tell your secrets. Deep down you've got to be willing. If you have a secret you'd never tell anyone, I can't force it out of you." Those are the ones I hunt, when they have the right scent; rich and with full copper notes. I make a show of leaning close to him and taking a whiff. "You don't have the smell, you're all leather and pomegranates since I took your secret. At most, you'll have a slight inclination to tell the truth for a few days"—I cock a grin at him—"depending how headstrong you are. I've had married men fess their adultery then walk straight back into a brothel."

Aben doesn't answer, but his eyes follow me as I pick my way across the clearing, pausing at two rocks nestled in the flattened grass. Both are smooth, one wide and flat, the other round and about the same size as my head. Residue cakes one side of each. I run a finger down the head-sized rock, hold it to my nose. Lavender and rosemary. "You were right about the mortar and pestle," I say, wiping my hand on my cloak.

My companion squeaks a response. Actually squeaks, like his voice has been caught on a hook and yanked out of water. I turn to find him standing rigid, the tip of a rusted knife jutting up at his throat. At the other end of the knife is a squat figure wearing old children's clothes, patched and threadbare.

"What you want?" the creature hisses through a frog-like mouth and its perfectly round eyes narrow into slits. Hair hangs limp and straggled from its brow, like it has been out in the weather too long. Behind it, a mound of sticks and firewood lay scattered on the grass.

I hold my hands out for peace. "Easy, we mean no harm. What's your name, friend?"

"Dalziel."

"And what are you, a boggart?"

"Broonie," the fae spits. "No boggart here."

My gaze wanders those ragged clothes again, then to the rows of scars on the back of his exposed forearms. Layers upon layers of them, turning his skin to knots of puckered scar tissue. He might have been a broonie once, but not anymore. Bad luck or perhaps a bad contract has transformed him from household hearth spirit to homeless sprite. Either way, he's old fae, from across the sea. My nose twitches, catching a lingering whiff of a copper secret. As if he senses it too, Dalziel's knife presses under Aben's jaw, all he has to do is stab up.

"What are you?" Dalziel snarls. "You look human, but you don't smell like one."

I open my palms to him and slowly crouch so we're closer to eye level. "I am a secret eater."

"Pah, lies. Eaters aren't real. Just stories."

"I assure you we're not. Not on this continent, anyway."

"Eater," Aben's voice squeezes out. He makes eyes at me, casting a meaningful look at my pistol.

Dalziel's grip tightens on his knife.

"It's fine," I assure them both. "Aben, broonies like Dalziel are harmless fae. A few pranks, nothing sinister. Dalziel, Aben is a harmless human, he wants to be friends."

Dalziel's knife eases off Aben's jawline, but still hovers close to Aben's throat.

"He'll trade you his shoes, in a show of good faith," I add.

Dalziel's eyes light up. "Oh, why didn't you say sooner?" It's impossible to miss the excitement in Dalziel's voice. He kicks off his worn boots, all cracked leather and flapping soles, and holds them out to Aben.

Aben shoots me a glare. "I will not—"

I cut him off with a glare of my own, until he sighs and reaches for his polished shoes.

"No buckles," Dalziel says.

Aben frowns a beat, then, "Oh right, iron." Even out here, everyone knows fae can't abide it. He loosens the buckles off, puts them in his pocket, and reluctantly holds his shoes out.

The knife drops away, sheathing back into Dalziel's belt. "My thanks, friend Aben." The boggart drops to his bottom and pulls Aben's shoes on with obvious glee. His feet, I notice, are scarred too—thin white strikes across each arch. The shoes are too big, but Dalziel's up and strutting around in them like Aben has handed him gold clogs. Then he turns on Aben, blinking his round eyes expectantly.

"Put on his shoes," I whisper to Aben, motioning to the discarded items on the grass. "It'll seal your concord."

Aben's face twitches like he wants to object, but under Dalziel's watch he bends down and slides his feet into the old shoes. His toes poke through the holes at the tip like they're a pair of sandals.

"Wonderful! Our friendship is set." Dalziel claps his hands and admires his new feet again. "Very nice gift," he says. "A nice gift indeed. Our friendship will be grand!"

"How long do I have to wear these?" Aben murmurs to me.

"Until we leave his domain." I gesture to the field.

Aben sighs, resigned to his fate. "What about you? Don't you need to trade?"

"I'm getting to it." I raise my voice, catching Dalziel by the shoulder as he hops about. Again, that copper whiff. Very faint. But it's there. I focus my attention on him. It's harder to work my power on fae, but I can if the secret is strong enough. And with the right kind of probing. "Friend Dalziel, why are you out in this field burning lavender and rosemary?"

Dalziel's eyes turn glassy, his face relaxes. Tranced. I grimace: I've pushed too hard. I ease off, releasing my hand from his grubby coat and coaxing him to sit at the edge of the pit. Dalziel blinks, shakes himself and starts building a fire, a house for the flame from his sticks and wood.

"What's with the lavender and rosemary?" I ask again, motioning to the two stones and the fresh bundles of herbs waiting to be pulped.

"To ease the bones," Dalziel says simply, as if the answer is obvious.

Aben and I share a confused look. "Your bones?"

Dalziel snorts. "Dead bones." He thumps his chest. "Not these. These still have plenty of life left in them. The bones under here." He stomps one foot, indicating the earth below.

Copper fills my nostrils. I'm getting close. I lean in, eager. "There are bodies buried here?"

Aben's face drains of colour. "Bodies?" he squeaks and he crosses himself. Funny how humans get all squeamish about these things.

Dalziel busies himself with the fire, lighting it with a practised strike from a knife and flint. He's been out here a while it seems.

"How many bodies?" I ask.

Dalziel considers. "Many. Dozens. Maybe more."

Another wick up my nose. My magic prowls in, hungry. *Closer, closer.* I press him a tiny bit more. "Who puts them there?"

Dalziel stiffens, back turning rigid, his hands clamp tight around his flint stone. *He knows.* Gods and spirits sure. He knows. Dalziel's eyes find mine, bathwater grey and glistening in the firelight. "Don't make me say," he begs. The hand around the flint quivers, and what I'd mistook for tense caution reveals itself: blind fear. It's so strong I could poke out my tongue and lick it off the air.

"Please," I say. "It's important." I gesture to the field. "And don't they deserve justice?"

Dalziel stares after my finger, eyes glazing over.

Damn, I've pressed too close again. For a fae as susceptible as this, he must have human ancestry in him, like me. Maybe not half-half like me, but it's there. Inside my chest, something I thought tough and hardened squeezes. It's not easy straddling two worlds. You never fully step into one or the other, it's always a balancing act between the two.

"My apologies," I say and shuffle back, my stomach giving a disappointed gurgle.

Dalziel opens his mouth, tries to speak, fails, then works his lips as if trying to chew through a particularly tough bit of bread.

Aben eases down on Dalziel's other side. His face is still pale, but his gaze is tender. He pats the boggart's back. "We're here," he assures. "One word at a time."

"I . . . c-can't!" Dalziel manages, spittle flying, straining to get the words out. It takes all his willpower.

Understanding clicks. I curse under my breath. "He's been Compulsed."

Aben lifts his head, concern rippling across his brow. "He's been what?"

"Compulsed. A spell. Stops him talking to anyone about this. Nasty stuff." Before I can think, I am up and pacing. Nervous habit. I swear again and cast my sights nightward. I would have been perfectly happy with a simple serial killer, but no. "We're dealing with wicked magic." I glance at Dalziel. "Nod if I'm right."

He nods.

"Shit."

There goes my easy meal.

"Anyone can use wicked magic," I explain to Aben. "You just need the knowledge." *And a spell book.* But the less people who know that the better.

Around us, leathers and needlework of his shoemaker's shop line the walls. It was the easiest place for us to confer out the way of prying eyes. Next to Aben, Dalziel looks miserable. The lamplight shows his limp grey hair, owl eyes dim and cheeks sallow from exhaustion. That's what a secret like this does to a person—fae or man. In this we're all the same.

Aben grips Dalziel's forearm and gives it a reassuring shake. "We'll find a way to remove the Compulsion, I promise."

A tick of annoyance twitches in my jaw. He is right. I'll grant him that. No one deserves to live with a copper secret eating them up from the inside. But Aben makes his promise with the conviction of one who has never dealt with wicked magic before.

Dalziel swallows and nods. "My thanks, friend Aben."

We sink into a stony silence. "So many people," Aben murmurs. We'd questioned Dalziel best we could on the way to the shop, keeping to the backstreets. The total count before Dalziel managed a nod: thirteen.

And those are the ones he knows about, I think but don't say.

Aben rubs his eyes. "How did no one notice?"

To this, at least, I have an answer. "Easy. Disguise their deaths as something else. Who in town has died recently? And what did they die of?"

Aben falls still, his fingers pinching his chin as he considers. "Sally Barton, fever. Bobby Ruthford"—his eyes dart up to mine— "fever. Frederick Sawyers." He swallows. "Fever. Those were all in the last month."

My gut knots. "All unrelated? No contact? They weren't family or neighbours? Or lovers?"

Aben shakes his head. "Not that I know."

I curse. "Then it's not a normal fever."

"But I *went* to Bobby's funeral, he was buried in the church cemetery," Aben objects.

My eyebrow cocks. "And did you see the body?"

Aben pauses, then shakes his head, uncertainty dawning on his face. "It was a closed casket."

An empty casket more like. No need to say it, it's clear from the horror on Aben's face that it's occurred to him too.

"But why bury them in the field?" Aben asks.

"Hiding—" Dalziel manages before the compulsion cuts his words short and reduces him to a coughing fit.

"It's all right Dalziel, I know," I assure him, patting the boggart's arm. With a glance to Aben, I add, "They're snatching the bodies before anyone gets too good a look and hiding them in Roper's field." My mind darts back to the woman who'd given up her secret on the town road; who'd sold her husband's horse to buy milk of the poppy. What had she said? *He went out searching for his horse and came back with fever.*

Where, then, had he gone? And what had he seen that he shouldn't have? I come to my feet. "The woman with the poppy addiction, where does she live? I need to talk to her husband."

Aben scowls, his hands clenching into fists on the table. "There's more than one woman with poppy addiction here. In case you hadn't noticed." Curious. A sore point I hadn't expected.

I raise an eyebrow at him and he sighs.

"My brother got mixed up in the trade. Didn't end well. Swore I'd stay the hell away from it."

Dalziel places a hand on Aben's forearm and pats it gently. "Please friend, this is important," the broonie croaks out, skirting around the edge of his secret. I suck in a breath, scenting the air on my tongue. I'm on to something. When Dalziel glances up at me and gives the faintest of nods, I know I'm right.

Aben sees it too. He closes his eyes, takes a moment, then releases his fists. "Describe her."

I do, and his brow wrinkles. "Sounds like Macey Gruber."

"And her husband is ill?"

Aben nods.

"Take me there."

We find the grave in Macey Gruber's front garden. Its earth is freshly turned and stinks of copper, the scent lies on the mound thick as a snowdrift. My hunger stirs with a faint gurgle. *Soon,* I promise it. From inside the farmer's cottage, a woman wails.

"We're too late," Aben says.

"Not necessarily."

When we knock, a bloodshot, tear-streaked face greets us. She's barely coherent enough to talk, but she opens the door and starts making tea. I sigh and take the teapot away and sit her down at the table. Her clothes are dirty, gravel soil still stuck to them. Five miles from town and on her own, she'd had to do the deed herself. My heart twists, thinking of another grave far from here and the mother I'd buried in it. That hurt never truly leaves you. It fades into the background, scabs over and scars, but never goes away. Not completely.

"It's my fault," Macey Gruber says, staring at her hands. There's dirt under her ragged nails. She fidgets, anxious in her own skin.

I rest my hands on hers and flex my magic. "Where did he go when he went looking for his horse?"

Macey Gruber stills, her pupils dilating. I don't like using my power like this, smothering people with it. I can't force people to talk, but I can make their tongues loose; fill their heads with haze until the world turns so dream-like the secret just slips out.

Macey sways, her head rolls to one side. "All the way to the plateau." She closes her eyes and relaxes into my magic like it's a warm bath. "That feels nice."

"Up to the fae kingdom?" Aben whispers. "I knew it! They did something—ow!"

Dalziel stamps on his foot. "Fae don't work wicked magic!" Dalziel protests, and he wants to say more, but the Compulsion chokes the words in his throat. He works his jaw for a moment, a vein pops in his head, cheeks flushing with anger, then gives up with a "humph!"

"It's outlawed," I explain to Aben. "Work wicked magic and you're cast out. Magic sealed. No longer fae. Few dare risk it. Is that what we're looking for Dalziel? An outcast?"

Dalziel shakes his head.

"Human then." At this, a copper scent curls off my words, strong and delicious. I'm closing in. I take Macey's hands again, give her a little shake.

Her eyelids flutter open. "Let me sleep," she groans. "It's all my fault. Let me sleep forever."

"Why is it your fault, Macey?"

A long pause and her red eyes, too red to be just from crying, study my face. "I sold his horse. His favourite." The smell of the old secret fills my nose like stale bread. Dry and ordinary. I've not asked the right question. "Who did you sell it to?"

"Vander."

The name drops into my belly like a bite of marinated pork. Full bodied flavour rolls over my tongue. Copper fills my nose. I breathe it in, chest swelling, my mind revelling in it. It's *here*. The trail's *here*.

"Vander, the *barkeep*?" Aben interrupts, incredulous. "What would he want with a farm hor—" but I hold up a hand for quiet.

"Why Vander? Why did you go to him?"

Macey swallows, on the edge of spilling it all. "Because he has the poppy," she whispers. "He runs it all."

Got you.

Copper hooks my nose, pulling my head around. A trail flares to life in my mind's eye, burning a path to my quarry like a line of gunpowder. It points straight back to town.

Dalziel grunts. Aben and I glance over to find him twitching on the floor, nodding furiously between his spasms. Once Dalziel sees we've noticed, he slumps, utterly spent. Aben hurries over, sits him up.

"Easy. Breathe," he says.

"Water," Dalziel croaks. "Please, friend Aben." Aben fetches a cup and the cold kettle from Macey's stove and Dalziel gulps it down.

"Stay here," I tell them, striding for the door. My trail beckons.

Aben's hand closes around my elbow. "I'm coming."

For a heartbeat I consider telling him no, that it's dangerous. Human my quarry might be, but he's got wicked magic at his disposal, and I can't protect Aben from it.

"Please."

His request turns to a bitter taste in my mouth. Not quite a secret—at least not the kind I like. It mingles with the copper, defiling it with its guilt. A secret blame then. That he'd turned his back when he should have helped. Of all times to grow a conscience. My gaze roves the room as I try to find the right words to explain why coming with me is a bad idea, the worst idea actually. My eyes light on the corner of a small envelope poking out of the pocket in Macey's dress. When I bend down to pull it loose, her hand catches my sleeve.

"Stay," she begs, rousing from her dream-state. In hindsight, working my magic on a poppy addict might not have been such a wise play. "Don't go." She claws at my clothes.

I detach her fingers one by one and slip the envelope into the fire at the hearth. It goes up in a heady whiff of burned poppy powder. "I have to," I tell her. The trail calls. But I don't like the idea of leaving her here alone. She needs more help than I can give.

Dalziel stands up with a grimace and dusts off his coat. "I will look after her," he says.

Aben cast me a doubtful look. "I thought you said he was a prankster."

"Broonies are not pranksters," Dalziel huffs. "We help." He pauses and the flicker of a grin crosses his wide mouth. "If the trade is right."

I study the squat fae. Maybe I read him wrong, perhaps there was more of the broonie left in him that I'd thought. After all, he'd been trying to appease the dead in Roper's field. If I gave him this chance, might he return to the fireside spirit he'd once been?

I crouch before him so we're eye level. "You would do this for me?"

Dalziel nodded, then held up one finger. "On one condition."

"Here we go," Aben muttered, attention dropping to his second-hand shoes. He'd not had a chance to change them.

"Name it."

Dalziel motioned me close, "Stop the bastard." His eyes snare me with their intensity and there's something pleading in them. Something he cannot say. *"Please."*

"I suppose it makes sense," Aben says through a yawn as we watch the saloon from across the street, waiting for the last of its patrons to stagger out. Our alley stinks of horse shit, cat piss and garbage, but it's the best we've got. Now that I've found the trail, the scent of copper hangs over the place, thick as soup. Coats the saloon like sticky paint. In my pockets, my fingers itch something chronic, begging for release.

"All those shipments from the coast. I thought it was just ale," Aben says. He rubs his face and slaps his cheeks to keep himself awake. "He has them bring it right up Main Street, you know. I can't count the number of times I've seen a cart full of kegs and the like parked out front with men unloading it—all of it in broad daylight! I never thought to question. No one has."

"No one alive," I correct him. If I had to guess, more than one corpse in Roper's field was there simply because they'd gotten too curious. A bit of wicked magic and they fell sick and died. Then whisk the body away and bribe the undertaker to keep the funeral casket shut. Job done.

Only it wasn't that simple. Wicked magic *always* had a cost.

My hands curl into fists as I think of Dalziel. Compelled to aid a murderer and not tell a soul. I can imagine how it happened. A contract of servitude to a smuggler in exchange for conveyance across the sea. Ten years, maybe twenty; a small price for a long-lived fae. Worth the risk for new life on a new continent, far away from the feuding and bloodshed of the old world. Only, his contract had been sold on to the likes of Vander once the ship arrived at port. It's a sad and all too common story.

At last, the final patron sways out the double doors and the lamp-lit windows turn dark. I glance at the moon; three, perhaps four o'clock in the morning.

I flex my fingers, feeling the prick of claws under my nails. Time to move, before this secret has a chance to escape.

We slink out from the alleyway. The moon's out and high, casting long drifts of shadow across the street. Aben follows doggedly behind. I'd tried to talk him out of coming, but he wouldn't hear of it. And from the stubborn set of his jaw, I'd known better than to argue, else he follow and give the hunt away. No, best he see this through to its end where I can keep an eye on him. With any luck, I won't give him nightmares.

Across the street and into the saloon. Aben catches the double doors so they don't swing behind us.

And there he is.

Waiting. The cold barrel of a '76 Winchester pointed our way.

"You picked the wrong night to be nosey, Eater."

Like I said. Some secrets beg. Some cry. Some do nothing at all. And some, when cornered with no way to run, turn around and bite.

Vander levels the shotgun at us.

The world sinks into fragments of time. A slick, copper-laden breath filling my lungs. I dive for Aben; pushing him to the floor.

Vander's rifle cracks. One saloon door erupts into shards of wood.

The next beat I'm up and running, leaving Aben reeling on the floor.

Vander aims his gun again. Too slow. Much too slow for my fae blood all frenzied with the hunt.

I dodge, my vision turning to a blur of hunger and shadow. A bullet whisks past my shoulder, snags a hole in the wall.

Vander's growl fills my ears, anger turning desperate. I close in, ten paces between us. He cocks the rifle again, aims for my chest.

Before I can think, before reason or judgement sets in, my body twists.

Jumps.

The bullet finds my gut. Buries deep and gnaws with a gusto that brings me to my knees. I stagger, clutching my belly.

"Ha, got you, fairy bitch," Vander snarls. He glances up to the balustrade where a small squat figure is waiting. "Another one for the field, Freda." The figure's perfectly round eyes fix on the scene below, frog mouth pinched shut. Another broonie. This one is softer than Dalziel, younger too, her hair thick and swamp green. But there are features I recognise. Dalziel's ears. Dalziel's nose. His kin through and through.

No wonder he was so insistent I end this.

She doesn't move.

"Freda!" Vander barks.

The broonie juts her jaw, squares her shoulders and stays still. Below, blood oozes from between my fingers. I'm too far gone to feel pain, but soon the weakness will seep in. I lurch to my feet.

Vander curses, snatches a switch-knife from the bar and scores it down his forearm. He utters something unintelligible under his breath. The blood oozing from the gash evaporates, exposing the open rent of flesh. Pressure washes over the room. I feel it wrap around my limbs and squeeze me still, right down to my itching fingers. *Wicked magic.* Damn, I'd gotten sloppy. I search for Aben but can't find him. *Double damn.*

"Freda," Vander growls.

Above, the broonie's legs jerk, pulling her down the stairs.

"Why all this?" I ask. My seized jaw slurs the words together. It's not much of a question but it's all I can think of to buy time. Some secrets can't resist bragging when they're exposed. I hope Vander is one of them.

Vander pauses, a slight curl in his lip. "What does it matter?"

"Matters . . . to me," I say, forcing the words through my teeth. "To the people left . . . behind."

Vander shrugs and nonchalantly flicks his knife open and shut. Open and shut. "Truth be I've forgotten why."

His words slide down my throat and into my belly in juicy morsels. But I want more. "Why use sickness then?"

Vander pauses, considering me. "Some couldn't pay, some wouldn't, some threatened to expose my operations. Bad business leaving them to talk." He comes closer, flicks his switch-knife out again under my jaw. "You really should have bought dinner."

It comes together in a heartbeat.

"You feed them cursed food." I swallow and fight to raise my voice. "An easy thing, I imagine, to cut yourself and work a spell behind a kitchen door instead of behind a bar." I still can't see Aben, but I hope he's listening.

Vander studies me, curious, as if I'm a puzzle he hasn't figured out yet. "It is."

"Why not poison?" It would be easier. I eye the gash on his forearm. If it took that much blood to work a binding, how much more to work a spell of killing? I think of Dalziel's scars; those hundreds of white lines scoured into his skin and probably Freda's too. Rage boils inside me.

"Poison's too expensive. No money in it." Vander's tone is dry, matter of fact.

All about the money, eh? That's the thing with wicked magic, it can get you what you want, but it turns you cold inside. Once, he might have been an honest merchant, but the magic sunk in, twisted it all up, turned his morals inside out. It's one cost few recognise until it's too late.

Vander's switchblade wanders along my chin and my jaw relaxes at its touch. I work my mouth open, testing this sliver of freedom he's granted. It's not much. He flicks his wrist, and the tip of his knife burns a line across my cheek.

"Ow!"

His eyes fixate on that first red line. Then the knife quivers close again, pauses above my other cheek, then shifts to my forehead, as if he's debating where to cut next. "To think of the spells I might cast with your fae blood," he whispers. And there's excitement there. A man enthralled in the power of magic. He presses closer and the scent of his sweat and blood fills my nose. Rich and coppery.

My mouth salivates. I bite down on my hunger. "You've fucked up."

He frowns, steps back, suddenly unsure. I suppose he's used to his victims begging—at least the victims he finished like this.

"You stopped counting us," I say, and grin.

Vander's eyes search me, then dart to Freda still standing at the bottom of the staircase. Realisation dawns on him in a slackening of his face, a strickening in his eyes. He whirls—just in time to see Aben plunge a meat cleaver into a leather-bound book.

Just like we planned.

It's no light cut, Aben throws his whole body behind the blow. The blade sinks through the cover as if it's made of butter, slices through the marrow of pages and thuds into the wood of the bar underneath. It sticks there like an axe in a tree stump.

His spell book is the source of his power. I'll distract him while you find it. That had been our agreement going in. I almost thought it hadn't worked.

"NO!" Vander's shriek turns my hairs on end. He lunges for Aben, even though it's too late. Far, far too late. His spell sloughs away, releasing my limbs.

Time to feed.

My fae blood boils. A burn building in my gut around Vander's gunshot. Copper swims up my nose, into my lungs, driving the hunger deeper. In a heartbeat, my *chelae* extend from my fingers, long flexible claws, strong as steel, sharp as swords. One set catches Vander in the boot, piercing through leather and sole to the floor beneath. He howls and buckles to cradle his trapped leg. My second set locks around his ribs in a cage, thumb and fingers pincering him still then drags him down in a sprawl.

I'm on him in a blur, straddling his chest. Pain flares in my belly. *Soon.* I tell it. *Just a little more.* Anticipation pulls my lips into a grin.

"Don't touch me!" Vander snarls, just once, before I lean close and brush my mouth over his. His lips are rough and scaled, with a hint of an old poppy on them. I kiss him.

Vander relaxes in my hold, eyes rolling into his head. *Lustitia,* my mother named this. *Judgement's Kiss.* Reserved for the worst and most delicious secrets. I open my mouth around his and suck out the blood-tangled untold. It slips from him to me, gliding down my gullet and into my stomach heavy-like, healing and filling me in a blink. Whole and deliciou*s.*

Sated at last.

My chelae retract. I release Vander; his head thunks to the floor. Limp.

"You killed him?" Aben asks into the silence.

I wipe my mouth with the back of a sleeve. "See for yourself."

Aben eases out from behind the bar, still holding the meat cleaver at the ready. His eyes don't leave me as he bends to check for a pulse. When he finds it, he blinks and his gaze breaks away as he runs a hand over the smuggler's chest, feeling the rise and fall there. "He's alive."

I snort. "I'm not a murderer."

Aben's cleaver drops to his side, forgotten. "What did you do?" He stares at me, searching. I smirk, it's not often I'm met with wonder. But I suppose Aben has seen enough this night to look beyond fear.

"I ate him."

"*Ate* him?"

"Him and his secret, everything that made Vander who he was." And come morning he'll wake as a blank slate. He'll never regain those memories. They're in my gut now, slowly digesting. A fresh start for a feed.

There's a humph from the stairs and a pad of feet crossing the saloon. Freda leans over Vander's sleeping form, pursing her lips. "Good as dead," she says at last. Then she lifts one foot and swings it hard into Vander's side. I wince at the crack of ribs breaking. Freda spits, straightens her tunic and turns to us. "My thanks."

I finger the bullet hole in the gut of my robe, frowning at the dried blood there. I'll have to get new clothes in the next town.

"You really can't stay?" Aben asks.

We're back in Roper's field. Dalziel and Freda are building a bonfire of herbs and bracken to calm the bones once and for all now that their murderer is gone. Dalziel practically dances as he does it. He is free, his daughter is returned and, if my hunch is right, they've found a new hearth to share at Macey's farm.

The widow watches Dalziel and Freda work, holding a bunch of lavender to throw on the blaze. A faint smile plays over her lips.

"No," I tell Aben. "Secrets to find, souls to eat and all that." *More wicked magic to hunt. It's never ending.*

As if sensing my thoughts, Aben produces the two halves of the spell book and gestures it at the fire. "Can I?" He asks. "I mean, is it safe to? I'm not going to get cursed, or jinxed for all eternity?"

A snort escapes me. "You won't," I assure him. "Without a wielder it's just a book. A dangerous book." *As for how Vander got his hands on it, that's a secret I'd like very much to know.*

That's the frustrating thing about secrets. They might nourish me, but they don't reveal the inner workings of their creators. The same way a person will never know the mind of the cow that became a steak on their dinner plate.

We sit together, watching the pages curl into ash until the bonfire burns low and the sun breaks over the grass.

Aben stands, still in his toe-holed sandals from Dalziel, and holds out a hand. "If you must go, know that my door's always open," he says. "Don't be a stranger."

I take it. His grip is firm, yet warm, and a pang echoes through my gut. Emptiness of a different kind. Funny as it may seem, I've come to like this rag-tag crew tonight. "You know," I say, slowly. "I might just hold you to that." A grin creeps across my lips. "You better have some good secrets to spill when I come back."

Aben grins. "Count on it."

About the Author:

Nikky Lee is an award-winning author who grew up as a barefoot 90s kid in Perth, Western Australia on Whadjuk Noongar Country. She now lives in Aotearoa New Zealand with a husband, a dog and a couch potato cat. In her free time, she writes speculative fiction, often burning the candle at both ends to explore fantastic worlds, mine asteroids and meet wizards. She's had over two dozen stories published in magazines, anthologies and on the radio.

Her short fiction has been shortlisted six times in the Aurealis Awards with her novelette 'Dingo & Sister' winning the Best Young Adult Short Story and the Best Fantasy Novella categories in 2020. In 2021, she received a Ditmar Award for Best New Talent. Her debut novel, 'The Rarkyn's Familiar', was released in 2022 and is the first of an epic fantasy trilogy about a girl bonded to a monster.

W: nikkythewriter.com | F: /nikkythewriter | T: @NikkyMLee | IG: @NikkyMLee

THE SCALES ALWAYS BALANCE

LJ McLeod

"The scales always balance." My grandfather always said that, even before the Alzheimer's. I thought it was the Russian equivalent of "Karma's a bitch." That is, until the day he grabbed my wrist, looked me right in the eye and said, "The scales always balance."

I would have pulled away, but Grandpa's gaze held a clarity I hadn't seen in years. He licked his lips, and his grip on my wrist tightened. "Her name was Katya. She lived down the road from me. She was beautiful—pale skin, long black hair, lips the colour of mulberries." His breath hitched and his eyes dropped to his lap. "Even when they found her broken, battered body in the stream behind our village, she was still beautiful."

"Everyone knew her husband did it, even if the *politsiya* could never prove it. He never moved. He just stayed in their house. Within a year there was another beautiful young woman living there with him. The *babushkas* in the neighbourhood shook their heads, but what could be done? This was during one of the harshest winters we had seen in a decade. Food was scarce for everybody.

"One day I was out hunting in the woods by the lake. If I could take down a rabbit with my slingshot, we would have meat in the stew that night. It had gotten dark, but I was too hungry to give in just yet. The first sickle moon of spring was in the sky, giving me just enough light to see by. It was so cold. When I first saw the white shapes moving in the distance, I thought I was hallucinating. As I got closer I could see the shapes were women. They danced on the bank of the lake, barefoot in the grass. One of them had long black hair and lips the colour of mulberries. It was Katya."

"Then what? Grandpa? What happened next?"

But the moment had passed. His eyes stared into the distance, at something no one else could see. Pushing him now would only upset him.

Before the disease, my grandfather had been full of life, always willing to lend a hand or an ear. He could fix just about anything with his pocketknife and his wits alone. Now he was someone else—a stranger that lived in our home. He had helped to raise me. Now it was my turn to look after him. Both of my parents worked full-time, and we couldn't afford care, so I was the only option.

It was time for lunch. Ham and cheese sandwiches were the extent of my culinary skills, so that's what I made. As I pulled the ingredients from the fridge, my grandfather wandered into the kitchen and searched through cupboard doors.

Unable to find what he was looking for, he moved on to the drawers, pulling out utensils in order to search further into the depths.

When I turned to see what he was doing, the countertop was strewn with scissors, tongs, and the kitchen scales. "The scales always balance, hey Grandpa?" I'd meant it as a joke. Or at least I thought I did.

His eyes cleared and he looked right at me. "The Unquiet Dead. That's what they were. You would say 'siren' or 'spirit'. In Russian, *'rusalka'* or *'rusalki'*, for there were five. Women who had died violent deaths. Women who could not move on. Women who hungered for revenge. They haunt the waterways, leaving only to dance under the sickle moon. They delight in drowning men and forcing them to dance until they die. I had thought them only stories, but there was Katya.

"As if the mere thought of her name summoned her, she turned and saw me standing there. Her eyes were all black, like midnight on a starless night. I couldn't move. They came for me, taking my hands and leading me forwards. We began to dance."

He stopped, when he noticed the sandwich sitting in front of him. He started to eat, and I sighed. I had hoped he would hang on a little longer.

"Let an old man finish his lunch," he said.

Satisfied that the Alzheimer's hadn't crept back in, I poured him a glass of milk, pulled up a chair and waited.

When my grandfather finished eating he sat back and, with a contented sigh, continued. "I had never killed a man before, but when I hit Katya's husband with that rock I thought for sure he was dead."

"Wait, you missed a bit!" I interrupted.

"Did I?"

"Yes! The *rusalki* had caught you and forced you to dance."

"*Da.* Just making sure you were paying attention. Now, where was I?"

"We danced until my feet bled. Then we danced some more. I knew I was doomed. My heart raced. It was hard to catch my breath. When I stumbled, they laughed. When I tripped, they pulled me upright. I'm not too proud to tell you that I begged. I pleaded for my life. I said I would do anything, anything, if they would let me go. As one, they stopped. Anything? Katya said. Her voice was like dead leaves on the wind. What else could I say? I was not ready to die. So they told me what I could do to live. The *rusalki* whispered it into my ear and I . . ."

His eyes glazed over and he was gone again. The story couldn't be real, yet I was disappointed nonetheless. This was something different to the usual stories Grandpa told when he spoke about the old days. I had heard about his days of hockey glory and the time he ran across thin ice so many times I could recite them myself. But stories of homicidal ghosts? This was new.

I cleaned up the dishes as Grandpa wandered into the living room and turned the TV on. It wouldn't be long now before he fell asleep on the couch. Once I had finished tidying up, I dropped onto the couch beside him. He still had that vacant look in his eyes.

"You never killed a man before," I began, "but when you hit Katya's husband with that rock, you thought for sure he was dead."

Grandpa's chest heaved and he blinked several times.

I took his gnarled hand in mine, squeezing tight enough to feel the calluses on his palm.

He squeezed back, weaker than I expected, and continued his story. "I looked down at his limp body and saw his chest rise. I wasn't a murderer after all. At least, not yet. I picked up Katya's *muzh* and threw him over my shoulder. He was heavy, but I had been cutting and hauling timber all winter. I was used to carrying heavy loads. It was dark and late. There was no one to see me carry him into the woods.

"Katya's *muzh* groaned as I walked. He did not wake. It felt like an eternity before I reached the lake, an eternity in which to contemplate my actions. I was trading this man's life for my own. Surely he deserved it after what he had done? And what did I deserve?

"I laid his body down on the lake shore. The *rusalki* appeared like dreams from beneath the water, with only their hair to cover them. They gathered on the shore around the man. Katya knelt by his side and laid her cold, pale hand on his cheek.

His eyes fluttered before focusing on her. "Katya? It's you! You're alive?"

She smiled, peaceful and benevolent. Without a word, she extended her hand and he took it. She drew him to his feet and it was only then that he began to realise. He took in his dead wife

347

and her naked friends and the panic blossomed on his face. Too late, it was too late. They had him now.

"The *rusalki* wrapped their pale arms around him and dragged him into the lake. He struggled, but their grip was iron. Inexorably he was pulled into the water, deeper and deeper until his head disappeared under the surface. There was a mass of bubbles and he was gone.

"That was the first. It was awful. Yet it wasn't as hard as I thought it would be. I was used to survival. This was just another thing I had to do to live. The scales had to balance. The next for revenge were the twins . . ."

The ring of the phone startled me. I jumped up and caught it on the fourth ring. It was my mother checking in that everything was well. After assuring her that we were fine, I hung up the phone and hurried back to the living room, hoping my grandfather was still cognisant enough to continue his story. He was asleep on the couch, mouth open and snoring softly.

Trying not to be disappointed, I grabbed the remote and started flipping through the channels.

"I was watching that," a grumpy voice said. Grandpa was awake.

"Where was I up to?"

Nervous anticipation fluttered in my stomach. "You were up to the twins."

"*Da*! The twins."

"Mila and Lena were only sixteen when their father drowned them, one by one, in their own bathtub. When their mother found their lifeless bodies, water still dripping from their long red hair, she lost her mind. Their father blamed their mother for their deaths and she was committed to an asylum. Those girls were so mad. Even dead, their anger was a palpable force that surrounded them.

"By the time I stumbled into Mila and Lena, their father was an old man. In the end I just walked into the hospice and took him. Nobody cared. Nobody was left to love him. He struggled, of course. He knew his time on the scales was coming. But he couldn't get out of his wheelchair, so his efforts were in vain.

"I wheeled him right to the water's edge. The *rusalki* appeared, Mila and Lena leading them. They pulled him from his chair, his useless legs dragging behind him. He wept, though he no longer struggled. They played with him, the twins. Holding him under the water, then allowing him to surface for a quick breath of air before pulling him under again. I made myself watch. It was the hardest thing I had done so far in my life, watching that man suffer. But I did it. I was killing him as much as the *rusalki*."

He stopped, his breath catching in his throat. His shoulders had slumped and he seemed smaller somehow.

"Why are you telling me this?" I asked.

"Because the scales always balance. Somebody should know."

His answer confused me even more.

He reached over and took my hand. It was something he had never done before. "This is not an easy story," he said. "I would understand if you didn't want to hear anymore."

I took a moment to consider this. My grandfather believed what he was telling me. Alzheimer's was a cruel condition, taking a person away, bit by bit. During some of his worst bouts, my grandfather had said some very strange things. But this story was coherent, even if it wasn't believable. I owed it to him to hear it. And I wanted him to stay himself for as long as possible.

I gave his hand a squeeze. "Tell me the rest."

"Natalia's story was the worst. Her brother was not quite right. He pulled the wings off flies and threw bottle rockets at dogs. Her family's cat went missing and its collar was found in his room. One day when their parents were out, he cornered Natalia and tried to have his way with her. When she fought back, he beat her. He choked her to the point of unconsciousness, then let her breathe, over and over. He broke her legs. He broke her arms. He pulled her nails out. When he tired of playing with her, he took her to the bridge and threw her body into the river. She was still alive when she went into the water. That bastard stayed to watch her drown.

"Her parents thought she ran away, and her body was never found. Natalia's brother grew into a powerful man, both of body and *vliyaniye*. How do you say in English? Influence?"

I nodded, so he continued.

"He ran a gang of thugs who sold guns, drugs and murder for the right price. He was a professional criminal and I was a poor wood cutter. Getting to him would not be easy.

"I took a loan with one of his goons. I told him we had no money for food or clothes and that we may soon starve. It was even the truth. He gave me money and a high interest rate and three weeks to pay it back. Three weeks and one day later, Natalia's brother and his bandits came to visit. He liked to participate in the punishments he ordered."

A shudder ran through him. I had never seen my grandfather flinch at anything in my life. This man must have been awful.

"My family wasn't home that night, I had made sure of it. We could not afford electricity, only candles, so the house was dark when they arrived. Natalia's brother had brought two of his men with him and it didn't take them long to break in. He went in first, eager to begin.

"When only one of the bandits remained outside, I emerged from my hiding place and hit him in the head with the back of my axe. The sound of his body hitting the ground made the man in the doorway turn. I swung my axe, and he grabbed it. I let go, grabbed his head and drove it into the wall. I watched him fall, not seeing the fist coming for me. It hit so hard I almost blacked out. I dove forward, catching Natalia's brother around the waist. We grappled on the living room floor. He was bigger and stronger than I, he should have won. However, he wasn't used to victims who fought back. He began to tire, just enough that I got an arm around his throat. I held on as he struggled and fought. Eventually he went limp.

"I took no risks, tying his hands and feet. The other men I left where they had fallen. I loaded Natalia's brother into my wheelbarrow and headed for the lake.

"He woke up before I got there, tipping the wheelbarrow and fighting as best he could. I ended up dragging him the rest of the way. Natalia was waiting for us on the lake shore. She tore her brother from my hands, dragging him as if he weighed nothing. She dropped him in front of her sisters, who gathered around to pinch and scratch and bite. At first he didn't scream, remaining stoic in the face of their torment. It wasn't until they started to bite his fingers off, joint by joint, that he broke.

"He screamed through the loss of his fingers, his toes, his ears, his lips and his nose. When they took his manhood, he lost consciousness.

"He woke up when the cold water of the lake washed over his skin. They dragged him out deep and watched as he struggled. He tried to swim. He tried to scream. They watched as his mouth filled with water and he slid beneath the water. The *rusalki* followed his body down, Natalia stopping to blow me a kiss before she disappeared under the water. I threw up, then started the hike back home.

Grandpa went quiet for a long time after that. He looked pale and drawn after sharing such a difficult part of his story, and I couldn't help but notice the tremor in his hands.

I didn't want to push him, but my curiosity was stronger than ever. "What happened to the thugs left at your house?" I asked.

My grandfather sighed and rubbed his eyes. "They were gone when I returned. I took the money I had borrowed and brought my family here, where they would not be able to reach us. I am not proud of what I did to get us here, but I do not regret it."

"Wait. What about the fifth *rusalka*?" I said.

Another sigh, this time the exhalation made him shrink in on himself. "Vanya fell in love with a man who did not love her back. When she discovered his heart belonged to another, she cut her wrists in the bathtub and bled to death. I could not help her." A tear ran down his wrinkled cheek. "I need to rest." He held his hand out for me to help him up.

I pulled him from the couch and walked him to his room. He settled onto his bed and turned away from me.

I let him be and went to the lounge room. I flicked through the channels, unable to settle on a program. My grandfather's tale had left me feeling melancholy and strange. How did he come up with such a peculiar tale? Maybe it was a fairy tale he heard in his childhood? It seemed very graphic to be just a delusion brought on by the Alzheimer's. And why would my grandfather imagine himself a murderer? It felt like there was more to this story than there seemed. I was also haunted by the plight of the last *rusalka*. How could she ever get her revenge and find peace if she took her own life? Would her sisters wait for her or leave her behind all alone? I knew it wasn't real, it couldn't be. Still, I couldn't shake this lingering sense of doubt. It lasted all night, from the time my parents arrived home, through dinner, which Grandpa didn't join us for, until I went to bed. Thoughts chased themselves around my head, questioning everything I thought I knew about my grandfather. Even in sleep I felt restless. Voices filled my dreams, strident and upset. I woke to my mother shaking me. Her face was streaked with tears.

"Your grandfather is missing."

"Of course," I muttered, then couldn't figure out why I had said that. My mother hadn't heard, she was already gone.

My father was talking on the phone to the police. I dragged myself out of bed and went into my grandfather's room. His sheets were rumpled and his bathrobe was gone. There was a photo propped on his bedside table that I had never seen before. It was of a beautiful woman with blonde hair and blue eyes. I picked the photo up and turned it over. 'Vanya' was written on the back.

It all made sense now.

"I know where he is!" I yelled, running out of his room and down the stairs.

"Where?" my mother cried from the kitchen.

I didn't stop. It was already too late, but I had to try.

Once out the back door, I took off at a sprint across the yard. There was a path through the trees that led to a park. A small river bordered the far side of the park. I ran all the way to its bank, stopping dead when I saw what I had feared—my grandfather's robe and slippers in a neat pile on the riverbank.

I stared at the river. There was no sign of him. He was already gone.

My mother arrived behind me and fell to her knees.

"The scales always balance," I murmured as she began to wail.

About the Author:

LJ McLeod lives in Queensland, Australia. She works in Pathology and writes in her spare time. She has been published in several anthologies and has been nominated twice for the Aurealis Award. In her spare time she enjoys diving, reading and travelling.

SCORPIO
OCTOBER 23 - NOVEMBER 21

THE ENDLESS CHASE

Tee Linden

The doe watched me at my campfire. She slinked through the cypress trees, her perfect, pale hide near glowing in the firelight. I sat on a felled tree and watched her from the corner of my eye.

It was winter. The winds off my father's sea were harsh that year and when I warmed my hands on the radiant heat of the fire, I could see the age in them. Even in those early days. No longer the hands of a young man. My knuckles ached more often than not.

The doe neared the campfire, as though taunting. Challenging me to pick up the still-strung bow at my heel. To nock the arrow. To shoot. My hunter's hands twitched. I knew the arrow wouldn't fly true. It couldn't. It was useless to try. It was madness to try. Dangerous, even.

Sirius sat at my side. He wasn't much more than a puppy then. My favourite. The bravest and fastest of all my dogs. Even he whimpered at the eerie doe with the rest of the pack. He curled his tremoring body against my feet.

The doe stalked. As fast as I could, I snatched up my bow and nocked an arrow. By the time the arrow was loosed, the doe had disappeared into the trees, melting into the deep shadows cast by the firelight.

As expected.

I smiled to myself. "Missed you again," I called, setting my bow down and my hand on Sirius' head to calm him.

I did not hear the change. I never did.

Her voice unpeeled from the trees and slithered towards me, accompanied by the sound of cicadas buzzing at the edges of her words. "Do you expect your arrow will ever fly true, Orion?"

"No," I said to the fire.

I was still wary around her then, though it's strange to think now. I had heard the stories of her. The first time I'd ever seen her, a doe as pale as snow, I had hunted her for days. Until my feet were blistered and I had no arrows with which to shoot.

"You knew the shot would not land before you loosed," she said, bringing the scent of night flowers as she drew near.

"Yes."

"Then why shoot?"

"That's part of the chase, isn't it?"

Silver sandaled feet stood beside me. Her shins were bare, pale as the inside of a shell. She wore a silver linen chiton and her cloak was deerskin. I risked a glance up to find her watching me with eyes the colour of brushed silver coin. A faint glow ebbed from her skin, like the moon behind clouds, and her black hair was braided with delicate links of chain. Her face was both ancient and ageless in the way of all Olympians. Artemis. Goddess of hunting, wild nature and chastity. Perfect and inhuman. Pitiless and beautiful.

"And what will happen," she asked, "if there comes a day you catch me?"

"I expect you'll kill me," I said airily.

That pleased her, a smile cracking the moon of her face.

She held her white wood bow, and I nodded to it. "Is the hunting good tonight?"

"Good enough even your arrows may find target," she taunted.

I took her teasing with good nature. Truth was, Artemis knew my skill at the hunt. It was why she spared me that first night. My relentlessness impressed her. Though far from the perfection of a goddess, I was known for those skills. Hunting. Shooting. Tracking. They had served me well and ill, in equal measure.

The two of us moved into the trees, my hunting dogs following.

We hunted like that for years, a pack, sneaking through the shadowy oak and juniper that grew over the mountains. She would come every other night. Mostly as herself. Sometimes as the glowing doe, beautiful and impossible to catch. We challenged one another. Shooting games. This deer, that boar. The chase. We both loved the chase. I think that's why we got along so well.

She admired my sight. It was far superior even to hers. My sight was a gift from Eos, the dawn goddess. I could spot a flea jumping from a boar's back a hundred yards away. A good talent for a hunter. And I admired her. I still do.

She's graceful, Artemis. She flows like water. Watching her nock and shoot is always a great pleasure, the movement eased by thousands and thousands of repetitions. Like watching a skilled hand at a lyre or a master work flat marble into lip and cheek and hair.

Always, she flips back the deerskin cloak and raises her bow in one fluid motion, silver tipped arrow at the ready. Her pale muscled arms grow taut. Her grey eyes narrow but never blink. Her stern lips thin when she concentrates, and she becomes still.

Then her moonlight arrow flies true and straight. Always.

I was used to godhead, yes, I am the son of a god. But skill and prowess filled every line of her body. My godhead bestows certain gifts, speed and strength and an unsinkable body, but it was nothing compared to Artemis. Comparing our talent was like comparing a grain of sand to blown glass.

That night, I watched her take a great leap off a rock, her deerskin cloak flying, nocking mid-air and shooting at a swooping owl. Artemis landed on the grass with a roll, and a moment later, the owl fell from the sky and pattered to the clover, a silver arrow struck through its skull.

"I have never seen such a shot!" I blurted in the darkness.

Artemis turned to look at me. Her features were hard and beautiful with pride. "Do not be surprised at my skill, Orion. My arrows never miss."

And she was right.

Every morning on that island, Sirius and I rose and made our pilgrimage to either the shore or the high mountains so I could watch Eos, the dawn goddess, untangle the night from the sky with her rosy-tipped fingers. The birds would chirp to her, as I settled into a seat on the sand, or tree, or rock. I always awaited Eos. I always touched the shafts of burnt skin on either side of my eyes when I first felt the dawn slip over me; my own private ritual.

I'd once been blinded by a traitorous king, and Eos had taken pity on me at the watery edge of the world. She'd restored my sight, refined it to rival a hawk's, and every day I thanked her.

After Eos had settled back into slumber, I moved back into the forest. I fletched arrows. Fed my dogs. Prepared camp or packed it up.

I remember it was noon, my shadow was small, and I was skinning goat when the world suddenly froze around me. The songs of the birds were silenced and every leaf in every tree stilled all at once. I gave a deep, laboured sigh, and stood with bloodied hands to face my interloper. It was not the first time he'd visited me, and it wasn't the last. But it was the most important.

He stepped in from nowhere at all, splitting the air like a flash of light. The twin sun to his sister moon. Apollo.

He was brown-skinned and sculptured where she was pale and soft, and his hair was silky gold where hers was thick black. His eyes were wide, blue afternoon sky. Even the ebony bow on his back was a perfect reflection of her white wood.

A gilded wreath shimmered in the sunlight, crowning a beautiful face filled with barely covered malice. "Orion." He said my name in a way that would send other mortals running. "I told you to leave this island."

"My home, you mean," I said.

"I told you to leave," he repeated.

While I had no wish to anger the god of light and prophecy, he hadn't left me much choice. "And I told you it is my home."

He did not like that answer. The very air crushed me down, tasting of metal as it forced me to my knees. Sirius whimpered, pressed down into the nettled grass beside me.

Apollo approached me, moving like silk in the breeze. His face shone, placid as he watched me choke and writhe beneath a great boulder of nothing.

Apollo's sulky, spiteful wrath was legendary.

Once, when trying to seduce Cassandra of Troy, Apollo had offered her his gift of prophecy. But when she refused him her bed, he'd spat in her mouth, cursing her so no matter how many true prophecies she spoke, no one would ever believe her.

Upsetting Apollo was the last thing I had mind to do. But the island didn't belong to Apollo. In title, this was my island. Artemis was its patron. And I had her protection. So eventually he released me, and my dog, and I stood, resettling my chiton and trying to quell the rage that grew like wild weed within. It held no use. It never did. Apollo watched me, empty and beautiful. His presence always filled me with burrs. I couldn't wait for him to be gone once more.

"She will not petition for immortality for you," he announced. "Zeus would never approve it. You are nothing, Orion, and you have done nothing to deserve being remembered. Your own father does not remember you exist."

Looking back, I think the cruelty was both unintended and conversational. Apollo had lived thousands of years with no understanding of pain, and so unleashed it without realising. But at the time, I felt it like a spear thrust deep into my belly.

Poseidon had hundreds of byblows. And I was born mortal; the immortality of gods made time difficult for them. In my life, I spoke with my father only three times. Each time I had to remind him who I was, and even then he only looked at me like a messenger of inconvenience.

"I have no wish to be immortal," I told Apollo.

"You are renown for your hunting skills. You are the son of a god, and a prince of Crete. She cannot improve your favour in what little life you have left."

I frowned. "I do not want anything from her."

He scoffed at that. Olympians are always jockeying for power and pride. Holding it, fighting for more, seeking retribution for any lost or injured. Especially Artemis and Apollo. I had heard a story that Niobe, a queen of Thebes, had boasted she was superior to the twin's mother, Leto, because Niobe bore fourteen children to

Leto's two. For that insignificant injury, Apollo and Artemis had hunted each of Niobe's children and shot them, one by one.

I imagine Apollo couldn't understand that I wanted nothing from Artemis. Least of all power.

The god approached me, his gold-sandaled feet weightless on the grass. "Artemis will not lie with you," he told me.

I cleared my throat. "Perhaps we just enjoy each other's company, Apollo."

Apollo looked like I'd spat in his mouth. "My sister does not enjoy the company of men. She never has."

I looked to him, in his jealous, interminable rage, and decided not to point out that he might be the reason why. "Mere mortals like myself who look upon your sister are transformed into deer and ripped apart by dogs," I said instead.

He stepped closer to me, peering down at me with blue eyes flashing cold. The gilded wreath in his hair, laurel wood, caught the sun like a still lake, flashing sharp as a blade.

More stories.

Daphne, a river nymph Apollo had pursued so viciously, had turned herself into a laurel tree to escape his advances. He'd taken wood from her desperate escape to make the wreath that sat atop his perfect head, and though there was much about Apollo to find unsettling, it was that wreath that unsettled me the most. The sight of the wreath always twisted my gut.

"It is unseemly for the goddess of chastity to spend nights with a mortal."

I disliked this whole conversation, and my skin prickled from being in his presence. I do not know how Artemis had withstood this for so long. I still don't.

"Your sister is a goddess," I said. Warning slipped into my words, though I knew it shouldn't be there. "She can make her own choices."

"If you seduce her," Apollo persisted, "you risk her vow to Zeus. And so her."

"If you are so invested in chastity," I glanced at his wreath, petrified body of a desperate nymph, "you could always take the vow yourself. Save some would-be laurel trees."

He stared at me, hollowed of empathy. I wondered at the time if he would kill me, despite his sister's protection. I had overstepped the crawling space reserved at a god's feet and I regretted it immediately.

The fallen leaves raised from the ground, floating upwards. The ropes of my intestines pressed up against my stomach, and my stomach to my lungs. I could not breathe, his entire being crushing every inch of mine. I watched him bug-eyed and silent, suspended in airlessness, about to drown in my own sour bile.

When he spoke again his voice had changed, growing deep, every word shaking the foundations of the earth itself. "Orion. I have a prophecy for you. Your death will be delivered by the sea." His smile was empty and unendingly cruel. "I will be there when it happens. I will laugh as I watch you die."

He flashed away, a lightning strike of anger. The leaves settled. The sound of birds returned. And I could breathe again.

I fell to my hands and knees on the nettled grass and vomited.

"Your father rages," Artemis said, as we stood atop a mountain looking out over the roiling sea.

I continued building a fire. "Why does he rage?"

"Polyphemus was killed," Artemis said.

"Who is that?" I asked.

She blinked, expressionless. "Your brother. The cyclops."

"Oh," I said, scratching Sirius' broad head as my loyal boy sat by my feet. The dog was older by then, no longer a puppy, and had outlived many of my others. "I never think about Poseidon's children as my siblings. It seems strange."

"You do not mourn?"

"How can I mourn someone I don't know?" Even as I said it, I realised I could. Since Artemis told me of Daphne, I'd mourned for she of the laurel wood. Yet I felt nothing for Polyphemus. "How old was he?"

"Older than me."

"That's old," I said with a smile.

She smiled back, shining like the moon. My stomach flipped.

It wasn't the first time I had felt that familiar bite of ardour in her presence. Love came easy but fickle for me. It flowed and ebbed like the tide. Love was just another chase. Eos. Merope.

The nereids that slipped from the sea, seeking me in my youth. All of them were easily loved and easily left. The feeling that filled me, looking at Artemis, was faded with age and use. I appreciated it for what it was, even if I could never act on it. I had no urge to be turned into a stag and gored by my own dogs.

She turned away, looking out over the sea again. I remembered Apollo's prophecy, turning it over in my mind. I couldn't imagine how the sea could deliver my death. Poseidon might not know me, but still; I was the son of the god who commanded the ocean. It gave me certain skills. I could swim from island to island without failure, without sinking; it's how I had swum to Eos at the edge of the watery world for her to restore my sight.

"Speaking of brothers," I cleared my throat. "Yours came to see me."

She sighed. "Apollo, I presume. He has been in my ear about you, like a giant, gold gnat. He is prone to jealousy."

"Jealousy," I repeated.

"Yes. Always. Since he was a baby. It was the nine days I had alone with our mother, when Hera banned Eileithyia from my mother's side." At the shake of my head, she clarified. "Eileithyia is the goddess of childbirth. Without her, Apollo was stuck inside. Eileithyia whispered to me on the winds, teaching me midwifery as to deliver him."

"As an infant. In nine days," I laughed.

"Yes," she said, fine chin raised. "There was no one else on Delos. Only me, and my mother. And then Apollo. The three of us against all the gods in Olympus and the Underworld. Against Hera herself, who wanted us dead. And still does. She always tries to find one way or another to remove our godhead."

When she talked of her mother or brother, she softened in a way that escaped the stories. When people spoke of Artemis, she was unbreakable as a shield, and as heartless as her silver-tipped arrows. The coldness makes a stronger goddess. A stronger story.

"Hera can remove your godhood?" I asked.

"Zeus can. Hera searches for a reason."

I thought on that, and on Apollo's words. *You risk her vow, and so her.*

Artemis looked to me. "What did he say?"

I didn't want to tell her about us arguing over her vow of chastity. Artemis was lenient with me, that wouldn't be denied, but the whole conversation seemed ripe for humiliation on her behalf. "A prophecy," I said instead.

A stillness hardened her, like freeze on a lake. "What kind of prophecy?"

"He said the sea will deliver my death," I said, saving her the rest of it.

She frowned. "You are a son of Poseidon. How could the sea kill you? You who can swim to the edge of the world? Who cannot drown or tire in the waves?"

"I don't know."

She continued frowning, watching me light the fire. "Well," she said stiffly. "You will just remain here. Never return to the sea and you will never die."

I laughed. She seemed so young at that moment. Endlessly young. Age brings wisdom, but Artemis was a goddess; she never aged. "I am mortal."

She blinked, expressionless and uncomprehending. The fire caught, scenting the air with burning oak.

"I will die," I said. "Of something. We all do."

I was at peace with that, in a way most mortals weren't. Looking back, I think it was because I loved the hunt. Death was a necessity.

But Artemis looked disconcerted, as though this has never crossed her mind. She was on her feet, grabbing her bow before I could stand. "I must go." She disappeared, lighting the night like starfall, disappearing from the world as easily as her brother.

The Goddess of the Hunt didn't return the next night, which wasn't rare. Then she didn't return for a few, which was rarer. Then a moon passed, waxing then waning. And still, she didn't return. Then another moon cycled. Then again. And a year passed. The baby kestrels lost their fluff, grew sleeker and flew. And then again, the next year. The olive trees bloomed and produced green, firm fruit, which ripened and dropped. And then again, the next year.

Eventually, heart-sore, I caught goats and brought them to her temple in the outskirt forests to sacrifice in her name. The gods can hear you at their temples, even on Olympus. Even Artemis, even during the day when she was deaf to me. The priestesses watched me from the temple, veiled and silent. They approached with garlands for the animals so I could dress them for her altar.

She never answered me. I stopped taking goats to her temple, and the wound of her abandonment slowly closed.

It was more than a few years later, when Artemis stepped out of nothing. Sirius and I were trekking up the White Mountains in the early morning, our daily pilgrimage to thank Eos. Much slower those days due to the stiffness that had gathered in my boy's aging joints. The flashing arrival of the goddess cracked the purpling sky. I flinched but didn't slow my journey, unable to think of anything to say, feeling my anger and hurt come to boil.

She strode along beside me for a moment, keeping pace, her face drawn tight as a bow. It was strange to see her under the chirping of dawn birds. I had never seen her so late.

"Apollo refuses to explain his prophecy," she said.

"Hello," I responded, the wound of her abandonment opening fresh and oozing.

She looked at me, confused, and I realised she didn't know how long she'd been gone. My father looked at me the same way when I'd told him who I was. She was a goddess, and not only did she not have to explain her sudden absence to me, she hadn't even noticed it. If I looked older to her, she didn't say anything.

I realised I was chasing a doe I could never catch and shook my head, at myself, at my self-inflicted injury.

"He wants you dead." She told me this plainly, as if discussing the weather. "He has told me to kill you many times. He is in a fit."

I said nothing. What was there to say? The discussion had closed years ago. She had left, and I had grown older, and I no longer even thought about Apollo's prophecy. But here she was, picking up the thread of conversation as though we'd been discussing it only the day before.

"I am patron of this island," she said with anger lurking in her voice. "And of you. The only person who can kill you here is me. He is angry about that. But he can continue to rage. And you will continue to live."

I knew this was untrue even as she said it. At that time, my hair was already greying. My skin had thinned and sagged. "Mortal life is not endless," I reminded her.

"Apollo has prophesised your death," she said. Her words were short and sharp. "If the sea delivers your death, and you never again touch the sea, then you can never die."

Not dying seemed simple for a goddess, I suppose. Not so for a mortal. Death comes for us all even when the gods do not wish it.

We never spoke of Apollo again.

Artemis visited more often after that, and I never questioned her years of absence. It meant nothing to her, and I was glad to have her presence again. I had been across the world; I had swum its breadth, seen its many shores of sand and stone and hard-faced cliffs. I had met many people but I had always felt an outcast. It's why I ended up on my island, alone, with a dog for a companion. An oddness about demigods was not uncommon, or so I came to know, much later in my years. We are not really anything, not gods but not normal humans either. We fit nowhere.

But Artemis soothed something fractious in me. There was a sameness about us. So, we hunted which always pleased us both. We challenged each other to shooting games. I showed her the baby kestrels, and she marvelled over the tiny fluffy bodies that would become such sleek, master-hunters.

Artemis and I argued only once in all the time we spent together on that island. It was years later, when she arrived while I was building a pyre on the shore for Sirius. His old, greyed body was wrapped in linen, laying on the sand, and my throat was thick with the pain of his loss.

Artemis appeared and, without a moment's pause for my grief, she howled with anger. The sound crackled like lightning, and the air rushed from me, emptying itself until I was on my knees on the shore, shells digging into my shins as I clutched at my throat. Sand stung at me like tiny wasps, slicing and burning my skin.

Anger made her fine features ragged and incandescent, and I could finally see in her the Artemis that felled gods on a boast, that turned men into stags for dogs to rip to shreds.

"What are you doing?" she shrieked, like knives in my ears.

"Artemis!" I choked. My face blistered in the heat of it. "Can't breathe!"

The air rushed back into my lungs and I gulped at it greedily, like a desert-traveller stumbling on an oasis. Sand fell like rain, pattering into my hair, against the raw skin of my shoulders.

She grabbed my arm and pulled me up, dragged me into the forest, where she glowed in rage.

My anger mirrored hers. I jerked my arm away. "Never do that again!" I cried, at the goddess who had never taken a direction in her life.

"I never took you for a fool," she hissed, her face twisted. "Do you wish to die? The sea delivers your death."

"I didn't go in the sea," I snapped.

"You were mere steps from it!"

She was furious, but the fury was mixed with shock and fear too. Emotions I'd never seen on her stern face before. She was scared. For me.

"I was dry," I said. "On the sand. I haven't been in the sea in years."

"Apollo's prophecies are riddles. He may not mean drowning and you told me yourself; nereids slip from the sea to find you."

I laughed at that absurdity, even in my sorrow over Sirius, even with blood drying in tracks from my ears. "You believe some soft nereid is going to slip from their feasts in the golden palace just to murder me?"

She blinked. Then, she laughed as well, jittery with relief. "No," she admitted after a moment. "They would not dare." A begrudging smile slipped across her lips, stealing her weakened expression. The tension between us settled to the forest floor.

She refused me the beach, as well the sea. The goddess herself collected Sirius' wrapped body, and convinced me to build my pyre at the top of the mountain instead of the shore. She carried him and I rebuilt the pyre. It took all night, and as the flames gathered, Artemis asked me if I wanted him laid to rest in the night sky.

"You can put Sirius in the sky?"

The flames that burnt my boy to ash lit Artemis and I both.

"I can," she said. "He will always be there, then. Chasing game through the stars."

My throat tightened and my face felt sodden with unshed tears. I remember that moment. Her pity and her kindness. "I would like that."

She just nodded, silver eyed and silent. We waited until the flames dwindled and then stood to watch Eos' pink hands of dawn unravel the night. Artemis observed me greet Eos, my daily ritual, with a nod and a touch to my scars.

"Why did the king blind you?" she asked.

"I wanted an impossible prize so he set me an impossible challenge."

"The prize was his daughter," Artemis said. She knew the story. Of course, she knew. But she had never asked about Merope before.

My lips pressed together. "Yes. He tasked me with clearing his island of all beasts. He thought I would never complete it. And, if I am honest, neither did I. But I did."

"If you thought the task beyond you, why did you try?"

"Why do I hunt the goddess doe when I know I cannot catch her?" I said with a soft smile. "Because it is in me; that need to hunt. It is part of who I am. And when he challenged me, I couldn't refuse. What I should have seen was that he *thought* it was impossible. He didn't want me to marry his daughter. I should have recognised that, and realised every beast I killed was a step closer to my own destruction. I didn't. I was young. I killed each beast I laid eyes on."

"Did his daughter wish to marry you?" Artemis asked, watching the sky blush.

"She said she did. But a hunter is not a good match for the daughter of a king and I am not a good match for anybody." I shrugged. "So when I completed his impossible task, he blinded me and told the people of Chios that I tried to flee with Merope."

"Why not kill him?"

"I thought about it. For years. It burned in me, that rage. Especially when I was young. That anger consumed my sightless days. I wasted years on that anger, dreaming of his death."

"What changed?"

I sighed. "I returned. After Eos restored my sight, I saw how the king had greyed. Merope had married. And all the animals were gone. Not the farm animals of men, but every other beast was gone from that island. I walked the hills. They were silent, and dead."

She watched me. "I do not understand."

I scratched my fingers through my hair, unsure how to explain. "I love the hunt, Artemis. The chase. They are as much me as my fingers and toes. But the hunt must end in death and so I must be careful where I direct my skills. He was an old man. Merope was a mother and a wife. When I saw what my hunting left, nothing but silence, I realised I must not hunt that which I don't want dead."

The sun rose but Artemis didn't leave. I was aware of it, because when the sun was high, Apollo could listen with all the sky.

"You were worried the hunt would consume you," Artemis said. "And her."

I nodded slowly. We always had so much common ground, she and I. We stepped in each other's footprints. "I could hunt everything." Those words echo even now. "I could hunt the entire world. I could kill every beast on this Earth. I think I realised that, when I returned to Chios with murder on my mind and saw the nothing I'd left behind. That endless, creature-less silence has stayed with me. It could so easily spread. And I didn't want to be the man who kills all he sees."

Daylight settled strangely on her. She lost her iridescence. She became flat. Like a stone carving erected at her temple. "You decided not to be the man who kills all he sees," she reflected. "Can one truly give that power up?"

"I did."

She looked out across the lightening sky, expressionless. "The other gods, they are always looking for a reason to knock me from Olympus. To make me mortal. So I can live and, therefore, die. They are jealous and cruel. They force me to guard my godhood endlessly, lest they take it from me."

Her gaze fell on our feet. "I must rise to every challenge, every slight, in case they find weakness. I must show them none. And so I am welcome nowhere, just as my mother was when she bore us."

The three of us against all the gods in Olympus and the Underworld.

I felt an echo of that in myself, though I would never dare to presume I knew what an ancient god could feel. So I said nothing.

She looked at me, weariness weighing heavy in all the features of her face. Tired, in a way no goddess should be. Her silver eyes were on me, unblinking and waiting. "You have always made me feel welcome, Orion," she said.

It humbled me. I knew it was a great confession. A weakness. Artemis was meant to have none. "I enjoy your company," I said in return.

She lifted her fine chin, indicating she'd heard me, if nothing else. "Would you hold my hand if I asked you to?"

I cleared my throat, taken by surprise. "Your hand? Will you promise not to turn me into a stag, and have me ripped apart by dogs?"

She looked at me. Clear eyed and unflinching. "Yes."

The day lit sky seemed to press down on my shoulders. But I took her cool hand and held it in mine. I remember her skin felt delicate and not like mortal skin at all. Like stroking the back of a lizard. No veins ran beneath her flesh. No wrinkles creased her, and no heartbeat pulsed in her dense flesh.

We watched the clouds drift as the sun arced overhead. She was silent. Unmoving. She didn't look at me but she held her chin high and defiant.

I had touched gods before. She felt different. Eos had rippled warm beneath my fingers, but the feel of her had faded with time. As had the slippery skin of sea scrubbed nereids.

But I remember Artemis, clearly, though all I ever touched of her was her hand, and only once.

Apollo came the very next day, as soon as the sun peeked above the mountains. I hunted boar in the forests that overlooked the calm sea, missing Sirius like I'd lost a leg. I hadn't seen Apollo in almost a decade and somehow I knew he would come.

"I heard your boast," Apollo said, his golden voice striking from behind me, startling the boars.

My prey fled into the forest and I breathed deep and turned to him. He was empty-faced beneath the glint of his gilded laurel. Nimble fingers played with his bow.

"My boast?" I asked him.

"I could kill every beast on this Earth," he said, repeating what I had told Artemis. "I am here to see if you speak the truth."

His listening in on our conversation riled me in a way I knew I shouldn't react to. It was bait. It was a challenge. It was the King, asking me to kill every beast on the island. He was setting me up for impossibility. I had learned that. I heard in his voice everything I had been too young to hear in the King's.

With one long, sun browned arm, he gestured toward the sea. I looked.

The calm of the water shifted. The waves rolled and warped, sloshing up onto the sand. Something was rising. Something large and malevolent and dark, from the depths of the ocean floor.

My skin prickled. My dogs cowered, whimpering behind my knees.

Great pincers emerged from the sea, and I stared in horrified awe. Then came the hump of a great chitinous back. Next was a bulbous tail, with a rosy-red stinger that drooled venom from a spike as long as my leg.

Water cascaded from the beast, in a hundred pale waterfalls. The creature seemed eyeless as it emerged, mouthless, and it had too many chittering, black-bristled legs.

A scorpion. It was as large as the temple where I'd sacrificed goats in Artemis' absence. The ugly creature's back was armoured plates of bronze, and its great segmented tail looped high as the trees. The scorpion blocked Apollo's morning sun, throwing me into stark, shadowed relief.

The sea will deliver your death, Apollo had prophesised. And there it was, death emerging.

The god's face was sweet and sour, pleasant and spiteful all at once. "Hunt and kill, little Orion."

"You cannot be serious," I snapped.

"You are the one who boasted you could hunt and kill any beast on Earth." His words were sharpened to a knife-edge. "So. Hunt. Kill."

"That is not of this Earth!"

"It is on the Earth now. So, great hunter, prove your salt. Or die."

When it moved, it chittered and clacked like a swarm. The trees by the shore bent and cracked, the sound of trunks falling echoing up the mountains. It was coming. For me.

"I refuse," I said, standing and backing away. "Artemis would not allow this; you cannot kill me here."

"If I cannot," he said as the scorpion crashed up from the shore. "Do you think a beast *from the sea* can't kill you?"

I erred. That thing could kill me. And as he foretold, the sea had delivered my death. I couldn't call for Artemis. She could never hear me during the day.

The scorpion was coming fast now, a behemoth, advancing up the mountains.

I wielded my bow. I nocked an arrow and shot; all one fluid, easy motion. The arrow flew, arcing towards the giant body, between the forward pinchers as big as boats, to where the eyes would and should be. A shot that would arch Artemis' fine brow in quiet appreciation.

The arrow bounced harmlessly off the monster's thick, chitinous shell, the way a drop of rain bounces off waxy myrtle leaves. The arrow fell to the dirt.

I looked to Apollo. He was glassy eyed and vacuous. He smiled a sweet smile that showed his glossy white teeth.

I ran.

The scorpion chased me for hours. We crashed through laurel groves, we shattered trees all up and down the White Mountains. The dogs fled. Apollo disappeared. I was alone.

I thought I could avoid the scorpion but it hunted me. It pursued me. Relentless. I had never been hunted before. Even exhausted as I was, I realised the deep irony in that.

I climbed many mountains that day. And the scorpion was so large it could follow me anywhere. The creature somehow sensed when I neared a cave, and always managed to get between myself and the safety of a cave's entrance. It knew to prevent my escape. I wondered how much of that scorpion was a beast, and how much was Apollo himself. He would enjoy watching me struggle and fade.

And I struggled. And faded. My breath was gone by the time I climbed a cliff-face, thinking the thing might not follow me there, thinking I could hold off until nightfall. Until Artemis returned. It was only mid-afternoon and my fingers shook as I clung to the rock. My thighs tremored and ached. But even up the sheer rock face the scorpion followed, slowly, slamming its spiny legs into the stone and burying them deep.

As slow as it was, I was slower. The sound of its jaws chattering made my ears throb. It was hungry for me. Apollo's sun stayed high in the sky, lighting me stark against the grey rock.

I remember the moment I realised I would not make it until sundown. The scorpion, like a huge spider, worked its way towards me over the rock, and I hung there, so tired, like a snagged fly in a web. I looked beneath me, at the cool blue sea and then back to the scorpion. It moved inexorably closer, chittering and clacking. The cliff stretched up into the sky above me forever. I was too tired to reach the top. I could not stay and I could not escape in time, not before the scorpion got to me. My arms tremored. I glanced to the sea below again, blue and foaming. I could swim to the edge of the world, of course. I was Poseidon's son.

I swallowed. Closed my eyes. And dropped.

The briny water covered me, frothing over my sweated skin. For a moment I wondered if I could drown, if Apollo's prophecy had changed me, but I was buoyant as ever. I floated. My energy flooded through me, as soon as I touched the waves. Energized, I swam away, looking back to see the giant scorpion dropping into the water after me.

I swam further from the island. The scorpion was slower in the water. It couldn't swim. Instead, it crawled along the ocean floor towards me, tail swinging like a battle flag. It needed no air; it needed only me. But it could not leap from the floor and I swam far enough out that it could not reach me. Its tail disappeared beneath the surface. I could feel the giant thing pacing far below me, kicking up sand and grit in the water. But it couldn't reach me. I laughed; my lips and tongue crusted with salt.

And I floated. And I waited.

I waited until the sun painted the distant cliff face orange, and the clouds were pink tufts in the deepening blue of the sky. The stars above, Sirius as well, sparked alive in the dying light.

Artemis was right. Apollo could not kill me.

The sky dimmed.

I saw her then. Suddenly. A glowing, silver figure high on the cliff. Artemis. The sister moon. Relief weakened me. And then beside her, a figure glowing gold. Apollo. The brother sun.

Apollo pointed at me, far out in the horizon. He was laughing.

My relief shrivelled like a grape on the vine. It took only moments.

To realise Artemis could not see the giant scorpion on the ocean floor.

To understand Apollo had manoeuvred me far out to sea, and that Artemis feared ocean-creatures would come to devour me.

For Artemis to raise her bow and loose a silver-tipped arrow.

I watched it come. Flying in a graceful, shining arc. I imagined how many beasts I would share this last sight with. Thousands of deer and boar and goats. The last thing I would ever see. I didn't bother to swim. I didn't bother to even attempt to avoid it.

Artemis' arrows never miss.

I was not of my body when she dragged me back to shore. I floated above her. Above my pale, sagging corpse with her silver arrow pierced through my skull. She could not hear me. Apollo stood by, stupid with shock. Artemis wept. She wept and wept like she wanted to raise the ocean with her tears. Her grief was born, a living thing ripped from her body. Her brother stared at her shuddering form and backed slowly away, his face indecipherable. He won, but at a cost he was incapable of imagining.

Only Artemis was able to dispatch me. And Apollo had made her do just that, by first seeding the idea something was coming from the ocean to kill me, and then fanning her fear. And he did it for her, I suppose. In order to guard her seat on Olympus she could suffer no weakness. I was a weakness. And he rid her of it. He used the sea to deliver my death.

But Artemis never forgave him. It was never her and him against the world again.

Later, Artemis hurled that scorpion into the sky, changing it into a constellation. Scorpio. She did that for me, before she placed me, whatever was left of me, in the opposite end of the sky, with Sirius at my heel.

I look down at my hunter's hands. They are made of starstuff now. But still they twitch. Each night I am ready to hunt, I grip my night-bow and chase until rosy-fingered Eos unravels the sky. I never run out of arrows. My quiver remains always full. And when I light up the night; Artemis is with me. She creates the shadows in which I hunt.

I glimpse the beast even now, chittering and chitinous amongst the stars. Sirius barks behind me, ready to begin the hunt again. The scorpion chases me, and I him. We belong there. We revolve around the Earth. Around Artemis. Sirius and the scorpion and me. Onwards and over. We never tire. I can set the whole power of my being to the task without worry. There is never silence or death. There is only the joy of the hunt.

The endless chase.

About the Author:

Tee is a writer living south of Sydney on the lands of the Dharawal speaking people. Her poetry and short fiction has been published in Australia and around the world.

When she's not puzzling out plots and characters, she's usually wandering around in the cemetery at the end of her street.

Find more of her work at teelinden.com.

Truthseeker

Mikhaeyla Kopievsky

The sands are shifting. The sky overhead turns dark and the emboldened wind hurtles the grains at me like a thousand tiny spears. I pull my keffiyeh higher, the soft cotton covering my nose and bringing with it the lingering scent of cardamom and cinnamon. The scent of the Red Bazaar . . .

"You are too angry. Breathe." The old woman shook her head at me, gold chains and bangles rattling with the movement and sparkling in the amber light cast from the stall's lamps. Around us, the bazaar heaved with activity and noise. It was mid-afternoon, when the crowds avoided the peak of Elanon's summer heat. When the lethargy that had accumulated over hours of tiling roofs or carrying bricks evaporated in the cool air of the tented avenues and the chilled mint tea spiced with cardamom or whiskey. "If you cannot control your anger, you will never pass the test. And you will never find him."

With my head bent against the onslaught of the wind-turned-corporeal, I step forward, pushing against the maelstrom. My heart thunders in its cage, not from the violent weather, but from anticipation. *They will feel your anger,* the old woman had said, *and they will respond.*

I imagine them hiding in the sandstorm—the Aqrabuamelu, the Scorpion Men—with their broad chests, dark skin, and arms as thick as the fabled trees of Gaia. In my dreams, they had worn breastplates blacker than the sky at midnight, and their tails flashed ruby-red, glistening under the twin moons like blood on a scythe.

But it is too early for them; they will come at the third trial, and I haven't yet reached my first.

A different shimmering flashes at the horizon: not the scales of the Scorpion Men, but staccato flashes of white light. With each step, the sandstorm grows wilder, clawing at the bare skin of my wrists as I hide my face behind my arm and press forward. Even through the folds of my keffiyeh, I hear its screams, the wailing of a mother cradling a still and silent baby, the wailing that had exploded from my own chest just one year ago.

The silk trader had found me lying unconscious on the muddy banks of the Nera, my veins full of the poppy milk I had drunk from the silver cup of my wedding. His eyes had been drawn to my orange kaftan trailing in the water, "like the river had stolen the sunset from the sky." I sobbed when I woke in the back of his caravan, my heart breaking all over again and no prospect of death's embrace to end it.

"You are too young to die," he said, his eyes sparking in the night's campfire.

I was too young to be a lot of things; too young to be a wife, too young to be a widow, too young to be a mother, too young to lose a child. "Only death will save me from this misery."

He stared at me thoughtfully, kind eyes sparkling in the firelight, his dark skin turned bronze. "Death is one kind of truth," he said, "but it is not the only."

I drop to my knees and crawl, tucking my head into my chest and pushing my shoulder into the swirling sand. It is a sick irony that would see me die out here, alone and unmourned, after the trader had delivered me from this same fate back in Asana. I had been ready to die back then, but he had given me a lifeline—an impossible story about the Scorpion Men and their Sun God of Truth. I cling to it now as my body falters and collapses to the desert floor. I curl in on myself, shielding my face from the storm, feeling the sand drifts pile up against my stationary body. This desert will be my tomb if I don't move.

A mighty roar thunders from my chest and the sheets of sand swirling around me retreat and fall, the air no longer thick, the sky no longer dark. Less than five body lengths away floats a mirror twice my height and girth. It reflects my surroundings perfectly, but my own reflection is compromised.

"The Sun God of Truth will not be found easily," said the old woman, riffling through the crumpled notes I had given her. "You will first need to pass three trials, each growing in difficulty, each

critical to making your way to the next." The money counted and stuffed into hidden pockets, she turned her scrutiny to me, frowning as she ran her gaze from my limp hair to my scrawny ankles. "You are not built for the warrior's test; you will suffer more."

"I have suffered more already."

She paused, cocked her head, and nodded. "The first trial will test your ability to know your true self. Truth has two faces, the one that looks outward and the one that looks in. You can not know the truth of the world until you first learn the truth of yourself."

The image in the mirror looks older than it should; dark circles around my eyes and a weariness that conspires with gravity to pull me down into the underworld. It remains still, even as I advance. I stare at my reflection as it looks down and away. It almost reminds me of my mother, the same stooped shoulders and worried frown that had followed me around as a child and aged her long before her second husband and fifth child arrived.

And then the image shimmers, weathered skin replaced with a youthful glow, the shuttered eyes now staring defiantly back at me. And just like the first reflection, this one is familiar. I remember her, the fearless goddess of my youth. The girl who free-dived from the Grand Arch Bridge into the icy Nera, who declined the honour to dance for the Vizaar at the harvest moon celebrations, and who fought off the winter wolves seduced by the plaintive cries of a hungry baby.

The sand ripples below the mirror as if twin snakes writhe just below the surface. And then the ground peels away, the sands coughing up two dull metal objects: a bronze stylus and a silver dagger.

"How do I pass the trials?" I asked, looking around the fortune teller's stall, searching amongst the silks and crystals for the kind of magical talisman that would guide me to the Sun God of Truth.

The woman slapped her hand down on the table. Smiling grimly, she plucked at her fine gold bracelet with a painted fingernail. "Each trial will confront you with something, and will give you a choice." The bracelet shimmers, tiny gold charms flashing in the light; hammers and scythes, papyrus stems, water jugs, rope knots. "Only choose one. Only touch one. Only use one. You can take whatever you want into the desert, but if you use anything other than what the trial presents to you, you will die."

Stylus or dagger. The options are as incomprehensible as the challenge—there is nothing to write on and nothing to stab. I step closer, eyes trained on the dagger. An accurate throw could shatter the mirror. But if I were to miss, would the trial be ended? I crouch down to reach for it; if fear of failure had ever mattered, I would never have stepped into the desert four days ago. My fingers are a moonbeam sliver away from the dagger's hilt when I pause and fall back on my haunches, the old woman's words rattling around in my memory. *The first trial will test your ability to know your true self.* Shattering a mirror of distorted reflections could be a repudiation of my false selves, but it wouldn't help me to accept my true self.

True self. I already know my true self—lost, empty, shattered. I am not weary like my mother was, nor vibrant like I used to be. I am alone. I am bereft. I am broken.

With trembling hands, I pick up the bronze stylus, its metal cool and heavy to the touch. I point it towards the sand, ready to write the words in the drifts. But the words are not enough, because I am not just broken, I am also a fighter. I pull up the sleeve of my kaftan, past the fine, white scar-lines of my previous death attempts, and drag the stylus across the pale flesh of my wrist. The instrument slices as easily into the skin as the dagger would have, carving out the Elanonian word for orphan, *YIHIXXYM.* The blood threads down my forearm, dripping from my elbow to sand. With the mirror still shimmering above, I stand on shaky legs. There are no more corrupted reflections, no fictions, just my true reflection.

I pull down my keffiyeh, and stare at the face that looks back at me. Wild-eyed and weary, but determined. I lift my arm, seeing the word carved into the skin transform in the reflection to its reverse. MYXXIHIY. Warrior.

The wound is a perfect paradox—neither descriptor true on their own, both true only when existing simultaneously.

The mirror shatters, sending tiny glass fragments raining down fire embers. Except these fragments don't scatter randomly: they fall in a perfect line that stretches toward the horizon.

The sand shimmers ahead, the impossible promise of water too much for my dehydrated mind to resist. My feet drag in the soft drifts, the resistance shredding already tired muscles. Death is stalking me and I am too slow to outrun it, and too sun-addled to outwit it.

"How will I know if I pass the trial?" I kept my voice low, worried that the fantasy of finding the Sun God would dissipate like the echoes of a dream if I spoke of it too loudly.

"You won't," the woman replied, pouring two short glasses of anais and mixing it with water to turn the alcohol milky, "until you find the next trial."

"But, what if I don't find the next trial?"

"Then you will die. Like so many others before you."

The illusion of water grows more insistent the closer I get. It's harder to rationalise away its rippling and reflection of the colourless sky, or its sweet, almost fragrant scent cutting through the dusty smell of barrenness. Harder still to hold firm the memory of the first trial, which slips further into the realms of a desperate fantasy.

"Desperate," the water whispers to me, the rippling on the surface growing stronger.

"Coward," it whispers again.

The water is shifting, the apparition morphing into three towering figures with translucent skin and amorphous features.

"You deserted your family," the first whispers, the voice a harsh gurgling as water falls in waves from the place where I imagine the mouth to be.

"I didn't desert them," I rasp, sinking to my knees as the delusion and exhaustion begin to overwhelm me. "I outgrew them."

"Liar," the middle spectre shouts, water spraying from its shimmering head and alighting on the burnt skin around my eyes. So real is the sensation, my hands fly up to touch the droplets, fingers coming away dry and warm instead.

"You abandoned them, and your duty," the third one booms. "You left them to avoid the weight of their expectations and dreams for you."

"Yes," I cry, the memory of their suffocating ambition too strong to deny.

"You were selfish and you were reckless," another bellows and I am not sure which; my eyes shut tight against the aberration and the memories. "You left the family that had sacrificed their own desires for your future, not for a greater purpose or a more noble cause, but for a flight of fancy."

It is impossible to not think of Richa. The same night I had fled from the harvest moon celebrations, I had run into the arms of my beloved Richa. A soldier in the Vizaar's army, he was handsome and brash and promised all the sorts of trouble and abandon I was searching for. We married three months later, just two days before he left for a far-off place and a foreign war. A wife one day, a widow less than a month later.

"You betrayed everyone for your desires and your sorrow," a gurgling voice calls. "You were selfish in your happiness and negligent in your grief. Turning them all away, turning inward, shutting yourself off behind your cold, dark walls."

"No," I whisper. Not everyone. My mother and father, yes. I had left them behind. And maybe I had broken their hearts— neither of them had spoken to me after I accepted Richa's proposal; hadn't seen me lay my wedding wreath or Richa's funeral wreath. Had never laid eyes on Arabella. Not that she had been alive long enough for them to have a change of heart, to forgive their daughter for the sake of their granddaughter.

My Arabella. The one I had never betrayed.

"Yes," one of the water sentinels counters, the sound of rushing floodwaters in the Nera. "Everyone."

"Not Arabella," I shout, opening my eyes and glaring at the unnatural abominations.

"Especially her," the one closest to me rumbles, water cascading down its liquid body and turning the sand dark.

"I loved her!"

"You forgot her. Wrapped yourself up in your misery and melancholy. Her cries weren't as important as yours, her needs a chore."

"I saved her."

"You saved yourself from another loss."

The cruelty of the accusation steals the air from my lungs. How dare they? It wasn't true. It *couldn't* be true. And yet, the indignant rage that had course through my veins like fire just seconds ago fails to flare again.

She had been so tiny. A little caramel-coloured bundle of squirming and cooing innocence. I had swaddled her slowly, fingers drifting over perfect skin and fuzzy hair. I had loved her; I love her still. She had been a good baby, rarely crying, sleeping well through most of the night. And yet, there had been times when her little hands had curled towards my fingers and I had pulled away, too tired, too lonely to have any energy left to be present for someone else. Nights when her little cries had spilled from the wooden crib in our draughty room and I had pulled the thick woollen blankets up over my head and stayed cocooned in the heavy embrace of a non-judgemental, undemanding, comforting sleep.

It had been a still, snow-covered morning when I awoke too late. The weak sun was already casting soft shadows on the timber floor, the hearth's embers still glowing a warm orange, and the crib beside me was silent. The memory of Arabella, her once rosebud lips turned an icy blue, still flashes with cruel clarity. I had wailed at the sight of it, screamed until my voice gave out and my chest could no longer support the wracking tremors that pitched my body forward and trapped my heart in a vice.

I had wailed, but under the scrutiny of these desert apparitions, the grief in my memory is changing colour and shape. It is less pure, less noble. More selfish, more indulgent.

Tears fall from my cheeks to join the wet sand at my knees. "I failed her. I failed everyone."

Water rushes around me, soaking my kaftan and soothing tortured skin. One water sentinel remains, its form trembling and swaying in the still, hot air of the desert. "You have proved yourself capable of learning hard truths, but the real truth still evades you. The sting-tailed guardians will test you further. To know the full truth, you must prove that you want it."

My feet drag through the sand, pulling me toward the mountains that have started to dominate the horizon, but my eyes continue to track elsewhere, looking for signs of another pathway. A way out. In these rare moments of lucidity, I can tell that I am wandering wild-eyed, remember that my rations are gone, my canteen dry.

I blink and the mountains appear closer. I distantly wonder how much time has passed unremembered, half-lived. Blessedly, the sun has retreated behind dark clouds and the beginnings of a northerly trade wind pick up. I pull the keffiyeh from my face and lift my face to the breeze, closing my eyes and savouring this final reprieve.

The wind turns colder, causing me to shiver and open my eyes. The mountain towers before me, engulfing me in its shadow. On shaky legs, I take a step forward and then another. The ground rumbles, throwing me off balance and sending me crashing to the rocky ground. I brace myself for an avalanche of rocks to dispatch me, but the rumbling ceases.

Looking up, I catch the glint of red and gold plates, shining in light that stretches from four doorways that seem embedded in nothing but the desert air. I shield my face, squinting to bring the vision into focus.

Four men, broad-shouldered and thick chested, tower above me; their charcoal-ringed eyes regard me without curiosity or menace. Dark hair curls around their temples and falls to their armoured breastplates in thick braids cinched with bands of gold. They are beautiful. And terrifying.

The red, black and gold of their breastplates segue seamlessly into tessellated abdomens that curve underneath them in sleek, powerful lines. Four pairs of black, slender legs spring from each of them and end in wicked points that stab at the sand. They appear as statues, except for their tails, which glitter like the blades of a scythe. Crowned with a red venom bulb and golden stinger, they flick around the Scorpion Men as though tasting the air.

"What do you desire?" The tallest Aqrabuamelu tilts his head at me. His voice is not the booming terror of the water sentinels, but rich and luxurious, like liquid amber or spiced honey.

"To see the Sun God of Truth," I reply, my voice rough and hoarse as I stand up.

The Scorpion Man's arm, broad and inked with henna, reaches out to open the door behind him a little wider. Through the opening I can make out the valleys of Asana, the afternoon sun a gentle benediction, its rays falling dappled to lush green fields and glinting off brooks that snake away from the Nera. "Why seek the Sun God, when you can step back into your life in Asana?"

"Or start a new one, here in Elanon," the one to his right croons. The door next to him opens wider, the view stretching out over Elanon's capital, to the vibrant city streets, the glass spire of the taj, and the canvas-covered Red Bazaar. People move about in that easy way of the contented and oblivious. I could get lost in that city, could let its bustling neighbourhoods and ever-present noise slough away my damaged life and tortured memories.

"Why choose a path you have already trodden?" a third asks, seduction dripping from his words. He pushes his own door wider; large swaths of green pasture and wildflowers stretch endlessly before me, a small village sits nestled in the shadow of a snow-capped mountain, and the brightly coloured ribbons from a maypole flutter on a breeze.

These Scorpion Men are not the monsters the trader or the fortune teller had made them out to be. They are stunning and seductive and offering me the choice of my desired futures with no payment but a few simple steps through a doorway. My tired body melts with relief, my parched throat swells painfully as I push down the unbidden sob of relief. They have released me from this perilous journey and saved me from the spoils of my reckless and hot-headed quest.

I turn to the final Scorpion Man, who has remained still and silent while his brothers have tempted me with their offerings. His eyes are brighter than the others, but he regards me with less interest. I peer past him to his doorway, but unlike the others, it is opened the tiniest of cracks. No light spills from the gap, his tail shrouded in shadow, its stinger appearing dull and colourless.

"What are you doing here, Kaeli?" Eron was surprised to see me in the Cynefin Clearing; he knew I should have been dancing for the Vizaar in the royal courtyard. He looked flushed in the orange glow of the fire, his hair messy and his uniform untucked. It was a well-known secret that the lower ranked Elanorian soldiers, excluded from the royal courtyard, were hosting their own celebrations that night; and I much preferred the haphazard abandon of roguish friends than the stuffy civility of Elanorian elite. I took the mug from his hands before he could stop me and downed the bittersweet liquid in two gulps. My parents would be

furious, but I would face their wrath tomorrow. For now, I just wanted to be free.

"You'll ruin your dress," Eron said, tugging at my emerald skirts. He looked handsome that night, unburdened from the responsibility that awaited him, older with the weight of what was to come, but not yet corrupted by it.

I knocked his hand away and handed back his mug, trailing my eyes across the raucous revelry. "Ruined dress, ruined woman."

He laughed, scoffing at the idea. Eron had known me as a child. We had grown up four houses apart, had shared the same wet nurse, had rumbled in the muddy banks of the Nera and nursed broken bones from falling off weakened branches in the Arto Forest. He knew I was no more ruined than the first fall of snow in winter.

"You look pretty tonight, Kaeli." His voice held a soft sincerity, floating on the bravado that liquor always delivered. I flicked him playfully on the ear and grinned. Eron had always been sweet on me, his glances and touches becoming more hesitant and less innocent in the two years since our adult rites. He grabbed my hand in his and pressed a gentle kiss on my palm.

For the briefest of moments, I considered what a life would be like with him; a good man, from a good family. A brave man, a gentle man. And then I had seen Richa—his bronze hair almost burnished in the firelight, the golden buttons of his uniform glowing like stars.

My hand disentangled from Eron's, my childhood beau forgotten. His lustre could never outshine Richa's

"What future do you promise me?" I murmur to the final Aqrabuamelu.

He shakes his head, his braid rippling like a snake across his shoulder. "I promise no future," he says, his voice deep and resonant. "It is not mine to promise or pre-empt."

The other Scorpion Men are whispering to me, tempting me with the desires I hold tight in my heart and barely dare to entertain. And yet, I keep my gaze on this last guardian.

"To know the full truth, you must prove that you want it."

"Will you let me enter your doorway?" I ask, stepping forward to him. This close, I have to tilt my head up to meet his gaze.

His tail segments ripple as the sharp point of his stinger draws closer. I flinch but do not step back. "Truth is not something that is offered," he says, blue eyes flashing, the stinger scoring a line down my neck. "It must be sought."

My head swims, details once clear turn hazy and amorphous. The sharp lines of the dark doorway are fading. I stumble forward, my hands bracing against something smooth and hard. I push past it, searching for the heavy weight of the final door. I stumble again, slamming hard into an unseen obstacle, no longer able to discern anything from the darkness and silence that suffocate me.

"Why do you come to me?"

I blink against the soft, warm light that spills through the cavern and illuminates a thousand crystallised spears that hang from the ceiling and jut from the floor. A throne made of golden blades radiating like a halo sits upon a floating dais. I try to train my eyes on the being that sits upon it, but the light is too bright and I avert my gaze, staring down at the dirt floor.

"I come to seek the truth," I whisper, heart smashing against my ribcage, responding with the answer the fortune teller had made me remember.

"What truth do you seek?"

I think of Arabella, her tiny hands reaching for mine, and of Eron, his earnest eyes searching for the tiniest of hints his affection could be requited. I think of my parents, honest and hardworking, left heartbroken and cold. I had come here to demand why fate had taken so much away from me—to ask why I had been so cruelly robbed of a husband and a child and a life of beauty and joy. To sate the shame that grows like a canker in my chest.

"Was it my fault?" I whisper, to the Sun God, to the ghosts of my past.

"That is not the truth you seek."

No, it is not. Because I know it was my fault and because the question I really want to ask, the truth that I need to know, is *was I worthy of their love, even as I shunned it?*

"This is the way of truth," the Sun God says, their voice a molten river of lava. "It always makes itself known to those who seek it. It is never as hidden as we imagine, never far from our grasp. It does not take a journey through the desert to find it, but a journey to the root of the soul. You do not need me for your answer, you already know it."

About the Author:

Mikhaeyla Kopievsky is an Australian speculative fiction writer and author of the Divided Elements series and Tasmanian Gothic. Her short stories have been longlisted for the EJ Brady Prize and published in Etherea Magazine and Deadset Press anthologies. Her debut novel, Resistance, was a semi-finalist in Hugh Howey's inaugural SPSF Competition and winner of a OneBookTwo Standout Award.

Born in Sydney, Mikhaeyla now livs in the Hunter Valley on Worimi land with her husband, son, two rescue dogs, four Australorp chooks, a hive of cantankerous bees, and the occasional herd of beautiful Black Angus steers. When she is not writing or reading, Mikhaeyla enjoys cooking with the produce harvested from her kitchen garden, going to the beach, stargazing, and training to be a ninja.

W: www.mikhaeylakopievsky.com.
F: https://www.facebook.com/MikhaeylaKopievsky.
T: https://twitter.com/MikhaeylaK.

SAGITTARIUS
NOVEMBER 22 - DECEMBER 21

THE TALBOTVILLE CENTAUR

Tim Borella

The pass office was to the right of the gaol's main entrance, where a large gate between two imposing bluestone turrets was open to admit a laden dray pulled by a pair of fine Clydesdales. The guard I followed was unimpressed at having been ordered to escort me, no doubt in his view just another time-wasting newshound. Down echoing corridors we walked, through barred gates, across the forbidding square and past the gallows—used less often nowadays but still quite ready to perform its function—and through a door in a high wall, into a compound within a compound. At last we reached the ugly stone building that housed the object of my interest.

My reluctant guide used every key on the large ring clipped to his belt to negotiate the series of locked doors leading into the gloomy interior, where the silence was cut only by our footsteps as we walked along a row of cells, all empty bar the last.

My first encounter with the prisoner was something of a disappointment. I had imagined a fearsome creature, and indeed he must have been at some time, to have ended up in this place reserved for the notorious and dangerous. But the figure I beheld was unimposing, slight even; an impression magnified by the outsized prison clothing he wore. His dark hair, long and wild at the time of his capture, had been hacked short, with strands of grey curving through it. He could have passed for one of the prematurely aged wastrels one often passed in Melbourne's dark laneways, and there was a corresponding stink in the cell to boot.

He had been brought in, still clad in the roughly cut hide of a stolen beast, following an extensive manhunt which was sparked by numerous complaints of unlawful interference with cattle, culminating in the death of a stockman who had attempted to thwart his actions. Months had now passed since his capture, and after an initial burst of excitement, the hubbub had just as quickly died down. The city was ever ready for some new sensation—the rumour of a new gold seam, murmurs of another royal scandal—so it was no surprise that the fickle focus of public attention had moved on. It would swing back if he were to hang, though, and I planned to be ready for that eventuality.

He sat huddled on the floor in the corner of the cell, even though both a hard bed and low bench were available. He did not raise his eyes when we entered, but he flinched as the key turned in the lock and I could tell he was watching me while pretending not to, a skill I myself was well practiced at.

Whether it was because the prisoner didn't appear capable of harming me, or that the gaoler didn't care if he did, he stepped back out of the cell and locked the door behind him.

"Shout out when you're finished," he ordered, already making for the guard's niche we'd passed on the way in.

I turned back to the man on the floor, who had shifted so he was now more side-on to me, his cheek pressed up against the hard bluestone. I stayed where I was, maintaining as much distance between us as possible in that small space. He was quiet but tense, his small sidelong glances and the rapid rise and fall of his chest giving him away.

"I won't hurt you, old fellow," I said, and felt immediately foolish. This was an accused thief and murderer, one who'd had the whole town talking, and yet in that moment not threatening but terrified. Perhaps it was just my imagination, but my impression was of an animal at bay.

I was fascinated by him, and found myself studying him as if he were an exhibit in a natural history museum. His feet were bare despite the cold, soles calloused and scored, and every inch of exposed skin bore some scar or blemish. The prison garb hid his proportions but there was a sense of wiry strength to him. A growth of coarse beard covered his jaw.

Without realising it, I'd crept closer until—with the speed of a striking snake—he jumped to his feet. I stumbled back, shocked, hands raised both in apology and in readiness for whatever he might try.

He was facing me, feet apart, dark eyes wide, nostrils flaring. For some seconds I was transfixed by his stare. It felt like an electrical signal passed between us, as if something beyond my ken was being communicated to me, and without rational basis, I understood my own eyes were sending a return signal, a message that I had not come to jeer or harm, but rather learn and understand.

Very slowly I retreated, until my back touched the iron bars. With that, he resumed his despondent huddle in the corner.

Approaching the guard's niche on the way out, I asked if I might trouble him with a question or two. At first he was cagey, but a couple of shillings and an assurance that any comments he made would be off the record saw a marked change in his demeanour. I started by asking him about the prisoner's routine.

"Well, he don't do much at all," he said. "Paced around a lot when he first came in, tried to rush out the door whenever he thought he had half a chance, but a touch of the lash soon settled that down. Wouldn't eat, neither—went about a week on just a few drops o' water. Oh—there's a strange thing as well! The beggar didn't even know how to use a cup, tried to suck the water out of the top rather than pick it up. He learned, though, I'll give him that. He ain't stupid, but . . . don't know how to put it, exactly. Doesn't seem to know anything much about anything. Can't talk, or won't, anyway. Even messed himself a couple of times, until we got him trained to use the bucket."

"I see," I said. "And how did you do that?"

A cruel smile creased the guard's stubbled face. "He don't seem to understand English, but—" he glanced at the short whip hanging on the wall, "—that there tends to break down language barriers without too much trouble."

Bishop set his tankard down and leant towards me across the dark wooden table of one of the Union Hotel's quieter booths. "I must tell you, Hawley, I think the whole story's a lot of rot."

"Maybe so," I said, "but you'd have heard the hysteria around town when they brought him in. Even if there's not a grain of truth in any of it, I'll bet I can put something together that will sell."

"Well, you've never let an absence of facts hold you back before, have you, old man?" he laughed. "Why start now, eh?"

"Why, I find that rather offensive!" I said, adopting an aggrieved look but unable to suppress a smile. My bookmaker friend and I went back a long way.

"You know, though," I continued, "there's something about this fellow that has me convinced he's more than just a common ruffian. I can't explain it, but now I've visited him a few times, I'm sure there's . . . I don't know, a kind of wild sincerity to him."

"Come on now," said Bishop. "The man can't even speak, can he? How can you comment on his character?"

I frowned. How indeed? And yet I was sure the odd communication between me and the prisoner was more than just a figment of my imagination. Still, putting that into words wasn't possible in the smoky ordinariness of our favourite watering hole. I tapped the dottle out of my pipe and reached into my waistcoat pocket for my tin, extracted an aromatic pinch, tamped it down and relit. My thoughts were as intangible as the rising smoke. "Yes, yes, you're right, I'm sure," I said. "Still, the whole improbable thing fascinates me for some reason. I just wish there was some way I could flesh the story out a bit. It seems to be all rumour and innuendo—my friend's cousin's father-in-law overheard someone say he thought he saw him, that kind of thing."

Bishop nodded and raised his hand to order us another round. "I tell you what, this may be an example of the very thing you're talking about, but I do happen to know a fellow." He paused, making me wait.

"And?" I said, intrigued but cautious not to take the bait too quickly. My friend didn't mind having a lend of a person now and then, though always good-naturedly.

"An old fellow, a cripple. A bit too fond of the drink, perhaps, but one can understand that. Hurt himself in a riding accident some years ago up in the mountains; in quite a bit of pain most of the time I gather, can't walk properly."

"Yes, yes," I urged. "Do get to the point."

"Well. I often see him poking about the racetrack. Not able to do much on account of the injuries, y'see, but the trainers all listen to him. Knows what he's talking about, one of those old bushmen who could ride before they could walk."

"And what does this have to do with—"

412

"Patience, old man. I'm coming to that." He took a sip of his beer and scraped the foam from his moustache with a quick movement of his bottom lip. "So," he continued, "this fellow—Dixon? Dutton? Something like that. Anyway, word is that when they brought your man in, the old boy was just about apoplectic. Went around telling all and sundry that this wasn't a man at all but a daemon, a half-man half-horse who'd been creating havoc up in the high country for years, wrecking fences and stampeding cattle over cliffs, running wild with the brumbies. Reckoned he'd seen him with his own eyes."

I raised an eyebrow. "Sounds like he does like a drink."

"Well, maybe so," said Bishop, "but I overheard him talking with a strapper about it, and while I grant you it sounded like a load of superstitious old poppycock, the impression I got was that he wasn't just spinning a yarn. He sounded serious, and as you know, I'm a fair judge of these things."

Indeed he was. Bishop was a good companion and a jocular fellow, but also a shrewd businessman. I'd not yet met the person who could fool him.

"So even if what he said was impossible," I said, "he himself believed it?"

"Precisely."

"Well, that's a good start, at least. I get the impression that the real facts of this matter will remain a mystery, but when this wild man goes to the gallows—as I suspect he will—there's going to be a resurgence of public interest, and I intend to be ready for it. Will you put me in touch with this . . . what's his name?"

"Dalton! That's it." Bishop stroked his moustache, then gave a quick nod. "Yes, if you like."

A few days later I sat on a crowded tram, rocking gently as the sturdy horses in front pulled us along the tracks. With my brown leather briefcase resting at my feet, I was squeezed in between an older woman with a pile of empty hessian shopping bags and a young man in patched working clothes—a builder's labourer or bricklayer, judging by his sturdy build and calloused hands. I always enjoyed riding the trams, as they allowed me to observe my fellow Melburnians in all their variations whilst going about my daily business.

This day was overcast, with the odd sprinkling of rain as we travelled the Flemington line, being overtaken by sulkies and carriages, halting regularly at the various stops. Tall poplars lined the wide road, and a steady breeze ruffled their leaves while providing welcome relief from the infernal flies that were an unavoidable by-product of the copious piles of manure scattered about the streets by our equine-powered transport systems. Steam carriages—unreliable things based on the principle the trains used for locomotion—had been seen wheezing and popping around town in recent years, scaring horses and breaking down at inopportune times, and there had been reports of vehicles powered by the new internal combustion engines becoming popular overseas. Social grandstanding being what it was, I suspected it wouldn't be too long before they'd make their way to us and perhaps usher in a cleaner, more pleasant future.

For now, though, it was horses I was focused on, particularly their relationship to the prisoner. I didn't know what to believe of the florid rumours I'd heard about him, but there must have been at least some basis in fact for the troopers to have brought him in. He had been charged with murder and other serious offences under the Crimes Act, including cattle stealing, and numerous other matters ranging from petty misdemeanours such as the working of animals without consent of the owner, to the abominable crime of buggery with an animal. I was somewhat perplexed as to what evidence the prosecution might use to bring about a conviction on that last matter.

The conductor's shout brought me out of my reverie and I stepped down from the tram, pausing first to check the road was clear. A pregnant woman had been knocked down and her legs broken not a week before by a reckless young driver laying on the whip, more interested in the girl beside him than the road in front. I had not heard what had become of the unborn child, but could only assume that nothing good could come of such a shock.

On foot, I made my way down several side streets leading towards the racetrack, nestled into a wide bend of the Maribyrnong. The houses got shabbier as I walked, until I came to the address Bishop had given me. The dwelling was modest but clean, of weatherboard and corrugated iron patched with various boards and sheeting that did not match the original. I hesitated for a moment, then knocked at the door. I was about to knock again when I heard stirrings from inside, and a stout woman with her hair in a bun peeked around the edge of the door. I introduced myself, and satisfied that I was not a threat of any kind, the lady of the house advised that I should go around to the back of the premises, where I would find 'Old Thomas'.

I thanked her and picked my way through the overgrown citrus trees crowded between the side of the house and the wooden fence separating it from its virtual twin next door. A scruffy piebald dog poked its head around the edge of the building in much the same way as the woman had done at the door, then retreated, granting me entry to the small back yard. In the far corner was a rough shed which wouldn't have been out of place in a farmer's paddock, walled in on three sides, the fourth sporting a thick curtain made from wheat bags held aside by being thrown over the structure's top corner. Smoke rose from a small fire in a circle of stones just outside the entrance, and beside it on a low wooden stool sat a white-haired man, hunched over with elbows resting on knees, gazing at the glowing coals.

I cleared my throat and he looked up, blinking owlishly a couple of times.

"Good morning, sir," I said, as if the man was a banker and I had come to his office to apply for a loan. "I hope you don't mind the intrusion. I'm Theodore Hawley, and my good friend Mr Bishop suggested I seek you out as someone who is knowledgeable on the subject of horses."

He sat up, a pained expression crossing his face as he moved, but I could tell he was pleased to have been described thus. "I do know a thing or two about horses, that's true enough," he said, the hint of an Irish accent colouring his words. "But what might you be wanting to find out about them from me, I wonder?"

Various items lay about in the hut, including an iron-framed cot and some pots and pans, and another stool.

"May I sit down?" I asked. "I'm a writer, interested in the experiences of cattlemen such as yourself in the high country. I do have a number of questions I'd like to ask, and I thought—if you don't mind, of course—we might talk for a while. Over a drink, perhaps?" I patted my briefcase, and the old fellow's demeanour brightened.

"Pull up a chair."

For the first half hour we spoke in general terms about his experiences as a younger man working cattle up in the hills and high plains stretching northward from Gippsland up into the alpine regions past Dargo and across to the Snowy River, where the weather could range from oppressive heat to bitter blizzard and a man needed his wits about him to survive, let alone keep vast herds of stock alive and safe.

I sipped from my tin mug of rum, while Tom, as he'd invited me to call him, took a more robust approach.

"Helps ease the joints a little," he said, setting his pannikin down on the ground beside him and gingerly shifting his posture.

As we talked, his observations moved from the factual—how he, the son of an immigrant labourer, had gained hard experience and come to be considered an expert in cattle handling in the alpine country—to more personal matters, like the effects of long spells alone with only cattle and horses for companionship; the certain knowledge that a serious accident or a snake bite would mean the end; the strange effects some places had on the mind so that stories of spirits and monsters that would seem laughable under normal circumstances became magnified to the point where men on their own could be driven mad by them.

He spoke of encounters with natives, common in his early experiences but rarer as men like he himself put up fences and denied them access to hunting grounds and waterholes in the quest to secure good pastures, or drove them like animals with whips and guns so there could be no question about who the ancient mountains and abundant high plains belonged to.

"And the horses!" said Tom, taking a good swig from his mug and looking away as if seeing a vision of his younger self galloping across a wide river valley in pursuit of errant strays. "Great mobs of brumbies, breeding up in the good seasons and hidin' God knows where in the winters. They could be a menace, cuttin' up the ground and fouling the waterholes, eating feed the cattle should have had, but by the Lord Harry, could the beggars run!"

The old fellow had been drinking freely but was not yet affected to the point where his perceptions were dulled and confused, and the time was now right to raise the subject I'd come to discuss.

"Tom," I said, "do you think there's any truth to the stories that have been going around about this fellow who's been brought in, the one they captured up near Talbotville?"

He quickly turned to me, his air of nostalgic reflection gone. "Oh, there's truth, all right," he said, eyes alive with intensity. I was afraid he might close up, but my instincts told me to continue questioning.

"Could you tell me a little of what you know?"

He was quiet for a time, staring back into the fire; then, he began to speak. "Most city folk don't know what it's like to live in the real world. They think what they see is all there is, but they are blind. I'm not talking about the kinds o' things my old mother—God rest her—used to go on about, spilling salt or never picking a white flower, but real things, things you see when you're properly on your own."

"And this man?" I said. "What about him?"

Tom ran his fingers over the grey stubble on his chin. "What about him? Well, Mister Hawley, I'll tell you this. I may be old and broken and a drunkard, but I am not mad, though plenty of people will tell you otherwise. The man you speak of, if he really is a man, is in league with the horses. He knows them, he speaks to them, he is one of them."

"And you have seen him?"

Again he was quiet, gathering his thoughts before continuing. "I'd heard talk for years, which I took as bungler's excuses for lost cattle, or else made-up fancies, like stories about bunyips and ghosts. Then, spring of seventy-three, when the weather was warming up and I was bringing a mob up along the Crooked River, I camped for a spell on a nice wide bend with plenty of feed. Nights were quiet, but after I'd been there a few days the cattle started getting stirred up for no reason. I'd get out of my swag and scout around, but apart from the odd wild dog, I wouldn't find anything.

"Then, this night, I woke to a mad rush. The cattle were everywhere, and for a minute I thought I might be trampled where I lay. Well, I jumped up and ran for my gelding, who I'd hobbled and staked, but when I got to him, he'd broken the tether and was lurching around fit to bust himself. The air was thick with the sound of pounding hooves, galloping horses, and in the moonlight a great mob of them circled around us like the devil himself was chasing them.

"I managed to get the bridle on my horse and throw the saddle over him and got on with no idea of what I might do, but I had to do something, otherwise the cattle would be spread from there to New South Wales. I rode out towards the front of that mob of brumbies with my stockwhip ready thinking I might be able to drive them off, but as I came at them, they turned away by themselves and raced off towards the hills."

"What did you do then?" I asked, caught up in his tale.

"Well, I thought I was all right, because they were gone and I'd be able to round up my cattle and go back to sleep, but when I tried to turn my horse there was no stopping him. I've ridden some hard-mouthed scrubbers in my time but Samson himself couldn't have dragged the reins hard enough to pull this fella up, and he was normally gentle as a lamb.

"We were racing along flat out and I thought about jumpin' off before he put his hoof in a wombat hole or smashed me into a tree branch, but I ain't never been one to bail, and half of me wanted to see what this mob of horses was up to, besides. The moonlight was bright enough to see, so I just hung on, and we kept going. After a while we caught up with the mob, and my horse ran alongside them like a fish in a school. Nothing I could do would turn him or slow him down, and I could have jumped on to the backs of the brumbies beside us, they were so close. The sound of their hooves—it was like thunder! Then, as we came alongside a rise, something made me look up."

I leaned forward, caught up in the mad ride with him.

"And there, up on the hillside, was another group of horses, and as we passed they came galloping down to join the race. And on the back of one, or maybe part of one, or so it looked to me, with his body cloaked in fur, his bare arms ready to strike, and his hair flowing out behind him like a mane, was this man, or beast. He flew down towards me like an angel, shouting in some language nobody'd ever heard, and as he did so the horses beside us turned at his command and pushed us off our course. I looked ahead and

I saw we were coming to the edge of a scarp, and yet those horses kept pushing us towards it."

"What happened then?" I said, breathless.

"We went right over the edge, my old horse and me," he said, eyes locked with mine.

I raised my mug and took a good mouthful, hardly noticing the burn.

When we had both recovered our equilibrium somewhat, I was able to tease out the rest of Tom's story. By some miracle, he had survived the fall, though grievously injured. He didn't remember much of the aftermath, but thought his horse must have taken most of the impact. Instinct, he thought, must have made him drag himself towards the river, where he was found just in time by another cattleman, and taken, barely alive, to help.

"But who *is* he?" I said, still lost in thoughts of the wild horseman. "How could a man come to be living with brumbies in the high country, a white man who knows nothing of our language or customs and who seems intent on driving us lock, stock and barrel out of the place? How could he even survive?"

"Oh, he did more than survive. He had everything he needed; food and clothing from the cattle he thieved and killed, and the command and trust of wild brumbies—who would throw the best horseman in a second—but carried him fast and freely so he could not be caught."

"But such a man could not appear from nowhere, could he?"

"That I can't say," he replied. "But there are two ways you might look at it. There's been all kinds of people pokin' around the hills over the years, from the Aborigines who were there long before us, to the prospectors and cattlemen, and the just plain ignorant who went up there in search of God knows what and perished. I know of young children who wandered away from their parents and no-one ever knew what became of them. Dead, probably, but maybe not. The natives could find a feed anywhere, moths and insects and roots where you'd think there was nothin' at all to be had, so perhaps he somehow did the same, or perhaps they took him in for a time."

"And the other way?" I said.

Old Tom took another long drink and put his mug back down. "Ah," he said. "The other way. Well, like I said, most people don't look around themselves too much, but when you're out in the bush alone and you see them stars so bright, you know there's much more. Those brumbies are new to this country, like us, but their spirit is old. We come along and push the country around, try and change it to suit ourselves, maybe there comes a time when it pushes back."

Three weeks after my meeting with Old Thomas, word came that the Talbotville Centaur, as the less reputable papers had come to call him, had been found guilty on all charges and was sentenced to hang.

I spent a lot of time trying to sort what I knew and had surmised of him into shape for a saleable story, but my thoughts kept returning to the old cattleman's tale, dragging my sympathies in two directions at once. On the one hand, there was no doubt in my mind that the man in gaol was indeed a thief and a murderer, guilty of crimes that had seen many before him mount the gibbet. But on the other . . . I had to see him once more in the flesh to settle the matter in my mind.

The next day, I made my way once again to the gaol and went through the lengthy process of gaining entry. Visitors were required to leave all possessions at the guardhouse, but on impulse I'd brought a bible with me, and this I was allowed to take in. The guard who had accompanied me on my first visit was on duty again, seeming quite cheerful.

"Not so sure this fella's ever been near a church," he said as we passed the gallows. "Oh well, the Lord moves in mysterious ways as they say, don't he?"

As before, he left me in the cell with the prisoner and went back to his station. The condemned man was crouched in his habitual position beside the wall, not looking at me, and I wondered if he could have been the one who sent Tom and his horse over the cliff, if indeed any of what the old fellow had said was true. I had no idea what I'd expected to achieve by coming there, and was overcome by a feeling of hopelessness as I studied the unkempt man who, in a few short days, would drop like a sack of wheat from the rope outside.

I lowered myself to the floor and sat cross-legged with my back against the bars. Now we were on the same level, he turned towards me and once again our gaze met. There was not the same spark of electricity as on that first day, but I felt an immense compassion for the poor fellow, a true outsider among his own species, one who could never belong in this crowded city and was perhaps better off leaving it once and for all.

I placed the bible on the floor and slid it partway across to him. What good it would do, I could not think, but there was little else I could offer. He looked from me to the leather-bound book and back again, and when our eyes met once more there was a calmness in them that had not been there a moment before. Knowing there was nothing more I could do for him, I got to my feet and called the guard.

The key clanked in the lock and the door swung open. I turned for a final look at the wretched prisoner, and just as I did so, several things happened at once. The bible was now in his hands, and he looked to me with a small jerk of his head as if telling me to move out of the way, and sprang to his feet. I reeled back as he jumped forward, swinging the heavy bible and landing a cracking blow on the guard's temple, sending him crumpling to the concrete.

The key ring still hung in the open door's lock, and I grabbed it, stepped over the unmoving guard, and took off down the corridor. After a moment's hesitation, the prisoner followed.

As we neared the guard's station, I sorted through the keys and found the one I thought opened the outer door. The coiled whip still hung on its peg and the prisoner's eyes narrowed at the sight of it. Then he went into a kind of trance, head bowed, staring at some point on the wall.

A moment later, the air was full of shouts and the whinnying and stamping of horses, followed by crashing and urgent whistle blasts. With nowhere to go but forward, I turned the key and opened the door, committing us to whatever might come next.

The yard was in uproar, with an overturned dray spilling its load onto the ground, and guards and an agitated driver ran around in pursuit of the team of horses that had been hitched to it but were now bolting around, pulling broken bits of harness behind them. Nobody noticed us at first, and my thought was to hug the walls, dodging the bedlam while making for the nearest exit.

I had run thirty yards when I sensed some change and turned back to see what was happening. Rather than following me, the prisoner had stepped out into the middle of the confusion and was standing boldly in the open. The guards, too, had realised he was there and were moving towards him with batons drawn, but as they did so, something I can still scarcely believe took place. Two of the four horses advanced on the guards, rearing and striking out with their hooves like knight's destriers, forcing the men to retreat. The other two came forward, one either side of the prisoner, and he grasped the mane of one and leapt onto its back. The other then joined its fellows and they formed a kind of shield, pushing forward while the prisoner, crouching low, was carried towards the main gate.

As he drew near, a strange sound grew from outside the prison walls, so unusual it took me a while to understand what it was; the vocalisations of innumerable horses. I could only liken it to the howling of wolves as they gave voice to their shared power.

The last I saw of the Talbotville Centaur was when he passed me, a bright elation in his eyes. He regarded me and I stared back at him. It may be foolish to ascribe meaning to that look, but if I had to swear, I would say we shared a fleeting communication as fellow primates before he was returned to his rightful place, and gone from my sight forever.

About the Author:

Tim Borella is an Australian author of speculative fiction. He contributes to AntipodeanSF, and has recently had stories published by Deadset Press, Horrorsmith Publishing, Third Flatiron Publishing, Nightmare Fuel Magazine and others. He's also a songwriter, and has been lucky enough to have spent most of his working life doing something else he loves, flying. Tim lives in Far North Queensland, on country recognised as the home of the Ngadjon-jii people. More information is available at tim-borella-author.mailchimpsites.com or on his Tim Borella - Author facebook page.

Arrow's Flight

Aveline Pérez de Vera

It is only by drawing the arrow backwards that one can release it forwards.

24th Emmesmonth, 2264
Space Station 3

"Archer, you're up!" said the commander of Echo Squadron.

Archer hawked into the spittoon, grabbed her remote-play goggles—giving them a showy spin around her fingers as she sauntered across the room—and wedged herself into the combat seat. The console was shaped in a large silver arc, with a tall, rotating seat through the middle; it resembled an arrow in a drawn bow aimed up at the ceiling. The seat was still warm from Taylor's body—the lifeless body they'd just carried out. Archer tried not to dwell on that possibility. Warfare had progressed, as it always does, but remote combat didn't mean remote casualties or remote dying. You had to hard-wire into the machines, and once plugged in, death's scythe travelled both ways.

Goggles on, her eyesight adjusted to the vast blackness of space, all the while flexing and rotating her thumbs to limber up. Archer had been picked for this squad on the strength, or rather the length, of those thumbs. Most people's thumbs reached just below their forefinger, but hers were longer, making them the second longest of her fingers. This meant she could operate the flight and firing mechanisms without having to curl her hand. A flat hand could operate for longer, and any army that could pull longer shifts required fewer soldiers. Fewer people on a space station was also a bonus. In a crisis, it meant that all of you might get to eat. So, longer thumbs, longer rations.

They should use that for their recruitment posters, Archer thought wryly.

She glanced to her right and to her left to get the lay of the tri-squad. Smith was gliding his soarer just behind her right flank, and Cooper was bringing hers up to the left, making Archer the lead between them. Basic. Cadet-level basic. Well, it was time to show those dirty Roaches that her squad was more than basic.

A quick low-level scan revealed the enemy amongst the debris of the last battle. They were just hovering below the planet that hung like a large blue ball in the blackness of space, lit from the right by a vast glowing sun. Archer knew that this fiery ball was something she could use to her advantage. A few short commands to her team saw them all manoeuvre their soarers towards the sun.

The plan unfolded with the precision of an atomic clock. The tri-squad held their nerve, making slow steady progress that would lure the Roaches out; their enemy being led to believe the soarers were not aware of them. Archer and her team executed a near-perfect last-minute turn that placed them face to face with their enemy, but with that bright sun now behind them. In the dazzling light, the Roaches couldn't see that Archer's squad had fired up their weapons to the max.

That'll show them something more than basic! The Roaches didn't see what hit them as the bolts of electricity arced across the black sky. Every Roach vessel, now glowing pale blue, drifted away—a dead weight in space.

It was textbook perfect, which is why Archer's death was so unfortunate.

By a stroke of bad luck, one of the ships with typical Roach sloppiness had rotated slightly off formation prior to the strike. The blue bolt from Cooper's gun not only found its mark, but reflected itself back across the void towards Archer's soarer from the unexpected angle of the hit.

In that split-second Archer knew it was over, that she couldn't disconnect herself in time. The flash started at her right temple, burning her ear and jolting down her throat. Trying to squeeze in one last breath, fire filled her lungs. Heat flared down into the pit of her stomach, where her nervous energy for so many years had writhed. Her left leg danced with the overload of borrowed power and her last conscious thought was of all that energy exploding out of her big toe. It took a fraction of a second, but it was long enough to reflect on a lifetime. Indeed, to remember many lifetimes.

Oh, of course! she thought. *I'm on fire—again.*

28th May 1940
L'Epinette, France

Heinz was not yet weary of this war. True, it had only been an official war for around one year, although for him it had been longer. He had joined the infantry as one of the many young and excitable recruits three years ago. The army was a solid career choice, his grandmother said. He looked dashing in the uniform, and he enjoyed the camaraderie. Heinz suspected he was good at being a soldier. Six months after he joined, he was promoted to Assistant Squad Leader. That happened at the time of the successful unification with Austria. He liked Austria, with its pure mountain air. It reminded him of his Alpine home. Not like this low mud-ridden plain they currently occupied.

A low quiet whistle drew his attention. Karl was crouching behind a house wall, rifle pointed down the dark empty street. Only the four remaining riflemen from the squad were on routine night patrol. Routine and boring, as the enemy had been steadily fleeing before the might of the advancing Panzer tanks and German infantry. Those weaklings would soon be cornered with the sea at their backs. The thought warmed Heinz on this fresh night. His squad didn't need to do anything more than maintain their position before the push continued tomorrow. But he was a conscientious leader, and he saw this as an opportunity for them to practise patrol manoeuvres.

At a signal Karl moved forward, and Heinz relocated to the opposite side of the road. They repeated the criss-cross motion a few times more. At the junction ahead they joined Werner and Gunther. All clear. They could now sweep back to the camp by the square, where their squad leader and the three machine gunners were, they hoped, preparing a half-decent meal. Heinz's stomach rumbled at the thought of food. Werner and Karl were holding a low conversation—something about the best way to set a house on fire. He smiled at their dedication. He had a good team.

They rounded the corner into the small square with its stone fountain. The old, worn fountain his squad mocked when they first arrived in the poor French village. This same unappreciated monument now saved their lives as the first bullet ricocheted off the stone, alerting them by a fraction of a second to the danger about to unfold. Instinct took over as they leapt for cover, weapons ready. Gunther and Heinz huddled behind the fountain. Werner and Karl each moved behind a house wall, rifles already firing.

The years of training and combat kicked in. They exchanged volleys, filling the square with noise and smoke. Heinz reloaded. *How was this possible?* There shouldn't be enemy troops nearby.

He estimated the enemy's number based on their firepower, and with a sinking heart realised that his small squad was outnumbered. If they were lucky, they would only be captured and imprisoned. Heinz ground his teeth. Why was there no support from the rest of his squad? No doubt the slackers had been caught unawares and were captured already. Well, that fate was not in his career plan.

Heinz was a good soldier: agile, alert, able both to take risks and to wait patiently, which is why his death during a routine patrol was so unfortunate.

In this modern world where war was ruled by all things metal, a soldier should be safe from assault by wood and feather. Heinz shifted only slightly to one side of the fountain to gain a line of sight to their camp. But he had exposed himself. In a brief break between the rat-a-tat of bullets, the low thrum and whistle of an arrow signalled his fate. He crumpled onto the ground, curled up in pain for what felt like an eternity.

Heinz cradled the feathery shaft with both hands as it protruded from his chest. His uniform that he so dearly loved was changing colour as his blood seeped into the wool, inching its way out into a growing circle. Dazed and confused, he thought he must be hallucinating as he looked up at a British officer holding an ancient longbow in one hand, and a sword in the other.

"Whoa! Mad Jack skewered one, lads! Would you get a load of that?"

More enemy soldiers were coming into Heinz's view. But these soldiers all had rifles, it was only the officer standing above him who clutched a bow. What confidence he must have to face guns with a bow and arrow. At least this defeat was not ignoble. Heinz coughed feebly, his mouth tasting of blood. The world was darkening as his breath slowed. He thought with sadness about his grandmother, his mountain home, his short life. And with his final heartbeat came the memory that drove his final thought—*My luck is ever cursed!*

16th August 1676
Rhode Island

Mitikwab stooped to clear the low tree branch without slowing her run. Her every fibre was focused on flight. She hated retreating, despite its familiarity throughout her life. She had now passed 40 turns of the seasons, and that was long enough to see her land and her people pursued towards oblivion. Mitikwab adjusted her bow lower over her shoulder so as not to snag on the overhanging branches. Her hand found its way to the smooth wood in the bow's centre which always gave her comfort.

She took pride in her bow, her namesake—bow, or arrow, or to stoop, or to serve. The Algonquian language was so fluid. And as one of its warrior chiefs, she could both bow and serve as well as fly like an arrow to clear the path for her people. But for now, she had to run, light as a doe, picking her way across ancient fallen trees on a downhill slope. She could just hear the equally light steps of her men fleeing with her, scattered amongst the forest. Soon they would reach the river.

As Mitikwab ran, her heart ached. What mistakes had she made that led to this retreat? If her husband had not been captured, imprisoned by the invaders, he may have persuaded her to a different course of action. But then, the bond of family was strong, and she would always support the younger brother of her first husband in this necessary war. The thought of one past husband led her to think of the three dead husbands that had followed him. Mitikwab was undecided if fortune had favoured her in love to now be married to husband number five.

She tried not to let her mind wander to memories of the child, though. That grief was still too raw. The great alliance of her current marriage, the joy of a child to unite their two large tribes, and the happiness his little laugh used to bring them had all unravelled around her this last year. But the cause was older. This war was about to continue for a third generation. That's how long the invaders, those who said they were just visiting, had stayed in her land. Her foot slipped, bringing her focus back to the present as she stumbled. But Mitikwab kept her balance and regained the rhythm of the run.

She could smell the river just before she saw it. They appeared as if by magic, stepping silently out of the woods, her men and herself, so few compared to the start of the raiding all those months ago. But they had had their victories, marked with plumes of smoke as each fledgling town burned. How the tide had turned: Mitikwab's people were now attacked as they tried to plant their crops, many slaughtered, others captured and facing a life of

436

slavery. Her thoughts were now dark, in contrast to the water which reflected the light sparkle of late summer. It's cool refreshing feel around her legs held the promise of revival. Once the river was crossed, they could regroup. They would keep on fighting for what was their birthright.

Mitikwab had learned to swim even before her memory of it had formed. It was one of her many strengths, which is why her drowning was so unfortunate.

The strong current unexpectedly pulled her down. She fought it, pushing her bow against the sandy riverbed to lever herself up towards air, towards life. But she was tired, and the current was remorseless, pulling her away from her precious bow, now stuck in the sand, both body and soul drifting further away from it.

As her lungs filled with water, Mitikwab thought of her favourite origin tale: the bow and arrow. The bow had been given by the mother moon, while the arrows were the gift of the father sun. Both were necessary for life, for the bow was a useless tool without its arrows, and the arrows could not fly true without the bow. She had failed. By trying to be both, she had been neither.

As the river took her, she remembered. *Oh, my poor baby!*

28th April 1453
Constantinople

In the still, dark night only one flame shone—from atop the Galata Tower. As the small fleet of ships rowed quietly by Galata's walls, Marco gazed again in wonder at Constantinople, the city across the river that was under siege. He had seen so many unbelievable things. The Ottoman ships being hauled across the hill behind Galata over greased logs was the most amazing thing. But before that, it was the huge chain stretching across the mouth of the river between Constantinople and Galata. The chain that was supposed to stop the Turkish ships entering the Golden Horn.

Well, it did stop them entering by water, but didn't take into account the ingenuity of the Sultan and his men. That was a week ago. A week on tenterhooks with enemy fleets now only a mile from each other on the same stretch of river. Going to war had indeed provided an experience of the world he could never have dreamed about from his small village on the island of Crete.

"Marcello—are you ready?" He bristled at the use of his boyhood name. Just because he was the youngest did not make him less of a man than the others. While he was too young to join the famous archers of Crete when they left home in the pay of the Venetian lords, he had escaped to Venice as soon as he reached manhood. But when he arrived, the Cretan Archers had already left for the impending war in the east. Then the Pope announced an envoy of three ships to support the fight against the infidel, and Marco travelled to Genoa in time to join them.

He gripped his bow tighter, remembering the triumphant battle on the Genoese ship as they had fought their way past the massed enemy ships outside the chain to be admitted into the Golden Horn. Marco was not a sailor. He should be with the other archers from home, who were positioned on the far side of the city defending its walls. When he made it through this battle, he would have some tales to share when he joined them. Nobody would doubt he was now a man.

Marco was startled out of his thoughts as the first volley of cannon fire began, so loud after their stealthy progress along the dark river. After that, in the smoke and fiery haze, he could no longer tell what was happening, only that it was happening with great rapidity. He fired off his arrows at the Turkish fleet, or where he thought they might be in the smoke. Sometimes a cry of pain erupted after loosing an arrow and he assumed he'd found an enemy target. Good, because the gunfire, cannons, and arrows were likewise finding flesh in his comrades.

Marco was reaching for the next quiver of arrows when a cannonball shot over the tall merchant ship providing them with cover and plunged through the heart of their galley. As the ship broke apart around him, he grappled to hold onto something, anything to delay the rise of the cold dark water. The last thing he heard were his comrades' cries before the blackness folded around him.

Then he gasped for air, discarding his weapons, armour, and heavy clothes between breaths greedily gulped in. The advantage of growing up on an island like Crete was that its citizens learnt to swim from an early age. Marco managed to keep afloat amongst the flotsam and jetsam and followed the sounds of the other men, both helping and being helped as they swam for the shore.

Blessed relief! He had avoided drowning. Marco said a quick Hail Mary as he crawled up the narrow beach to slump in tired relief with around two score other men, barely half of the ship's crew. As his strength returned, he sat up. Looking out in the dawn light at the wreckage of the Papal fleet, Marco's heart sank. Not just in shame at the lost battle, but because he was looking across the river to the walls of Constantinople.

In the confusion of battle, Marco and the survivors had swum to enemy land. It was such a simple mistake, and one which would lead to his unfortunate death.

The Ottomans wasted no time in rounding them up, and their justice was merciless. Marco was young and not the man of the world he supposed himself to be, for it did not dawn on him at first what the long wooden poles were for. As they were made to lie down in a line along the shore, the piercing screams of his comrades foretold his fate. As his impaled body was raised up in view of the horrified Christian army watching from Constantinople's walls, Marco lived just long enough to think *My God, what have I done to deserve such a fate?* And then, in a final flash he remembered.

Winter, 401 BCE
Armenia

Akhilleus and his men took cover behind the trees as the last of the paltry arrows clattered along the path from the hamlet. His blood was still thrumming after the skirmish with the local men half an hour ago. Farmers made poor soldiers, but good sport for a seasoned squad like his Cretan Archers. Akhilleus had volunteered them for this food raid, not just for the black-market potential in an army that was starving, but also because he had grown bored of always running away.

They had been running since Cunaxa. He shuddered at the memory of that last large battle, ransacking the corpses as they lay rotting in the summer sun before their hasty retreat. The Cretan Archers had survived that battle, which was not surprising. If you didn't live, then you didn't get paid. A mercenary's life was that simple. And now, months later the snow lay thick around them, their bellies rumbled constantly from hunger, and their feet felt every league walked in retreat from those dusty Mesopotamian plains. Now the battle to win was that of survival; to get home. This army of ten thousand hungry exiles needed to reach the sea.

Akhilleus surveyed the homes, barns, and huts with an expert eye. The women and children were no doubt cowering inside the large house. A lecherous grin crossed his face in anticipation of both sport and food. Why some chose to defend while others gave up and shared their food, wine, and women, he could not say. Over the course of this long march, they had met with both kinds.

"Give us your food," the archer yelled across the winter silence. Did they understand his words? Well, they would understand his actions. He dragged out a young boy captured from the earlier skirmish and marched him closer to the larger hut, his knife hovering under the boy's ear.

"Food! Now, or he dies." Akhilleus had no intention of letting the boy live, not when there was such good sport to be had. The silent youth was on the threshold of manhood, and yet the archer noticed with glee the stain of tears on his dirty cheeks. He hoped he'd picked a mummy's boy, and that mummy was watching now from the hut.

Nearby, animals bleated in fear, and somewhere a woman sobbed. The archer's blood roiled within him. He needed release. Akhilleus gave the signal and one of his men approached, a freshly hewn spike balanced over his shoulder. At least wood was in rich supply at this forlorn outpost. This time the silent boy did cry out, as they impaled his body in clear sight of his home. His cries were matched by wailing from within the hut, echoed by the jeers and curses of the raiding party.

The archer walked slowly around the upright corpse surveying his band's fine work. The kill had raised all his appetites: for food, for death, for a woman. As if rewarded by divine intervention, a flurry of skirts left one of the distant huts. The woman, crouching, fled towards the far woods. Akhilleus gave chase, excited at the prospect of the hunt, the short, ragged bursts of his breath matching his flying feet.

The woman's sobs left a trail as clear as her footsteps in the snow, leading him like an arrow to his quarry. The forest sloped down a gentle hill to where a cold black river eddied and swirled. As the archer closed in, he could see that her crouched posture protected a swaddled baby. He surged forward, the desire for maternal ripe full breasts and soft thighs driving his thoughts of conquest.

With a desperate cry the woman waded into the river, seeking protection in its icy flow. As she pressed deeper into the surging water, she slipped. Her scream turned into a gurgle as she fell and was tugged downstream by the current. Her arms thrust the child above her head, a last despairing attempt to save at least one of them.

Akhilleus watched in stony silence as they both went under, never to resurface. *Well, I'm still hungry, horny, and now even more foot-sore!* As he trudged back up the hill, the archer's mind turned to the hostages still inside the larger hut, sparking a new plan. This one would warm the cockles of the heart.

The bonfire was grand. They shot the fiery arrows in dazzling arcs of light across the darkening sky. The little suns of flame soon ignited the roof of the main hut. The archer heard the panicked screams from within, but there was no escape from this fiery death.

His men had barred the door and windows from the outside. Let them all burn from head to toe.

This is too easy. Too basic! The archer's admiration of his work was interrupted by a movement at the corner of his eye. An old woman was creeping towards the burning house, a vain attempt to rescue her family. He howled with laughter, and with one smooth movement raised his bow, arrow nocked, and let loose a spinning shaft. The old woman turned in surprise at the loud laugh, the arrow finding its way deep into her chest. She crumpled onto the ground.

Sauntering over to where she lay, a curled-up ball of pain, the archer sneered down at her frail form.

"Did you think you could outrun my arrows, grandmother?" He smiled. This one seemed to understand him. "You could have avoided all of this. We will still take what you should have given us, and look what you have lost in return!" He spat in her face. The smoke from the fire made his eyes water, but he felt no sympathy.

"You not win," the old woman wheezed in broken Greek, her teeth stained with blood. "But as you curse my family, so I now curse you." She hugged the arrow in her chest, as if it were a friend who would share and lessen her pain. With effort, she released her grip, skin loose with age and thin as paper, as she jabbed an accusatory finger at him.

The archer looked down into dark eyes that glowed with a fury spanning eons. He involuntarily took a step back from the dying crone.

"I call upon the Gods. Witness my bargain. You, archer, shall not die . . ." A wracking cough interrupted her.

"Well, that's a bit of a boon, old hag," sneered Akhilleus, feeling the need to show some bravado before his men. "Giving me eternal life, are you?"

"Shall not die . . . by natural means," she rasped in an effort to finish. "By the father archer Hayk, by the mother goddess Nane, all that you have done will come to pass again. And again. As it was taken, so shall it be repaid. Long may you serve your sentence, archer. Often may you be reborn. Often may you die in pain."

The old woman fell back, dead. On the dark horizon a lightning bolt shot from the purple heavens, shaking the winter ground. The pact was sealed, the fate of the archer had been set, its course as straight as an arrow.

About the Author:

As a linguist working in data analysis, Aveline has always loved patterns and words. Drawn to narratives emphasising time and place, she creates speculative fiction flavoured by history and geography. Her greatest desire is to time travel – until then, writing and regular travel will suffice!

Aveline has visited more than 70 countries, but during lockdown spent her travel money building up an inspirational library of fine books. Her stories have been published in Deadset Press' Zodiac series 'Leo' *and* 'Sagittarius', *Black Ink Fiction's* 'Fantasy on Four Feet', *and PS Publishing's* 'From the Waste Land' *– a centenary tribute to the T.S. Eliot poem.*

After many years in the most liveable city of Melbourne, on Wurundjeri Woi Wurrung land, she is now based in the never-tiring city of London, where she lives in an open relationship with her books.

Follow her explorations at www.travellinwithAveline.com.

ABOUT DEADSET PRESS

Deadset Press is an independent publisher of incredible speculative fiction. We provide publishing pathways for emerging writers from Australia and New Zealand, and aspire to shine the light on unique and diverse voices.

You can learn more at:

www.deadsetpress.com

ALSO BY DEADSET PRESS

#